Wild Times

A HopePunk Novel

David Bridger

Beaten Track
www.beatentrackpublishing.com

Wild Times
Published 2021 by Beaten Track Publishing
Book 1, *Quarter Square* © David Bridger 2011 from Carina Press
This rewritten edition © David Bridger 2021
Book 2, *Golden Triangle* © David Bridger 2013 from Carina Press
This rewritten edition © David Bridger 2021
Book 3, *Full Circle* © David Bridger 2021

Paperback ISBN: 978 1 78645 488 1
eBook ISBN: 978 1 78645 489 8

Beaten Track Publishing,
Burscough, Lancashire.
www.beatentrackpublishing.com

Dedicated to the memory of Toni Morrison.

"This is *precisely* the time when artists go to work. There is no time for despair, no place for self-pity, no need for silence, no room for fear. We speak, we write, we do language. That is how civilizations heal."

– Toni Morrison

Contents

BOOK I
QUARTER SQUARE

You're lost, aren't you?

I'M CURLED UP on the stage, listening to rats scratching in the darkness high above. At least, I hope they're rats. The thought that something else might be stalking about among the rodents up there, its claws clicking on the dusty floor, brings my old fear of wolves bursting to the surface.

Stupid phobia. I've never even seen a wolf in the flesh, and there's no way one would be prowling the roof space of an abandoned theatre in Plymouth.

No reason to think the creatures above me are anything other than rats.

It'll serve Tony right if his building is infested. I might call the local council tomorrow and tell them. After all, I *was* supposed to be surveying the place today. Might get a pest-control inspector in and make it official before Tony even knows he has a problem.

On the other hand, I'll probably walk away and leave him to his rats.

The place smells old. Not damp. Not rotting. Just dusty and very old. I roll onto my back, give my scalp and beard a good scratch, and try to concentrate on the noises and the smell of dry centuries. I prefer them to the sound of my thoughts and the stink of betrayal.

But the scurrying rats and deep darkness offer no distractions. My haunted mind slides back to the source of my misery, the bright hotel room to which I returned twelve hours ago and found my naked wife riding my naked best friend.

I can't blank out the memory of her hair swaying across her back, or their moans of pleasure as I walked into the room, or Tony's grunt when Carole twisted off him to crouch by the other side of the bed.

"Joe!" they gasped in unison.

They tried to talk to me, but I didn't want to hear any of their shit. Tony took a step towards me, covering his genitals with a pillow and spouting some pacifying crap, until I punched him in his lying mouth.

He went down, spitting blood, and had the sense to stay down.

Carole wrapped herself in a bed sheet and stood tall. She raised her chin to me, as if offering a second target.

How could she think that? I've never lifted a finger to her. She might have felt better about her own behaviour if I had hit her, but that isn't my style.

Even hitting Tony isn't my style. I'm not a violent person.

I sigh into the darkness. So here I am, alone in a strange city, at the lowest point in my life, spending a night on the dirty stage floor of my *friend's* latest auction purchase, with nowhere else to go and no one to turn to. Great.

New noises break into my thoughts, footsteps and low-pitched voices from somewhere inside the building. Sounds like men are walking up the corridor from the fire exit towards the foyer on the other side of the wall from me.

I scramble around for my boots, grab the heavy lamp without switching it on, and push open one of the double doors a crack.

Three lithe, muscular, young men dressed in dark clothing file purposefully across the moonlit foyer. Their supple movement puts me in mind of cats. They don't break stride as they approach a blank wall, but before he hits the old plaster, the front man snaps his fingers, and a door appears in the wall.

My jaw drops, but I manage to stay silent.

The finger-snapper holds the door open for the others, then follows them through and leaves it to swing shut behind him.

I hurry across the foyer to catch the door before it closes, open it carefully and slip through, then stand on the pavement and stare out to where a modern office block should be but isn't. In its place, a raggedy square of half-timbered Elizabethan houses surrounds a small public garden.

Is it a film set or something? Coloured lamps twinkle in the trees, and the warm night air carries the murmur of voices. Someone barks a friendly laugh. A violin plays a jig, and dancing movements flash on the other side of the high bushes. People are having a party in the garden.

I squeeze my eyes shut and shake my head, but when I look again, the square is still there, under a three-quarter moon so bright it throws strong shadows. I reach behind to touch the door, just checking, and lean towards it as if I'm standing on a cliff edge.

Soft footsteps sound on the cobbles, and a woman of about my age rounds the nearest corner, clicking her fingers to whatever music is in her earphones. Full-figured and curvy, Rubenesque, beautiful, she's a real person in a possibly unreal place. She's wearing a pink T-shirt with a retro Debbie Harry image and black skinny trousers tucked at mid-calf into lightweight combat boots. Her dark, bobbed hair has pink streaks. She crosses the road and shoots me a pretty smile as she removes her earphones. The music is tinny, with a jazz beat.

"You're lost, aren't you?" Her voice is clear and sweet, her skin colour like someone from a Mediterranean country.

Southern Spain or Portugal, perhaps. Her brown eyes promise warmth and kindness.

I inhale her light scent and stare across the square. “I don’t know.”

She starts singing.

But first: coffee

RUNNING ON A dry riverbed, stumbling over rocks and logs and other obstacles hidden by the night, terrified for my life, I'm surrounded by the pounding and scrabbling and thunderous panting of the monster behind me, and I know there will be no escape. In the end, when hot breath hits the back of my neck, I can't help it. I glance back. It drags me down, hauls my head back savagely to bare my throat, and its hideous jaws gape.

*

Dusty sunlight streams through the theatre's high windows like diagonal spotlights into the gloom. I start my daily coping routine, which entails lying quietly for several minutes while I seal the nightmare in its box. I'm determined to fight this fear and kill the monster that has hunted me in my dreams for as long as I can remember.

I replace the horror with pleasant scenes from my earlier dream. The old Elizabethan square, the garden hung with lights, people dancing to violin music, and the lovely woman. Her voice and her delicate scent, like freshly cut oranges and lemons, seemed so real both in the dream and remembering it now. The entire experience did. Does. Except for the magic door.

Well, that's something I can check out. I sit up and pull on my boots.

The foyer wall is as blank and featureless as it was yesterday during my survey. No matter how I prod and poke, there's no opening or even any edge I can prise to make one.

Shaking my head and feeling foolish about chasing a dream, I leave the magic door and the woman where they belong. It's time to deal with real life.

Thirty minutes later, after washing and tidying myself in one of the old dressing rooms, I leave the theatre with a clean face mask on and walk uphill from the mediaeval Barbican Harbour to the modern hotel on Plymouth Hoe.

I watch Carole and Tony eating breakfast for a minute before they notice me.

They look more like a married couple than Carole and I ever did. Well-dressed in similar styles and exuding the same casual confidence, they are like two peas in a pod. How come I've never noticed that before?

Too busy with my own stuff, I suppose. Certainly, that's how it's been for the past year or so. Too concerned with the new direction my life has taken and always on the defensive against Carole's complaints about the changes.

She sees me first, and Tony's shoulders tense in response to her expression. I pause by their table without making eye contact and tell them, "I'll wait upstairs."

A face-masked waiter notices me and moves to lay another place at their table, but I shake my head. This time yesterday, I was enjoying a full English here. Today, I don't belong.

Somehow it doesn't feel right to go into the room I shared with Carole, but I don't have to wait in the corridor for long. I guess their appetites for breakfast are no better than mine. Carole opens the door, and I make a beeline for the armchair with a view from the window.

I don't want to look at them. And I don't remove my mask. It's an unspoken statement. I'm not in their bubble anymore.

"I'm sorry, love." Carole is close to tears.

I stare out at a yacht sailing across Plymouth Sound. It's a picture-postcard view. "Don't call me love."

"Joe..." Tony whines.

When I glare at him, he glances at my white knuckles on the arms of the chair and licks his bottom lip. It's swollen and shiny.

"I'm not going to hit you again. You're not worth it. I'll say my piece and you'll say yours, and let's get this finished."

They don't speak.

I return my attention to the little yacht out on the Sound. "How long's it been going on?"

"For a while," Carole admits. "We're in love, Joe. It isn't just sex. We'd never do that to you."

"How. Bloody. Long?"

Tony bites the bullet. "Two years."

"We were going to tell you," Carole says. "Honestly, love. But it was never the right time."

"Well, now it is. Tell me."

"We want to be together," Tony says. "We didn't want to hurt you."

Enough is enough. I stand and prepare to leave.

"Wait." Tony extends his hands, fingertips splayed and quivering as if I'm a hot plate and he doesn't want to get burned. "We can't leave it like this."

"We should sort it out," Carole says.

"We can sort out the legalities later," I reply. "Right now, I don't want to talk to you."

"Carole and I are going to live together," Tony blurts. "We're going back to London today. What will you do?"

What the hell do they expect me to do? Sit in the car with them? Make small talk? Hang around the house like a spare part while Carole packs up and leaves me?

Well, none of those things are going to happen. That much is certain. But what *am* I going to do?

A woman's song echoes in my memory.

"I'm staying here."

"Plymouth?" Carole's tone holds a familiar London-centric assumption. "Why?"

"The theatre," I say to Tony, determination and something else, something I don't recognise, building inside me. "You don't really want it, do you? I'll take it off your hands."

"It's a dump. What will you do with it?"

"None of your fucking business."

Tony shrugs. "If you put it straight back into auction, it's worth half a million as it stands."

I nod towards Carole without breaking eye contact with him. "It's worth a Carole. I'll sell her to you."

I sense her clenching her jaw. It must nearly kill her to stay silent in response to my deliberate and very unusual sexism. For the first time in years, I don't feel responsible for her unhappiness.

Tony stiffens. "If that's how you want to play it."

Typical him. An instant decision and no haggling. He never wanted the theatre anyway. It's the least attractive property in a job lot he bought at auction last month. He calculated as soon as we saw inside the building that a conversion to apartments would return little profit. My demand will enable him to offload two liabilities while keeping the asset he wants.

"Arrange the transfer," I say over my shoulder as I leave. "Address the paperwork to me at the theatre."

I make it around the corner from the hotel entrance and out of sight of their window before I give way to tears.

Leaning against the sea wall, facing a stiff, salty breeze, I unhook my mask and face the full force of their betrayal. I don't stand with my shoulders shaking, so a passer-by wouldn't know there's a problem, but my pounding heartbeat makes my throat ache.

Our marriage has been difficult for some time, and it's mostly my fault. I, not Carole, moved the goalposts. She wasn't the one who abandoned a good salary and excellent prospects in order to work at making a dream come true.

As she never tired of telling me, she'd married a chartered surveyor, a junior partner in a family business, not a carpenter, and certainly not a bloody eco-protester.

She ganged up with my parents, and they all poured hot disappointment over me from the moment I announced my decision.

Tony scorned my life change. "Thirty-one's a bit early for a male menopause, isn't it? Carpentry's your hobby. Get a grip, for fuck's sake."

It dawns on me that betrayal by my best friend hurts more than betrayal by my wife, and somehow this realisation makes me feel a bit better about things.

Truth be told, Carole and I fell out of love a long time ago. But a friendship as solid as Tony's and mine should last a lifetime. We've been like brothers for twenty years.

That's why I punched him. Not for screwing Carole. For screwing me.

For pitying me.

For knowing exactly what he wants and taking it instead of overthinking everything, which is what I always do. What I'm doing right now, in fact.

I've spent my entire life wondering who I'm supposed to be. I went through the motions with a good degree, a good middle-class career, and a good marriage to a clever and ambitious woman. But none of it was ever solid for me.

Only my dreams have ever had any substance. I dreamed of working in wood from sustainable sources to protect the environment. And I dreamed of a great love that none of my real-life loves have ever lived up to.

I've never found a soul mate. But two years ago, right after our first Covid lockdown, I finally took the step I was dreaming about when I binned my salaried security and set up as a self-employed carpenter.

Working in wood hasn't made my life blissful. Nor has turning up at protests time after time, chaining myself to bridges, getting punched and kicked by the police while the corrupt politicians they work for allow our world to burn so that the obscenely wealthy people *they* work for can extract their maximum profits from the destruction.

Carpentry and protesting are only two parts of the whole. What's missing in my life is the third part, a lover as wonderful as the soul mate of my dreams. That's what I yearn for. But at least in her absence I'm now working at what comes naturally and feels right.

My phone vibrates. I know who it is before I look at the display. *Carole.* I watch the screen flash until voicemail kicks in. Then I hurl the phone, high and spinning, into the sea.

It's time to pull myself together. I need coffee.

Then I'll need bedding, cooking and eating stuff, basic toiletries, and some cleaning gear. A camping shop will be the place to start equipping myself for my new life.

But first: coffee.

I replace my mask, turn my back on the past, and walk into the city.

Quarter Square

BREAKFAST IS A bacon bun and a big coffee from a fast-food place. I sit outside to eat it while seagulls scream overhead and street dancers perform in the shadow of a department store. Three acrobatic men with rippling muscles throw a dark-skinned woman between them in high flips and somersaults. At the top of every dangerous loop, the woman's dazzling white dress catches the sun and makes her fly, bringing a smattering of applause each time from people who've stopped to watch.

I snap the plastic lid off the cardboard cup and sip the scalding liquid. Not coffee. Whatever it is, it isn't coffee. I snap the lid back on and dump the muck in a bin. Now I know what I need to make my day better.

Down the road is a decent-looking café, and behind its counter are shelves of vacuum-packed ground coffees and machines and stuff.

"A strong black coffee to drink in, please, with two bags of ground Italian Roast and your biggest French press to take away."

Carole calls ours a cafetière and always smirks when I say French press, which is what Mum and Dad called theirs when I was a kid. Whatever.

The café has free wi-fi, and I want to let my activist friends in London know I'm okay. They deserve a message so they don't go worrying about me doing a disappearing act. Only I threw my bloody phone into the sea. But the guy behind the counter kindly lets me use his to send a quick email.

Hi Bill

I'll be working away for a few months. Hope you and the kids are okay. Will let you know when I get back.

Simba

Our protest cell stays anonymous in our online communications. Bill is Karen, a retired teacher about the same age as my parents. She's Scottish but taught for many years in a London high school, retiring from there a short while before the first Covid pandemic. The *kids* are a young woman called Pen and her boyfriend, Poke, whose real names I deliberately never learned despite getting arrested with them more than once. I have the impression they're postgrad students.

The four of us met at my first ever protest, which was also Bill's first, and after that we became regular protest partners.

Bill's disabled with arthritis so doesn't go getting herself arrested like we do. As far as she knows, the authorities aren't aware of her real identity, and our emails only ever contain arrangements for meeting. No secrets or sensitive stuff. Ours isn't that sort of cell. I chose Simba for my username on a whim and keep to it more for Bill's security than anything.

It was Pen and Poke who introduced me to the concept of hopepunk, during a long conversation while we were chained to a bridge and stopping traffic in that part of central London one bitterly cold December day. Pen's mention of *hygge* as one of its components is what attracted my interest, but hopepunk turned out to be far more than that. Their approach was literary and for the most part concerned recently published novels, which is where I got the idea that they're postgrads, probably in modern literature.

"It's a storytelling template for resistance," Poke said.

Pen gave him a pointed look as if he'd quoted someone without attribution or something. Her, perhaps?

I thank the café man for the use of his phone and order another bucket-sized cup of black coffee. Like all the retail and hospitality workers and many members of the public I've seen in this city, he's wearing a fabric face mask. Different places respond to the pandemics in different ways. I like what I've seen of Plymouth's approach. The café man's mask features some funky design like a computer game graphic.

"Go on," I encouraged Pen and Poke on the bridge that cold day. We'd all been wearing masks too, but pre-Covid, they were intended to thwart the police's face-recognition technology.

Poke had the hump, so Pen took over. "Artistic movements sometimes seem to appear out of thin air, almost ready-made. But they often result from big cultural changes, especially in response to big political shifts."

It occurred to me that I was receiving a lecture one-to-one that she would normally deliver to a class of undergraduates.

"Hopepunk is such a movement," she continued. "It was born in 2017 when the American writer Alexandra Rowland posted on her Tumblr that the opposite of grimdark is hopepunk. You know what grimdark is?"

"Doom-and-gloom fantasy fiction."

"Yes."

"Like our reality." Poke was over his hump. "With neoliberal governments here and in the States for all of our lives. Then, when the world was already in enough shit, they put Trump in the White House and Johnson in Downing Street, purely to show us they could, and laughed at the danger of climate disasters."

"They're gone now, though."

His look was intense. "Yes, but the establishment always gets its favoured candidates elected. And you know who isn't gone? Millions of people who voted for those two dangerous clowns. That's who we have to persuade, the misled millions."

Pen nodded. "What Rowland and others say is that grimdark isn't compulsory. And neither is pessimism in response to it. Hopepunk encourages optimism and determined activism. It says we have to keep fighting, no matter how unlikely our prospect of victory might appear."

It didn't sound all that new and different.

"There's more." Pen listed and described a few novels. "It's about cooperation, with gentleness and conscious kindness. Self-awareness. Bravery and strength, yes, but while caring for others. Softness. Comfort." She winked, knowing my soft spot. "Hygge. And empathy. Always empathy. It's anti-cynicism. You know the hero's journey?"

I didn't.

"Classic fiction model involving a chosen one, a noble warrior hero battling evil and leading his people to victory over a massive enemy. Aragorn in Lord of the Rings. Well, hopepunk doesn't have a chosen one. Or if it does, they're more likely to be a facilitator than a great warrior. Someone who inspires, encourages, supports, or enables people to work together and keep fighting the evil, no matter what. Samwise Gamgee."

"The act of choosing hope and cooperation over despair distinguishes the movement," Poke said. "It's how we'll win this war without innocent people getting hurt."

I liked that, and still do. It speaks to me. And it has hygge.

By midday, I'm back in my theatre, properly caffeine-fixed and sorting out my living space. Two of the six old dressing rooms have cold running water, but only the bigger of them has an intact handbasin and a flush toilet, so that room chooses itself for my bedroom.

It will need alterations. A cold-water birdbath is okay during this May heatwave, but the English weather can turn at any time of the year, and I have no intention of living like this for long. At the very least, I'll buy a space heater and get a decent shower unit installed.

Swept out and mopped down, with the camp bed and sleeping bag set up in one corner and the camping stove sitting on a trestle table across the room, it feels like an okay place to nest while I lick my wounds.

That's what I need. A nest. It's what I always needed, even as a boy, and then later at university where Carole used to make fun of the cosy hobbit-hole I made of my room there.

Years later, when we married and moved into our first home together, her style of furnishing and décor was smart. Modern. Minimalist. And I was fine with that. As long as she left my workshop in the garage alone when during our first winter there it quickly became my cosily heated soft bolthole.

I've always needed the warm and cosy. I fell in love with the concept of hygge on a family holiday in Denmark when I was a boy and brought it home with me long before it ever became a thing outside of that country.

"Ha-oooo-ga!" Carole used to exaggerate its pronunciation like her version of some submarine's surfacing klaxon when poking fun at my desire for a comfortable hidey-hole.

Bless her.

I take an evening walk down to the mediaeval harbour. In the queue for a bag of fish and chips, I read a tourism leaflet that says the Barbican was the only part of Plymouth to survive the Blitz in World War Two. According to the leaflet, it was 'the place from where Sir Francis Drake sailed, from where the Pilgrim Fathers departed to settle the New World (the Mayflower Steps) and where Britons danced in defiance of Hitler's Luftwaffe'.

The area certainly oozes charm. Even from within my emotional numbness, I can appreciate its visual qualities. Narrow, cobbled lanes of Elizabethan buildings radiate from the harbour and give the place a higgledy-piggledy character.

It's easy to forget that a modern city enfolds this bohemian quarter against the sea.

I eat my fish and chips on a harbour wall bench and then sit outside a bar on the ground floor of a converted old warehouse to wash down the meal with a long, cold beer.

Two young women are spinning big fire-string things for an appreciative circle of passers-by near the Mayflower Steps, while along the road, an artist is doing rapid business sketching charcoal portraits of tourists.

Yes, it's charming. I wish I could enjoy it. But I'm still numb to everything. I don't belong anywhere or to anyone.

The air is heavy with summer smells of beer and cigarette smoke, diesel oil from the harbour, food from all directions, and a hundred different perfumes and aftershaves. It tastes like life and makes me feel even more of an outsider.

As I watch, the Barbican changes character from a daylight tourist trap to a nighttime party place. At nine o'clock, I leave the streets to strutting boys and whooping gaggles of girls and retreat to my dusty, old theatre.

Surveying the inside of the building by the light of a battery-driven lamp isn't the most efficient method, but I repeat the process to keep my mind busy. And because I'm more invested in it now.

Will Tony's idea to convert the property into apartments work? Or can I do something else with it?

I'm not sure it's ever been used for its intended purpose. Or any purpose. Stacks and piles of building materials sit here and there under centuries of dust. Despite ornate scrollwork across the curved front piece of the upper circle and gold paint peeling from plaster cherubs everywhere, the place feels more like an unfinished construction project than a former working theatre.

My theatre and me, perennially unfinished business, both of us trying to figure out what we want to be.

Eventually, inevitably, I find myself in the foyer, looking for that bloody door again and still haunted by the lovely dream woman's song. I fail to find the door, scorning myself for trying to substitute a fantasy for lonely sadness, and go to bed.

When I stretch out on the camp bed, I realise the bedroom has no ceiling. I can see straight up to the false roof, fifty feet above me, and the rats are still scratching up there. I'll check it out in daylight tomorrow.

As soon as the intruders break into my dreams, I pull on my boots and jog to the back of the arena and get there as a boy and girl pass through the magic door. The foyer smells of chips and vinegar.

I step into the square and cross the road cautiously, wary of attracting attention.

The garden is busy, filled with people of all colours and ages. Lanterns glow in the trees. A folk band is playing some manic tune with maybe a Russian origin while several couples whirl about and a wide circle of seated revellers clap along. The youngsters I followed through the door join them and open their paper bags of chips. No one is masked.

A second group of people are sitting slightly apart from the main crowd. They're cooking and eating around a low campfire. One of them is the lovely woman, and she is looking directly at me.

I move out from behind my bush as if I'm not spying on her while she walks towards me. She's so beautiful I nearly forget to breathe.

"Hello." Her light scent fills my mind. Her voice warms me like central heating from a good slug of brandy on a cold day.

I find my voice. "Hello. Is that a magic door?"

"Yes." Her eyes twinkle with humour.

Is this happening, or am I dreaming? Maybe I'll find some sort of rational explanation if I stick around. "Are you going to send me away again?"

"Send you away?"

"Like you did last night, singing, charming me, whatever it was you did."

See, I tell myself, here's the thing. I don't believe any of this is actually happening, but at the same time I totally believe this woman is real and last night she sang some sort of enchantment onto me.

She tilts her head and studies me. "What's your name?"

"Joe. What's yours?"

"Min."

It's like someone dropped a pebble into deep water somewhere far back in my memory. But the sensation lasts only a second because she's talking again and drawing me back to the present.

"How did you find us?"

I nod at the theatre. "I just moved in."

"Ah, I see." She glances back at the garden and starts walking towards an open gateway in the perimeter hedge. "Would you like to meet some of the others?"

Her four companions watch our approach. A lean man of about sixty dressed up like Plymouth's answer to Davy Crockett, an old woman in a dark bundle of skirts, and a couple in their twenties wearing skinny black jeans and T-shirts with studded belts and their hair dyed black to match.

Min sits on a cushion and gestures for me to take a place among them. "This is Joe," she tells her friends. "He's all right."

How does she know?

"Evening, Joe. I'm Andrew." The old man has a gravelly American accent. The turquoise stone threaded into his shoulder-length white hair sways away from his jawbone when he reaches across to shake my hand. He nods towards the old woman. "This is Flo. And these two are Jimmy and Fliss."

The others say hello as I sit cross-legged on the grass opposite Min. Then Andrew and Fliss resume, I assume, a conversation about fixing a roof, while Flo massages Jimmy's right forearm. A big blackbird sits on Flo's shoulder, observing me intently.

Jimmy catches me watching his treatment. "Hurt it last week and haven't been able to work."

I wince in sympathy. "What do you do?"

"I'm a juggler."

The old woman releases his arm. "A couple more days. Don't rush it."

"Ta." Jimmy hands her a coin. "Flo's our fixer," he tells me, then nods at the blackbird. "Ouzel's her assistant."

"What do you juggle?"

He grins. "What have you got? Clubs, knives, and swords mostly. Fire sometimes, if the crowd's worth it."

A piercing whistle sounds from over near the theatre, and two young women burst into the garden, laughing and skipping through the gateway. They dump their haversacks on the ground and join the dancers.

Jimmy waves to the new arrivals with his good arm. "Cindy and Debs are our fire girls."

I recognise them. "They were down at the harbour earlier, spinning fire on ropes. They're good."

"They're called *poi.* The fire ropes."

"Are you all performers?" I ask.

"Some of us," Min says. "We have all sorts here."

Flo and Ouzel are staring at me. They're starting to make me feel uncomfortable.

"What do you do, Joe?" Fliss asks.

"I'm a carpenter."

*

He works in wood.

Min studies the serious young man while images tumble through her memories and her heart thumps so hard it makes her throat ache.

He works in wood, and it feels so right.

Can it be him? Finally, after so many years?

Can it?

Flo leans to her and murmurs, "He's clean."

Virus-free, she means. Good to know, confirming what Min sensed from the first, but that isn't what's pulling her to him like a magnet to its partner.

*

Her stillness draws me in.

I forget about the unsettling old woman and her blackbird. Everything else blurs around the edges of my vision. The music fades into the distance.

I know only Min. I don't struggle against the pull. I'd be happy to fall into those warm, brown eyes forever.

Then she says something to Andrew, and it's as if my inner ears pop clear. What's going on? Is she enchanting me? How else can I explain the powerful need that filled me for those moments?

"Joe's living in the theatre," she tells Andrew.

"Why?"

"Sorry." I have to switch my brain back on. "Why what?"

Andrew's gaze is steady. His eyes are morning-sky blue, and the deep crinkles at their corners suggest a lifetime of studying horizons. "Why are you living in the theatre?"

"Thinking I might do it up."

They all glance at one another. Andrew looks uncomfortable.

"What is this place?" I ask Min.

"This is Quarter Square. It's a haven."

With these eccentric types dancing, playing musical instruments, eating and talking and laughing, it feels as if I've landed in a Roma camp in some fantasy film. "You all live here?"

"Most of us. Some move around a bit, stopping for a while in various havens along the way."

"There are more havens?"

"Yes."

"This takes some getting used to."

She chuckles. "I know."

The violinists call her to sing with them.

She waves back. "I won't be long," she promises me.

I admire the swing of her hips as she walks away.

"She's a beautiful woman," Andrew says.

"She is."

The band plays a sad piece, full of soaring violins and a slow, melodic drumbeat. Min closes her eyes and sways with the music, apparently in a world of her own. Then she sings in a strange language.

Her voice transports me. I close my eyes too and fly with her, glimpsing swirling visions of snow-capped mountains, a city of polished marble, and rivers flowing across green plains to a sea.

I don't know how long the song lasts, but at its finish, I return to myself refreshed, as if I've enjoyed a long sleep. The band plays something livelier, and a passing dancer sweeps Min into the stream.

"You know," Andrew says, "that theatre is the last anchor for this place."

"Hmm?" I murmur, watching Min dance.

"We're losing it." He waits until he has my attention. "Over the centuries, building developments around here have destroyed all the anchors except the theatre. It's the only structure left standing in the footprint of an original building. The only physical link to the outside. If that theatre goes, Quarter Square goes too."

I'm about to reassure him that I have no intention of removing the building, but he continues.

"All those changes in the outside world have affected the square. It hasn't lost its shape, but the texture of the place is damaged."

The houses surrounding us are clearly outlined in the bright moonlight. None are in as good a condition as I'd thought at first glance. The black-and-white-timbered chocolate-box prettiness of the place hid the fact that several buildings are crumbling at the edges.

"Nowhere is solid," Andrew says. "Not unless it's used regularly. People have died or moved away, and the place has gotten unreliable." He scans the surrounding rooftops. "Oh, we can keep repairing it, bit by bit, but no one wants to spend all their time maintaining the neighbourhood."

Jimmy winks at Fliss.

"This square is disappearing," Andrew says, "and these kids don't care."

Jimmy flutters the fingers of his good hand. "If we have to, we'll move on. There's always somewhere else."

Andrew fixes me with his forceful stare. "See? We're losing it."

Min returns from her dance, breathless and glowing. Seeming to sense a tension in our group, she looks from me to Andrew and arches a questioning eyebrow.

I've had a thought, but there's no way I'm ready to discuss it until I can think it through. It isn't my habit to blurt out ideas without weighing them first. And to be honest, I'm not completely sure this is my idea at all. Feels like my world has been placed on a tilting board and is sliding out of my control.

Old Flo and her bloody blackbird are still staring at me. Are they playing with my head? It won't surprise me if they are.

No, I'll say nothing about this strange idea.

Min has other plans. "What?" Her eyes twinkle, and a smile tugs at the corners of her mouth.

"Andrew's nagging Joe about the theatre," Jimmy says.

She focuses on me. “What is it?”

I want to tell her. But I don’t want to say anything until I have a clear head. But I want to tell her. “The guy I got the theatre from planned to convert it into apartments.”

Andrew groans.

“I only just arrived here and haven’t decided what to do with the place,” I continue, “but I’m thinking, could I renovate it? As a working theatre, I mean. Would that help? If you could all perform in it for a paying audience, would that help keep your community alive?”

“Bloody hell,” Jimmy breathes.

I could say the same thing.

Andrew gives a long, low, interested whistle, while Min and Fliss grin, and Flo kisses Ouzel on the beak and murmurs something to him.

“I’d need help.” I’m talking myself into this and thinking maybe it isn’t such a daft idea after all. Not completely strange. Probably. “You’d have to provide money for materials and as many labourers as possible, especially at first when we’re clearing all the junk out. But I don’t see why not.”

Jimmy’s eyes are wide. “That’s very cool.”

Min regards me with something like quiet pride.

My cheeks flush.

Insiders

ENJOYING AN EVENING meal with a group of our friends, I look around the living space of my cousin's new home.

It's a simple dwelling, furnished with the turned timber pieces I made as a wedding gift for him and his wife. Through the window shutters we hear the rumble and tumble of our merchant town coming to the end of its working day.

Someone says something funny, and we all laugh.

Before our mirth dies away, a massive blow bursts the door off its hinges, and a hideous beast springs into the room. Everyone screams. It is man and wolf at the same time, standing on its powerful hind legs, its head brushing the ceiling, with a fury of madness in its bloodshot eyes and saliva splattering from its fangs.

It charges at me and rips out my throat.

*

After breakfast, I find a public telephone and arrange for a skip to be delivered outside the theatre the next day. I get back to find Min, Andrew, Jimmy, and five other residents of the square have turned up and started to collect rubbish from all over the building.

They've brought dozens of candle lanterns. For the first time, I see the arena the way its designer meant it to be seen.

It's horseshoe-shaped, with a tier of private boxes on the side walls aligned with the upper circle of the auditorium. The orchestra pit is full of rubble. I've estimated the building to be about two hundred years old, and left-over construction materials stacked about the place appear to confirm this.

The only signs of more recent times are some twentieth-century additions backstage, a fifty-foot steel wall ladder up to the roof space, and the flush toilet in my bedroom. These suggest that someone once started doing something with the building but didn't get very far.

Andrew agrees. "I guess the insiders back then made it difficult for whoever tried to change the place."

"Insiders?"

"Haven people."

"I suppose that makes me an outsider."

He wrinkles his nose. "Everyone has to start somewhere."

I stoop to pick up another armful of rubbish to dump in the open space at the front of the arena.

Andrew lays a light hand on my arm. "Don't worry, son. You're doing a good thing here. You'll be on the inside before you know it." He bends to pick up a pile of junk.

"Hey," he calls over his shoulder, "we talked things over last night after you left. We agreed to help towards the cost of materials."

"That's why there aren't too many of us here today," Jimmy says. "We're having a fundraising push. They're all out, taking advantage of the good weather."

"Not you, then?"

"We thought I might be more use to you here. I've worked on building sites, so I'm your first labourer. And my arm is nearly better." He throws me a scruffy salute, then points to a big man carrying his own weight in sawn timber to the stack of usable materials we're creating in the centre of the stage. "That's Big Luke. Good as gold. He'll be our heavy lifter."

I wander backstage and peer up into the shadows. The roof space bothers me. I know there will be nothing unpleasant or scary up there, but I need to check it out for my peace of mind.

If I don't, I won't thank myself when every night I lie in bed staring up and imagining things. I stand at the bottom of the ladder and struggle with the idea of climbing it.

Jimmy appears at my shoulder. "Want me to check the loft?"

I should do this myself. His arm isn't completely healed. "Is your arm okay?"

"It's fine, honest. Go on. I want to take a look up there." He adopts a pirate drawl and a wild-eyed grin. "There might be treasure."

It's my job. I shouldn't let him do it. "Would you mind?"

"'Course not. Lend me your torch." He hooks my lamp over the back of his belt and shinnies up the ladder like a monkey. At the top, he pushes the hinged hatch cover back with a loud bang and hoists himself into the darkness.

The back of my neck prickles. A cold, damp shiver runs up and down my torso. I've never experienced one of my nightmares while wide awake, but blanking out mental images of a wolf savaging Jimmy to death comes horribly close to the pounding dread that always accompanies them.

His face appears in the hatch opening. "Lots of rats up here but nothing else." He coughs. "It's bloody filthy, mind."

He slams the cover shut behind him and comes back down, favouring his injured arm as he nears the bottom rungs of the ladder.

He sees my frown at that when he reaches solid ground. "It's a bit sore, but we don't need to bother Flo about it. I'll rest up again, and it'll be fine. Okay?"

"Okay."

He winks as he hands me the lamp and leaves me at the foot of the ladder.

I'm pathetic. I should have gone up there, not let someone do something I was too scared to do myself. Shame burns my cheeks. I close my eyes and vow never to do anything like that again.

Never. From now on, I will face my fears and fight my own battles.

I step into my room to grab a long drink of water, swallow my shame with it, and get back to work.

When we're ready to break for lunch, I realise I haven't seen Min for hours. Jimmy says she's working out back in the dressing rooms, and I find her finishing off my bedroom. She and an older woman have spent all morning washing the walls and floor in there, and they've done a far better job than I did when I moved in. The room is spotless.

"You deserve it," is Min's simple response to my sincere thanks. "And we'll get you some soft fabrics for in here. Make it nice and cosy. Now let's go find some food."

That evening, she comes to collect me, filling my bedroom with her delicate scent. "We're having a party in the garden tonight. Would you like to come?"

When we reach the blank wall in the foyer, I stop her from snapping her fingers. "Do you think I could learn how to do that?"

"It's easy. Once you know the door is there, all you need to do is break the glamour. Click your fingers."

Yeah, right, just like that. But I do as she suggests. When I click my fingers, my hand tingles with pins and needles, but nothing else occurs. I shake my itching fingers.

"Try again. This time, see the door when you do it."

I click while visualising the magic door. The tingling happens again, and the door appears.

"Yay." She pulls it open. "Now you can come and go as you please."

I thrill from head to toe when she links arms with me. We walk in step easily and fit together as if we've been doing this all our lives. Her delicious citrus scent makes me feel fresh and clean.

The party is well under way. Children are running around. It hasn't occurred to me that there might be families among the insiders. Do they party like this every night? What about school next day?

The youngest ones look about three or four. I see no babies. The global birth rate is still in its post-pandemics low, and it looks like that applies for insiders the same as for outsiders.

We head to what I think of as the elders' campfire, where Andrew introduces me to the young black woman massaging Jimmy's forearm.

"Meet Tara, Flo's apprentice. Tara, this is Joe."

Tara is lithe and strong, sitting cross-legged in a long cotton dress and open sandals. She raises her head of intricate plaits and welcomes me with a calm smile.

The campfire is bigger, its glowing coals filling a shallow trench two feet wide and ten feet long. A dozen or so people kneel around it, cooking, and Andrew and Min introduce me to each of them.

People respond with varying degrees of warmth, which doesn't surprise me. Inevitably, some will doubt my integrity.

The only properly cold welcome comes from three dancers, Dish, Blue, and Sab, who are the quiet men I followed into the square that first night. Someone mentions that they're a street act with a Spanish acrobat called Delores. They seem to prefer their own company.

Delores is friendly, flourishing a bottle of red wine while she practises her heavily accented English on me. She's delighted when I recognise her as the spectacular flying dancer from the shopping centre.

But her warmth towards me doesn't spread to her partners. They look right through me and remain silent in my presence.

I hope things will turn out okay, even with people who treat me with such open suspicion. This is their home, and I'm some outsider who's strolled into their lives promising rescue. I want to be accepted into this community where no one is telling me what to do and how to live. I want to belong here. But I need to be patient.

Fliss takes my hand. “Dance.”

“I don’t dance.”

“Yeah, you do.” She hauls me to my feet.

The next hour disappears in a whirl of dancing like nothing I’ve ever done before. When the music slows and the cooks call everyone over to the fire, my cheeks ache from laughing.

Beer and wine have been flowing freely all evening, and the group I return to is merry and loud. Someone shoves a can of beer into my hand, and someone else hands me a plate of roasted chicken pieces. “Help yourself to spuds and salad.”

A second fire has been lit away from the cooking fire. People sit around it, eating, drinking, and talking. Still sweating from my physical jerks, I sit beside old Flo.

Jimmy and Fliss wave to me from the other side of the fire, and Flo gives a single short nod as if she’s made a decision. “You’ll do fine.”

Ouzel ducks his head in agreement and chuckles away in her ear. They’re not doing their stare routine on me anymore. My head stays clear.

Maybe that was some sort of preparation to wash my memory, in case I turned out to be someone they didn’t want around.

While I eat, I study the people gathered in the garden. There are about eighty of them, twice as many as last night. Quarter Square is more like a secret village than the strange circus troupe I thought at first.

Beyond the fiddles and drums and tree lights of the garden, and the silhouetted Elizabethan houses that enclose it, is Plymouth’s Barbican. Out there is all the hustle and bustle and heavy air of a summer evening in the old harbour. Inside here is peace and lightness, music and magic.

High above, on the opposite side of the square, a movement catches my eye. The chimney and ridge tiles on one of the houses shimmer briefly and then fade away.

Of course. Everyone is eating or making music or dancing. No one is maintaining the structure and fabric of the place, which Andrew said is an ongoing task. It comes home to me that the square would disappear forever without their magical repairs.

I find myself looking for Min all evening. Our eyes meet often, and every time, I feel like I'm glowing.

After a while, I become aware of a young white man I haven't seen before who also keeps making eye contact with me. His stare isn't friendly. He has a teenaged boy in tow.

"That's Will and his apprentice Danny," Flo says. "They're magicians. Been working the streets up in Bristol all this week."

For some reason, I can't stop watching Will, although I try to do it surreptitiously. He's the sort of person I instinctively never like, supremely self-confident and always smiling with those dark eyes in that predatory way. He is suave, elegant, easy in his own body, and with well-groomed good looks. He must spend hours getting his hair swept back like that and keeping his little beard trimmed perfectly.

But the thing that really pisses me off is his manner around Min. He keeps touching her, draping his arm across her shoulders or stroking the back of his hand against her cheek in a proprietary way, and watching me the whole time to make sure I'm seeing it.

His message is loud and clear. He is Min's lover.

Min notices this silent exchange yet does nothing to deny his message. She doesn't reciprocate his affectionate touches, but neither does she push him away, and she continues to make friendly eye contact with me.

Instinct tells me Will's behaviour is for me alone, that he heard about me when he arrived back from his week in Bristol and feels threatened by the quick friendship Min and I have struck up.

Instinct also tells me that Min wouldn't put up with his mauling of her if they weren't intimate.

I'm off-balance.

Have to be honest with myself. The whole thing makes me deeply uncomfortable and jealous as hell. Thoughts of Carole and Tony keep surfacing, regardless of how I push them back under.

Jimmy and Fliss flop down again, flushed and still laughing from another dance, then canoodling and giggling quietly. Their happiness makes me happy.

Fliss whispers something to Jimmy, who glances at me before he nods to her.

"We're going to bed soon. Would you like to come with us?" Fliss pitches the question for my ears only. Not from any sort of shame, I guess, but as a courtesy to me.

Jimmy's smile is welcoming.

There's no ambiguity here. They're inviting me to make up a threesome in bed.

I'm not opposed to the concept in theory. I've always been attracted to men as well as women. Some men. Not to men nearly as often as to women, but in sufficient numbers to be self-aware of my interest.

That's where it has always stopped, though. Attraction has never developed into action. And my feelings have always remained private.

I've never been very active, sexually, with people of any gender. Certainly, I've never been promiscuous. Fumbling with two or three girlfriends was the extent of my explorations before university. Then I met Carole there, and that was pretty much that.

Sex for its own sake never gets me fired up. I have to really warm to someone before I'm interested in having sex with them.

Have to love them, in fact. I accepted years ago that I only want sex with someone I love.

With Carole, well, nowadays I think with her, I mistook comfort for love. It worked for a while, but looking back, it was doomed from the start.

Fliss and Jimmy are smiling encouragement at me. Waiting patiently for my answer.

I like them. The last thing I want is to hurt their feelings. They're attractive, both of them, and fun. But I feel only friendship, and I don't want to complicate things.

"It's no, isn't it?" Fliss says. "Don't worry. It's okay. We're not upset."

She must be reading my body language. I'm grateful for her gentle kindness and hope she's telling the truth about not being upset. When they leave a minute later, Jimmy gives me an understanding smile, and Fliss squeezes my shoulder. "It's okay."

I wonder if Carole ever wanted to ask if I'd like Tony to share our bed. And how things might have worked out if she had.

He was my friend. Valued and trusted. That's why the betrayal hurt so badly. But I didn't love him. It wouldn't have been right for me or him or Carole. They wanted each other. I was on the outside of their love.

And I'm okay with that, because now I have a new life, a second chance, and from my new vantage point, I feel released like a strong spring from the captivity of my old life.

Danny sits next to me and starts chatting. He's a friendly lad of eighteen or nineteen, about ten years younger than Will, whom he talks about like he's some sort of film star.

It irritates me, but I understand hero worship. It's how I used to feel about Tony when I was struggling to stay focused long enough to graduate from university, while he'd already joined his family business and was enjoying early success as a young property developer.

Will comes to sit on the other side of Danny. In my peripheral vision, I see him lean in to murmur something in Danny's ear, and I can't help but notice the stiffening of the boy's shoulders and the sideways glance he gives me.

I ignore what's going on. Will whispers something more to the lad, grins at nothing in particular, and saunters off to dance with Min.

Danny doesn't move away immediately, but his attitude turns noticeably cooler. I decide to win him around, not only because I like him and want to be liked, but also to thwart Will's game.

The man himself comes to stand beside me later, when I'm talking with Andrew. He waits for a gap in our conversation. "You're a builder then?"

I match his steady look and pause before answering. I hate to admit it, but his voice is melodic and pleasant. I can't quite place his accent, which sounds like a warm blend of West Country and Irish. When I reply, I keep my voice cool. "And you're a magician."

"You're going to do up the theatre for us. Out of the goodness of your heart. And we're supposed to believe you."

I eye him down to the ground and back up again, feeling the familiar brain fog creeping in, the same as when Flo and Ouzel did their number on me last night. "Believe what you want, and don't bother with your Vulcan mind-meld shit. It doesn't work on me."

His knowing smile says I'm a liar.

Andrew watches him walk away. "He's a firebrand, that one. Give him time."

I nod but decide to call time on myself. The evening is spoiled.

Later, lying on my camp bed, I try to resist the disappointment crowding in on me. Most of the insiders have been friendly, and I have no reason to think that will change. Will's jealous. He doesn't trust me. He doesn't believe my motives. But mainly he's jealous about Min and me. And he's just one man. Sod him.

I'm not worried about Dish, Blue, and Sab, either, because the acrobatic dancers don't mix with anyone, never mind me.

But I can't stop Will from getting under my skin, and I don't try to fool myself that my sensitivity has nothing to do with my jealousy over his relationship with Min.

I try not to imagine what they might be doing together right now.

*

Hiding in a dark city alleyway, buried beneath a stinking pile of food scraps and domestic waste, ignoring the vermin that shove around me and nuzzle against my tightly compressed lips and squeezed-shut eyes, hearing only my own heartbeat hammering in my throat and ears, I know the monster is coming.

A heavy shuffle sounds close by. The rats in the midden heap freeze.

A terrible grip takes me by the scruff of my neck and hauls me out, and I stare into the raging red eyes of my nemesis, my final thought a silent thanksgiving for my lover's safety.

To work

A DEEP BOOM VIBRATES through the building and wakes me with a start at eight o'clock. By the time my feet hit the floor, I recognise the crashes, bangs, and hydraulic squeals in the road outside. Our skip is being delivered.

I'm not the only one who's been alerted by all the noise. On my way to the front door, I'm joined by four insiders.

Jimmy salutes. "Ready for work, boss."

"How's that arm?"

"It's good."

I raise an eyebrow.

"No, really, it's fixed and I'm right to go."

"Good. Let's start shifting that rubbish."

He checks we can't be overheard. "We didn't upset you last night, did we? Me and Fliss. I'm sorry if we made you feel uncomfortable."

"No. Honestly. I was worried I'd upset you."

"You didn't." He grins with relief. "We're good then."

I leave them to their dusty work and wash my hands and face. Today, I want to get around all the timber yards and builders' merchants in the city to get a feel for the different places and order all the tools and materials we'll need.

I call into the square to see if Min wants to come with me, but she's busy teaching in the garden.

It's interesting to see all the kids together in one place. The youngest ones, sitting cross-legged with their scruffy exercise books on the grass under a tree, look like any class outside on a summer's day in any real junior school.

I wander over and catch some of Min's lesson.

"The *Mayflower* sailed from Plymouth in September 1620 with a crew of thirty plus one hundred and two passengers. Thirty-two of them were children.

"Next time you're down by the Mayflower Steps, take a look at the bronze plaque on the wall across the road. All their names are there. It wasn't a big ship, just a fat-bellied, creaky, old wooden boat with sails. There wasn't even enough bed space for everyone, so some passengers had to sleep in boats on the upper deck.

"It took them sixty-six days to reach America, and it was an uncomfortable crossing. Most of the passengers had never been on the sea before, and they were already scared before they left, especially the families with little ones.

"The weather was already turning bad while they were still in Plymouth, but they'd run out of money for mooring fees and food stores, so they couldn't wait it out. They had to go."

Her descriptions are vivid. It sounds almost as if she'd been right there, watching the ship leave the harbour. I tell her so when she sends the kids off for a break.

"Maybe I was." Her eyes glitter with mischief.

"Those kids are a credit to you."

"Thank you, but it isn't down to me alone. We all muck in." She nods over to a bench where Linda, one of the insider mothers, is using tattered *National Geographic* magazines to teach the older group.

I recognise Linda from my first evening down at the harbour. She's the artist who was doing rapid charcoal portraits for tourists.

"As far as the outside is concerned," Min says, "these children don't exist. They're totally free. No one out there knows their real names, and no one ever will. We each have our own list of aliases. If the police want a name, the kids know to give a different one every time. That's why you won't see many insiders with tattoos. Distinguishing marks can make things difficult."

"That's why the kids stay in the square during normal school hours," I realise.

She nods. "To avoid drawing attention. And that's why they need to know how to read and write, at least. Anything that makes them stand out from the crowd is dangerous. They need to look and act like outsider children. It'll be a lot easier for them a few weeks from now when the outside schools close for summer."

She calls them back from play and settles them under the tree again as I leave for my shopping trip.

I spend five hours, and nearly a thousand pounds on my credit card, buying tools and materials and arranging for everything to be delivered as soon as possible.

The timber yard smells like heaven. I spend twice as long there as I need to. I usually do in these places, wherever they are, and always leave them in a good mood.

Back to the city centre to buy a Cornish pasty for lunch, and I'm attracted by the deep, breathy, plaintive notes of a woodwind instrument somewhere nearby. I follow the mellow sound into a tree-lined pedestrian area, where Andrew is playing a pipe of some description. His tune is slow and thoughtful, sad even, although not mournful. I'm pretty sure it's a Native American flute. I've never seen one before but have heard them played on the radio.

A young couple drop coins into his upturned leather cowboy hat on the pavement as they pass and smile back at the little *thank you* trill he adds as they walk away.

He's certainly an engaging character, and his music is hauntingly beautiful. I slip back around the corner so as not to disturb him.

I'm enjoying getting to know Plymouth, especially because I know Min will be at home when I get back there.

Home. That's how I'm thinking of the square and the theatre and my cosy little nest in the back of it that Min is furnishing in soft fabrics of deep reds and blues.

Hygge.

I've never felt so free in all my life

THE TOOLS AND timber arrive next morning while a gang of insiders are filling our second skip with rubble and rubbish, and I get to work.

I estimate it will take three months to complete the structural repairs, mostly on my own but with some labouring help from Jimmy and as many insiders as can be spared from the fundraising.

They've agreed to keep me supplied with food and coffee so I can concentrate on getting it done as fast as possible. This haste is for my benefit. Payment in kind is all very well, but sooner or later, I'll need to start earning real money from outside work.

For now, though, my full focus is on the job in hand. I clear a space on the stage, set up two sawhorses and select lengths of oak, maple, and ash to build a monster eight-by-three-foot workbench.

A big job needs a big bench.

I've bought a manufactured clamp for one end of it and plan to make a heavy-duty second one by hand for the front edge, complete with dogholes and a quick-release lever. Now I tack my bench sketch to the nearest wall, strip off my shirt, lick my new carpenter's pencil, and start measuring and sawing.

The smell of fresh sawdust is exhilarating, and I ride the customary rush of happiness, so completely in my element that I've sung all the way through my blues-rock repertoire before I surface from the rapture.

When the final planed length of maple sits alongside its brothers and a dozen bar clamps, all ready to be glued together like a huge butcher's block for the bench worktop, I wipe sweat from my face and chest with my balled-up shirt, stretch my back with a long luxurious groan, and hear a giggle from somewhere in the wings.

Min, Cindy, and Debs have been watching me. I don't know how long for. The poi girls' amusement is obvious and appears to be directed at Min rather than me. Her shining eyes seem to say more than the smile she's trying not to show, and she arches an eyebrow at the girls. They jostle friendly shoulders against hers before giggling off into the darkness backstage and leaving us alone.

We stare at each other across the stage until, eventually, one of us has to say something.

"Care to lend a hand with this? I need someone to help clamp these pieces together so I can glue them." I don't need any help with it, but she isn't to know that.

"Sure."

And that's how Min becomes my carpenter's assistant.

I subcontract the electrics and plumbing to two local tradesmen Jimmy recommends and put them to work immediately, installing a water boiler and shower in my room. They get the unit fitted and operational by the end of that very day, which makes me happy.

Ten minutes into my inaugural shower after work, I think of Carole and realise I'm not even slightly sad without her. My mental image of her is replaced by one of Min, who's invited me to hear her sing in a jazz club this evening. I grin and break into a driving blues song, stamping its bass drumbeat in the shower well.

Min's gig is brilliant. Her voice is incredible. She brings the house down.

We leave the club arm in arm and walk into the city centre, where she says some of the insiders will be performing for evening strollers. It feels natural for us to walk this way in perfect rhythm. I love the intimacy of our bare forearms pressing together and our gentle shoulder-to-shoulder bumps every second step. Her scent fills my head, and I resist the strong temptation to fold her into my embrace and kiss her.

I wonder how she would respond.

It's a lovely evening, and there are plenty of people out walking. Sure enough, we find a small crowd gathered in the middle of the pedestrian shopping precinct, applauding Will and Danny's magic act.

Min slows as we approach, clearly intending to stop and enjoy the act, but I keep moving.

She catches my eye and smiles.

I smile back, all innocence. "What?"

"Nothing."

We stroll through a wide paved area between department store buildings, where two more insiders are busking for a growing audience. When we get close, one lowers her violin and calls Min over to join them.

"I'll help them out," she says. "You go on. We'll be here for ages if the audience is generous."

I cross Royal Parade and leave the city streets behind as I head down towards the harbour. Within a few hundred yards, the roads change from concrete paving to cobblestones, their lighting from electric orange to moonlight and shadows, and I imagine I'm travelling back in time four or five hundred years.

I've only been living in the Barbican for a few days, but already I love it.

I turn the last corner by the theatre and walk straight into a gang fight, a vicious brawl happening in one of the tight crossroad spaces between terraces of crooked old houses.

Forty or fifty men are beating one another savagely with fists, boots, baseball bats, and even a couple of tyre levers. Knives too. The fight takes place in near silence, apart from grunts and scrapes and heavy blows. It seems almost unreal.

It's a scene from a film, surely? A remake of *Highlander* or something? That's the impression I get from the whole thing, a battle of the clans.

But even as that thought suggests itself, I know what I'm seeing is horribly real.

And these aren't teenaged boys having a punch up after a night on the beer. These are adults, big, heavy men like bikers, battle-hardened warriors battering and stabbing one another right there in front of me.

I stand frozen to the spot, appalled, too scared to even twitch in case I draw attention to myself.

One of them staggers from the mob with the ornate handle of a knife sticking out of his abdomen between his clenched, bloody hands. He crashes into me, and I clutch at him automatically as we fall to the ground. He sprawls on the cobblestones and stares up at me in mute agony while I smell his rank old sweat and watch the life leave his eyes.

Police sirens sound in the distance.

The combatants disengage and melt into the shadows, still stealthy but for the clink of weapons and the scuff of heavy boots, taking their dead and wounded with them, except for the one lying across my legs.

They've left me holding a dead man.

While sirens wail closer and closer, I sit there in shock, waiting for someone to come and take charge of the nightmare I've walked into.

Then Will is there, shoving his hands under my armpits from behind and lifting me to my feet while Danny rolls the heavy man off my legs. I stare at them mutely, not knowing what to say, but they're not interested in conversation. They drag me away and we make it inside the theatre before the police arrive.

As I close the front door, four fighters hoist the dead man between them and disappear into the darkness as if they were never there.

We stand and listen to police cars screeching to a halt, doors slamming, and men shouting.

Danny nudges my arm. "You might want to change your shirt. There's blood all over it."

I touch the sticky wetness.

"Don't hang around," Will tells Danny. "Exeter early in the morning, remember?" He strides away without a word to me, up the sloping corridor to the foyer.

My eyes are growing accustomed to the gloom, and I glare at his back as he leaves.

Danny grips my shoulders and shakes me. "Come on, Joe. Pull yourself together. You need to burn the shirt. We don't want to be linked with shit like that."

He stays with me while I change. Then we walk into the square, where I throw the bloodied shirt on the fire and sit next to Flo.

She and the others watch calmly as the shirt burns. No one passes any comment.

I stay late in the square, long after most people have gone to bed. Flo, Ouzel, and I sit in companionable silence for hours, talking occasionally but mostly just enjoying the fire and listening to the night.

Flo breathes slowly and rhythmically with her eyes shut as if meditating. Her presence is healing.

Maybe she feels me watching her. I don't know. But one time she lays a gnarled hand on mine. That's all she does, but instantly, I'm filled with peace. My anxiety about the fight evaporates. She leaves her hand there and I'm comforted by the contact.

"I've never felt so free in all my life," I say.

Her dark eyes shine in the firelight. "Me neither."

This is Flo Crow

MIN CROUCHES BESIDE my bed and wakes me soon after dawn. "Flo has died."

I struggle to take in what she's saying, still smelling woodsmoke in my beard and feeling Flo's warm hand on mine.

"Come on." Min pulls me to my feet. "She liked you. Come and see her."

I splash cold water on my face, and we go back to the garden.

And there's Flo, sitting peacefully next to last night's smoking ashes, where I left her two hours ago.

Ouzel sits on her shoulder and regards her assembled friends calmly. He doesn't complain or even flutter when Big Luke lifts Flo's body and carries her from the garden like a sleeping child.

"Would you like to come to her funeral?" Min asks me.

"Yes. Where?"

"In the Wild."

I've never heard of the Wild before, but this isn't the time to start asking curious questions.

We all follow Luke down an alley between two houses, across a wooden footbridge over a stream, and into a forest. The mood is quiet, but no one seems particularly upset, despite having lost one of their friends. Even Tara, Flo's apprentice, strolls along as if we're off for a walk.

I can't understand their lack of emotion. I'm deeply affected by the old woman's death, close to tears, and I've only known her a few days. How can the insiders not care? What are they going to do? Dump her in the woods?

Min squeezes my hand and I'm heartened to see her eyes glistening too. Thank goodness for that.

My body gives a vigorous jump, as if I've fallen asleep and woken with one of those multiple muscle jumps. It's odd.

We walk a long way into the forest before we stop in a clearing, where Luke lays Flo on the ground.

Ouzel flies to a nearby branch and watches.

People find places to settle, while three of the women attend to their friend. Fliss and Cindy straighten Flo's body into a comfortable position, tidy her clothing, and place her head on a pillow of woven grass and flowers. Tara takes a jar of red powder from her shoulder bag and rubs the dull colour gently into Flo's brow and cheeks, hands and feet.

The clearing fills with strangers. All around, people step from the trees, greeting various members of the square respectfully and talking quietly in groups.

"Friends and relatives from other havens," Min tells me. "From all over the West Country by the looks of them. Those are Flo's cousins from Bodmin Moor." She nods at the latest newcomers, a group of twenty or so people who enter the clearing and move among the mourners, handing out stone flagons. "Cider," she says. "Be careful. It's rocket fuel."

I smile my thanks to an old man when I accept a flagon from him.

"Hang on." I turn to Min. "How did they know about Flo? And how did they all get here so fast on foot? She only died a few hours ago."

"We're in the Wild," she says. "Time and distance don't always work the same way here as they do outside. Not for everyone, anyway."

She shakes her head to fend off any further questions. "I don't know. If you want theories, you should talk to Andrew." She taps a fingernail on the flagon I'm cradling. "Are you going to open that?"

Tara is sitting cross-legged above Flo's head. When everyone is settled, she claps for attention and speaks clearly. "I am Tara Hand. Flo Crow is my friend. She grounded me and taught me as healer and midwife. We've birthed five new babies together. We always thought my first birthing of an old one would be hers, and here we are."

She puts her fingertips to the old woman's temples and says tenderly, "Go with love, my friend." Then she looks around the clearing and announces, "This is Flo Crow."

People stand to speak their memories of Flo, while Tara maintains a serene presence beside her mentor and everyone else sits in respectful silence, passing around flagons of cider. There are many people, so the speeches go on for a long time.

I lean back against a tree and get pleasantly mellow while words of love and fellowship flow, feeling a sense of belonging I've never known before.

Min sings for Flo. Her song starts low in some lyrical foreign language and builds to a stunning soprano celebration, as if she's climbing the mountain of Flo's life with her.

Sunlight flashes in the treetops. For a second, I think a golden angel has landed there to listen.

Min stays in the heights for some time before returning to the lower slopes with softening refrains, and then she finishes with a whisper of childlike joy that carries clearly.

Andrew plays beautiful tunes on his flute while various groups take turns dancing around Flo's body. When Min pulls me to my feet to join the dance, I sway, surprised at how drunk I am. After our dance of respect, I slump back against the tree and my mind buzzes sleepily.

A movement in the undergrowth across the clearing draws my attention when a lion's huge head pushes through a clump of foliage. He studies me calmly for long moments and then withdraws back into the greenery without a sound. I recognise him from my boyhood dreams. His presence at Flo's funeral fills me with a deep sense of well-being.

Lamps are lit at some point, and I drift off, comforted by the cider and lulled by the murmur of a hundred quiet conversations.

When I open my eyes, Flo is standing up.

My heart lurches. Shock wakens my brain sharply.

Her old body remains supine on the ground. She is still dead, as far as I can tell, but she is also standing on tiptoe, smiling broadly, stretching her hands into the air and showing none of her aged stiffness.

She is a young version of Flo.

I gasp with delight at seeing her spirit.

Ouzel launches himself from his branch and flies directly to Child Flo's shoulder. She kisses his beak and giggles.

Everyone in the clearing studies her keenly. It feels like the world is holding its breath.

Child Flo looks round at all her family and friends with a blissful smile, gives Tara a big hug, and skips away into the woods with Ouzel fluttering on her shoulder.

Silence hangs in the air, and then everyone is clapping and cheering.

Music starts simultaneously from three different places and the tunes blend together. There is singing and dancing and laughter everywhere.

I hug Min and cry happy tears. In my bones I feel her sweet humming.

Cayal

Next morning, Min wants a cooked breakfast to soak up the cider effects. She invites Joe to walk down with her to Cap'n Jaspers on the inner harbour wall.

The café is quiet. It's too early in the day for tourists and definitely too early for the regular crowd of bikers, for which she is grateful and assumes Joe will be too, so they get one of the bench tables all to themselves.

Joe gazes past his boots into the dark, oily rainbows lapping against the harbour wall, lost in thought, while Min buys breakfast and watches him out of the corner of her eye.

"Look at me." She deposits a plate of bacon rolls and two mugs of coffee on their table and brushes wood shavings from her shirt. "Sawdust everywhere. No wonder I keep dreaming about joinery. You have a lot to answer for, mister."

Joe inhales steam from his coffee. "You're a natural. Should have been a carpenter." He bites off a chunk of bacon roll.

"Well, maybe, and I do like the smell of fresh wood shavings. That's your smell. You should bottle it." She chuckles. "But usually, I prefer my dreams to be more fun than doing woodwork." She opens her roll, folds a bacon rasher, and pops it into her mouth.

Joe stares across the harbour to the marina, where hundreds of yachts bob against jetties. "Dreams can tell us stuff sometimes, can't they? Guide us, I mean. I had a significant dream last year. It led me here, indirectly."

Min's mouth is full. She raises her eyebrows and makes a rolling *go on* gesture with her forefingers while she chews.

"When I was a kid," he says, "I used to dream about a lion."

Her heart sinks. She hides her dismay by swallowing her bacon and blowing across the surface of her scalding hot coffee.

Joe's gaze is distant. "He was a male lion in his prime. In my dreams, he'd watch me walking to school. I'd look over my shoulder and there he would be, always in the same place, sitting tall, watching me. I wasn't scared. I knew he wouldn't harm me. I thought of him as my lion, even after the dreams stopped when I moved up to secondary school." He chews his last bit of bacon roll.

She waits for him to continue.

"Early last year, it happened again. I didn't see him. I had a lucid dream in which I remembered my childhood ones and realised I am my lion. He's a symbol of my spirit."

He is searching her eyes, looking, she imagines, for a sign of amusement.

She knows he is seeing only seriousness there.

"That's when I decided I couldn't carry on fantasising about leaving the old job and setting up on my own. I had to do it. I had to do it right then and sod all the risks. Lion spirit. So I did it. And here I am."

"Here you are." She smiles to hide her anxiety.

They sip coffee and watch the lock gates opening to allow a yacht into the harbour.

It always unsettles her when he talks about his lion. Every time. Not that she'll freak him out by saying so at this early stage, of course. And she can always cope as long as the lion stays in his dreams.

"I saw him yesterday in the Wild. My lion."

Her heart sinks again, like a rock dropped into quicksand, but again she doesn't reveal it. "That doesn't surprise me."

Again, he looks to see if she is teasing him.

"Sounds like he's your spirit companion," she says. "If you're going to see him anywhere, the Wild is the most likely place."

He holds her gaze. "Do you have a spirit companion?"

She studies his innocent, serious, honest face, and decides to let the conversation take its natural course. "Yes. His name is Cayal."

He copies her pronunciation. "*Kai yal.*"

"He's a noble spirit," she says. "Peaceful, powerful, and gentle. My best friend. My Cayal."

"Have you met him in real life?"

"You can't half tell you're a newbie. People don't ask people things like that, you know."

He winces. "Sorry."

"I'll tell you, because you need to know some of this sort of stuff. And I trust you to keep my story to yourself. Okay?"

"Okay."

She suspects he's more excited about her trusting him than hearing her story.

"Cayal comes to me in dreams, and, sometimes, in my waking life. When he's with me I truly come alive. When we're together, if I think back to the times I've been without him, it's like remembering a dream, as if I've been functioning okay but not firing on all cylinders. Sometimes I go a long time without seeing him. But I know he will always find me again."

She stares across the harbour, aware that she's mirroring Joe's mood when he told her about his dreams. "He always finds me."

*

Her dream man is very real to her. And there's a kind of purity coming from her when she talks about him, so my instinctive jealousy makes me feel childish. "What's he like?"

"Magnificent. Huge. Not in body, not a physical giant, but in spirit. Bigger spirit than anyone else I've ever met. He's majestic."

A noisy family clatter about happily as they occupy the table next to ours, unhooking their masks ready to eat and drink.

Min stops talking, and we share The Look. It still thrills me.

"Shall we go back?" I suggest.

We return our plate and mugs to the counter and head back to the theatre. As soon as we're clear of people on the streets, I encourage her to continue her story.

"He's the most wonderful person I've ever known." Her voice falls away, and she studies the cobbles ahead of our feet. There's a faint blush on her cheeks.

"You love him, don't you?"

"I love him. We're beautiful together. Too beautiful to describe." She halts and touches my arm. "This is private, Joe. Okay? This stays between us."

"I'll never tell a soul."

She stares into my eyes. "I trust you."

A shiver runs right through me at the intensity we are sharing.

We continue up the lane, our forearm hairs brushing together innocently, deliciously, and the theatre comes into sight around the next bend.

The sudden blast of a motorbike engine bounces off the walls of surrounding buildings and is gone instantly as its rider speeds past the bottom of the lane.

I tense instinctively and wince at the loud noise.

"Will told me about the big fight outside the theatre the other night."

Yeah, of course he did. I roll my eyes at the mention of his name and catch her sympathetic smile before she hides it. The subject needs changing.

"What is the Wild? Yesterday, it seemed so solid and real, but today, it's like remembering a dream. Is it really as dangerous as it felt in there outside of our gathering?"

"The best person to ask about that is Andrew." She smiles fondly. "He's a bit of a scholar."

"I will."

For the rest of the day, while I strengthen the leg joints for my bench with countersunk screws and teach Min how to fashion walnut plugs for a decorative finish on each one, I wonder about this Cayal character who fills her dreams when he isn't around in the flesh.

I also wonder where Will fits in between her and this towering love of her life.

Does he know about Cayal?

I put these questions aside. They're unanswerable and only confirm my status as an outsider in the most important sense of the word. I focus instead on my thoughts about the Wild and decide to ask Andrew about it this evening.

The Wild

THE GARDEN IS quiet at first. Min has a second gig in the jazz club, and the other performers are taking advantage of the fine weather to extend their working day. Later in the evening, people dribble back in, and things liven up.

I sit across the small fire from Andrew and watch him conduct one of those concentration sessions with Fliss and Linda, repairing bits of the square.

Linda selects certain faded sections to sketch as if they're in good condition, and then somehow all three of them transfer each charcoal image on Linda's sketchpad to the actual buildings. They say little while they work, but their focus is intense. They finish the session with closed eyes and slow breathing, holding hands in silence.

I can't figure out how it works. I'm studying Andrew when he opens his crinkly eyes and returns my gaze with amusement.

"What?"

"Sorry. I was just trying to work out how you do that."

"It's magic." He chuckles. "And you want to learn." It isn't a question.

"Yes. Will you teach me?"

"Maybe. You might be able to learn my kind of magic."

In my head, Freddie Mercury is singing the soundtrack to this conversation.

"Or you might have a better chance learning some other kind," Andrew continues. "Not everyone can learn any of it, you know. Doesn't matter how they try, some people never get it."

"I understand. Can we try?"

"Yes, but not tonight." He looks at the women sitting either side of him. They both look drained. Him too. "I'm tired now. We'll give it a go tomorrow."

"Thanks. My job will be a lot easier if I can pick it up."

"I don't think so. Not how you mean anyhow. If you're talking about using magic to renovate the theatre, forget it. You're doing a good job with your hands and tools, with your fine skills, and once the work is finished, it'll stay finished. Making a magic structure is one thing, but maintaining it is a whole nother thing."

He inhales deeply and holds the breath for a while before exhaling steadily through his nose. His shoulders sag with the release. "It takes a lot of energy to keep things upright."

Fliss and Linda share a tired *you're not wrong* look with him as they stand and leave us to our conversation.

"How many kinds of magic are there?" Freddie's still there in my head, bless him.

"That's like asking how many magic users there are. The answer is many."

"What different kinds do people here use?"

"You know, people don't tend to ask questions like that in polite conversation around here. I'm not offended, but some might be. Okay?"

"Okay. Thanks for telling me."

"You'll figure things out as time goes on. Be aware, though, that a lot of folks will let you see some of their magic while keeping some hidden. This is not a community of open books."

"Got it."

"Some kinds are more obvious than others. You already know about Min's song magic, I think." He smiles innocently across the fire.

My face floods with warmth. "Yes."

"Surface magic is easy to see when you know it's there," he continues as if he hasn't noticed my embarrassment. "Like glamour. All the kids use that on the street."

"Glamour?" Min said the word once, about the secret door, but I don't know what it means.

"Illusions. Making something look like something else." He nods at Will in the centre of a rowdy group of newcomers as they settle at the far end of the big fire and flip tops off bottles of good German beer. "Will's entire act is glamour. He and Danny use it to mask the real magic."

Will goes still and stares at us, apparently having heard his name somehow through all the noise.

Andrew seems unaware of the sudden tension. "Flo and Tara's healing talent is magic, of course. That's as obvious as any you'll find."

He falls silent, staring into the glowing embers, looking old and tired.

Ask him now. "What's so dangerous about the Wild?"

Someone starts playing a fiddle, and people get up to dance, but Will remains sitting where he is, leaning forward slightly, his dark eyes shining like coals in the firelight.

He calls out to answer my question in that bantering, challenging voice that drives me mad. "Nasty things in there, Joe. Things that'll get you. Things that'll eat you."

I regard him calmly for a moment, trying as always to hide my irritation, before returning my attention wordlessly to Andrew.

He speaks as if Will hasn't interrupted. "The Wild is dangerous because it's lawless. It's a different world."

"Give me a clue."

"Here's the thing. Magic is a marriage of hope and rebellion. It's everywhere in the world. Always has been. But in most of the world, it's unknown. People stopped using it, believing in it even, thousands of years ago, and hundreds of years ago, and tens of years ago. It seems that each culture and each generation rejects magic a bit more than the one before. Some cultures more or less than others, but the general trend is to ignore magic and eventually to forget it."

Linda brings him a bottle of chilled beer, beads of perspiration rolling down its dark-green glass. He accepts it with an elegant kiss of her hand.

"In every culture, though, in every generation, there are people who don't ignore it. Some of them stick around in the normal world and they are often persecuted because of what they know, what they practise. But many don't stick around. They go into the Wild."

He takes a long, slow drink.

"Also, there are times when a culture that uses a certain kind of magic is conquered by another culture that won't accept the native magic. Alongside the migrations and wars in the history books, there have also been migrations of magic. There are feuds and wars in the Wild too. Some have been going on for centuries. You'll find people from any era you wish to name. Roman Britons? They're there. Ancient Britons? They're there too. Prehistoric people? Yeah, but don't go looking for them, will you? Some of the earliest ones *will* eat you." He chuckles and winks.

"Do only humans live in the Wild?"

"No, and I think you guessed that already. There are other creatures. Lots of them."

"What kinds?" I'm on a roll. I don't know if I'll find him in such an informative mood again, and I'm not about to waste this opportunity to learn. I visualise the golden angel I thought I saw for a second in the sunlit treetop yesterday. "Just magical versions of normal animals like we see in the outside? Or are there fantastic creatures too?"

"There is every kind of fantastic creature."

"Ha!" Will bursts into mocking laughter, and even Andrew pauses to look at him, but Will's scorn is for me alone. "That's right, Joe baby. There are monsters in there. Monsters and werewolves and vampires, and they're all gonna come and get you."

"There are," Andrew insists.

"Yeah, right." Will turns his sarcasm on Andrew. "So how come none of us has ever seen anything like that, old man?"

Andrew turns back to me. "Some dickheads think their reality is the only reality. That their knowledge is the only knowledge. Even so, such things do exist."

I'm about to reply when a new commotion heralds Min, home from her gig. Her eyes shine *hello* from forty feet away, but before I can return her smile someone gets in the way.

Will has jumped to his feet, and he grabs her, sweeps her towards the dance and keeps her spinning around in that skilled way of his.

She squeals happily and they join the dance.

I watch them in my peripheral vision, hoping jealousy isn't burning a visible hole in my face. I try to come up with something intelligent to say to Andrew, but the music changes and I catch Will's eye.

His face is towards me, his chin resting on top of Min's head as they circle slowly to a romantic melody. For a moment, a split second, his face changes. A wolf is grinning at me.

Time shudders to a halt. A heavy pulse pounds my eardrums, once, twice, and the moment threatens to last forever.

Then Will's normal sneer is back on his normal face, and the dancing couple disappear into the crowd while my blood runs cold.

Your heart is a lion

I CAN NEITHER MOVE nor utter a sound. Only a few feet away, on the main road, hundreds of people stand chatting outside the opera house. A cry for help would bring at least some of them into this shadowy side lane, but I am frozen with terror and cannot even squeak.

After an eternity compressed into an instant, the monster crosses the distance between us in two huge strides.

It has my throat in its jaws. The last sound I hear is my own destruction.

*

I wake early. Once my determined mental and physical banish-the-nightmare routine is completed, I consider Will.

Yes, he pisses me off. And, yes, his wolf-face stunt scared the shit out of me. Does he know about my phobia? How could he?

Andrew said something last night about glamour hiding the real magic. Might mind-reading be Will's real talent?

I don't think it is. He simply responded to the way the conversation had turned. He can't know I'm terrified of wolves.

Moving on deliberately from the scary stuff and leaving Will's annoyance factor out of the equation, I realise he's like lots of other insiders with his blind spot about the Wild.

Clearly, insiders consider themselves to be freer than outsiders and more in the know. They feel superior, actually, and the youngsters definitely think they're more street. Well, they *are* more street.

Do I sound embarrassingly middle-class and middle-aged using that expression?

Probably.

Yes, even in my head I do.

Anyway, if Will is an example, insiders also tend to think the Wild doesn't matter much to them and their way of life. Despite all the differences between them and outsiders, their connections to the normal world appear to be far stronger than their connections to the Wild.

Insiders aren't so different from normal people in their worldview. They might mock outsiders for being blinkered by their failure to see havens or do magic, but at the same time, many insiders fail to see the significance of the Wild that I understand instinctively. And which Andrew's knowledge confirms.

Not Min, though. She doesn't say much, but I get the strong impression she knows all about the Wild.

Sometimes, when I look deep into her eyes, I think she has access to all the knowledge in the universe. Quite often, I feel she definitely knows everything there is to know about me.

I luxuriate in thoughts of her, pushing the dutiful nagging about getting up and getting on with the job to the back of my mind. And all my thoughts lead me to the fact that I'm falling in love with her.

Whoa!

But there it is. This isn't a rebound thing. I've hardly thought of Carole since we started work on the theatre. Or Tony. When I'm with Min, it's almost as if my old life never existed.

The only time I've ever felt this way before is when waking from one of those soul mate dreams. In those brief moments before the delicious knowledge slips out of reach, the memory of a powerful love is identical to the feeling that's blossoming in me now.

A fiercely hot shower doesn't distract me from my fantasies or stop the sudden stomach lurches. Nor does it wash away my sense of impending doom when I consider Min's relationship with Will.

And that's before I even go near the subject of her perfect love, Cayal.

I toast a slice of bread and eat it while I dress. When I wander out onstage, I find Andrew sitting on a sawhorse, waiting for me.

He nods at my newly built bench. "Impressive."

"Thank you."

"Ready to learn some magic?"

"I'm ready."

"We have the place to ourselves today. It's sunny out there and the tourists are swarming, so all the insiders are out earning money. First thing we'll do is find out if you can pick up my kind of magic."

Hello, Freddie.

"I call it *threading*," Andrew says, "which is the nearest English equivalent I can find for the Diné word *bitah*. Fliss and Linda call it *seeing*, but it's the same magic."

"Dye-nay?"

"The language of the Navajo in Arizona. They helped me find this magic."

"Are you Navajo?"

"I'm Californian." He stands behind me and places his fingertips on my temples, directing my line of sight to a pile of rusty old scaffolding poles on the far side of the stage. "Tell me what you see."

"Scaffolding."

"Concentrate. Look at the rust."

I do so.

"Tell me what you see."

"Rusty scaffolding."

"I'll show you what I see." He takes away his hands but remains close behind me. "Watch the scaffolding."

I do. Maybe I'm going to see some spectacular trick. Is he going to renew the old iron?

The shadows around the pile of poles begin to lift. It isn't like a light shining in the darkness. It's more as if the air itself starts to glow.

The scaffolding has my full attention. The poles are outlined with faint light, each one delineated as if someone has traced it with a fine-tipped pen. So are the stage floor below and the wall behind. Everything is connected by fine golden lines.

"What do you see?"

"It's like everything is coming alive." I find myself whispering and clear my throat.

"Everything already is alive. Always has been, only now you can see it."

I look to the back of the auditorium, below the circle, where the deep darkness is now illuminated by countless fine, golden threads joining and delineating all the edges inside it. I assume Andrew has followed my gaze and is lighting the place up for me.

"Watch the scaffolding again. Focus on the rust."

There are tiny movements within the corrosion.

"Look closer."

I do, squinting with the effort, but nothing changes.

"Okay, you can't zoom in. Go over there and see it."

The threads part like water when I walk through them. No, not like water. Like air. I reach the scaffolding pile and study a single pole. The movement is easier to see close up. It's like millions of tiny golden dancers, grabbing partners and holding on. The air above them shimmers as if their iron dance floor radiates heat.

"What is it?"

"Molecular activity. Oxidation."

"So you're not making it happen?"

He barks a laugh. "You think I have time to waste making things rust? All I'm doing is colouring in what's already there so you can see it."

I nod at the golden lines in the air between us. "What's all this then?"

"I told you. Molecular activity. It's what the universe is made of."

He waves me back towards him, and all the illumination disappears. When I reach him, he puts his hands on my shoulders and turns me back to face the scaffolding again. "Now you know it's there, can you see it on your own?"

I stare at the bloody scaffolding for about ten minutes while Andrew sits on a sawhorse and watches patiently, but not a single golden line appears. Eventually, I give up and turn to him with a shrug. "Doesn't look like I've got it."

"You haven't given it much of a chance. I was fourteen days in the desert before I saw it." He chuckles at the face I pull. "Patience isn't your strong hand, eh?"

"Well, you know."

"Tell you what. I'm going down to Cap'n Jaspers and eat. You sit here and concentrate. Or not. Up to you."

"Tell me about the desert."

"What about it?"

"What happened to you there? How did you find the magic?"

"It was a long time ago. I was about your age. How old are you?"

"Thirty-three."

"Younger, then, but not by much." He stares out into the arena as if into the past. "The initiation is eighteen days alone in the desert. Nothing happened for my first five days and nights. Not a thing. I was in a world of emptiness, wondering if anything would happen at all, but the old Navajo woman who prepared me said it would probably be that way."

He touches the turquoise stone threaded into his hair, rolling it between forefinger and thumb. "She gave me this sacred stone to hold on to while I waited. On my sixth night, something flew high over the desert in a big arc from east to west. It glowed like a spaceship re-entering the atmosphere, but it wasn't that. Wasn't a meteor neither."

"What was it?"

"An angel." He closes one eye and peers at me with the other.

"An angel."

"Yes."

"How do you know it was an angel?"

"Because I met him nine days later when he walked out of the Wild. He was hurt, torn up real bad. Stayed with me for a night. I fed him, patched him up the best I could, and next day he went back into the Wild."

He smooths his thick white hair. "That was the first I knew of angels and the first I ever heard of the Wild. Forty years on, I'm still learning. Anyhow, the experience opened my inner eye, and I found the threading magic."

He raises a sardonic eyebrow. "So don't tell me it ain't working for you after ten minutes, okay? I'll be in Cap'n Jaspers."

He glances over at the scaffolding as he steps down from the stage, and the pile of iron that has probably lain undisturbed for two centuries suddenly spills across the stage floor. He chuckles to himself as he walks out of the theatre.

I don't have his magic. It isn't that I don't have the patience. I simply can't feel anything, and somehow, I know this magic isn't in me. Maybe I have some magic and maybe I don't. But if I do, I'm pretty sure it doesn't involve golden lines.

I get to work and select blocks of timber from the stack I've set aside to build a backdrop frame for the stage. An hour later, I'm busy sawing wood when Andrew returns with Tara.

"Thought so," he calls from the back of the arena. "No patience, you youngsters." He clumps up onto the stage. "Tara thinks she might be able to help."

"We need somewhere clean and quiet to sit." She looks at the sawdust and shavings carpeting the floor.

I find my soft broom in the wings and sweep a small area clean.

"It'll do." She sits cross-legged and gestures for us to join her, then produces from her shoulder bag a black felt pouch and a handkerchief-sized black felt cloth, which she spreads flat on the stage between us.

"We keep this simple," she explains, rattling what sounds like marbles inside the pouch. "We ask a single question, and we get a simple answer. Okay?"

"Okay."

She closes her eyes and breathes steadily. The silence grows deeper, as if everything is waiting.

Then she opens her eyes and looks directly at me. "Does Joe have magic?" She plunges her hand into the pouch and pulls out a smooth black pebble painted with a white symbol that resembles an open eye.

"That's the Sun," she says. "The answer is yes."

"I knew it," Andrew murmurs.

Tara replaces the Sun and stirs the stones again. "What is Joe's magic?" She turns the pouch upside down and empties the stones onto the felt cloth.

We study them, each one painted with a different symbol in white or red or blue.

"You are very old," she says.

"Thank you."

"You are a lion."

There's something in this.

"You work in wood."

Well, duh. I look around at all my timber and can't help giving a quick eye roll.

Tara taps the back of my hand to get my full attention. "Your heart is a lion. Your *magic* is in wood."

Andrew picks up a small cut-off cube and hands it to me.

Tara touches it. "Oak."

It is oak.

She presses a fingertip lightly to the middle of my forehead and holds it there. "You see things. You are a protector, a provider, and a healer. Not my kind of healing. You heal through action. You bring truth and balance, and sometimes it hurts. Sometimes pain accompanies you. It isn't clear to me if you bring the pain or it brings you. Maybe it's a coincidence you arrive at the same time. I don't know."

Her eyes glaze over. "Out of pain you will help to bring truth and balance."

Andrew and I exchange a look.

Tara blinks and takes her finger away. "You are oak," she says with a note of finality.

I don't know what to say.

Andrew grins as they get to their feet. "There you go. You're oak. We'll let you play." He links arms with Tara, and they leave me in silence.

There's no doubting her sincerity and talent, but I don't have a clue what she's talking about.

I put the little block of oak in my pocket and hum a happy tune as I lock the front door behind me on my way to get my brunch from Cap'n Jaspers. Whatever all this wood magic and everything means, it feels good.

Let me give you a hint

"JOE...OH," CINDY AND Debs call in sweet, two-part harmony as I hit Southside Street. They're across the road, spinning poi for face-masked tourists on the wide cobbled area in front of the old glassworks.

People in their audience notice me, and I grin back and wave. I'm an insider!

The grin stays put while I stroll round behind the Navy Inn, but it drops at the sight of a long line of motorbikes at the kerb and dozens of leather-clad riders standing around drinking mugs of tea outside Cap'n Jaspers.

My stomach flips and my pace slows. Am I really so hungry? Probably not.

But it doesn't look like the gangs from the other night. These guys are more the kind of law-abiding enthusiasts I used to meet all the time during my biking days at university, when my friends and I rode out into the countryside most weekends.

I get close enough to see for sure. Yep. They're talking bikes, of course, and there isn't a single outlaw type among them. All wearing masks. I nod hello as I pass and feel perfectly safe admiring their highly polished machines from my table while I eat a quarter-pounder.

I take the other route home. Jimmy is juggling for a small crowd up ahead on Quay Road, sending a set of silver balls high into the air in a never-ending arc and singing a nonsense song with the cheekiest grin I've ever seen outside an Artful Dodger film.

Fliss moves with a pretty smile among the gathered tourists, collecting coins in a plastic bucket and exchanging a friendly word here and there. She sees me passing by on the harbour wall and shouts, "Hi, Joe!"

"Day off, boss?" Jimmy doesn't falter or miss a catch. I bet he could juggle those balls with his eyes closed.

"Early lunch break. I'm making a start on the backdrop frame today."

"It's gonna get bloody hot out here this afternoon. I'll come and give you a hand in a bit."

People are looking to see who Jimmy is calling to as I wave and walk on, and again I get that warm thrill of belonging. Friendship. *Family.*

And, again, the stupid grin falls off my face when I turn the corner alongside the theatre and bump into Will. Great.

"Ah, Joseph." He grips my arm above the elbow. "A word."

I glare at his hand until he removes it, then meet his stare and wait for him to speak.

He flicks sawdust from my shoulder with his fingertips. "About Min."

"What about her."

"Back off."

"Fuck off."

He narrows his eyes. "You don't want to fuck with me. Be warned."

"What are you gonna do, dickhead? Pull faces at me again?"

"She's mine, right? Accept it. Back off or you'll be sorry." He looks me down to the ground and back up with a sneer of contempt.

The horribly familiar buzz starts like a whisper in my brain and grows rapidly. *No!* I shake it from my head and slam him against the wall.

He exhales with a *whoosh*. There's whisky on his breath.

I pin him with my left forearm across his throat and draw back my right fist. "I told you, that hypnotism shit doesn't work on me."

He's laughing. I smeared him all over a rough stone wall, and yet he's laughing like a defiant schoolboy at the back of the class.

"Are you growling at me?" He can barely get the words past my chokehold, but he's still giggling. "Seriously, *growling*? What the hell do you think you are now?"

I don't know what he's talking about. He's a weird one. I shove him aside and point a finger in his face. "Min can make her own decisions. You stay out of my way."

He bursts out laughing again as I stalk to the theatre door.

I shut out his stupid laughter and relish the cool peace and quiet inside the building, but before I reach the arena, someone raps on the door I just closed. If the idiot has come back for more, I'm ready to deck him. I stamp back down the corridor to fling the door open.

But stop myself before I get there. I'm not a violent person. Punching Tony was childish. Understandable in the circumstances, some might say, but it isn't me. It made me feel bad about myself afterwards. I won't let Will goad me into a repeat of that mistake.

Whoever it is raps on the door again.

I open it calmly.

Two policemen in full black urban battle gear regard me through their emergency services respirators. I associate ESRs with getting punched and kicked by Met officers when I'm on protests. At least these two aren't hiding their shoulder numbers, so they're probably not planning to beat me up. Not yet, anyway.

"Joseph Walker?" the taller one asks. His voice sounds slightly metallic through the ESR mouthpiece.

"Yes?"

"Are you Joseph Walker?" he insists.

"Yes. What do you want?"

"I'm PC Turner," the other one says. "This is PC Peterson. Can we come in for a minute?"

I let them in and follow them to the auditorium, glad no insiders are working there.

Peterson looks round with interest, while Turner doesn't take his eyes off me. They're not showing a scrap of skin anywhere but are still careful not to touch me or anything inside the theatre. I suppose I can't blame them. They must encounter all sorts of situations in their job.

Is this all about the gang fight the other night? "What's going on?"

"Is anyone else here?" Turner's tone is brusque.

"No. What do you want?"

Peterson completes his examination of the arena and turns his attention to me. "Are you married to Carole Walker of 39 Hunters Close, Islington, London?"

I'm getting a very bad feeling about this. "Yes."

He nods. "Joseph Walker, I am arresting you for the murders of Carole Walker and Tony Evans. You do not have to say anything, but it may harm your defence if you do not mention when questioned something which you later rely on in court. Anything you say may be given in evidence. Do you understand?"

I stare at him with my mouth open.

"Where do you keep your clothes?" Turner wants to know.

"Carole's dead?" The world is crashing down around me. "And Tony? How did they die? Why would anyone think I killed them?"

I'm in a cold sweat. I glance back and forth between them and realise I must be wild-eyed. Right now, the thought at the front of my mind is that I don't want to appear guilty. But instantly I remember that Carole and Tony are dead, murdered, and my instinctive selfishness *does* make me feel guilty.

I take a steadying breath and swallow hard to relieve pressure building in my ears. "What the hell is going on? Are you bastards going to tell me what happened to them or what?"

"Let me give you a hint," Peterson says. "When I said you don't have to say anything, what I meant was *don't say anything*."

"Where are your clothes?" Turner asks again. "And the keys to this place. I'll lock your front door when we leave."

"Key's in my pocket. Clothes are in the back."

I give him the key, and he goes to find the dressing rooms, and that's that. We're on our way. Peterson leads me outside and into the back box of their police van. It's a reinforced glass cube with bolted-down bench seats, everything hard and smooth and easily washable. Turner appears with a sealed brown paper bag, which I guess contains all of my clothing he could find. He locks the theatre door and drops the key into an evidence bag, then they get in the front cab and remove their ESRs. Their seats look comfortable.

"Where are we going?"

They don't even look at me.

They chat to each other all the way up to London, but I can't hear them. The intercom must be switched off. I suppose the paperwork is easier with no conversation to record. We stop once for a toilet break, in the same services where Carole and Tony and I stopped last week on our way down to the West Country.

That day was a lifetime ago.

I can't stop imagining various ways in which they might have been killed. However I try, I can't erase the picture of them having sex in the hotel room when I walked in. That isn't how I want to remember them, but there it is.

Were they murdered by someone with a grudge against Tony? It has to be that because for the life of me I can't think of anyone who might have a grudge against Carole.

Except me.

Or maybe it was some random violence. That kind of thing happens all the time, right? Madness.

I hope they didn't suffer. I hope Carole wasn't scared. Maybe they were lucky and didn't see it coming. Just stepped from happiness into oblivion. That would be the best way to go.

We reach London in the late afternoon and drive directly to Islington Police Station, not far from our house.

Turner hands my possessions to a custody sergeant, who is also fully covered and wearing an ESR. He logs everything meticulously then takes me to a medical room and directs me to stand on a big sheet of paper and strip naked. He places the clothes I've been wearing in a paper bag, along with the floor sheet, and hands me a white paper suit to wear.

Then I'm introduced to a forensic medical examiner, likewise fully covered and wearing an ESR, who checks that I'm free of injuries, takes a sample of my DNA, and tests me for the Covids. During the examination, he asks when I last slept and ate. I assume he's checking my fitness for interrogation. I pass my medical, and the custody sergeant, now free of his ESR, locks me in a cell.

I sit on the bed and go back to wondering how and why Carole and Tony were murdered and who could have done it. I think briefly about a suicide pact but reject the idea immediately. It's ridiculous. The truth is, with me out of their lives, their futures were rosier than ever before.

I wish I'd answered Carole's call that day instead of chucking my phone in the sea. I wish I could talk to her one more time, to tell her I'm not angry with her anymore, maybe to remember some happier times together and say goodbye as friends. I hope against hope that however they were killed it happened instantly without pain or fear.

A policeman brings me a paper plate of egg and chips, with plastic cutlery and a plastic cup of milky tea. While I'm eating, it strikes me that I didn't get a chance to tell Min and the others what was happening.

Maybe someone saw me being arrested. I hope so. It kind of grounds my emotions to think of my new family knowing I wouldn't disappear on them without a word. I like that they will be concerned about me. The thought brings a lump to my throat.

Quite a temper

THE UNIFORMED POLICEMAN comes back and takes me to an interview room, where he tells me to sit. Another one stands silently inside the door while we wait.

I study the room, including the double-cassette tape recorder fixed to the wall at one end of the desk, the big pane of darkened glass set into the wall opposite me, which I assume is a one-way window, and the two little film cameras, one above the window and one below it, both aimed at me from different angles.

The clock on the wall above the door says 5:00 p.m. when two plain clothed detectives walk in. The man sits opposite me and the woman beside him.

Before a word is uttered, the woman unseals two cassette tapes and places them in the recorder. She turns the machine on and says, in a clear North London accent, "Interview with Joseph Walker. Present are Detective Chief Inspector Ian Dawson and Detective Sergeant Jennifer Smith."

Dawson speaks directly to me. "I'll remind you that you are under arrest and being interviewed as a suspect in the murders of Carole Walker and Tony Evans. Do you wish to have a legal representative or an impartial witness present in this interview?"

Although his soft Scottish accent makes him sound unthreatening, I'm under no illusion about the danger he poses to me. As far as he's concerned, I'm a murderer.

"No."

"You may change your mind and ask for one at any time."

"Thank you."

"What I'd like you to do," he says, "is account for your movements over this past week."

"I will. But first, tell me what happened to Carole and Tony."

"I will. But first, you need to account for your movements over this past week."

"When do you want me to start from?"

"Any time you like."

"Okay. I take it you know I stayed in Plymouth on Wednesday, when Carole and Tony came back to London." I pause for him to confirm he does know this, but he regards me silently, so I carry on talking.

"I spent the rest of Wednesday buying bedding, clothes, food, and stuff. Thursday morning, I started work on the theatre. And I've been working there ever since, until the policemen picked me up today."

I shrug and look innocently at him. I've had plenty of time to think about this and have decided not to mention the insiders. They have nothing to do with any of this. They don't deserve to have the police invade their world simply because my life has suddenly turned into a nightmare. "So what happened to Carole and Tony?"

Dawson shakes his head. "You need to give us more first. Tell us about your trip to Plymouth."

"We went to the West Country to look at properties Tony bought in a job lot at auction. One in Somerset, three in Cornwall, three in Devon. The theatre in Plymouth was last on our list."

"Why were *you* there?"

"Tony asked me to survey the buildings."

"You're a builder, are you?"

"Carpenter. Formerly a chartered surveyor."

"And Carole? Why was she there?"

"She decided to make a holiday out of the trip. That was the official version. Of course, now we all know she was there because she was shagging Tony."

"So I understand," Dawson says. "This was the first you knew of that situation?"

"Yes."

"You found out about them on Wednesday and that's when they decided to come back without you? And you decided to stay put in Plymouth?"

"I found out on Tuesday. I slept rough in the theatre that night and went back to talk to them on Wednesday morning. That's the last time I saw them."

He removes a few sheets of printed paper from his file and shuffles through them, glancing at me over the top of them from time to time. He keeps me waiting before saying quietly, "You have quite a temper, don't you?"

"No."

He studies the papers. "Tony's post-mortem revealed recent dental work. His dentist says he went in for treatment to a damaged crown on Thursday morning. We also spoke to his solicitor, who told us his client had a cut lip when he visited Thursday afternoon to instruct him that he wished to transfer ownership of the theatre to you. The solicitor says Tony told him you punched him, and why." He raises his gaze. "Do you still say you don't have a temper?"

I shrug.

"For the tape," Smith announces, "the suspect shrugged his shoulders."

"I walked in on them shagging. Not exactly a normal situation. I don't normally have a bad temper. What happened to them?"

But Dawson isn't ready to tell me. He takes me back to my verbal account and examines it. He walks me through everything I've said so far, taking each small section in turn and encouraging me to remember more and more about it before moving on to study the next section.

He's making me commit further and further to my story and manoeuvring me into spaces where I will have to invent things on the spot if what I'm saying is concocted and rehearsed, inventions I'll then have to remember accurately when he re-examines me later. He's calm and meticulous, like a surgeon, cutting deeper and deeper.

My main difficulty is keeping the insiders out of the picture. I manage to do it but suspect these lies of omission make me look guilty, so I compensate by talking in great detail about my dealings with builders' merchants and subcontractors and the timber yard.

"I bought lots of stuff in Plymouth last week. All the credit card receipts are in my wallet. They'll prove I was where I say I was. Take a look at them."

"We are."

Explaining my whereabouts during Flo's funeral gives me the most trouble. I'd lost track at the time, but calculate now that it took place on Saturday, and today is Monday.

Still Monday. It's been a very long day.

Anyway, I didn't see anyone on the outside from Friday evening until Sunday morning and have no receipts to cover that thirty-hour period.

The fact that I'm being interviewed in Islington tells me the murders must have occurred here, and thirty hours would have been long enough for me to get from Plymouth to London, kill them both, and return to Plymouth. The time gap worries me.

But Dawson doesn't probe this weakness. He allows me to explain it away as time spent working alone in the theatre. From that, I assume the murders must have occurred before then.

Thursday night? Perhaps. I'm tired. My brain is buzzing from being interrogated for two hours and I don't trust my powers of deduction.

He pulls a slim folder from his file and rests his fingertips lightly upon it. "We want to talk to a Plymouth man of about your age and height, but thinner. Wears black clothing in a rather theatrical style. He has longish dark hair and a little Van Dyke beard. Sound like anyone you know?"

Shit. I shake my head. "No one I can think of."

"Doesn't sound familiar?" He purses his lips and shakes his head too, as if sympathising and trying to jog my memory.

"No."

"That's odd." He slips a glossy ten-by-eight photograph from the folder, places it image-up on the desk, and announces an evidence number for the tape.

It's a good quality shot of Will and me outside the theatre. I have him pinned to the wall and am threatening him with my raised fist. Both our faces are clearly visible.

"Oh, *him*." My mind races through various possibilities.

"Yes, *him*." Dawson raises his eyebrows and waits for whatever I come up with. For a moment, he looks, I think, incredibly tired of having people lie to him.

"He's a nuisance who heard I'm taking people on and keeps pestering me for labouring work. I needed a couple of tradesmen and found the ones I want. He has no skills anyway. Eventually, he got a bit nasty," I nod at the photo, "and I told him to back off."

"This is another example of you not having a temper, is it?"

I sigh. "Look. Things took a nosedive last week and, yes, maybe I've been more touchy than usual. Surely that's understandable, no?"

The detectives turn to each other wordlessly. They don't buy it.

Tough. I've chosen my story and now I have to stick with it.

"No stranger to a police cell, are you?" Smith studies a document. "Five arrests in four years." She waits for me to comment.

"Protests. The environment and social justice. Passive resistance. Your boys in blue have knocked me about, but I've never reacted violently. Your records will tell you that."

"What's it all for?" she wants to know. "If you're not just after a scrap, why do you do it when you know you'll keep getting arrested?"

Do they really not know that getting arrested in numbers is one of our tactics? I recite the three-minute presentation of facts I learned from an Extinction Rebellion newsletter.

"Mass extinction has begun. A million species are in danger of disappearing forever. One in four of all our animals, birds, and insects are on the brink of extinction.

"The world's climate is changing faster than it has in sixty-five million years. Back then, ninety per cent of all species vanished forever. It may be happening again.

"This time, humans are responsible because we're ignoring the signs and the science. Governments have refused to take positive actions within their power, allowing relentless consumerism and irresponsible industry to pillage and pollute our world."

Their faces are blank.

It isn't what they want to hear, but at least I'm giving them something. For all I know, the message might even get through to them. I continue to the end of it.

"Three-quarters of our land and two-thirds of our oceans have been significantly changed by industry, farming, and overfishing, leading to wildlife disappearing at an average of sixty per cent across species populations in only fifty years.

"The insects that pollinate our plants are dying. No pollination means no food. The bugs that protect our crops from pests are dying, increasing the risk of famine and disease.

"Oceans are acidifying and heating up, which is killing a quarter of all ocean species, further destabilising all life on Earth.

"This isn't science fiction. It's real and it's happening right now. Governments and industry aren't acting fast enough to safeguard our future. They won't act at all unless we pressure them to.

"Together, normal people like you and me can bring about great change, but only if *we* act now. If we wait any longer it will be too late."

I learned these facts to tell magistrates when I appeared in court, but this isn't the first time I've recited them to police officers. Because you never know.

Dawson and Smith respond with the same professionally neutral expressions I'm used to seeing.

"Your most recent arrest was nothing to do with the environment," Dawson says. "It was at a Black Lives Matter rally. You might be a lot of things, but you're not black. So tell me that wasn't just an excuse to kick off one Saturday afternoon."

"Do you really think only black people believe black lives matter? Climate breakdown and racial injustice are two symptoms of the toxic system that's driving us to extinction."

He reads down his page. "Defund the police?"

"Myths can be unmade."

"What myths?"

"In this instance, the one that says so many aspects of state assistance for people in need have to be provided by the police. That so much state funding must be allocated to your organisation at the expense of health and social workers. Wouldn't you and your colleagues like to let all that non-policing work go and get back to your proper jobs? And do you *like* your uniformed people being militarised?"

Smith rolls her eyes.

Dawson doesn't, but it looks like he's heard enough of my stuff. He produces another folder and announces its evidence number. "You asked what happened to Carole and Tony." He opens the folder. "This is what happened."

I stare down at two photographs of carnage.

Carole and Tony lay torn apart in our old bedroom at home. There's blood everywhere. Blood and guts and flaps of skin and clumps of hair. Everywhere. Soaked into the bed and carpet and even splashed all over the walls and windows. The bodies are unrecognisable, but it's definitely our bedroom and the police are telling me it's Carole and Tony.

I can't take the horror. Can't believe what I'm seeing. My heart thumps massively. My mind rebels. I shove my chair away from the desk, from the photographs.

Dawson's mouth moves, but I can't hear anything except blood drumming fast in my ears.

He and Smith study me while I reel from the shock.

It takes me a while to get myself together. I sip tepid water from the plastic beaker Smith hands me and focus on Dawson's face to keep my gaze away from the photographs.

"I didn't do this. I couldn't do this. Please, hurry up and find a way to know I didn't do this, so you can start looking for whoever did."

I'm not a terrorist

"OKAY." SMITH CLOSES the hideous folder. "Help us to help you. Tell us about you and Carole."

"What do you want to know?"

"Everything. How long have you been married?"

"Twelve years."

"Why do you think that happened between her and Tony?"

"I think you're asking the wrong person."

"We can't ask them. Why do you think it happened when it did?"

This one is easier. "I changed jobs two years ago. Neither of them was very keen about it. In fact, that's an understatement. My whole family thought I was having some kind of breakdown."

"Who do you mean?"

"Carole and my parents. And Tony, I suppose."

"Where are your parents?"

"Florida. When I left the firm, Dad sold up in disgust, and they took early retirement."

"You don't get on?"

"We share a mutual disappointment."

"You're a self-employed builder?"

"Carpenter."

"And you said your old job was...?"

"Chartered surveyor."

"Junior partner in a successful little firm, in fact."

"Yes."

"That's quite a downsize. So, were they correct? Were you having a breakdown?"

"No."

"Come on, Joe. You're making me drag this out of you like I'm drawing teeth. I thought you wanted to help."

"Okay." I sit forward and meet her calm stare. "This is how it was. Carole and I met at university. We both studied maths for our first degrees, although with different careers in mind. I planned to join my father's firm and she was heading into the city."

The memory of her fierce ambition gives me a private smile.

"She worked hard and was very good at her job. It involved project management, hiring and firing, with quite a big team under her. She was always busy and must have been well regarded in her industry because headhunters stalked her all the time."

"Firing?" Smith interrupts. "Did she do much of that?"

"Not individually, I don't think. Not personally. But her last project was working out how to run the business with far fewer people after the fourth pandemic wave." I frown. "Or fifth. Anyway, it meant lots of contracts weren't renewed."

"Did she ever mention any names? Anyone who might have felt hard done by?"

"No." I can't remember a single name from Carole's work. Not even her colleagues. What does that say about me? "Sorry."

"No problem. We'll ask there. Carry on."

It's an interesting angle. I try to remember what I'd been about to say.

"Well, she was a go-getter basically, and she always expected me to go-get too. I played the game for as long as I could, but even by the time we were married, straight out of university, my plan was to get out of surveying eventually. I had this dream of working with wood from sustainable sources, turning my hobby into a business and being my own boss. It wasn't a secret. Carole knew all about the dream, but apparently, she never thought I'd do it. She was shocked when I said I was actually going to leave the firm."

I flash back to that bloody awful family dinner when Carole announced my intention before I was ready, and everyone shouted at me like I was a difficult child.

"She really worked on me. They all did, her and my parents and Tony, but I put my head down and carried on. It was stormy as hell at first, but once they realised how determined I was, the rows stopped.

"Even then, I knew they were talking about me behind my back. I was okay with it. I understood. They expected my business to fail within its first few months. They were convinced I couldn't have chosen a worse possible time, with the first pandemic and the economy struggling so badly. But I was doing something I loved, and it worked out okay for me."

I look back and forth between them. "That's it. I don't know what more I can tell you."

"You think that's when Carole and Tony started their affair?" Smith asks. "When you made your big life change."

"Yes."

Dawson takes the reins again. "Money isn't important to you?"

"I need it to live, same as everyone does."

"But you're not a greedy man?"

"I don't think so, no."

"It's plain luck, then, that you've ended up owning a two-million-pound house in Islington and a half-million-pound property ripe for development in Plymouth?"

Bloody hell. He's right.

Smith is doodling on a writing pad. She stops and looks up. "How did you feel when you caught Carole and Tony having sex?"

"I was pissed off."

But that isn't the whole story. I remember that lonely night on the stage floor only a few days ago and recall my emotions. I mean, I'd found my wife in bed with my best friend, and what concerned me most was *how could she think I'd hit her?*

Not *why was she doing my friend?*

Not *how could Tony do that to me?*

Not even *why were they being careless enough to get caught so easily?*

No, what I'd wondered was how come she didn't know me better. When it was pretty clear from the circumstances that I'd been missing one or two things about her. And about Tony.

I remember my numbness when I realised the part of my life that included Carole and Tony was over.

But it didn't break my heart the way I might have expected it to. Considering my immediate strong attraction to Min, I had to question whether I ever really loved Carole.

Smith is waiting for more.

"I was hurt and pissed off with both of them. They were the people I trusted most in the world, and they betrayed me. For two years. They should have told me what was going on."

"Tell us about Tony," Dawson says.

"He was a wheeling-dealing property developer." I smile sadly when I recall Tony's job description in his own voice. "Always on the lookout for a good deal. I expect he could be ruthless in business life, but I never saw that part of his character. We were best mates ever since school. Like brothers." I shake my head. "I didn't think he even liked Carole."

They watch me in silence for several seconds, then Dawson calls a break.

It's seven o'clock. We've been going at it hard for two hours. My head's buzzing.

They leave me in the interview room, and the silent policeman comes back to stand inside the door. He brings me a cup of sickeningly sweet tea, which I sip while waiting. It makes my teeth itch. Why don't they ever ask if I take sugar?

When they return, Smith switches on the tape recorder and Dawson gets straight down to business.

"Tell me how you got blood on your jeans and shoes."

It must have been the fight outside the theatre, when Will and Danny dragged me inside before the police arrived.

I keep my features blank. "No idea. It could be anyone's blood, from any time. I've worked all over London this past year, including three months on a building site in Camden. People get injured. How much blood?"

"Specks. But it's blood all right."

"Look. It's not mine, or Carole's or Tony's. I know it and you know it. I don't know whose it is, and to be honest I don't know where we're going with this."

Dawson gives a decisive nod. "We'll talk again tomorrow."

The uniformed policeman takes me back to my cell, locks the door, and they leave me alone for the night.

*

Sitting at my writing desk, I enjoy the moon shadows cast across the rug from the tall many-paned window at my back, and the pool of warm yellow light from my desk lamp, and the faithful fountain pen in my old black hand.

Will there be many more words for me? I don't know. I've written millions of them in my long life, for hundreds of speeches and thousands of sermons, and I'm tired, if contentedly so. Friends are urging me to retire from the struggle for civil rights in America and enjoy my model making, and the idea is becoming more attractive by the day.

My decision is nearly made. I'm accustomed to living alone in this silent house. I can look back with satisfaction on my achievements. My only regret is never having found the soul mate I've always dreamed about. In the quiet of my retirement, I have no doubt she will continue to visit me in my dreams.

Now it is time for another decision: what shall I cook for dinner this evening?

The moonlight is blotted out, and in the same instant the window smashes. Glass showers across the room. I twist in my chair to see a monstrous ungodly shape reaching for me.

*

My lover and I roll around on her immense bed enclosed like a big open box of intricately carved cherry wood latticework, beating each other with plump cushions like naughty children, leaving outside for these brief sweet moments the promise and threat of the uprising my academic brothers and I are planning in Wuchang. I am Chinese. She is not. She pulls me closer and lifts her face for a kiss. She is Min.

*

Walking along the road from my English childhood home towards school, I pass the place where my lion watches me in my dreams. It feels good. Safe. I don't look over my shoulder, but I trust him to be there. His quiet courage fills me.

*

I hadn't expected to sleep at all, but I wake at dawn in a calmer state of mind. The numbness and sadness about what happened to Carole and Tony remains, but I trust I will be cleared, and I look forward to going home to Quarter Square.

After scrambled eggs on toast in my cell, I'm taken back to the interview room.

Dawson and Smith are already there. They take me over my movements during the week and check my story with the version I gave them last night. Their demeanour has changed. I hope it means they believe me.

When two quiet taps sound behind their heads, as if someone has tapped a coin lightly against the darkened glass, Smith announces a refreshment break, and the detectives leave the room.

Dawson returns after the break, but without Smith. In her place is a man with a stern, craggy face and an expensive suit. Oozing the natural authority of a moneyed birth, an elite private education, and a suitably high-flying career, he introduces himself as Sebastian Merritt from the Home Office.

I glance at the tape recorder, which no one has turned back on, and then at Dawson, whose face remains blank.

"Let's talk about people you know," Merritt says. "Tell me about your family and friends."

"Carole and my parents are my only family."

"We spoke with Carole's mother and father. They don't have a very high opinion of you."

"I know."

"How do you feel about that?"

"I don't care. They thought Carole was marrying down. I think they're ridiculous snobs. That's it."

"What about friends?"

"Mine?"

He gives a slow nod without breaking eye contact.

"There was Tony. He and I have lots of friends and acquaintances, but mainly it was the two of us."

"Your activist friends?"

Bill smiles in my mind's eye. So do Pen and Poke. "I don't know anyone by name."

He lets that pass. "What about colleagues at work? Bosses. Staff. Tell me everyone you can think of."

I don't know where he's going with this, but I do what he wants the best I can. I tell him about colleagues and acquaintances from my surveying days and temporary workmates on various building jobs. I tell him about local shopkeepers and neighbours and everyone else I can think of.

"Might anyone harbour a grudge against Carole, or Tony, or you?"

I went through this with Dawson and Smith yesterday. "I don't know."

"Search your memory. Can you think of any strange people or events in the recent past? Or further back perhaps?"

I try but can't come up with anything.

Merritt's disapproval is evident. "How do you vote?"

"I beg your pardon?"

"Do you vote at all? With all your activism, I expect you're an anarchist?"

Home Office? I don't think so. Special Branch more like. Our country's secret police, even if individual officers in the organisation might balk at the description. If it walks like a duck and talks like a duck, it's a duck.

My father accused me of being an anarchist. He meant it as an insult, as Merritt obviously does too. I don't consider it that. I've met anarchists in meetings and on protests. Quite liked some of them. It isn't my path, but I understand where they're coming from, and I respect their opinions.

"Are you a soldier? Do you consider yourself to be at war?"

"No. But I do believe the extreme right wing in this country and the USA has been waging an undeclared war on our democracies for several years."

"Why would they do that?"

"To create dictatorships."

"We are at war, then? You and your comrades are fighting a war to stop that happening?"

"I'm not a terrorist."

His smile is deliberately infuriating. Performance art. "So, if you're not a terrorist, and not an anarchist, which party do you vote for? Labour?"

"I did while Corbyn was leader of the party."

He doesn't try to hide his sneer. "Ah. Proper little rent-a-mob then."

I don't dignify that with a response.

"Before Corbyn? Since? Not Labour, then or now?"

"Not in the New Labour years. Or now. I don't vote for neoliberals."

He arches an eyebrow. "How did Carole vote?"

"Labour."

"She didn't have a problem with *neoliberals*?" He enunciates the word as if he's dangling it in front of his face and peering at it with private amusement.

I shrug. Carole's support for New Labour was indeed a touchy subject in our marriage, so we avoided it. Especially the illegalities and atrocities of the Gulf War when we were at school, which I couldn't forget once we were old enough to vote.

"How did Tony vote?"

"We never discussed it." For the same reason. Touchy.

"Property developer. Probably a tory, eh?"

"We never discussed it."

"I expect he was. Their voting habits must have been frustrating, Carole and Tony, for a man of the hard left like you."

Hard left. How pathetic are these people? "I didn't kill them."

He stands without a word of warning or goodbye, to either Dawson or me, and leaves the room.

Smith returns immediately, and the detectives turn the tape back on to wind up the interview.

At eleven o'clock they release me, and I walk free. I'm not allowed inside our old home, the crime scene. Not even into my garage workshop. But I am allowed to collect my van from the driveway. And they say I have to let them know if I plan to be anywhere other than Plymouth in the foreseeable future.

On my way to the house, I remember Dawson's remark about my owning it all now. House prices in Islington must have trebled since we bought the place, straight out of university and with both pairs of parents giving us generous wedding-present sums towards a big deposit. If Dawson reckons it's worth two million, I expect he's done his homework. When Carole's life insurance pays out it will clear our mortgage and I'll own the house outright, as well as the theatre in Plymouth.

Although with a murder investigation underway I don't expect the policy will pay out any time soon. And in any case, except for the sale of the house providing renovation cash for the theatre, I'm not interested.

Without even looking through the windows into the house, I collect my van and set off for Plymouth.

I'm under surveillance. The black car that follows me back to the West Country makes no attempt to hide.

I don't know if it's him

I REACH PLYMOUTH AT four in the afternoon. Twenty-eight hours have passed since my arrest, and I'm drained.

The black car sweeps past when I pull up opposite the theatre. I give its two shadowy occupants a sarcastic wave as they turn the corner.

Min is sitting in the garden with Andrew and some other insiders. She runs to me and hugs me hard, even crying into my chest a bit, I think, but drying her eyes before I can see for sure.

They've all been worried about my sudden disappearance. They listen to my story about the events in London, and more people arrive as the word spreads about my arrest. I have to repeat everything five or six times until everyone has heard it.

They're all concerned, but Min is horrified. As the insiders discuss what I've told them, and the conversation takes on a life of its own without any need for my input, she takes my hand and leads me away from the others.

We settle in the quiet spot under the tree where she teaches the kids, and she makes me tell her everything again in great detail.

She sits thinking for a minute. Then, "Tell me about all the policemen."

"The ones who interviewed me?"

"Yes. Start with them."

It's obviously very important to her. I tell her about Dawson and Smith. I don't know why, but she wants more, so I describe everyone I came into contact with since I last saw her. The two Plymouth officers who arrested me and took me up to London, the custody sergeant, the various silent policemen who fed and guarded me, Merritt—

"Who?"

"Some guy called Sebastian Merritt. Claims to be from the Home Office but he was very interested in my politics so more likely Special Branch. Seriously up himself."

"Tell me about him."

I recall everything from Merritt's interrogation. I tell her, word for word, what he asked and what I answered.

"What does he look like?"

"About my height. Dark hair. Strong jawline. Sharp eyes. A good head of hair for his age. Fiftyish." I scour my memory for other details that might lurk there. "Long fingers and bony wrists." I glance at my roughened hands and bruised fingernails and remember how I kept them under the desk after noticing Merritt's manicure.

"I don't know if it's him," she whispers, almost to herself.

"Who?"

"Tyac."

I blink. "Who's Jack?"

"Not Jack. Tyac." She spells it for me.

"Sounds like Jack."

She smiles bravely through a film of tears. "Yes, I know."

"So who is he?"

"An old enemy."

"An old enemy of yours?"

"An old enemy of ours."

Huh?

"I need to tell you something." She looks around to make sure our conversation is still private. "It's a big thing." Her eyes bore into mine.

"Go on, then." I keep my tone light but get the feeling this is going to be a serious talk. I have no idea where we're going.

She glances around once more, then takes a deep breath. "We've known each other before."

I smile. "I feel that way too."

She squeezes my hand. "It isn't only a feeling. We *have* known each other before. We've been lovers for thousands of years."

What the hell am I supposed to do with a statement like that? A neutral expression is the best I can hope for, but I don't know if I'm managing it.

She sings in a low voice, just for me. I don't recognise the language or the tune, but the spirit of her song slows my heartbeat.

Visions of a purple mountain range come to me, their lower slopes decorated with cultivated terraces and a pretty settlement of white stone buildings shining in the sun. A big circular temple with many columns supporting its domed roof stands proudly on a hilltop, above a river-threaded plain that stretches to the dark sea in the distance.

I see Min, many times in many different places in that beautiful land and always smiling. Always smiling at me. She holds my hand, and the action is mirrored in the visions.

We have always been together. We have always been in love.

Her song reaches its end. She gazes at me. "That was us you saw, Joe. You and me, together in the land of our birth, thousands of years ago."

She's telling the truth. I know it in my marrow, but it's difficult to accept.

She makes sure no one has wandered too close. "I'll tell you how it is with us. I am immortal. You are reincarnated repeatedly. We fell in love in Atlantis, when I was a priestess in the temple of Cleito and you were a woodsman called Cayal."

"Cayal," I whisper.

"It means golden lion."

We share The Look.

"Is Min your real name?"

"Minsilvia."

The way she says it makes me tingle. "What does it mean?"

"Daughter of the sea. Which is ironic because I can get seasick in a puddle."

That strikes a distant gong, somewhere in the deepest cave of my forgotten memories. I start to remember fragments, as if it's all a dream, and Min allows me time to come to terms with the knowledge.

"Where was it?"

"The mountaintops of Atlantis are now known as the Azores. Most of the land was lost in a cataclysmic flood when the sea level rose after the last Ice Age."

"And when was it?"

"We first knew each other thirteen thousand years ago. We lived together again and again for a thousand years on Atlantis, before it was lost."

The memory of a memory trickles into my mind. I focus on it, letting it solidify, and gasp when the certain knowledge hits home that I was poisoned to death. "Who is Tyac? Why did he kill me?"

She holds me tight. "He was a powerful man, a priest in the silver temple of Poseidon. He loved me. He was determined to have me, but I rejected him because I loved you, so he murdered you."

I absorb the information.

"I can show you, if you want me to."

"Show me."

Her new song begins softly, and the memory swells in me.

At a fountain in the centre of a circular courtyard paved in yellow stone, surrounded by ornate pagodas and trellises, sunlight dances in the falling water, and the scents of a thousand different flowers float on the sea breeze.

The sun is low in the evening sky. Its heat is gentle. I sit on the low wall of the fountain and eat my supper while waiting for Min to finish her duties in the temple.

The ache in my stomach starts small, almost as soon as I swallow the honeyed bread, but it grows quickly and hits me like the kick of a mule.

I double over in agony.

I've been poisoned. I know it. I fall off the wall and can't stand again. I'm numb from the waist down, and my upper body is going the same way.

I want Min. I'm dying. I want to hold her close one last time before I go into the darkness. I lift my head with difficulty, look up at hundreds of stone steps towards the temple on the hill, and crawl to them.

On a normal day, I would skip up those steps in no time at all, but now I don't know if I can make it. I pray to my family god, the great lion Maahas, and beg him to help me.

It takes an eternity. I soil myself on the way but I'm beyond shame. I only want to see Min before I die.

Eventually, somehow, I reach the golden entrance steps of the temple. I'm a stinking mess, an empty husk, crawling on my belly and leaving a smear of blood and shit across the polished marble floor of the cool interior.

A woman's voice has been droning a ceremonial song. Now it falters. My sight is fading fast, and only the white blurs of priestly robes are visible, but I guess the singer is Min's mother, Shira, high priestess of the temple.

A hush falls over the holy ones as I drag myself towards the altar.

"Cayal!" Suddenly Min is here, turning me carefully and resting my head in her lap, her tears falling on my blind face. "What's happened?"

"Poison," I gasp.

"Tyac!" she screams. "This is your doing."

"It is." The hated voice echoes from the walls of the temple. "It *is* my doing. Who do you think you are to consort with an uninitiate? Who do you think you are to break our rules?"

She trembles violently. Her voice breaks. "You have killed him."

"Min." My voice is no more than a breath. "Forget him. Hold me. I love you."

She strokes my face with tender fingertips. "I love you, Cayal. I will always love you."

Shira's voice cracks across the temple. "Tyac, who do you think *you* are, to murder an innocent and boast of it as if your victim doesn't matter? This dreadful act will not go unpunished."

The sound comes of several pairs of footsteps running and scuffling.

"Hold him," Shira commands.

Fury strangles Tyac's voice. "I curse you, Minsilvia. I curse you to immortality, to barrenness, to an eternity of loneliness without your peasant lover and without a family to comfort you."

Min stiffens.

"And I curse you, Tyac," Shira proclaims. "You are banished from this land forever and I curse you to take on the nocturnal nature of the first animal you see after leaving our borders. I curse you to immortality as a restless man under the sun and a beast in the darkness. Cast him out!"

There come further sounds of struggle. Tyac continues to shout in rage as he is manhandled from the temple.

I can't understand his words and I don't care. My time is near.

Min holds me close and whispers in my ear, "Come back to me."

"I will."

A new scent reaches me, and new hands help Min support the dead weight of my body. Shira's voice is close. "Cayal, my daughter's love, may you be born and reborn again and again for as long as her immortality curse lasts, and may you find each other again and again, so that you may remain together in love."

Min kisses my forehead as I die.

Now, thousands of years later, I know the pain once more as terrible agony spreads from my stomach through my body. I slump forward to lay with my head in Min's lap. "What happened to Tyac?"

"The first beast he saw that night was a wolf."

I jerk nearly upright, convinced that this time my heart really has stopped.

She holds me and steadies me. "I know. I know all about it."

I rest my head in her lap again, enjoying the sensation of her stroking my temples, and wonder about all those lives I've lived. I can't remember them, but the memory of my first death is sharp and the crushing sadness of tragedy weighs me down. I cry quietly into Min's breast while she holds me.

People approach. She waves them away.

"This is how it works. If I'm with you when you die, I know where you will be born in your next life, although I never know when. Usually, you find me. Or, rather, you stumble across me, and I recognise you. If we're not together when you die, we can struggle to find each other when you're reborn. That's happened several times, especially during wars or periods of social upheaval. We've endured three long separations when I searched for you while you lived strings of lives in sadness and longing without ever knowing why."

Her tears fall on my face, as they did thirteen thousand years ago in the temple. I gaze up into her lovely eyes and remember those times of deep sadness. No specific circumstances, but a dreadful emptiness stretching across lives.

She dries her eyes. "When we meet, it takes time for you to understand our relationship. I never push your understanding faster than what comes naturally to you, although sometimes a situation forces me to accelerate your memory. Like now."

"How many lives have I lived?"

"I don't know exactly. Two hundred maybe."

"How many have we lived together?"

"Many."

"Tell me about them."

She chuckles. "You always want to know this. Every time."

My distress is fading, but I stay cradled in her arms, where I belong. "I've always liked Arthurian legends and Celtic art. Was I ever involved in any of that stuff?"

She laughs. "The Arthurian chivalry stories are fictional. They were copied from a myth cycle that originated in Brittany hundreds of years before the Romano-British era they claim to represent, adopted by Britain's new rulers after the Norman invasion and adapted to fit their twelfth-century worldview. The mediaeval depiction glorified a courtly way of life that you despised as elitist and damaging."

She grins. "And the nineteenth-century Celtic revival was an invention that bore very little resemblance to the ancient Britons that people now call Celts."

"You were there, through all those things."

"So were you. In the early English period you're talking about, you lived seven lives as master carpenters working for Saxon warrior chieftains whose people assimilated the Britons, and later for the Saxon kings who reigned over the land. It was a good era for you, for us, but I'm afraid there were no royal round tables or knights in shining armour." She aims an amused wink at my romanticism.

"Was I ever a Viking?"

She blinks at that. "No. We were Saxons then. Vikings were the enemy. Although we did have sixty happy years in Denmark in the eighteenth century, when you became a locally celebrated woodcarver. We took in laundry. In the winter months, we sat by the fire, me repairing garments for our townsfolk and you carving little wooden animals."

I like that. "Hygge."

She lifts a pendant from inside her T-shirt and unfastens its fine plaited leather thong. "You made this for me."

It's a fat dolphin, shaped sensuously in oak, only an inch long but with a joy of movement in its simple lines. It shines with oil absorbed from her skin over three hundred years. One side is flattened, and into it are carved the letters M I N, blackened with those natural oils. I stroke the little piece with the ball of my thumb and try to remember those happy years.

She fastens it and lets it drop back inside her T-shirt. "When we lose track of each other, this dolphin and my memories are all I have of you."

"Have we ever had any children?"

There's a tiny pause. "You have."

Ah, yes, Tyac cursed her to barrenness. Touchy subject? She disguises it well, but I think it hurts. I won't mention children again. "What about my most recent lives?"

"I haven't seen you for more than a hundred years. We lost each other after the Wuchang rebellion in China. I've traced you twice since then, once in America and once back here, but both times you'd already died. Last time, you were an exciting young scholar of Atlantis. The trail of your research led me to you after your death forty years ago."

Her body tenses beneath me. "Both times you were murdered."

"Tyac."

"Yes. He hates us. He's followed us through the ages, sometimes catching up and attacking us and sometimes losing us for generations. He's murdered you many times, even when you were only an infant."

"Is he a werewolf?"

"Yes," she whispers. "That's exactly what he is. And he might be this man Merritt. He's expert at changing his human appearance and attaching himself to government bodies, royalty, or organised crime. He likes any organisation that will allow him to work in the darkness. He often achieves positions of power, although he never seeks fame or reveals himself to the public eye. He uses those positions to gain knowledge, always with a single aim, to find us."

"I wonder if he was Jack the Ripper. Tyac the Ripper."

"We wondered that at the time." She gazes into the past for a moment, then blinks back to the present. "In any case, whether or not he is Merritt, he's on our trail again. From what you said about the murder scene photographs, I'm certain Tyac killed Carole and Tony."

Tyac

MIN HAS A gig, and I don't want to spend the evening dealing with questions from concerned insiders, so we leave the square together.

I manage to keep my hands off her as we walk without words down through the arena and across the stage into the cool darkness beyond, but the moment we enter my bedroom, she turns to me and we melt into each other.

It's our first kiss in a hundred years. Our tongues join in the passionate dance I've dreamed about forever.

She tastes divine, like honey, like a fresh new growth of meadow grass on a bright summer's day, like heaven.

And she's real. Not a dream, but a strong physical presence in my arms, hands pressing the back of my head and neck, jamming my face into hers. She matches my passion, moaning breathlessly and kissing as if she wants to eat me.

We come up for air and gaze into each other's eyes, our hearts pounding in unison.

She rests her forehead against my chest. Her voice vibrates inside me. "My Joe, my Cayal, my love, do you have any idea how I've longed for you? You've been in my dreams every night since we were last together. I've never stopped searching for you, yearning for you to come back to me." She lifts her face and smiles through glittering tears.

I hate myself for asking but can't go any further without knowing. "What about Will?"

"What about him?"

"You're lovers, aren't you?"

She holds my face and kisses me again, once, her lips closed and full. It's like a seal, a declaration and a confirmation of her love. "Will and I have had our moments from time to time, but we're not an item." She peers up at me. "I do take lovers when you're not around, you know. It's been a century, Joe. You don't think I should spend all those years completely alone, do you? Would you want that for me?"

"No," I lie.

"I understand, my love. Honestly, I do. But when we're without each other, we live with deep loneliness. We both have other people in our lives when we're apart. It helps."

She strokes my temples with her thumbs and gazes deep into my eyes. "When you come back there is no one but you."

I kiss her again and ask the question that is burning a hole in my brain. "Do you love him?"

"Yes, as the loyal friend he is. He's as jealous of you as you are of him, but get beyond that and you'll see he's a good man."

She hugs me. "Please don't worry. *You* are the love of my life. Friends like Will and Tara are loving company for me when I'm alone, but you have my heart forever."

"Tara?" That one has passed me by unnoticed.

"Yes. She's lovely. Why, would you have me limit myself to men only when I need love and companionship in your long absences?"

"I suppose not." I slip a hand under her T-shirt, the thought of her making love with Tara adding an unexpected new buzz to my excitement.

"That's good, because you've been a woman many times. When you carved my dolphin in Denmark? You were Greta."

My jaw drops and my hand stills on her breast.

She laughs. "This one always gets you, whichever gender you've come back as."

Obviously, there's going to be a lot more of this situation to get my head around than I've realised.

"Make love to me," she whispers.

I can't breathe.

"We've waited too long. Make love to me now."

We drop our clothes where we stand and come home to each other, become one on my camp bed.

"I love you." We say it together.

Afterwards, we sleep with our limbs still entangled.

Eventually, she stirs. "Better get a move on or I'll be late for my gig."

"No." I don't want to unwrap myself. I nuzzle her neck with a playful growl. "More."

She rises on one elbow and places a gentle hand on my shoulder. The laughter is gone. Her serious, direct look wakes me up fully. "We have to leave here. You do realise that, don't you? I'll sing in the jazz club tonight because they owe me for three nights and we need some cash to get us clear of Plymouth, but by tomorrow morning, we need to have disappeared."

"You don't have to work tonight. I have money."

"I suppose you mean bank accounts and plastic. Forget them. You may as well carry a big *Here I Am* sign around. We have to get off the grid. Quickly."

I frown and gesture around at the theatre. "What about this place?"

"Nothing else matters. Whatever we do in our lives that brings us together, we're only doing those things in order to find each other. Once we do, everything else falls away. There is only you and me."

"I told the insiders they can perform here. I promised I'll get it ready. They're relying on me."

"Trust me, they'll be fine. You've offered this place to them, and they will use it even though you won't be here. I know these people. I love them. You're not letting them down, and even if you were, they'd get by okay without you."

This new start isn't going the way I expected. Not at all. I drop back onto the pillow.

"What?"

I shake my head.

"Talk to me. What are you thinking?"

I speak slowly, opening my soul and saying the words as they surface. "All my life, people have told me what to do. Everyone has always known better than me. They all manoeuvred me into whichever position they thought I should be in and told me what I should be doing, who I should be. I played their game for as long as I could, but last year I broke free. Tried to, anyway. Carole and Tony were still pulling my strings, but I didn't know that until last week." I close my eyes and for a moment see them again in that hotel room.

"When I found Quarter Square, when I found you, my life turned around overnight. I'm free here. I make my own decisions and live the way I want."

She sighs.

I stroke her cheek. "I love it here with you. It's heaven."

"It won't be heaven when Tyac turns up." She kneels beside me and grips my upper arms. "He's hunting you. I guarantee he killed Carole and Tony to flush you out. That's how he works. Somehow, he'll be involved in the murder investigation, or at the very least monitoring it. Please believe me. If we don't run, he will find you."

She shakes me, her eyes glinting with tears. "He *will* find you and he *will* kill you! Again! He fucking will, Joe, and I'm not going to let that happen."

It's my turn to sigh. I hate this, but I know when I'm beaten. "Okay."

She splashes cold water on her face and dries it with my towel, then hunts for her knickers. They're under the bed. "Tonight, as soon as I get back, we run. Okay?" Her voice is muffled as she pulls her T-shirt over her head.

"I brought my van back from London."

"And a police tail with it." She pauses with her jeans hauled halfway up her thighs. "We'll use the van to get away from here, but we'll need to dump it before morning."

She buttons her jeans and pulls on her socks.

"I'll come with you now."

Right boot stamped in and laced. "You're tired. If we're going to drive through the night, you should sleep now while you can." Left boot stamped in and laced.

I can't deny it. I need sleep.

"See you in three hours. Sweet dreams. I love you." With a quick kiss and a smile, she's gone.

I take a long hot shower, shampooing my hair and beard twice, chuckling because beyond everyday cleanliness I haven't taken so much care with personal grooming since I was a teenager, and certainly not while I was with Carole.

I've grown the beard in this past year. She hated it. For me, it symbolises freedom from the constraints of commercial life. For her, it probably symbolised rebellion or something.

In any case, Min likes it.

While I shower, I sing Carole King's 'You've Got a Friend'.

I've always sung this old favourite when I was sad, wishing I could find that friend. I've been quietly sad all my life without even realising it. Min called it the loneliness deep inside. It was the sense of missing someone I didn't even know I was missing.

Now I sing the song with joy because the ache has gone, and I step out of the shower still humming it happily.

There are two men in my bedroom.

My heart jumps into my mouth and I nearly stumble back into the steamed-up shower cubicle.

Sebastian Merritt is sitting on my bed, leafing through my sketches for the theatre renovation. He looks up at me innocently.

On the other side of the room, blocking my exit, stands a stranger I assume is his driver. A strong, silent type with a dark crewcut and a heavy five o'clock shadow, he fills the space.

"Hello," Merritt says as if we've met by chance when passing on the street.

"What the fuck are you doing in here? Get out."

"Calm down." Merritt exudes that infuriating air of comfortable authority.

Naked, wet, vulnerable, I resist the urge to hide behind my towel as I dry myself. "What do you want?"

"I want you, Joe. I want you to come and work for me."

I squint at him. What the hell is he on about?

He gestures at his sidekick without taking his eyes from me. "Fisher and I work for a government department you won't have heard of. We investigate magic. Magical people, creatures, and places. Yes, they exist. I think you know they do."

I concentrate on getting dressed.

"The murders of your wife and her lover show all the signs of a werewolf attack." He leans forward to study my face. "And you don't seem even a little bit surprised by that statement."

"You're mad. I'm wondering how long you plan to sit around in here before you piss off and let me get on with my evening."

"Very good. Whatever you say, though, I know you are involved with magic. I've been around it long enough. I can smell it." He shuts his eyes and inhales deeply, a showman in perfect command of his audience. "I smell it on you."

"You need therapy."

He talks over me. "Magical activity is on the increase in the West Country, around this Barbican Harbour part of Plymouth in particular. My department has been monitoring it for months."

"What do you mean by *magical activity*?"

He chuckles. "Come on board and you'll find out."

"You're barking."

"What do you plan to do for money, Joe? It's been a while since you earned a regular income, and now you're down here and you've got this place to sort out. No business contacts or friends or family. What will you live on?"

"I'll manage."

"I'm offering you a full-time position. A good salary plus benefits."

"Stuff it. And get out. You're boring me."

"I'm not going anywhere. You really should be my friend. You don't want to be my enemy."

"You're full of shit. You don't believe in bloody magic any more than I do. This is some bullshit to keep me under observation. It's about my politics. That's all you're interested in. You're bloody Special Branch."

"Special Branch," he sneers. "I asked about your silly politics to throw those detectives off my own scent."

"Bollocks. This is all so you don't have to honour my legal rights. If you think I don't know what you're up to, you're even more stupid than you look."

Merritt shoots to his feet, and Fisher tenses, ready to spring if I make a wrong move.

"Be careful how you talk to me, young man," Merritt warns. "We know you've had an upset, but I don't take rudeness like that from anyone."

"How's this, then? Leave my property now or I will call the police." I glare at him with my forehead thrust forward and my fists clenched at my sides. My aggression is more about fear than anything else, but I hope they won't pick up on that. Might Merritt be Tyac? Can werewolves sense fear?

He shares an amused glance with Fisher. "Do you want to know who the highest authority in your life is, Joe? It's me. The police will do whatever I tell them to do. There's only one department that will protect you. Mine. Don't go fooling yourself by grasping at false security, will you?"

He and Fisher leave without another word, and I follow them to the main door. Fisher disappears around the corner. An engine starts, and the black car eases from the shadows.

"See you soon," Merritt says.

I close the door firmly.

*

Sprawled on the marble floor of the Golden Temple with my head in Min's lap, blinded by the poison and with all my other senses dimming rapidly, I hear Tyac shouting, his hated voice receding into the distance as guards bustle him from the building. A salty tear splashes on my lips and Min shakes with grief.

*

Suddenly awake on my camp bed, reliving random nightmares despite my best efforts not to, I know they are real memories. While I'm sweating and trying to get my heart rate under control, more memories arrive. I don't want them, but they come anyway.

I focus on the silence. I'm here now and I'm safe. I'm back with Min and we have a chance of happiness together. Focus on the safety. Focus on the silence.

I breathe steadily, recalling my first night in the theatre and my fears about noises in the roof space. Can't not grin. If I knew then what I know now, a few rats scratching about up there wouldn't have worried me.

There are no noises. For the first time since I moved in, there are no rodents scuttling or pigeons cooing. There is complete silence.

I hold my breath and listen, trying in vain to detect the slightest sound.

It feels like the theatre is waiting for something.

There it is: the unusual sound that woke me in the unusual silence and set my nerves jangling. A scrape somewhere high above, a pause, and another scrape.

Then comes a new sound, the quiet but easily identifiable crack of a seized window being forced open and a thick membrane of old paint layers breaking when the wooden surround is parted from its frame.

Someone is opening one of the windows set high in the wall just below the roof space.

A big, dark shape climbs through the window, its movements smooth and fluid and powerful. I recognise it from my nightmares.

My stomach drops into my bowels.

The monster is coming to get me.

It rocks its huge head slowly from side to side and then springs across a ten-foot stretch of bare brick wall to the iron ladder that runs up to the roof space. It lands on all fours with its snout pointing to the ground, and without a pause it runs headfirst down the ladder, all the way down in seconds.

Fear paralyses me.

The monster launches itself from the ladder, springs over the partition wall, and lands squarely in the middle of my room.

Galvanised by terror, shaking violently and tasting bitter stomach acid, I scramble back on the bed as far as I can go and cower in the corner.

The werewolf glares at me with insane intensity, its bloodshot eyes like hot lava in the gloom. Its stink fills my nostrils, a heavy mix of damp earth and raw flesh that makes me gag. It's bigger than I remember from my nightmares. It fills my vision.

Its belly jerks repeatedly beneath its shaggy fur. It's laughing at me. Mocking me.

I'm going to die.

In a split second, it picks me up like I'm a rag doll, slams me against the wall with a hammering force that knocks the wind out of me, and draws back one of its massive, clawed paws, ready to strike.

I can't breathe. Can't make a sound. Can't even think. I wait for the fatal blow.

It doesn't come.

Instead comes Min's beautiful voice. She stands in my open doorway and sings a song of power and enchantment.

The werewolf drops me and steps back with a frustrated snarl that makes me cringe.

Min continues to sing, drawing the monster's attention. It moves like a sleepwalker, swivelling its head towards her and its body following suit, but remaining in the same place until a new tone in her song commands it to walk to the partition wall.

When she pauses for a breath, it pauses too and twists its terrifying head back to me. Then she sings a high note, and they continue their strange dance of enchantment. Her song forces it to leap high and grab hold of the ladder. Its ascent is ponderous, almost thoughtful, as if it's dazed.

Again, she pauses for breath when it reaches the top and, again, it pauses in its retreat and glares back down at me.

Her song comes stronger than ever. It forces the monster to lift the window, climb through, and disappear from view as the window slams shut behind it.

I try to thank her, but she silences me with a raised hand and continues to sing, her voice powerful even as her body sags under the strain.

I guide her onto my bedside chair without interrupting her song. She leans on me. I put my arm around her back and give her shoulder a squeeze of support.

Eventually, she falls silent and slumps against me.

I listen carefully. It feels like the theatre is listening with me. Normal sounds of the night are still absent, but there are no sounds to suggest the monster is returning. Then, from a distance but carrying clearly through the night air, comes a long howl of rage.

Min falls off the chair.

I catch her before she hits the floor and help her to the bed, then hurry to fetch her a glass of water.

She takes two sips, three, and tries to focus on me. "We must leave."

"You can't even walk."

"Doesn't matter. He knows how weak I am right now. He'll be back as soon as the charm wears off. We have two days maybe, three at the most. He's killed you before when I weakened myself too much to stop him a second time."

Where the hell can we hide?

"Take me into the Wild while I recover. It's our only chance." She holds up her arms as if they weigh a ton. "We have to go now."

Always running

I GRAB MY VAN keys.

Min shakes her head and winces like she has a horrible headache. "We have to run into the Wild."

"But we were going to drive out of Plymouth and ditch the van. We agreed."

"That was before. It's too late now. If we stay on the outside, Tyac will use the police network to keep tabs on us while he recovers from tonight. When he's ready, he'll know exactly where we are. In the Wild, he'll have to track us on his own. It'll give us two or three days to get clear."

This doesn't feel right at all.

"Believe me. We have no choice, and we don't have time to argue about it. You have to trust me." She holds up her arms again. When I help her to her feet, she rests her head on my shoulder. "Anyway, the forest is your natural home. We'll be safer there than anywhere."

Is it? This is the first I've heard of that.

Tyac's enraged howl has woken the insiders. They're all crowded together in the garden. Will and Danny have arrived home and are saying they think the howl came from the far side of the harbour, over by the fish market.

"That's good," Min murmurs into my neck. "It means he didn't run into the Wild. He'll go to ground somewhere on the outside."

Conversation stops when the insiders notice me assisting her.

Tara runs to us. "What happened? Are you okay?"

Min's trembling. I help her to sit beside the fire. I feel totally useless. I too am shaking with shock and fear. Everything is wrong. I should be able to protect her, especially after she saved my life, but I don't know what to do.

Kill Tyac. That's the only way to stop this nightmare. *Kill the monster.*

Yeah, right. Where's the nearest anti-tank missile when you need one?

Tara kneels in front of Min and clasps her hands. "Tell me what's wrong."

Min says to me while they all look on, "We have to tell them. They need to know about the danger." She scans their anxious faces. "A werewolf attacked us."

Over the immediate uproar, she continues to explain. "He'll be back. We're running into the Wild to escape him. If he comes through here, you stay away from him. It's us he wants, Joe and me. Don't try to stop him. He'll kill anyone who gets in his way."

The commotion would be comical if not for our terrifying situation, and the noise of complaint and astonishment continues until Andrew calls for quiet.

"Whatever's happened," he says, "you can't go into the Wild. Whatever dangers you think will find you here, they're nothing compared to what's in there."

"Stay," Big Luke says. "We'll protect you."

There's a chorus of agreement and encouragement.

Except from Will. All through the fuss he stands at the back, taking everything in, not missing a trick.

Min answers everyone's questions while Tara ministers to her. She tries to do it without revealing too much of our story, but these people are canny, and they probe until she has no option but to tell them the truth.

Will listens in silence. I can see him putting the picture together. All along he's been jealous of Min's affection for me.

From his reactions to her story and the sympathetic looks she gives him, it's obvious he's in love with her, and she knows it.

Now I understand his behaviour from the moment we met. Scared of losing his love, he's been fighting to keep her the only way he knows.

Min gives them a brief version of what she told me earlier, enough for them to understand our situation and the danger our continued presence in the square would bring to everyone.

There are still a few grumbles of resistance, but they're more distressed complaint that reasoned argument.

Will and I exchange a look. It isn't warm, but it's a ceasefire and maybe a truce.

With Tara's help, Min has recovered sufficient strength to stand, although she's still weak and wobbly. We're ready to leave. Everyone hugs her. Many of them hug me too, and Linda thrusts a haversack packed with food into my hands. Jimmy hugs me like he's never going to let go.

Will hugs Min the same way and is still holding her hand when he fronts up to me. "Keep her safe."

"I will."

"You'd better." His anguish is clear to see.

I feel his stare on our backs as we leave. Poor bugger.

Everyone accompanies us to the edge of the forest, and they stand in a tight group to wave goodbye as we go into the Wild. We don't go very fast because Min can barely walk in a straight line. A hundred yards into the trees, I get another one of those muscle jumps and stop in my tracks.

"Don't worry about that," she says. "It happens when you enter or leave the Wild."

"I remember it from Flo's funeral. On the way in, anyway. Not on the way out."

"You were drunk on the way out."

I can't deny it. "So where are we going?"

She squeezes my hand. To find some old friends who will help us."

Thank goodness.

"Who are these friends?" I ask when we stop to rest for a bit.

"A Neolithic tribe."

"Seriously? Stone Age people?"

"Yes. You've met them before. You might even remember when we get there."

"Where is *there*?"

"This time of year, they'll be in the part of the Wild that roughly equates to Dartmoor. But we're not going straight there. The most important thing is that we don't leave an easy trail for Tyac. He'll be following us, all right, but we need to slow him down."

I have no idea what direction we've been travelling during our night trek, and I'm surprised to find the ground quite hilly inside the forest. I spend most of my time making sure she remains on her feet, and I trust her to know where we're going.

My instincts scream that I should be doing more than following her lead. That I should be doing something, anything, to protect her.

Kill Tyac.

Yeah, right.

"What's the point of running to these people? Aren't we taking danger to them instead of to the square?"

"There's nowhere safer for us than with the Axe. Thousands of years ago, a wise woman of the tribe developed a magical ward of protection that Tyac can't break through. It makes him sick when he tries. They pass it down from generation to generation and always fortify their settlements with it. If we can reach them before he finds us, we'll be safe from him as long as we stay there. They'll be safe too."

Sounds good.

She stretches out and pats the ground beside her. "We should sleep. Two hours, then we'll leg it again."

I lie down and she snuggles into me.

Feels like my eyes have only just closed when she's shaking me awake again. "Come on, my love. We have to go."

Dawn is breaking through the trees overhead. We creak and groan as we get up and help each other to jog on our way.

As the day goes, we travel through water often. I'm glad the weather is so good because we're always wet.

"If we ran upstream," she pants, "our scent would be carried downstream. We always have to go with the flow to avoid leaving a trail behind us, even if it isn't in exactly the direction we'd like to go." She pauses to catch her breath. "You know all this woodcraft. I mean, you've known it before. It's your thing and you taught it to me. You'll soon start to remember it."

"Tell me what I need to know until I remember it."

"Okay. Physically, he holds all the cards, so we have to outthink him. While you're still fresh to this, he'll probably expect us to run directly away from him in a straight line. Terror does that to people who are being hunted. The only way we can escape is by doing things he doesn't expect."

"That's why we're zigzagging so much." I climb out of the stream and haul her up its little bank.

"Yes. Also, fugitives tend to seek high ground. They feel if they can put a mountain between them and their pursuers, they're home free. And there's always the chance they might see a possible escape route from up there. It's not safe, though. Going around a lump in the landscape might take longer than going over it, but if we show up on the skyline, he's got us."

She jogs along a well-used wildlife path beside the stream. "He'll expect us to take the easiest routes, so we'll do the unexpected, even if that means doing everything the hard way. We'll make good time on paths like this, but soon we'll leave it and go through undergrowth for a mile or two in a different direction."

"How can we throw him off our scent?"

"We can't. He's a wolf at night. Well, he's a man-shaped monster with the strength and speed and hunting instincts of a huge wolf. Best we can do is slow him down, so we can reach help before he catches up."

"Okay. How do we do that?"

She jogs on for a minute until her breath comes easier. "We'll break our scent every time we change direction, by walking backwards over our own tracks for ten minutes or climbing a tree and going sideways for a while across decent sized branches. Then we'll come back down into nettles, brambles, that kind of thing. It won't stop him, but it won't be the obvious route. We can't do anything about his tracking ability as a wolf, but we'll do everything we can to confuse him while he's a man during the day."

"At least he can't climb trees when he's a wolf."

The look she sends over her shoulder makes my stomach flip. "He can? Fucking hell. Can't we just hide?"

"When we're tired and hungry and hurting, that's all we'll want to do. The closer he gets, the more we'll want to crawl into a hole. He knows that."

"But you can enchant him again, can't you? If he catches us, you can sing him away like you did last night?"

"I told you, it won't work again so soon. Even taking my own recovery requirement out of the equation, I don't know how long it has to be between enchantments for the next one to work."

She stops and turns to face me. "But you have a trick he doesn't know."

"What trick? And why are we whispering?"

"Your wood magic."

"Tell me about that. Tara said I have it, but I can't feel it. How does it work?"

"Let's take a breather and see if we can get you started."

We slump to the ground. I lean against a tree trunk on one side of the trail, while she does the same facing me with our legs touching.

She picks up two fallen twigs from the ground. "You can do lots of stuff." She crosses the twigs and holds them like a diviner's rod. "You could join these together as if they've grown that way naturally. Try."

I pick up two twigs and hold them the same way. Nothing happens. I shrug. "How?"

"I don't know how you do it. You just do. Let's shut up for a bit so you can concentrate. See if you can find it inside yourself. Believe me, it's there."

Several minutes pass, but nothing happens. I don't even know what the ability will feel like if I find it. I try to still my thoughts, calm my breathing, and relax my muscles.

"Close your eyes," she suggests.

I do so and try to focus on nothing.

"There you go."

The twigs in my hands are joined.

"How did I do that?"

She chuckles. "I don't know, magic man."

"I wasn't even thinking about doing it right then. I tried to clear my mind."

"But you picked up those twigs with the intention of joining them. That's the closest I can come to figuring out what it is you do." She gets up. "We'd better get moving."

I practise joining twigs every time we stop, but mostly our day is an exhausting succession of climbs and descents, running along streams and struggling through tough undergrowth. I'm totally lost. I simply have to trust she possesses some sort of homing signal that is taking us in the general direction of this tribe she relies upon so much.

Sometime after twilight, she stumbles over a root in the ground and nearly falls. "Enough. I'm done. We need to stop for the night."

She sees my expression. "I'll be no use if I push myself too far and too fast for a sensible recovery. There's no knowing when my magic will be good again, but let me sleep tonight and I hope that at least I'll be back to my normal physical strength in the morning."

She leads me off the trail, and we sit on the ground beneath a big tree, staring at each other.

"How did you meet the Axe?"

"They were here when we first arrived on these islands."

"When was that?"

"Six thousand years ago."

A big raindrop splats onto a broad leaf somewhere, then more drops fall through the canopy overhead. I start to weave a sheet of grasses and flat leaves, using my beginner magic to make us a shelter. "Why did we come here? Where did we come from?"

"Before we came to Britain, we lived for two thousand years on the river plain where the North Sea is now. You know that used to be land, joining these islands to mainland Europe, yes?"

"Yes."

"We lived many lovely lives on that plain. Before then, Tyac hunted us all over Europe and Asia for four thousand years after Atlantis was drowned. One time, we fooled him and sent him east to Russia while we escaped south into Sumer, Iraq now, where we lived for a century among Atlantean descendants."

She stares into the past and smiles fondly. "The Sumerians called us Atlanteans *Anunnaki* for our magic. It meant *those who came from heaven*. When Tyac tracked us there, we gave him the slip again and ran north for months, until we came to the Great River."

I'm hungry for information. Without knowledge, I'll always be his quarry. "How did we escape him that time?"

"We were in Eridu. It's easier to live invisibly in a city. You died peacefully of old age in my arms, gazing out across the Lower Sea from our little villa."

I see a moonlit panorama. It feels more than my imagination. "On a cliff."

"Yes. You loved that view." She strokes my cheek. "And you were reborn as a baby girl to my maidservant, Phyra, a year later in that same villa."

"What was she like?"

"She was from an Atlantean family. Her grandparents were our dear friends, and I offered to employ her when she married Hud, your father. He was an orphaned street acrobat. They were only twelve. Her parents went mad."

"I bet they did."

"By the time you could walk and talk, our bond was strong again. You knew things no normal child would. When you were seven years old, you remembered who we are."

I enjoy the peaceful seascape in my mind's eye.

"There was an earthquake. Hundreds of people died, including Phyra and Hud and all her family except you."

In disjointed flashes, I see broken buildings smoking in the dawn light, broken bodies buried in haste, grief and shock everywhere, and people whispering of something else, something terrible moving in the ruins at night. "Tyac was there."

Her nod is grim. "We'd had a bad feeling, you and I, as the Anunnak community grew. Before the earthquake, people were trying to recreate our ancient Atlantean culture. They were working from oral traditions thousands of years old and getting it mostly wrong, but it was becoming recognisable, and we knew sooner or later Tyac would come to investigate."

I remember hurried encounters with fellow survivors of the disaster, frightened conversations, rumours spreading like wildfire, and dull shock growing into panic and terror.

"Three mornings after the earthquake, people spoke of a wolf-monster eating bodies. We left everything and ran. It helped that crowds of refugees were already on the road out of the city, and Tyac wasn't accustomed to searching for a mother and her girl child, which is what we posed as during our escape."

She looks thoughtful. "I don't think Tyac has ever realised that sometimes you are a woman. When you're born female, it's always a huge relief for me. In those lives we are safe from him."

I get it.

"We travelled thousands of miles, into and right across what is now mainland Europe. By the time we reached the Great River..."

"You mentioned that before. What great river?"

"It started in the Northern Lake, way up beyond what is now Scotland and Scandinavia but back then was a mountainous region all across the top of mainland Europe. It flowed south for hundreds of miles and then west to a wide estuary where it met the Atlantic Ocean. The rivers we now call the Thames, the Rhine, and the Seine all flowed into it. We first saw it near where the Kent coast is now, and as mother and daughter, we joined a small band of hunter-gatherers on its banks.

"A few years later we moved west along the river and lived as a couple for years with a different community, and when you got older we settled in another one again with me as your daughter. You died an old woman and were reborn a boy.

"It was a difficult birth, that one. You survived it but with a damaged arm, and your mother died. Her people were pleased for me to adopt you. They were even more pleased when, despite your disability, you developed carpentry skills and made superior hunting tools for them.

"When we moved on, we did so as an adult couple, and then again years later as an ageing father and his daughter. We've been through that routine so many times I've lost count. We returned to some communities along the river several times over, without anyone knowing we'd lived with their ancestors. But we only get a chance for those peaceful transitions when you have a long life and Tyac doesn't find us."

"He didn't find us then? Never came close?"

"We enjoyed two thousand years of freedom, living in hundreds of different groups and always avoiding Atlantean descendants."

She smiles into the past. "Those were the happiest of all our lives. The climate was gentle, and it was a good place to live, with great grasslands and forests, marshes and lakes. There were elephants twice the size of modern ones, and sabre-toothed tigers." Her eyes shine in the silver moonlight filtering through the canopy above.

I try to remember those lives but can only picture things from her words. The sabre-toothed tigers in my mind look like illustrations from a children's book. Maybe the only real memories strong enough to stretch across lives involve my terror of Tyac.

"It came to an end," she says quietly, "as it always does, when we heard stories of a wolf monster attacking communities."

I reach back and feel the dread. It isn't difficult to find but is likely an accumulation from many centuries of running. Always running.

"The people we were living with at the time were already on the move, migrating away from rising floodwaters that were fast filling the fertile plains. It felt like Atlantis all over again. We left them where the Thames joined the Great River. They walked north while we canoed west, right past fearful stories of Tyac as he moved east along the river's south bank. We abandoned the canoe, let it float out to the ocean, then climbed the hills and made ourselves a home in Dartmoor Forest with the ancestors of the Axe tribe we're on our way to see now."

She looks around at the dark forest. "The Wild didn't exist in those days. Or rather, the outside didn't exist. There was no separation. Everything was wild."

"So the Axe are from the Stone Age. Like cavemen?"

"Not cavemen." She rolls her eyes in mock frustration. "Neolithic farmers."

The rainfall doesn't last long, but our shelter is finished in case it starts again. I weave a mat for us to sleep on. At least this is something I can do for her, although for the life of me I can't imagine how my wood magic is supposed to help us escape Tyac.

"They were good people." Min's slurring her words a bit with tiredness. "The ones we're going to see are their direct descendants."

"Why did they move into the Wild?"

"A new wave of immigrants arrived."

"Who?"

She purses her lips. "Beaker people, I think. Can't remember exactly, and all their culture names were different back then to what you'd know them as now. There have been so many immigrations. Whoever they were, it was some bunch of Bronze Agers who arrived from the Continent and started clearing Dartmoor Forest. The Axe had to choose, leave the land of their ancestors and find another home somewhere else in the outside when so much was changing everywhere, or move into the Wild and continue living as their tribe had lived forever. No contest."

"How do you know all this?"

"We were living with them at the time."

"How long has it been since we last saw them?"

She squints. "About three hundred years."

"What makes you think they'll remember us?"

"They will."

"How can you be sure?"

"I'm their goddess."

I stare. What on earth will she say next? "You're a goddess." I can't stop my stupid grin.

"Yes." She grins back. "And you are my consort."

I shake my head at this new craziness. "So they'll know you, but how come they'll remember me? You said I don't look the same in every life. And, anyway, it's been three hundred years."

"I always see something deep in your eyes, and sometimes there are physical similarities too." She curls a lock of my beard around her fingers. "But to a stranger, no, you won't look the same now as you did last time. The Axe will know you because you're with me. They expect my consort to accompany me."

"Well, Goddess, your palace awaits."

We snuggle up inside the hide I've made. She rests her head on my chest and from her breathing I can tell she's ready to fall asleep. I hold her, feeling her heartbeat and breathing in her fragrance.

"What should I expect when we meet them?"

"They use sign language a lot, especially when they're hunting, signing with only one hand." She lifts her left hand from my stomach and flicks her fingers rapidly through a brief series of shapes.

"What does that mean?"

"It means go to sleep."

She drops off quickly. When I'm sure she is sound asleep, I work my jaw and pinch my cheeks, determined to stay awake and guard her.

The earth releases its sweet scent after the rain, heady and intoxicating. I ease myself out from beneath her and sit cross-legged with my eyes closed, breathing slowly, drawing

the ancient smell deep into me. It fills me with peace and at the same time it heightens my senses.

The forest isn't as silent as I thought. The night is filled with sound. Random noises form shapes in my mind that I try to interpret. Some feel like they're related. My mind classifies them as stealthy movements in several different directions, and they're coming closer.

Doom drops in my stomach like a brick. My eyes fly open, and I try to look everywhere without moving my head. If something bad is coming, I want to see it before it knows I'm aware of it.

I'm unsure when to wake Min. Sooner rather than later, I think, to give her chance to come around if we have to run. Or fight. I reach to shake her shoulder and see a face in a nearby bush.

My hand freezes in mid-air. Blood pounding in my head is dulling my hearing.

The face disappears. I don't know if it was there at all, or if my fear is playing tricks on me. I study the bush while my heart rate calms and my hearing returns to normal.

Nothing. It's just a bush.

Another face. And another. Popping into view and peering at us from the undergrowth foliage only twenty feet away.

I jump to my feet and stare around wildly.

Min jerks awake, startled.

One of the faces pushes an inch or two through its bush and becomes clearer. Is it a child? It's about the size of one, and there's something childlike about the shape of its big eyes. But those eyes don't have a childlike expression. They look old and hostile. And the skin of its dirty face is leathery and wrinkled.

Five ugly faces now. One of them pushes all the way through into the open. Then three more appear, all of them glaring at us.

We are surrounded.

Min scrambles to her feet and grabs my hand.

I cast around for a stick or something to use as a weapon but find nothing, so I release Min's hand and prepare to fight.

A new noise comes from above, like slow wing beats that go from quiet and distant to loud and close in the space of a few seconds, until they hover overhead.

What now?

I can't see the creature, but from the flurries each wing beat causes in the highest tree leaves, it has to be something big. The uglies have disappeared. Whatever is above us, they don't want to tangle with it.

Min sings a few notes. Her voice isn't strong, but it's as pure and clear as ever.

The wing beats depart in the same direction from which they arrived and at the same speed. Silence falls around us.

I peer at Min. "What was that?"

"I don't know. I mean," she looks at the bushes, "I don't know what those creatures were. Never seen anything like them before." She stares up. "And I don't know what that was either, but I'm glad it came."

"What did you sing to it?"

"I said thank you."

I hug her. "I know you don't *know* what it was, but what do you *think* it might have been?"

"It isn't a thought really. More a feeling." Her voice is muffled against my chest. "It felt like an angel. Not that I've ever met one knowingly, but if I did, I think that's what it would feel like."

I shake my head in wonder. "That's what it felt like to me too. Not at the time. When it was here I was scared. But now it's gone, remembering it…"

She hugs me tight. "Yes."

Hunted

STIFF AND GROGGY, we're on the move again before dawn. I go to destroy the shelter, but she stops me. "Leave it for him to find and investigate. Anything that delays him is to our advantage."

I frown and not for the first time at one of her decisions. Now and then I wonder if being immortal means she doesn't have to worry about acting too stupid to live. But the thought is ignoble. And she does possess all the memories I lack. I have to keep trusting her to know what she's doing.

Twenty minutes after leaving our overnight camp, we retrace our steps for ten minutes then climb a tree and set off in a different direction. Walking backwards with heel-to-toe placements makes my tendons ache, but I'm getting better at it.

She's more sprightly moving through the treetops than she was yesterday, but we still go cautiously to avoid a catastrophic injury and indirectly towards wherever it is she's taking us.

We talk as we travel, and she helps me remember more about my magical talent.

"There's this trick you've used before to help us escape from him. You call it *growing*. You sort of blend us into a tree, or a log, or a beam or something. Anything wooden that's big enough, although you always say you prefer a living tree." She sighs. "I hate it."

I'm surprised. "Why?"

"It's like the worst kind of claustrophobia imaginable. It terrifies me. But it's saved us many times."

"Saved me, you mean? He never kills you, does he?"

"He can't kill me, but he breaks my heart by killing you. That's what this is all about."

When we stop at midday to let me catch up on the rest I lost during my attempt at a night watch, I try to blend myself into a tree.

"You normally stand and lean your back into it. Apparently, you connect with its rush of life."

The potential to connect is there. It's like being filled with a thrumming flow while also being alert and aware of everything the tree feels. Through this tree I can sense what other trees in the vicinity feel, but I can't do anything close to what Min described as blending into it.

I practise *growing* during the night while she sleeps, improving as the hours pass and using it to listen out for wildlife moving, near to and far away.

In the very early morning, I feel a party of humans and dogs jogging. The sensations are so strong I can almost see and feel boots thudding on the earth, leather armour rubbing and squeaking, clunks of wooden shields, clinks of iron weaponry, and dogs panting hard. I can even count them. Twenty-six men and twelve dogs. I wake Min to tell her about the war party.

She sits up stiffly and rubs her eyes. "How far away?"

I have to think. "Quite distant."

"Tribes have always fought each other in the Wild. People are pretty much the same wherever they live. We'd better take care we don't walk into a battle." She peers into the trees overhead. "And we'd better get going."

"It isn't dawn yet."

"Even so." She stands and stretches. "Tyac will have recovered by now. He'll be coming soon."

We stop again at noon to eat the last of Linda's food and allow me a quick nap. She's eager to be off again as soon as I wake, but I insist on trying one more time to grow into a tree. If this is such an effective trick against Tyac, I want to master it.

I rest my spine against the bark, close my eyes, still my thoughts, and become one with the tree in my mind. This, my tenth or twelfth attempt in twenty-four hours, doesn't feel any different to all the others.

Min gasps.

I open my eyes to see what's alarmed her. My eyelids work slowly.

She's staring at me, her eyes wide.

I try to ask what's wrong and discover my lips can only move slowly too. I don't have the breath to utter a single word and don't seem to need it. I feel the tree around me. It touches me everywhere, outside and in, hollow and solid at the same time. I taste the living wood. I've become part of it.

We stretch our roots deep to drink from the earth and welcome clean sunlight feeding our leaves and the soft breeze tickling our uppermost branches.

Vibrations from other creatures moving in the forest come to me through the wood, and without conscious thought I translate those vibrations into sounds.

With a focused effort, I lift my right hand until it breaks free of the bark. Nothing splinters. It makes no sound. I swivel my eyes without moving my face to see my hand and arm covered in bark, appearing as a limb of the tree.

Min shudders. "I can't bear this."

I crook a finger to beckon her, but she shakes her head and hugs herself.

It takes considerably more effort to extract myself from the tree than it took to blend with it. When I finally make it back into fresh air, I stretch and shake myself, blinking rapidly and working my jaw. My mouth is dry. It takes time to work up some saliva. "Come on, then. You said this has saved us from him many times."

Her eyes are sharp with fear.

"I managed to do it alone, but that's no good. If he finds you, he'll find both of us. We have to do it together."

"You can't imagine how awful this is for me. It's natural for you, but I'm terrified. Imprisoned inside a living tree, unable to breathe or speak or move at all. It's a nightmare."

"Are you saying you won't do it?"

She doesn't respond for several heartbeats. Then she grips my hand, closes her eyes, and takes some deep breaths. "Keep hold of my hand. Don't you let go of me in there."

We choose the biggest tree around and stand with our backs against its bark.

"Ready?"

"Just do it. And don't bloody let go of me."

This time it's easy. I simply relax my breathing, still my mind, and grow us into the tree. I squeeze Min's fingers, and her answering squeeze comes back in slow motion.

A new vibration comes to my attention, a man running steadily many miles away. My tree sense translates the vibrations so that I see him as a camouflaged shape moving among other camouflaged shapes. Breathing heavily, he crouches to study the ground.

I ease us free from the tree.

Min falls to her hands and knees, gasping for air. "I hate that."

"Tyac's coming."

She's instantly alert. "Where is he?"

"Near the cave we passed yesterday, searching for our trail where we climbed over the nettles."

"Let's go."

We jump down into a stream and follow its current.

"We might make the Axe village tonight," she pants, "if we keep going after dark."

"Do you know exactly where it is?"

"No, but I'll find them okay when we get into the area."

"Can't risk it. He's too close and moving too fast."

"He'll move a lot faster when he's a wolf."

"Run."

An hour later, we climb high and go through the treetops for a hundred yards before shinning down a big old oak tree into a clearing and setting off in a different direction to the one we were going before our climb. Then we double back to the clearing as night falls.

I don't need to grow into a tree to sense the monster now. By touching bark, I can hear him coming. He's found our midday resting place and is splashing along the stream we followed this afternoon. He's hot on our trail, and his vibrations terrify me.

After making sure we're leaving no sign of our presence here, I lean on the oak. "You ready?"

"Ready as I'll ever be." She shoots me a brave smile. "We're going to be in here all night, you know. Don't move until well after dawn. Even if you think he's gone and we're safe, keep us in here." She tries to hide her shudder. "He's a clever bastard and a lot better at this than we are. Okay?"

"Okay."

We step up to balance on two thick exposed roots, with our backs against the bark. Min gives me a tender kiss on the cheek, and I grow us into the oak.

It's difficult to measure time accurately inside the tree, but maybe thirty minutes go by before Tyac makes his appearance. I hear him coming all the way. Creatures of the forest go still and silent as he approaches and stay that way until he passes them by. Min and I aren't the only ones paralysed by the fear of him.

He trots along the trail we followed and passes the tree we climbed to the east of us. But after only a few feet, he skids to a halt, drops to all fours, and snuffles around our tree of ascent. He seems to fly up that tree, ripping out leaves and branches and hurling them behind him. His trip through the treetops is just as frenzied and destructive. The hundred yards it took us twenty minutes to cross, he spans in three or four.

Again, he charges a few feet past our departure point, then he swings around a supple treetop and lands squarely in the uppermost branches of our oak tree.

I hear his powerful heartbeat and feel the pressure of his paw pads, the sharp denting grip of his claws, and his breath on my leaves. If I could shiver in my immobility, I would do so when hot saliva flicks from his fangs onto my innocent bark.

He plummets in a controlled fall and lands heavily in the clearing on all fours, visibly alert, massive muscles bunched under the coarse hair of his back and shoulders.

I give Min's fingers a slow squeeze.

Tyac sniffs the ground extensively, then rears up and trots away on his hind legs in the direction we took earlier.

I follow his progress with all my senses as the forest goes silent in waves around him. He reaches the spot where we turned back and doesn't waste any time investigating that area before returning to us.

I squeeze Min's fingers again to warn her of his imminent reappearance.

He enters the clearing, his ears cocked and his huge head swinging from side to side as he stalks directly to our tree. He inhales deeply. He must know our scents intimately. He circles our tree and then circles the clearing on all fours, sniffing and snuffling the ground closely, investigating every tree and shrub.

Finally, he stands in front of us and looks directly into my face. I'm grateful he doesn't know it. I'm grateful I can't tremble. I press Min's fingers and stare back into the monster's bloodshot eyes, only inches away.

He prowls the clearing again and tests several places for our tracks before returning to our tree. He peers at the bark, the thin crust of living wood that's the only thing between him and us. He leans forward to sniff it, and the stink of his breath assaults me with its stench of carrion and death. Then he licks the bark as if it's a delicacy to be savoured.

If my bowels were free to move, they would.

Eventually, he leaves the clearing.

We stay put, sealed inside our hiding place while I follow his movements. Which isn't difficult, because in his rage he rips every bush and scars every tree along his path. He roams a long way, zigzagging randomly, before he stops moving, although the creatures of the forest maintain their silence.

When he moves again, he does so stealthily. There's another heartbeat in his vicinity, and at the same moment as I realise he's stalking something he hits it hard. I know terror on behalf of the deer he's hunted, even as its heartbeat stops.

I warn Min with my fingertips before he drags the deer into our clearing, where he tears it to shreds and eats it in plain sight. He throws the remnants aside as he stands, belches, and wipes a bloodied front paw across his muzzle.

Wolves howl in the distance.

He cocks his head to listen, then trots away.

I follow his progress. He travels in a straight line and jogs at a steady speed. It's very fast compared to even our best running speed.

I press Min's fingers for the hundredth time, imagining her reining in her terror. I don't know if this will work, but I do my best to soothe her mind by transmitting calm thoughts and feelings to her through the wood.

Tyac doesn't return. He keeps moving away from us for several miles and then goes to ground. I detect no further movement from him, and eventually lose any sense of his location. I assume he's asleep.

We stay in the tree until sunrise.

When finally we step free, Min falls into my arms and sobs. "I felt your thoughts. They were soothing like your voice. Thank you, my love. I'll never get used to that, but thank you for your thoughts. They helped."

The Axe

WE'RE JOGGING THROUGH broken patches of knee-high grass beneath a dense tree cover when my skin tingles all over and I pull up sharp.

"Don't worry about that," Min pants. "It's the ward. Feels strong and fresh. We can walk now. We're nearly there."

Two miles farther on, we stand upon a rise of ground and watch leisurely activity inside an enclosure below. The Axe settlement covers an area the size of a football pitch and consists of assorted wooden huts inside a high circular fence of split logs.

"I thought we were looking for their temporary camp. This looks pretty permanent to me."

She shrugs. "It is temporary. Kind of. They're nomadic herders, and they follow traditional routes. That's how I knew roughly where to look for them in summer. Every time they return to one of their camps along the way, they tidy it up." She frowns. "Does look well established, though, doesn't it?"

I count thirty-seven huts of various sizes laid out in a horseshoe shape, with its open end aligned to the palisade gateway.

At the innermost point stands a substantial oval-shaped building with an apex roof of timber shingles, but all the other huts are circular constructions with low-hanging conical grass roofs. Tethered goats are grazing the edges of some of them.

Eighteen people are visible in the open ground between the huts, and a bunch of shrieking kids chase one another around two of the huts. Like the adults, they're naked.

"Will said there are cannibals in the Wild."

She chuckles. "I'm sure he did. Don't worry, love. The Axe won't eat you. Honestly, they're not cannibals. Look, they've got cattle penned over there. Anyway, you're my consort, remember?"

"Let's hope they remember."

"Come on, wimp. Let's go and meet some old friends."

People notice us the moment we walk through the gateway, and excitement spreads through the community. Within minutes they're crowding us, the entire tribe it seems, and they're not as fully naked as I thought. The women are bare-breasted, but all the adults are wearing loincloths. Everyone smells warm and earthy and fresh, like they belong to the forest.

And I needn't have worried. They're happy to see us, many of them clapping with delight and several women singing together in a drawn-out single note. There's no doubt they know exactly who Min is.

Seven women are carrying babies on their hips or at their breasts. Min moans with joy and kisses each of the infants, her eyes shining. The mothers are delighted.

Everyone falls silent when a tall, splendidly built man makes his way through the jostling bodies. I admire his impressive mane of light and dark greys, which matches his beard and chest hair and is all set off to great effect by his deep tan.

"Welcome, Min!" He spreads his powerful arms wide. "Your presence honours us." He bows to her and then directs a head tilt to me. "Welcome, Cayal."

Min acknowledges his courtesy with a regal inclination of her head. "Thank you for welcoming us, Chief. What is your name?"

"I am Shad."

"Shad, in this life Cayal is named Joe."

"Welcome, Joe," he says, and my name ripples in murmurs through the assembled people.

"Prepare a dwelling for Min and Joe," Shad says.

I like his style of leadership. No bombast. Just confidence.

Three women peel away from the back of the group and disappear inside one of the huts, then reappear with their arms full of folded woven blankets and stone storage jars. A boy trots into the hut with a broom, and clouds of dust billow from the doorway into the air.

Apparently, we are to be accommodated in the tribe's storeroom.

"They speak English." I keep my voice low.

"What did you expect? This is the Wild of Britain. There are other languages in the Wild. Original languages, with the kind of developments you would expect after hundreds or thousands of years. You'll hear Welsh in Wales and Gaelic in Scotland, plus many more, but the common language nearly everywhere is English."

I'm dead on my feet. Now we're safe I want nothing more than to sleep. She's wobbly too.

Shad is a perceptive man. "Min and Joe need to rest. Clear a way for them."

We're led to our hut and ushered inside. Two women help us out of our clothes, wash us reverently but efficiently, and present each of us with a clean loincloth, while two more prepare a grass bed on the swept floor of hard earth. They don't linger, but take away our dirty clothing and leave us alone to settle in.

I must have been asleep before I closed my eyes. No idea what the time is when I wake, or how long I've slept, but for the first time in days, I feel well rested and safe.

Truly safe. It won't last forever. Sooner or later we'll have to leave Axe territory. But Min said we're a hundred per cent safe inside the protection of their ward and I believe her.

I stare up into the shadows beneath the low roof.

The inner wooden planking of the circular walls continues to the apex of the roof, but the upper planks aren't butted closely like the lower ones. Scraps of animal skins, soil, and grass roots show between the gaps, and I recall the goats grazing on the other side of the compound. These dwellings are living, organic constructions.

There are no adornments or decorations, but I wouldn't expect to see any in a storage shed. It's well built and dry. With a little care and attention, someone could make it a nice cosy home.

Distant sounds carry in from outside, almost as if underwater. I suppose people are staying away from our hut to allow us a good rest.

Those kids have probably been herded somewhere else. I can only imagine their intense excitement when adults told them a goddess has come to visit.

My goddess. Her head rests heavily on my chest. I stroke her back tenderly.

She stirs. "Mm."

I kiss her head.

She opens her eyes. "Hello, my love. Sleep well?"

"For the first time in days. Weeks maybe. You?"

"I always sleep well with the Axe."

"Why don't you spend more time with them?"

She props up on one elbow. "We get them into trouble. They never complain. They're brave and always consider it an honour to help us. But there's rarely been an occasion when we've come to ask for their assistance that hasn't resulted in at least some of them getting hurt. They're so lovely. I hate bringing danger to them."

She lowers her lips to mine. Her hair brushes my face as we kiss. "They'll leave us alone until we reappear, you know."

We don't talk. We look and smile and touch, and the mask I wear for the rest of the world slips away. We make love as if we have forever and not a care in the world.

Later, when we're ready to appear in public, she shows me how to tie the loincloth securely. The intimate moment is like a continuation of our love-making, and I don't try to hide my goofy grin. This is how our lives will be from now on.

We step into the sunlight and a rush of adoration fills me. She is a bare-breasted goddess. I understand exactly how the Axe feel about her. It's an honour to stand at her side. And she's still wearing the dolphin pendant I made her.

The kids come running to us, followed by their mothers and a couple of fathers who herd the jabbering children away and smile apologies for the fuss.

A statuesque woman with silver-streaked long hair strides across the compound to us. Her well-defined muscles and beautiful breasts are spectacular, but it's her effortlessly commanding presence that arrests my attention.

She goes straight to Min and without pausing for hello throws her strong arms around her.

Min shoots me a look of surprise but returns the hug with equal warmth.

The fabulous woman holds her at arm's length and studies her. "Welcome, Min. I am Anya. Shad is my husband. Meeting you is the greatest honour of my life."

"Thank you, Anya. I'm honoured to meet you too. This is Joe."

I expect a handshake, but instead get a bearhug so vigorous it takes my breath away. Embarrassed by the instant thrill I get when her hard nipples rub and press against my bare chest, I glance over her shoulder at Min, who grins with mischievous understanding.

After releasing me, Anya grabs us both by the hand and declares, "You must be hungry." She leads us towards a cooking fire that's burning in front of a big hut. "We have food prepared for you."

As we approach the hut, Shad pushes its animal hide door curtain aside and steps out. "Come," he says. "Eat."

The hot smell of roasting pork hits me. It's a huge boar on a spit being turned slowly by a boy, its fat dripping into the glowing embers below and sizzling fiercely. I can't remember how many days it's been since I ate a proper meal. My stomach growls and my head swims.

Anya gestures to two vacant places on a prettily woven grass mat by the fire. We sit there cross-legged while she takes her place beside Shad.

Several adults and two children are chatting around the fire, glancing at us constantly. Is this a communal fire for the whole village, or are these people Shad and Anya's family? I don't have to wonder for long.

"My son, Karn." Shad slaps the muscular shoulder of a mahogany-tanned man of about my age, who raises a hand in a friendly greeting.

"Karn's wife, Keira." Shad points to an equally muscular thirty-something woman. "Their oldest daughter, Songa," he nods at a dark-haired woman aged about twenty carrying an earthenware jug to us, then to the grinning boy turning the spit, "and their youngest son, Sing."

Keira hands us cups, which Songa fills with light amber wine.

"Songa and Sing are named for you," Anya tells Min.

Min's smile lights my life. "You have a lovely family."

"We have more," Anya says. She points across the fire at a strapping young man who is struggling to contain two boisterous four-or-five-year-olds. "Songa's husband and their children, Du and Pynta."

"You have a *big* family." I laugh, sizing Shad up and trying to calculate his age. He's a fit, strong man. Difficult to say exactly, but I guess he and Anya are five or ten years younger than my mum and dad. About fiftyish, and already great-grandparents.

Shad laughs too. "Bigger than you see here. There are more."

Anya tells Min, "Today or tomorrow you will meet our daughters, Vua and Tae, who will love you and serve you."

"They've taken Songa and Sing's brother and sister to teach them some of the forest beyond our boundaries," Shad says, pushing the tip of a dagger into the boar. He withdraws the knife, presses its blade flat against the flesh to check the juices are running clear, and bellows, "Let's eat!"

Songa prepares two plates of food for Min and me. The roasted pork comes with a sweet apple sauce, pulped and juiced crimson berries, root vegetables that might be yams or wild potatoes, and a salad of leaves and tender shoots, all to be washed down with more of the pale amber wine.

After the sparse rations we've survived on in the Wild, it's a feast.

While Karn is carving meat and people are dishing up and sharing food, others bustle into place around the fire and the level of conversation rises.

Min and I share a blissfully happy smile.

They're generous hosts. Several people try to press more food on to us when we clear our plates, and it would be churlish to refuse. An hour later, I lean back against the side of Shad's hut, feeling like I've eaten my own weight, and unintentionally release a big belch.

Min elbows me with mock horror, but a chorus of belches follows mine, and everyone laughs in appreciation of my evident appreciation.

I'm very happy and suddenly very drowsy, filled with deep contentment and wanting nothing more than to curl up to sleep with Min in my arms. We make our excuses and walk hand in hand across the compound to our hut.

I sleep dreamlessly and wake refreshed, unsure for a moment of where I am. Then I feel Min's sleeping presence beside me, and everything comes flooding back.

The hut is warm and dark and as silent as night, but when a breeze lifts the edge of the door curtain, it shows slivers of early evening light.

I reach to stroke Min's hair, not wanting to wake her, but my hand touches another body. Two little people are on the bed with us. Du and Pynta are nestled into Min, sound asleep and breathing in unison. Pynta snores softly.

A lump forms in my throat. It's a picture of pure trust. Those kids only met us today, and already they're sleeping in Min's arms.

It comes as no surprise. She's had the same effect on me.

The children wake when she stirs. They yawn and smile shyly while she hooks her hand behind my neck and pulls me down into her kiss. The kids get off the bed, and we look to see what they're up to.

Pynta gives us a charming wave from the curtain and disappears outside, while Du sits cross-legged on the floor at the foot of our bed, drawing finger pictures in the earth and humming contentedly.

"I understand why you love these people. They're wonderful."

"They are. They've changed quite a lot since last time we were here, though. For a start, they no longer use sign language in social situations. And they're very healthy."

"Why wouldn't they be?"

"I'm not sure. It's just something. I've never seen them so strong. They're shining and bursting with health and vitality, aren't they? I mean, have you seen the women's tits?"

"Well, yes." I smirk. "Can't help it really."

"They're like glamour models. Every one of them full-breasted and, well, pert."

"And that's wrong?"

"Not wrong. I'm enjoying them as much as you are. But it's different. Think about it. When was the last time you saw a TV programme about the Third World that had full-breasted women everywhere?"

She waits.

I shrug.

"Doesn't happen, does it? Except for mothers feeding babies. By the time they hit middle age, they're usually flat and drooped."

I glance to make sure Du isn't watching, and stroke one of Min's beautiful nipples, which puckers and hardens. "Never mind their tits," I growl low. "I have yours."

From the far side of the compound, Songa calls for Du. There's no alarm in her voice, and the lad doesn't seem to have heard his mother. He continues drawing and crooning.

"Pynta will tell Songa he's safe with us," Min says.

I'm about to suggest that we might want to be alone for a while, when Du makes a gurgling noise and topples over sideways.

Min sits up. "Are you okay, my love?"

The boy twitches but doesn't reply. He makes another gurgling noise then goes still and quiet.

"Du?" Min speaks louder. "What's wrong?"

As if he's dreaming, he gets to his hands and knees. His eyes are squeezed tight shut and he's trembling.

"Joe, he's having a fit."

I scramble to the bottom of the bed while Min gets up and hurries around to the boy. We reach him at the same time, and I touch his shoulder. His skin is clammy, covered in a light sheen of sweat.

"Du?" Min says. "Shall we take you to your mummy?"

I stoop to pick him up.

He snarls and snaps at me.

I whip my hands away and jump back out of reach.

The boy crouches on all fours. Coarse hair sprouts thickly on his naked back, in a grey line all down his spine, and more is sprouting everywhere else on his body. He glares at me, and his eyes change. His innocent little boy gaze becomes darker, bloodshot, colder, and somehow inhuman.

This is terrifyingly like last night.

Something cracks, like bones snapping inside him. We stare as his body emits more snaps and now wet squelches, and, underneath it all, a panting growl of pain.

He changes rapidly, the entire process from start to finish in about two minutes. His face lengthens into a snout, and his pointed ears twitch. Black claws burst from paws where his hands used to be. His back writhes with a final loud crack, and he shakes himself vigorously then lifts his head to stand proud and whole.

He is a grey wolf cub, as tall and leggy as an adult German Shepherd dog.

Min's backing away on foot, but I scramble away across the bed, desperate to put space between me and the wolf. We meet at the head of the bed and huddle together.

Du shoulders the curtain aside and pads out of the hut.

We follow him to the curtain and peer out, holding hands tight as if that's going to protect us from the nightmare we've witnessed.

The compound is lit by a full silver moon rising through the trees. Dozens of wolves occupy the settlement, with not a single human being in sight.

There's a first time for everything

We huddle together and tremble while trying to plan an escape and watch the wolves at the same time.

It's difficult to count how many there are in the compound because they keep coming and going, but we estimate fifty.

"I think it's the whole village," Min whispers.

"The tribe is a werewolf pack. Didn't you know?"

"Of course I bloody didn't. Think I'd bring you here if I knew?"

A gang of young wolves tumble into view from behind Shad and Anya's hut, biting and snapping and rolling over one another.

"They're the kids, aren't they?"

She sighs. "Certainly looks like it."

An older wolf snarls at the youngsters, and they skitter out of his way in a rush. Most of them move to a safe distance before resuming their play, but one strays too close and gets pinned to the ground and growled at for his trouble. He offers his belly and freezes, then runs back to his playmates as soon as he's released.

The adult wolf is massive, standing four feet high, seven feet plus from his nose to the tip of his tail, and with a broad chest. His coat is a mix of light and dark greys. He must weigh 250 pounds.

It's Shad. I have no doubt of that.

A slightly smaller but still solidly built adult nuzzles into the shaggy ruff of his neck, and he licks her ears.

"That's Anya," Min whispers.

"Yes." There's no mistaking the silver streaks in her glossy coat. "What are we going to do? There's no way they'll let us sneak out of here."

"I'll sing to them."

"I don't think so. You don't know how they'll react."

"I've calmed wild animals before. Even a werewolf, remember?"

"Ever calmed a whole pack of them?"

She smiles bravely and stands up. "No, but there's a first time for everything."

I hold her wrist. I do *not* want her to go out there. "They're not coming near this hut. We're safe in here, I think. For now, anyway. Let's not antagonise them."

She kneels. "Okay. But if things get bad, I'll go out there to sing and you stay in here."

"You say you're immortal, but if you got injured badly enough could you die?"

"No. I've been injured badly before, and it can take a long time, sometimes months, but in the end everything heals."

I give it a minute. "If you go out there to sing, I'll stand right at your side. If we're going to get attacked, we'll get attacked together. Two of us might stand a better chance than one."

"Let's hope it doesn't come to that."

She's only trying to mollify me. I know she has no intention of letting me go out with her to face the pack.

We'll deal with that when the time comes.

The werewolves ignore our hut completely, but that doesn't ease our fears. We both twitch every time one of them so much as glances in our direction.

A group of them trot quietly out of the village and return a while later, dragging the carcasses of a red deer and a boar. The pack fall upon the kills in a savage frenzy, ripping the dead animals apart and eating the meat raw. There's lots of snarling and snapping at each other. It looks fierce, but this is probably normal dining behaviour for them.

"They're not monsters like Tyac."

"No," she says. "They're real wolves."

"Still fucking terrifying, though."

She hugs me.

Two wolves return from the forest and nuzzle up to Shad and Anya, who accept their subservience with a sort of benign dominance.

The newcomers yip, paw the ground, and curl their backs repeatedly, as if communicating an important message, and all four wolves keep staring out into the surrounding forest then glancing at our hut, which increases our anxiety to the limit.

Shad raises his face to the sky and howls a long, pure note, which the entire pack take up.

As dawn breaks, the wolves settle into groups of hairy lumps, all ears and limbs. Their breathing slows, and the widespread twitches and subdued dream yelps suggest they're all sleeping.

This is what we've been waiting for. "Ready?"

"Let's go." But before I can get to my feet, she grabs my arm. "Look."

Several wolves are stretching into unnatural positions in their sleep. Then more of them. Within seconds, the whole pack is a writhing, twisting, bone-grinding, skin-stretching, moaning mass, and all that's visible is a hideous mix of fur and twisted flesh.

The change happens quickly. None of them even wake up. By the time the first horizontal sunbeams shine through the trees, the Axe have returned to their human forms.

They sleep on peacefully, cuddled together in pockets of innocent nakedness.

"Maybe we don't need to run at all."

I squint at her. "Are you serious? You think it's safe to hang around?"

"I do. I've no idea how they became werewolves or how long ago it happened, but they didn't harm us in the night, and I'm certain they never will when they're in human form, no matter what else they've become."

Shad stands tall, stretching his arms high and wide as he gives a mighty yawn. I'm not in the least surprised to see he's hung like a fire hose. He steps into his hut and reappears, tying his loincloth, then strides straight across the compound in our direction.

We shrink back as his shadow falls across the gap at the edge of our door curtain and his voice comes through. "Did you sleep well?"

Min thrusts the curtain aside and shouts, "How were we supposed to sleep? We were terrified. You know it's a werewolf monster that hunts us. You must know this from your history. How do you think we felt seeing you all change into wolves?"

He narrows his eyes.

The quiet everyday sounds of the waking village roar in comparison to our silent face-off.

"We thought you knew about us."

We duck out through the doorway, and Min arches a disapproving eyebrow at him.

He casts his eyes down. "If we had known you were unaware of what we have become, we would have prepared you."

"I know you would." She relents and touches his shoulder. "So prepare us now."

His relief at her forgiveness is huge. "The story tells of a youth coming home from a journey. He left as a boy and returned as a wolf."

"Does the story say how he got bit?"

"No. Only that it was of his choosing."

I doubt that, for sure.

"When the people saw how the change made him strong and improved his hunting skills, they all wanted the same. They held council and decided to take the bite."

Min and I exchange a dubious glance.

"We became strong warriors."

"You already were strong warriors," she says. "I've always been proud of the Axe."

He basks in her approval and beats his chest once with his big fist. "Stronger than before, even."

"So you thrived."

"We did. Since long before the days of my grandfathers, we have been the fiercest warriors in the forest. This makes us prosperous and safe." He spreads his arms wide to take in the whole village.

"I'm glad for you." She sounds polite but not really very glad.

"Today we will feast in your honour. But first, Anya has prepared our sweat house." He leads us behind their hut and past a roaring bonfire to an igloo-shaped stone building with a heavy leather door curtain, which he holds open for us to enter.

Anya is sitting on a raised, slatted, smoothed wooden bench, on a ledge of hard packed earth, by a fire pit that contains a bed of hot rocks. When the door curtain falls closed behind us, she leans forward with a ladle of water from a bucket at her side and throws it across the rocks. They sizzle fiercely and add new steam to the clear clouds of it already filling the space.

I breathe deep, instantly exhilarated, feeling better even than I ever did when I went in the sauna at my old local gym.

Anya is fully naked, her splendid body shining in the firelight. So, now, is Shad. He sits beside her, and they gesture for us to sit on the smoothed bench opposite theirs.

We don't need asking twice. In seconds, our loincloths hanging with theirs from wall hooks, we sit enjoying the intense heat and admiring their nakedness as openly and comfortably as they are admiring ours.

Anya throws water on the stones six or seven times more in the next hour. By then, my mind is rested and utterly peaceful. But although I've sipped about a pint of water from the shared ladle, my stomach is growling like some beast underground when finally she declares it is time to eat.

Shad flexes his great arms and chest. "Yes!"

We tie our loincloths as they lead us out into the morning and around to the big building at the back of the palisade. By the time we reach it, our shiny clean sweat has dried in the fresh air.

We walk through the entrance and find the tribe assembled inside, singing a tribute to Min, worshipping her in song, an appropriate form of worship for a goddess with music magic.

The spoor of an unknown creature

SHAD LINKS ARMS with us and we walk the central aisle between bench tables filled with people. "I still regret the fear you must have felt last night, but I hope you know we would never hurt you. Nothing has changed about that. The Axe will always protect you, with our lives if necessary."

He escorts us to a pair of matching thrones. I take my seat beside Min as if I've been doing it all my life, and grin when it occurs to me that I have, in fact, been doing this all my *lives*.

Shad returns to the doorway to talk with some people, and I take advantage of the lull to study the hall. It's oval-shaped and of similar construction to the domestic huts, but with two sturdy upright poles supporting the apex ridge instead of a single central pole.

Beside the nearest upright stands two life-sized wooden statues of godlike figures. The female one bears such a resemblance to Min it takes my breath away.

She smiles. "The other one is a pretty good likeness too."

The other carving is of a man with a full beard, naked but of a loincloth.

"Me?"

"You've always loved your face fur." She studies the statue. "That was you last time we visited the Axe. They think the world of you, you know. They respect your wood magic."

Her eyes widen. "Do you know what? I think they've settled permanently here now they're, you know..."

"Wolves."

"Yes. And I suppose that's why they've stopped using sign language. Wolves don't have fingers to sign when they hunt."

The hall fills with people who join the hymn, except for two newly arrived women who conduct an animated conversation with Shad and Anya.

When the entire tribe is assembled, Shad brings his urgent conversation to a close, and his family takes their place at a table on a raised platform opposite our thrones.

Everyone except Min and me is singing the hymn. Its rhythm, melody, and harmonies are pleasant. When it ends, Anya sings on alone.

Hers isn't the most tuneful voice there, but it's powerful and the song is striking.

Min nudges me. "This is the protective ward."

Anya finishes with a single shouted word, which the people repeat as one voice.

Min looks over the assembly with love and affection. Then she starts to sing.

I can't take my eyes off her. I share the adoration the Axe tribe feel. I've never heard anything like this in my life. Not in this life, anyhow. I don't understand her words, but the rhythm sounds familiar, and the song moves memories in me like smoke stirred in air.

Her voice soars. The emotional journey I experienced when listening to her in the garden last week was nothing compared to this.

She takes me to new places inside, lifts me and shows me visions of such splendour they remove conscious thought from the process of seeing them. I feel the visions but have no words to describe them and don't try to find any.

She sings for a long time. I don't know if the Axe can understand her words any more than I can, but everyone is clearly entranced by her voice. I want to hug them all. Her song fills me with love. My heart swells and my mind soars free.

It's a holy experience.

Eventually, she brings us down from the heights and sends a discreet nod to Shad, who lifts his arms for attention. At the same time, she returns to the hymn the people were singing when we came in.

Shad circles his hands once, then lowers his arms, and everyone joins the hymn.

Min sits down, smiling. She links fingers with me, and my entire universe thrills even more.

After one more round of the melody, Shad brings the joyful singing to a close. "Eat!" he roars.

Everyone bursts out laughing.

Min kisses my cheek.

Breakfast arrives on wide platters. The people dig in as if they're famished. Their metabolisms must be amazing.

Anya invites us to step down from our thrones and sit with her family at the top table, where she introduces us to her daughters, Vua and Tae.

They are the powerful warriors who spoke with Anya and Shad before the ceremony. They continue their hushed conversation with their mother while everyone else shovels food, until during a lull in the clamour one of them says something that sounds like *Tyac*.

"What did you say?" I can't hide my alarm.

Several people glance over.

"I'm sorry." I lower my voice. "What was that word you said?"

Vua checks with Anya, who blinks her permission.

"Last night, some of our wolves found the spoor of an unknown creature around our perimeter. This morning, Tae and I went out to check it."

Tae continues. "We think it is Tyac."

Min's ears prick up, and she turns from her conversation with Karn. "Tyac?"

Vua nods. "His legend comes down to us as part of yours. We know of no other creature that could have left those tracks and marks."

"Is he hunting you?" Tae asks.

"Yes."

"We will protect you." Anya is unruffled.

I share Min's confidence in these people and their wholehearted commitment. They will do everything in their power to save us from Tyac. But I also understand her concern about involving them in our troubles.

A light draught blows across my bare back. Min and I shiver in unison.

Anya speaks to a boy, who brings us a pair of short, lightweight, woollen cloaks. I tie mine loosely around my neck. It keeps the chill off while leaving my arms free to move. Others in the hall are wearing similar garments, so I don't feel odd, even though they remind me of the sort of bed jackets old women wear in historical dramas on television.

Anya ties one on too, and I can't help noticing again how magnificent she is. The werewolf gene certainly does make everyone strong and healthy.

Is it a gene? A virus? Is it permanent through the population, or do they have to pass it on to each new generation by biting their children? And do they change every night or only at the full moon like now? I guess we'll find out if we stick around long enough.

My old terror of wolves, which occupies the front of my mind whenever I think of Tyac, has mellowed into curiosity around the Axe. They're such loveable people. When they aren't being wolves. And even when they are, probably.

Min returns to her conversation with Karn and tells him about the war party I heard a few nights ago. "I suppose it's the usual tension between Tin and Hare, yes?"

Karn grunts through a mouthful of food.

Min tells me, "There's this feud between two families that's been going on in the Wild for a thousand years. Since the Norman invasion. The Hare family of Dartmoor Forest is headed at present by Queen Fiona, while King Owen rules the Tin family from Bodmin Moor. Roughly speaking, it's Devon versus Cornwall. Used to be open warfare, until five hundred years ago when they reached an uneasy stalemate. Not so much open war these days as a power struggle."

Shad interrupts. "It's been open war these past ten years."

She sighs. "Has it been bad?"

He roars with laughter. "Bad? No, it has been very good."

People laugh with him, and he beats the table with his fist. "Good for the Axe. We are famous warriors. Tin and Hare bid against each other to recruit us for their battles."

Things have changed even more than Min thought.

Shad leans into her. "This is why the bite is so good for us. We flourish. No one can beat us."

"What caused open war to break out again after so long?" Min is evidently trying not to sound dismayed.

"It started with a skirmish between people from two fishing villages on opposite banks of the River Tamar. You know Hare always controlled the River Plym and Tin controlled the Tamar?"

"Yes."

"Well, Tin still has a strong hold on the Tamar upstream, but Hare aims to take the wide stretch where the two rivers meet the sea."

Min and I mouth *Plymouth* to each other.

Shad nods enthusiastically. "Yes, in the outside, it is called Plymouth. And Hare wants it."

Min clutches his hand. "They're not going to invade the outside?"

"They are. There's a small in-between place in Plymouth, on the edge of the outside. Queen Fiona plans to use it as a base. If she takes this place, this..." He looks to Anya for help.

"Quarter Square."

Shad continues, "If Fiona takes this Quarter Square, it will open a broad corridor for her troop movements from the Wild to the outside, and she will gain control of the harbour. Then she will push upriver. It is a good plan. A bold plan. But it will fail." He grins, enjoying the anticipation of our next question.

I ask it. "Why?"

His chest swells with pride. "Because in this battle, we will fight for Owen against Fiona. Any day now. We are waiting for the word to take Quarter Square ourselves and stop the Hare advance right there. That quiet little place will become a famous battleground."

Min's voice shakes. "Shad, please, this is terrible."

"What, Min? What is terrible?"

"Quarter Square has been my home for years. The people who live there are my family."

Shad's confident grin dissolves.

An attentive hush spreads through the hall.

Min's eyes brim with tears. "Please, Shad, I love those people. Will you help me find a way to save them?"

Something has set wind blowing in the trees

THE BREAKFAST FEAST becomes a war council. Everyone in the tribe has a say, although some voices carry more weight than others, but there is no strong dissent. Only minutes pass before Shad declares the decision.

"We will help Min. We will fight to defend her friends in Quarter Square against Hare and Tin."

The ragged cheer that follows has hardly started before it's interrupted by a strong new voice from the doorway. "We will, will we?"

People part to make way for a tall, massively muscled man with a presence as powerful as his physique.

"Ban." Warriors growl his name and clap him on the back as he passes them.

After sweeping his gaze across Min and me, he embraces Anya and leaves his arm around her shoulders when he fronts up to Shad. "What is this, now? We are going against Tin in spite of our contract with them for this campaign?"

Shad's nod is emphatic. "We are going to fight against Tin *and* Hare to protect Min's loved ones in Quarter Square."

Ban arches an eyebrow. "Then you have picked the right time to do it. I ran through the night with Owen Tin's message. He bids us to take Quarter Square tonight."

A murmur passes through the crowd.

Anya sits, still holding on to Ban's hand over her shoulder. "My baby brother," she tells Min, love and pride shining in her eyes.

"Tonight?" Shad asks. "So Hare will be moving into Plymouth soon?"

"Some are already there, and the remainder of their force is moving now. They will attack an hour before dawn tomorrow."

Anya peers up at him. "King Owen knows Hare's plans very well."

"He has spies in Fiona's camp. And he says Fiona has a spy in Quarter Square who told her of increased tension in the settlement. I do not know what has occurred there, but something has set wind blowing in the trees."

"It's Tyac," Min says. "He attacked us in Quarter Square a few days ago. We escaped him, but it caused fear and alarm among our friends. I bet that's what they're talking about." She inclines her head to Ban.

He returns the greeting with a bow. "Min." His serious grey eyes meet mine. "Cayal."

"In this life, Cayal is called Joe," Min says. "Tell me, who is Fiona's spy in Quarter Square?"

"I do not know. If I had a name, I would give it to you." He turns to Shad. "We should talk."

They walk from the hall together, two impressively powerful men in the prime of their lives, leaving behind them a groundswell of anticipation.

Min reaches across the table and touches Anya's hand. "What will happen?"

"Exactly what Shad said."

"Ban doesn't seem very happy about the change of plan."

"Ban will do what is best for the tribe." Anya's pride shines again. "He always does. His reactions do not necessarily mean he is unhappy about the change. Part of his job is to discuss plans with Shad and suggest alternative ways to look at a thing."

Min's floundering a bit. "Is he your...beta?"

"I do not know this word."

"Like a second in command," I suggest. "I thought that would be you." I hope I'm not stepping on anyone's toes, but Anya clearly exercises personal and social power.

"I am chief, as Shad is chief. Neither is above the other." She grins fiercely. "And Shad is the last person who would ever forget that."

I believe her. "So what is Ban's position?"

Anya frowns. "It is difficult to find a single word. He makes things happen. If there is trouble between people, he stops it. He is strong. Everyone is strong, so internal conflicts have the potential to sever ties within the tribe, but Ban is stronger. He makes people fight together, not against each other." She shrugs. "Yes. Like that."

Enforcer? He certainly looks the part.

"This is all new to me," Min says. "The Axe never had anyone perform such a function before."

"We are wolves now."

Wolves. For the first time in my life I'm not scared of them. Tyac is a different thing altogether. He's still terrifying, but he isn't a wolf. He's a monster. The people of the Axe are genuine wolves. Around them I feel safe. Protected. At home.

A long night run

THE PLAN IS for Shad to carry Min on his back and Karn to carry me. We're going to ride big wolves through the night, all the way back to Quarter Square. This will be interesting.

"Today will be quiet," Anya says. "Everyone is resting, preparing for tonight."

The camp does indeed look deserted.

She and Shad stand outside their hut, arms around each other's waists. They share a look before Anya says, "We invite you to share our bed today."

Shad nods his agreement. There is no doubting the invitation is genuine.

My swallow is a gulp.

"Perhaps you need to discuss this in private," Anya suggests.

"Thank you." Min takes my hand, and we stroll across the empty compound. "Are you okay?"

Am I? I'm shaking inside at the enormity of their invitation, and the enormity of my instinctive response to it.

"First thing I want to say," Min begins, "is that you mustn't even think of doing anything you don't want to do."

I search her eyes. "Does that mean you want to sleep with them?"

"Second thing I want to say is this. You know we both take lovers when we're apart. Sometimes for your entire lifetimes. There have also been some lifetimes when we've been together while both enjoying other lovers too. Sometimes all in one bed at the same time."

There's my answer. She's up for it if I am.

She hurries on. "It isn't compulsory. Some lives you like that. Other lives you don't. I never pressure you or try to influence you. Whatever comes naturally to you in a lifetime is perfect for me."

She allows herself a mischievous little smile. "Have you caught your breath yet?"

I chuckle. "Yes."

"And?"

I close my eyes for a moment while blood thuds in my throat. "And, yes, I would like to share Shad and Anya's bed with you."

Our body language must be easy to read because when we turn back their faces light up.

It's glorious. Unbelievably wonderful. Min always has been and always will be the love of my life, of all my lives, the shining sun of my existence. But today, in that dimly lit hut, I fall in love with Shad and Anya too.

It's more than sex. It's fantastic sex, but so much more. It's emotionally intense. Powerful. A consummation.

When all of us have made love with all the others, more than once each, different ways and in all the combinations I can imagine, when we have given everything of ourselves, we sleep entwined together like wolves.

*

Ban isn't happy. Not one bit, and he makes no effort to hide his displeasure. He submits to Shad, bowing his head for the chief to place a hand palm down upon it, but his shoulders hunch in anger and his face is dark.

He avoids eye contact with Min, while glowering in my direction. His tribe is in danger, both from Tyac in the next few hours and from the probably vengeful King Owen of Tin further down the line.

And we brought these dangers, Min and me. No wonder he's glaring.

But he accepts Shad's decision, which is also the majority decision, and I don't know which of those carries more weight, and he accepts the task Shad and Anya have entrusted to him.

"Ban will shepherd the youngsters and mothers with babies by a different route," Anya explains. "He will come to us in a wide circle to protect them and keep them well clear of Tyac."

Because Tyac will be coming to *us*. I shudder.

Min squeezes my arm.

"Wait." The meaning of Anya's words hits me. "Everyone is coming to Quarter Square? You're all leaving this village?"

"Yes." Shad swings one arm around my shoulder and the other around Min's and hugs us tight. "We leave no one behind."

That must be what Ban is so angry about. And it isn't the plan I heard the tribe agree upon at breakfast. It must be Shad's plan. His alone.

"Surely you only need to send warriors to fight the battle," I say. "Why drag the whole tribe along?"

Shad chuckles. "Trust me, Joe. I know what I am doing."

I shrug off his heavy arm and face him. "No, Shad. This is wrong. You're putting everyone in danger, and there's no need for it."

He lifts his eyebrows. It isn't a friendly look.

"Send a war party. You said yourself no one can beat you. Why take the whole tribe? What's the point?"

"My decision, Joe." His tone carries a warning.

"It's the wrong decision. You're going to remove all these people from the protection of the ward. *Tyac* is out there, for fuck's sake. If Min and I stay here with your tribe, he'll stay in this area. When your war party leaves for Quarter Square, he'll let you go. It's us he wants. Me and Min. If you put your tribe between him and us outside the ward, you'll be putting them all in danger. For nothing."

"*My* decision, Joe. My people, my decision." Shad's nostrils flare. He thrusts his head forward and plants his massive fists on his hips.

I look to Min for support, but she pulls a stressed face and says nothing.

Shad lifts his right arm towards me at shoulder height, parallel to the ground.

I stare at his flattened hand. What?

He jerks the hand imperiously and glares at me.

He wants me to submit to him? Like Ban did? No way.

He jerks his hand again and gives an ominous low growl.

I growl back.

"Joe," Min pleads.

Anya nods her serious agreement.

I don't believe this.

Shad tucks his chin into his shoulder above his still raised arm. Undoubtedly, his next move will be to hammer me into the ground.

Our confrontation has attracted the attention of the entire tribe.

This isn't the same Shad I made love with. The Shad who kissed me tenderly when we awoke all curled up together less than an hour ago. Well, it is, but it's also Shad the chief of these people, Shad the leader of the Axe wolf pack. He has to dominate me. He has to be *seen* to dominate me.

With seething bad grace, I bow my head.

He presses his hand on it, none too gently and for longer than I consider reasonable. When he removes it, he studies my burning eyes curiously, almost playfully, all his aggression gone. Satisfied, he and Anya turn and walk away.

I tremble violently, filled with rage and nowhere to put it. Min busies herself talking with two of the children, but I catch Ban's eye, and we exchange a nod of understanding.

The Axe prepare to leave, planning to move out as soon as they change into wolves when the sun sets.

Min and I dress in our laundered clothes, separately because she's keeping out of my way, and then join the tribe in the compound. Mothers are fussing around the little ones as Ban gathers them together. Older boys and girls are releasing the goats from their tethers and the cattle from the pen.

"They don't expect to come back from this," I observe.

"I know." Min appears drawn, stressed beyond tears. "Look what they're giving up for us."

"Come with me." I touch her arm and go back into our hut.

*

"This is wrong," he says. "You know it is. There's going to be a tragedy tonight, and I can't believe you won't help me prevent it."

She's unable to meet his challenging stare. "I can't."

"Of course you can. You're their goddess. Order Shad to change his plan."

"It doesn't work like that. They honour me as their goddess, but I don't rule them. I doubt they'd take any notice if I tried."

"You'll never know if you don't bother."

She grips his arms. "I do know. I've known the Axe for thousands of years. I know how they think and how they react to threats. This is typical of them. They're going to put their lives on the line for me whether I want them to or not. I'm their goddess, and they'll do whatever they deem necessary to ensure my safety."

"But..."

"But nothing. You think I like this? You think I wanted to come here and put them all in danger? You were *there*. What other option did I have?"

Her tears spill over. "You saw how Shad responded when you challenged him. If I try that, even if all I do is question whether they can succeed in a battle with Tyac, I won't only be questioning Shad's authority as chief. I'll also be suggesting the whole tribe is weak and not worthy of me. It's my duty to accept it."

"You won't say anything because you don't want to hurt their pride?"

"Pride? How condescending are you?" Anger churns within her and she swipes her eyes dry. "It isn't pride. It's their culture. Their *identity*. They've been headstrong, brave, fond of grand gestures, faithful, and utterly fearless like this for six thousand years. And that was before they became fucking werewolves so all that is probably times ten now."

She's crying again with frustration and fear and pending heartbreak. "And there's this too. I love these people, Joe, but you mean everything to me."

He steps back. "Don't put this on me."

"I can't watch you die. Not so soon. I can't do it." She drops to the ground and hugs his legs. "I've seen it too many times. And we've been apart for so long. I've only just found you again. I can't bear it." She clings to his legs and sobs.

Joe helps her to her feet and holds her tenderly, obviously pulled in different directions like her and hating it as much as she does.

"I know I'm selfish." She talks into his chest. "But if others have to die, even people I love, so you can live, then so be it."

He stiffens in her embrace as if appalled by the thought she has spoken aloud.

A distant howl comes from far away in the east, and the skin crawls from the base of her spine to her scalp.

"We will protect you." Anya and her daughters are in the doorway. She beckons Min and Joe out then places a hand on each of their shoulders.

The warmth of her grip almost reassures Min. She wants to believe her. Surely even the mad savagery of Tyac won't be enough to beat a whole pack of wolves. Will it?

She turns her blotchy face to Anya. "I love your people, and I love you even more for wanting to help, but you know some are going to get hurt."

"We are ready to die for you." Anya stares hard at her.

"We are," Vua and Tae agree.

Shad joins them. "It is true," he rumbles. "We would all die for you. Tonight, I think some of us *will* die for you, and it will be our honour. You are our goddess."

Min shakes her head and looks around the tribe, her tearful gaze pausing on each of the children.

"We will protect the young ones." Shad squints at the sky. "It is nearly our time. Will you sing for us?"

Anya hugs first Ban and then Shad, kissing her husband tenderly.

Min sings a sad song in the Axe's old language while they wait for the sun to go down.

*

Like last night, the children change first. Parents murmur soothing words to the youngest ones, holding them and smoothing their hair as pain racks them briefly. In minutes, Min and I stand tall in a moving sea of big wolves.

The only ones I can identify by their markings are Shad and Anya, but the two dark females shadowing Anya's every move must be Vua and Tae.

General Anya and her two lieutenants. Those three females are as magnificent in wolf form as in their human shapes. They herd the pack to form up and take the lead in the main gateway, while Shad tastes Min's fingertips and rubs his flank against her hip.

She cocks her leg over his back, settles comfortably behind his shoulders, and grips his mane.

Another wolf waits beside me.

"Karn?"

He nibbles my fingertips delicately.

I climb onto his back. It's like mounting a small horse. He feels awesomely strong and powerful beneath me and smells like a big dog on a hot afternoon. I take fistfuls of coarse hair and use my inner thighs to adjust my seat as he pads forward.

When we reach the head of the column, Anya barks once, and the pack moves through the gateway in a long line, while behind us the big black wolf I assume must be Ban is leading nursing mothers and youngsters along a trail at the back of the village.

No matter what happens in the next twenty-four hours, the tribe is unlikely to see their home again. King Owen will destroy the village in revenge when he finds out they've betrayed him. If Min and I think that's probable, the Axe must know it with certainty.

We move fast. Trees flash by, and it dawns on me what this means. It's barely sunset, and the Hare attack on Quarter Square is planned for an hour before dawn. In order to arrive there in time to defend the place, we'll have to cover in a few hours the same distance it took Min and me three days to travel on our way here.

Although I expect we'll be taking a direct route tonight.

Our progress is amazingly quiet, considering there are scores of great animals running at speed through the woods. The loudest sound in my ears is my own panting, which is a mixture of fear and occasional jolts of pain.

It takes time for me to get used to the motion. I keep adjusting my position, trying to find a comfortable seat on Karn's back.

Eventually I discover that by bending my knees and gripping his flanks with the insides of my knees and calves and sometimes even insteps as well as my thighs, I can get into the rhythm and move with him. My groin stops taking hammer blows every time he leaps over a fallen tree or something in our path and lands heavily at the sprint, and I'm able to settle down and enjoy the ride. In a manner of speaking.

The village is half an hour behind us, and we've covered tens of miles when a distant crashing sounds from somewhere over to our right.

Tyac is coming. He's coming fast.

I renew my grip on Karn's mane.

The first attack happens so quickly I almost miss it. There's a crash and clamour in the undergrowth as we sweep past, then a brief scuffle from somewhere near the back of the column, and it's over. I look back and catch sight of a badly wounded wolf being dragged off the trail and into the bushes. No one stops to help him. Our flight continues at the same pounding pace.

Tyac's second attack takes out another wolf.

His third meets with more resistance. Three wolves turn on him, snarling and snapping and tearing at every part of him their sharp teeth can reach. The furious defence slows him, but only slightly, and we leave another dead wolf on the track behind us when he crashes back into the forest.

"They'll all be killed," Min pants beside me.

I don't answer. *I told you so* would be cruel and petty. Also, useless.

Wolves mob and maul Tyac every time he attacks, but he's bigger and stronger and faster than any individual member of the pack and he keeps on coming. The pack's numbers fall, one by one, and casualties are left behind.

The eeriest part of the whole horrible thing is that pauses between the attacks are nearly silent. Grimly so. Nothing breaks our breathtaking speed. Obviously, the plan is to keep moving, no matter what happens, to keep Min and me out of Tyac's reach at any cost.

I glimpse him through the flashing trees as we run. He's twice Shad's size and runs upright on two legs like the monster he is rather than on all fours like the wolves carrying us. He is insane and utterly terrifying.

We thunder through the night, our progress marked by the dead bodies we abandon and the bloody smears they leave on trees and foliage. Our sound carries in heavy vibrations in the ground more than as noises in the air.

Even in my fear, I marvel at the pack's discipline. Anya remains calm while she marshals her fighters. I guess we're about halfway back to Quarter Square when she falls back in line, while Tae and Vua take her place at the head of the column.

Min and I twist our necks to watch her filter back to the middle of the line with several other fighters.

"I don't like *this*," Min says through gritted teeth.

Shad gives an angry huff beneath her. I think he doesn't like it either.

I don't like any of it, but Anya's revised plan makes more sense to me than Shad's original one. Why lose individual wolves to the monster if a pack of them together can fight him off?

And why has it taken them so long to figure this out? I wonder if their famous success as mercenaries owes more to the fact that their adversaries are usually frightened humans pitted against huge wolves than from any sort of superior strategies or tactics.

Tyac's next attack is met with such firm resistance he fails to take out a single wolf. Maybe this is going to work after all.

After that failed attack, we run unhindered for about an hour, although I catch sight of him flashing through the trees that flank us, sometimes one side and sometimes the other. This isn't over by a long way. And I ache everywhere.

I start to recognise features in the landscape from our first day of flight into the Wild. The return journey has taken the pack only four or five hours, and I dare to hope we might make it back in one piece.

We're only a mile from the square when Tyac attacks from above, running through the treetops and dropping directly into our path. We're on him instantly.

He flashes his spittle-flecked maw of vicious teeth at me, and I punch him hard on the snout as we charge past.

Wolves drag him down and mob him. Anya and her warriors hit him in a mass.

The remaining wolves close around us, and we sprint for the edge of the Wild, leaving a screaming carnage in our wake.

The Battle of Quarter Square

THE PACK LIMPS into the haven on bleeding pads and scares the hell out of a pair of youngsters who are necking by the fire. Word spreads quickly, and insiders gather in the garden. While Min explains the events to everyone, I sit with the wolves sprawled together in a heap.

The acrobats, Dish, Blue, and Sab, crouch under the old apple tree and glower at us.

"Don't know what their problem is," I tell Shad. "They never liked me from the moment I arrived here."

He butts the hard bone top of his head against my hand, and I realise I've been stroking behind his ear like he's a dog. He doesn't seem to mind it, but he's far from relaxed. He and his wolves study the acrobats intently. The air between the two groups quivers with hostility.

Jimmy approaches with caution and sits beside me. "I'm glad you're okay. We've been worried sick about you and Min." He eyes Shad warily.

"These people saved us from that bastard Tyac. Lots of them died on the way here to stop him getting us."

"They're werewolves too?"

"Yes, but not like he is. These are the good guys. And if you think they look awesome now, wait until you see them as humans."

Voices sound across the garden as insiders stand in pockets, trying to deal with the news.

"This is crap," Andrew insists. "No way Queen Fiona would hurt anyone here."

Other conversations fade as people turn to him, and Min's question carries clearly. "Andrew, what do you know about Fiona's intentions?"

His eyes dart left and right. "Well, nothing. Obviously."

"Tell us." There's no accusation in her voice. She sounds like an understanding Mother Confessor.

He closes his eyes. His breath trembles.

Min takes his hands and croons a quiet tune to him.

People exchange unhappy stares while Jimmy and I stroll over to the main group.

Min stops singing. "Tell us what we need to know."

Andrew's brimming eyes implore her to believe him. "She wanted to know all about the haven. She cares. No one cares anymore." Tears spill over and roll down his cheeks.

Min opens her arms and hugs him. Angry mutters break out among the insiders, but she shakes her head at them over his shoulder and holds him while he sobs.

I clear my throat. "They'll be here in an hour. We'd better get ready."

Nearly an hour later, Will and I patrol the square together, checking everyone is okay and looking for potential weak points in our hurriedly agreed plan.

Fliss and Linda kneel in the middle of the garden with a subdued Andrew, holding hands and meditating. Their sketching and threading magic will be the backbone of our defence. Everyone knows to watch out for their safety.

Five teenagers stand nearby, ready to defend the sketcher-threaders and armed with some of the sheets of heavy timber I fashioned into full-body shields. I also made dozens of heavy spears. Each teenager has one of them in hand and a few more within reach on the ground.

Will's still muttering in amazement at the magic he and Jimmy saw me perform with wood in this past hour.

Making the weapons released some kind of muscle memory in me. When I hefted the first spear, its weight and balance perfect, I knew I've done it before. Not only have I made them, I've wielded them.

Anticipating the battle to come invigorates me like the promise of imminent sex. Energy powers my limbs, fires my senses. I want to run out there and find the enemy now. It's an alien emotion in this life, but it must have been familiar in at least some of my pasts.

Tara sits cross-legged by the smaller fire, briefing her four recruited medical assistants with calm assurance. She smiles when Will and I pass, and mouths *oak* to me.

The rest of the adult insiders are divided into two main groups and armed with an assortment of weaponry from spears to juggling clubs, knives, and swords, and most of my woodworking tools from inside the theatre. Big Luke leads the group at the far end of the garden, while Cindy and Debs whirl their fire ropes slowly at the front end near the theatre door.

Jimmy has gathered all the insider children in his and Fliss's front room, where Min is singing soothing songs to them. He bears two spears. "I'll stay here and protect the kids."

"Me too." Delores joins us with a spear in her hand.

Min comes out and hugs me hard. "Be careful. I love you."

"I love you."

She hugs Will too, and then goes back in to sing with the children.

I stand on tiptoe to look over the hedge into the garden. The acrobats are no longer under the apple tree, which Will and I agree is probably a good thing. I've been concerned their unfriendly but innocent blood might get spilled when the wolves are in a fighting fury.

"They're in our house," Delores says. "Don't know what's got into those boys tonight. They're in a nasty mood."

"Maybe they don't like wolves." Will bares his teeth in a nervous grimace. "Can't say I'm too comfortable around them either."

"They're here to help. Let's go see them." I stroll to the gate and sense Will hesitating before he follows.

Shad stands up on all fours as we approach.

Will edges behind me, and my amusement shames me. Who am I to scorn someone's fear of wolves?

"Not long now." I don't know how much human speech Shad understands in his present form, but I'm sure wolf senses make his grasp of the situation better than mine.

I'm scared and elated at the same time. Getting high on adrenaline. A wild grin keeps stretching my face. I strip off my shirt, throw it under the apple tree, and grip my spear. *Bring it on.*

Shad's ears prick forward, and he spins to the theatre. The pack rises as one, fur all fluffed up as if they're ready to spring at something.

Will starts to say something, but his gaze wavers over my head and his jaw drops open.

Figures are climbing into view in a line along the roof of the theatre and its adjoining buildings. They range out in menacing silence, silhouetted against the pale early morning sky, and stare down at us.

So this is the Hare army. I recognise them. Not as individuals, but as a type. They look like a biker gang, like the men who fought that deadly battle I walked into outside the theatre last week. The other combatants must have been Tin soldiers. I wonder which family the one who died in my arms belonged to.

They have bows and arrows. They're aiming them.

"Cover!" Big Luke yells.

Will and I pull up two shields each and hold them vertically like a wooden wall to protect ourselves and the wolf pack. Others do the same thing all over the square, and just in time before a heavy rain of arrows thumps into the shields. The force of the blows surprises me, and so does the second flight seconds later.

Will grunts. "This is bad."

"It'll be okay." As far as I can see, everyone is huddled behind the shield walls and fully protected.

"They'll be down among us soon, and these lumps of wood will be useless."

"We've got these guys to help us." I grin, first at Will, then at the wolves, and shout, "We can take these bastards, can't we?"

Shad howls his answer, long and low, and the rest of the pack howls with him.

No more arrows thump into our shields, but some individual shouts something from the theatre roof. I can't make out the words, but the tone is ominous. I sneak a look around the side of my shield.

It's a thin, bald, angry old man, dressed in a cape of feathers. He points an ornate staff forward at arm's length.

"A wizard."

"Huh?" Will squints at me behind his shield.

"They've got a wizard with them. Or a witch or something."

The old man's voice takes on a new note of command. He points his staff at the houses behind us and bellows a single word.

Everything pauses, and then a woman screams.

"That's Delores." Will spins around in a crouch.

Something heavy crashes over and through the top of the high hedge. Something moving very fast. Three huge jaguars tear into the wolf pack right behind us. The pack falls upon them. In an instant, our immediate vicinity is a snarling, snapping, ripping, biting, blood-splattering nightmare.

Will and I scramble away from the melee and watch in horror, only remembering to hold our shields firm when a third flight of arrows strikes from above.

Another imperious call comes from up there.

It's matched by a similar call from Andrew. He's sheltering with Fliss and Linda behind a semicircle of shields, but they're facing the Hare wizard, and Andrew shouts something directly at the old man.

They duck when a storm of arrows thud into their wooden wall but stand tall again straightaway and glare up at the roof.

The wizard waves his staff both ways along his battle line, and the archers take aim again, but this time all their arrows fall harmlessly only a few feet from their bows.

The wizard screams in rage, and something invisible batters into our magic team. They and their shield wall protectors stagger back a step, but they hold firm again; Linda keeps sketching rapidly, and Andrew barks a defiant laugh.

"They're coming down," Big Luke shouts.

The archers have abandoned their bows. They bump and shuffle down the sloping roofs, drop to the ground, and draw swords as they run at us.

Our wolf pack is being ripped to pieces. They've fought the jaguars with everything they have, but five of them lie dead and all of them are mauled.

Shad and his daughters snarl and snap as they back away from two huge cats advancing on them.

I drop my shields, grab a spear, and run at the nearest one. It's awesomely powerful. It turns on me at the last moment in a blur of speed and drives itself onto my spear point as I ram hard and force the sharp stake into its chest. The animal's great weight and momentum slams me back, and the butt end of my spear wedges in the ground behind me.

The jaguar screams hot spittle into my face then dies and falls heavily on me. It's like being crushed under a velvet-coated car.

The fight between wolves and jaguars continues all around me and next to me and over me. The dead one's weight traps my legs, but Will drags me clear and helps me scramble away.

"You're fucking mad!" he says, laughing wildly.

"Come on." I grab another spear and ram it into the flank of the cat Shad is fighting. Will rams his spear in alongside mine, and we hold on while the huge animal screeches in pain and rage. We push hard against its struggles, trying to keep it away from us.

Shad and his daughters rip out its throat and it falls dead at our feet.

The other wolves round on the remaining jaguar and back it to the apple tree, where it roars and lashes out at them with its massive paws until their combined weight bears it down. It disappears beneath them, its screams mixing with the wolves' savage snarls.

The enemy soldiers are among us. Everyone is fighting. Cindy and Debs walk forward steadily, spinning their poi faster than the eye can follow, flashing fire in the faces of the Hare soldiers, breaking the assault on their group as insiders circle around and catch the attackers in a pincer movement.

Big Luke leads his insiders at the run and clashes against the main force.

Will and I join Luke's fight when the Hare numbers are greatest. I wield my heavy spear like it's an extension of my arms, which is exactly how it feels.

At first, I try to club and repel rather than stab. But the Hare are experienced warriors armed with all kinds of wicked blades, so I find myself fighting for my life and killing them as savagely as they're trying to kill me.

Our spirited defence takes the attackers by surprise, but they rally to the shouted orders of their wizard. The ensuing violence is brutal, almost overwhelming.

Min's voice carries across the noise. Her brief burst of song is urgent.

"Min!" Will and I shout at the same time. We break free of the fight and sprint around to Jimmy's house, where he and Delores are trying desperately to hold off twenty Hare soldiers while Min clutches her throat and staggers around as if drunk, glaring mute hostility at the wizard on the roof.

We charge into the soldiers from behind. I stick my spear through the nearest Hare back and unintentionally hoist him into the air. He scrams as he arches. I throw him off the end of the spear into a group of his comrades and stab at them all repeatedly. One of them catches me a glancing blow off the top of my head with a club, and another slices my forearm with a blade, but I feel only rage and they both go down beneath my feet.

A brawny Hare warrior swings his arm around Min's neck and drags her backwards towards the garden. I can't reach her. There are too many soldiers between us. I stab and kick like a madman, but the man keeps dragging her farther away.

Will flies at him and uses his spear like a club. It snaps across the warrior's back, and he throws Min down. Will stabs at him with the broken shaft of his spear, but the big man grabs it with one hand and pulls Will to him while he swings his machete with the other.

The terrible blade seems to move in slow motion. It slices Will's throat wide open. His blood jets and showers Min as his body crumples to the ground.

Tae and Vua hit Will's killer and tear him to pieces. Shad and the rest of the pack rip into the other soldiers surrounding me and kill them in seconds before streaking back into the garden to attack the remaining Hare force.

I run to Min. She's cradling Will and rocking him. I rest my hand on her shoulder for a moment. Then I leave her to mourn in private and run back to the garden.

The battle has come to a bloody end after the wolves piled in. The only surviving attacker is the wizard. He points his staff down at Andrew in a menacing gesture before turning to disappear.

Andrew hangs his head.

My legs won't support me anymore. I slide down to sit on the grass with my back against the apple tree.

Strong words

TARA STANDS OVER me in a dazzle of rising sun. "Are you all right?"

I nod. I'm not all right. I feel terrible about the violence I've seen. The violence I've done. About my ravenous hunger for it at the time, as if I were someone else entirely, someone savagely happy to kill and maim others. I'm far from all right, but I nod anyway.

"Sure?" She places a comforting warm hand on my arm.

"I'll be okay. Thanks."

She squeezes my arm and moves on to the next exhausted insider. She and her assistants have already treated the wounded, including the wolves as they changed back into human form and all their injuries became apparent. Only twenty-four Axe warriors have survived.

We had to fight. Had to save our friends in Quarter Square. Negotiation wouldn't have worked. The time for peaceful talks was gone long before those Hare soldiers appeared on the roof, if that time ever existed at all. Some battles have to be fought. But I don't want to be in any more of them.

I don't like warrior me.

"I didn't know, you know." Delores takes Tara's place in the sun halo.

I squint up at her. "That your acrobats were giant jaguars working for Hare?"

"Yes. If I'd known, I never would have hooked up with them and brought them to the square."

"I know." I understand why she wants to talk, but right now I have nothing for her. For anyone. I'm hollowed out.

People bring clothing into the garden and help the Axe warriors to dress. Big Luke and Jimmy are piling Hare bodies on carts and wheelbarrows. Others are laying out our dead insiders on one of the lawns.

I haven't seen Min since Will died.

A new commotion disturbs the subdued mood when the Axe mothers and children arrive. Ban strides naked into the garden with Anya's wolf body cradled in his powerful arms. He has eyes only for Shad.

He lowers his sister's body tenderly to the ground and crouches beside her, stroking the fur around her neck and murmuring something to her. Then he straightens and swings a haymaker punch that knocks Shad flat. It would knock most men into next week.

Shad gets back to his feet and works his jaw. "Ban."

"Half of our warriors are lying dead out there."

"I know. There are more of our dead here."

Ban half turns away and swings another massive punch, but this time, Shad stands strong and deflects the blow with his forearm.

"I am hurting as badly as you are," he growls. "I gave you one hit because you needed it. You want another one, you will have to earn it."

The two big bruisers stand toe-to-toe and glare at each other for long moments before Ban turns on his heel and strides back into the forest.

Shad lifts Anya and buries his face in her neck fur. When he raises his head, his tears are flowing.

So are mine. My heart is breaking.

"Come," Shad tells his people. "We will care for our fallen."

Min stands over me. "I can't sing for them, but I want to be there when they tend to their dead. Are you coming?" Her throat sounds raw and painful.

I wipe my eyes and squint up at her. "They didn't need to die."

"What?"

"If you and I had stayed in the Axe village, Tyac wouldn't have attacked them on their way here. He wasn't interested in them. It was us he wanted. They would have arrived here alive, and there would have been enough of them to take the Hare army. Possibly without any casualties. I said this back there, but no one would listen. If they'd all got here in one piece, they might even have been able to take those jaguars without losing anyone."

Her voice cracks in a hoarse whisper. "If we had stayed alone back in the village, the ward would have faded, and Tyac would have got in."

"We wouldn't have been alone. They needed to send a war party here, not the entire tribe. If Anya was the only one who could sing the ward every day, she could have stayed with us. They would have managed fine when they got here."

Angry tears blur my vision. "Anya would still be alive. *Anya*, Min. If the war party had arrived here at full strength, maybe Will would still be alive too. And all the others."

Min stares at the ground. A tear drops into Will's dried blood on her shirt.

"*And* we were leading Tyac right back to our friends in the square." I wipe my eyes again with the back of my hand, smearing the sticky blood on my face. "You know what, love? I'm sick of other people making decisions for me. I'm sick of people assuming they're qualified to do that. It isn't going to happen anymore."

She lifts her head. "You mean me."

"Among others, yes. I love you, Min, but I won't let you control me anymore. The spoon-feeding me with only as much information as you think I can handle? That stops now. Overruling my judgement on the basis that I only remember one life? That stops too. If you love me, love me for who I am now, not who I once was."

She watches the Axe leave. "You coming?"

I have some thinking to do. "Say goodbye for me."

*

The silence inside the theatre makes my ears roar. My tools are scattered across the garden, leaving me a solitary hand axe and three wood chisels on the bench. I'll have to go around and find them. Not that I'll be doing anything more to the theatre while Tyac is still coming after me.

I stand centre stage and gaze out through dust mites dancing in shafts of sunlight, but my mind is elsewhere, and I see only violence and blood, terror and pain.

Rage explodes inside me, and I hurl the axe across the stage. It thumps into a solid vertical beam at just above head height. For a second, I imagine the beam is Tyac's head.

Some battles have to be fought.

"Got one of them for me?" Andrew speaks from the dark arena. He shuffles up onto the stage, carrying a duffel bag over one shoulder and his flute pouch over the other. He looks as if he's aged twenty years in a single night. "Know what they're calling you out there?"

I shrug.

"Lion man." He peers at me. "You don't know, do you? You were roaring all through the fight. Roaring like a lion."

What fresh bollocks is this? I was just shouting in the heat of the moment.

"Tara saw it in her stones, didn't she? You're a lion."

Whatever. I nod at his bag. "Leaving?"

"Yep. Can't stay now they know I betrayed them."

"Will you go to the Hare?"

"Hell, no. That bitch read me like a book and used me."

I understood. "All you wanted was for the square to carry on."

"More than that. I had this vision for the insiders to see the wider world out in the Wild and for the square to be a place where people would come together. I told Fiona that. She said she understood. The last thing I expected was that she'd attack us. And I didn't know about those fucking cat acrobats working for her neither."

"Where will you go?"

"Dunno. Somewhere the Hare wizard can't find me."

"Tin?"

His expression says not. "I'm so sick of it all." He stands passively while I hug him, then he leaves without another word.

I stay under the shower for a long time after all the blood has washed off and swirled down the drain. Hot water blasting on my aching muscles helps physically, but it doesn't improve my frame of mind.

I make a pot of coffee, my first in days, and lean in the front doorway to take in the sounds of another innocent Barbican day getting started.

"Lion man." Jimmy joins me. "You okay?"

I shrug. "You?"

He mirrors my shrug. "It'll take some getting over."

"Fliss?"

"Same."

A seagull cries overhead. Answering calls from the harbour echo up the narrow lanes.

Jimmy gestures over his shoulder. "Don't feel bad about the theatre. I can't do the stuff you do, but I'll do what I can until you come back when it's safe."

How long will that be?

He nods at the row of parked motorbikes up the lane. "Maybe we should put them in the square. Those dead Hare guys don't need them anymore."

It isn't a bad idea. "I'll take one for Min and me."

"Take two. She can handle a bike."

I nod at my van across the road. "That's no use to me anymore. Too easily traced. If you want it, it's yours."

"Thanks."

"You'll need to get it some different number plates. Keys are in my bedroom."

He holds his hand out awkwardly. "Look after yourself.

I pull him into a hug. "You too. Stay safe. We'll come back as soon as we can."

I get another mug of coffee and return to the doorway to enjoy the seagulls' song, but my peace crumbles when the black car draws up at the kerb and Sebastian Merritt climbs out.

"Good morning." He brushes past me into the building. *My* building.

I follow him when he strolls into the auditorium and up onto the stage. He glances around the place with a coolly interested air as I place my coffee on the bench.

"Major activity around here last night, Joe. Major. Are you ready to talk to me about it?" He turns his sleek smile on me.

I catch him off balance, run him backwards across the stage, slam him into the upright beam, and pin him there with my hand squeezing his throat hard. The axe handle juts from the timber above his head, but I'm careful not to look at it directly.

If this bastard is Tyac, can I kill him while he's a man? Can I grab the axe and split his fucking skull open? Yes. I glare into his eyes and know I can kill him.

He knows it too. For a flicker of an instant, his eyes show fear. Normal fear. Normal human fear. And I know in my gut that he isn't the monster.

I hope I'm right, anyway, because I release him and step away. "No, I don't want to talk to you at all. Leave me alone."

He's smooth. I'll give him that. He adjusts his tie, straightens his lapels, and smiles as if I haven't laid a finger on him.

"You will. Unless I'm very mistaken, you're starting to realise how way out of your depth you are with whatever's going on around here. Then there's the murder investigation. I've steered it away from you for the time being, because I think you're a good investment and I know you didn't do it. But my patience isn't endless. It will take only a call from me to point DCI Dawson back in your direction. Think about it, Joe. We need each other."

He flips a business card between his manicured fingers and offers it.

I ignore it.

He clicks it down next to my coffee on the bench. "You'll be in touch."

I watch him walk up through the arena and listen as he leaves the building.

*

"You were right to let him go." Min's voice is hoarse, her throat horribly sore. She steps from the wings. "He isn't Tyac."

Joe releases a frustrated sigh. "Tyac's still out there."

"He always is, my love."

"Not for long. I've had enough of running. I'm going to kill him."

She's horrified. "I understand how you feel, but we have to run. It's the only way."

"We'll run for now, but only because I don't want to bring any more shit down on Quarter Square. We'll find somewhere safe to rest and recover. Then I'm going to hunt that bastard down and kill him." He looks around the theatre. "And then I'll come back and keep my promise to the insiders."

She runs across the stage into his arms. "Please. You've been like this before, and it always ends badly. Always. He loves it when you go for him."

"He won't love it this time."

She leans her forehead against his chest. "You've said that before too. When you get like this, you scare me nearly as much as Tyac does."

"I'm sick of people dying to protect me. It isn't right. But you won't change anything about it. So I will."

Her shoulders shake, and her tears dampen his shirt. "When you consider the horrific deaths I've had to watch you suffer at Tyac's hands, is it any wonder that I'll do whatever is necessary to keep you with me?"

He strokes her hair. "If we keep doing what we've always done, we'll keep getting what we've always got."

It's the lion in him. Always. Whenever it's born strong in one of his lives, that life is always tragically brief. She hugs him and weeps.

*

Footsteps clump down through the arena. Shad, Vua, and Tae have appropriated pairs of biker boots and they're not yet used to walking in them. They thump up the stairs to the stage and stand before us in their newly acquired clothing.

Min wipes her eyes.

"The people of Quarter Square have offered the Axe a place to live here in gratitude for our help last night," Shad says.

"That's good."

"Not for me and my daughters. We're coming with you."

"With us?"

"I expect you will leave immediately to get a head start on the monster?"

Min and I nod.

"Wherever you go," Shad says, "we go too. We will protect you. This is our pledge."

Min tries to clear her throat. It sounds painful. "What about the tribe?"

"Karn and Keira are their chiefs now. As for Vua and Tae and me, our place is with you. You are our goddess. We owe you our lifelong allegiance."

"Yes." The sisters affirm it with quiet strength.

Shad looks at me. "Also, I owe you my life. I will not forget."

"Come with us," I decide. "We'll leave now. But we're not running forever. I'm going to find Tyac and kill him."

Shad glowers. "*We* are going to find Tyac and kill him. Together. For Anya and all our kin."

Vua and Tae growl their agreement.

Min moans in distress.

I hold my arm out towards Shad at shoulder level, parallel to the floor, palm down.

He lifts his eyebrows.

I jerk my hand and jut my chin.

He thinks about it. Then, slowly, he bows his head and steps to me.

I place my hand on his head and hold it there. "We'll hunt him down and kill him together." I can hear the war growl in my words. "Now, *that's* a plan."

BOOK II
GOLDEN TRIANGLE

Ready?

I GUN MY BIKE ahead of Shad's at the bottom of a long hill, and the snarl from my exhaust smacks back at me from stone walls edging the empty Pennine road.

Shad growls alongside effortlessly. His heavy Triumph cruiser doesn't have scary g-force acceleration like my Suzuki, but it's more comfortable for a long haul and better suited to his powerful body. In his open-face helmet and flying goggles, he looks like he was born on a big bike. He bares his teeth at me in a fierce challenge as he pulls ahead, and we tear up the slender ribbon of road to crest the hill neck and neck.

There's no joy in his grin. It's pure competition. His need to win is as strong as ever, although I never see any pleasure in it for him. Anya's death kicked the joy out of his life.

Min and I invited him to share our bed, the way he and Anya invited us to share theirs on what none of us knew was to be Anya's last day alive. We invited him with love, respect, and compassion. He declined, with equal love, respect, and compassion.

We told him the invitation will always be there. When he's ready, if a time comes when he is ready, he won't need to think twice about it. We'll be pleased, and in our union, the three of us will honour Anya. He knows that. And we understand why he isn't ready to join us yet. There's no more he or we can say.

Sheep-grazed fields roll away across the moors in every direction. Ahead of us, Rivington's sandstone buildings glow under a pink September sunset. We swing right at the next crossroads and lose sight of the village.

Our first day on the new job has been a long one, shifting a house-sized mound of construction rubble and contorted old iron railings in a scrap metal merchant's yard. I ache, but it's a good muscle ache and we've made a satisfying dent in the mound. Plus, the money's okay. As good as can be expected for two strangers seeking casual work with no questions asked.

I miss carpentry. It hurts like a hole in my life, and the yearning is reduced only a little by my new hobby of carving small figures from old fallen wood. Min likes them. That's something.

I also miss being involved with the protest movement. It's horribly frustrating to be out of the communication loop, trying to filter drops of truth from the floods of government lies on the TV news channels. And on a personal level, I miss seeing Bill, Pen, and Poke's friendly faces at our protests.

But knowing Tyac's undoubted ability to monitor communications networks, I'd be stupid to make contact. And I'd have to be suicidal to attend any protests in person.

It took no effort at all for Min to persuade me of this logic when we went off grid, in spite of the protest movement having been an important part of me before all this started.

I focus on the road ahead. The bright point is that Min and our family are at the end of this ride. And, hey, at least while this job lasts, Shad and I will enjoy our daily commute.

My earpiece trills. I tap the phone button on my helmet. No need to check who's calling. Only Min has my number. "We'll be home in ten minutes."

A muted female voice says something in the background at her end. Tae or Vua. "I'll call you back in a sec," Min says before the line goes dead.

Probably found something interesting online. Min taught them to read and they're hungry for information. They trawl weird and wacky websites every day, searching for anything that might be a mention of Tyac.

We've heard nothing of the monster since that terrible night in June when he killed Anya and nearly half of the Axe pack. But he's out there. He'll never give up the hunt. Sooner or later, he'll find us again.

We're not ready for him. One day we will be, and I guarantee he won't know what's hit him then, but until Min recovers her song magic, we're missing a vital weapon in our armoury. So we've spent the summer running and hiding.

We prefer cities and big towns, where it's easier to be invisible. But last week we hit trouble in an east coast town and had to leave in a hurry. An outlaw biker gang runs that town. We moved on as soon as we found out, but not soon enough to avoid their biggest bastard picking a fight with Shad, who did what comes naturally to him and beat the hard man into a puddle of blood and snot. In public.

We could have taken the whole gang. I don't look for violence, although after my experience of hand-to-hand fighting in the battle for Quarter Square, I don't have a problem dishing it right back to anyone who threatens my family. Some battles need to be fought. Mostly, though, I'm not needed, because when Shad and his daughters go into action, even in their human forms, they hit like a hurricane.

But fighting a stupid turf war isn't part of our plan to lie low and keep quiet, so we crossed the Pennines and have rented an old farmhouse in the West Moors. Where Min's getting her hygge on and making us a warm nest of comfort and cosiness. Where Shad intends to build a sweat house out back before winter sets in. And where, all things being equal, there will be a big dinner ready for Shad and me to help make it disappear.

My phone trills again at the same time as an air horn blows two loud notes behind us. It's a flashy pick-up truck with a four-seat cab, all metallic red paint and chrome and spotlights. The driver waves an impatient demand for us to get out of the way.

Shad tucks in behind me as I tap my phone button.

"Where are you?" Min sounds tense.

"Five minutes away."

"Those bikers from last week are riding up and down the road right outside the house. Tae and Vua have shifted in case it kicks off before you get here."

"Two minutes."

The line goes dead again, and I look back to signal urgency to Shad.

He's fifty feet behind me, slowing down, allowing the pick-up driver to get past him. Then a shotgun barrel pokes through the pick-up's rear window and fires.

Shad's fuel tank explodes. It blows him and the bike clear off the road and over the wall.

Shad!

The truck accelerates to me with the barrel still poking out.

I rev up and fuck off.

Even though the truck is fast and they have the advantage of surprise, I could leave them in my dust if I wanted to. But Shad needs me. I fumble my escape and allow them to catch up.

The driver sneers at me as he inches past. His head is polished bald, and he wears a heavy Zappa moustache. He's one of the outlaw gang members from last week. The ugly little bastard in the back with the shotgun is another one. When his finger tightens on the trigger, I lock my back brake and twist the wheel to lay my bike down.

The shotgun blasts over my head as the bike and I smash into the road surface at forty miles an hour. The bike slides alongside the truck with sparks flying everywhere, but I only glimpse it for a second. My right shoulder screams. I don't know how far I'm rolling and bouncing along the road before I slam into the stone wall.

*

Min carries a high-backed armchair into the kitchen, from where she can see the front and back doors. The sun is down, and it'll be dark soon, but she leaves the lights off.

She's so sick of violence. In thirteen thousand years she has witnessed too much death and destruction but learned long ago to predict it and get out of harm's way. She's managed to keep Joe safe from it as much as possible throughout his many lives. But this time is complicated.

This time, *he* is complicated. And headstrong. And violence follows him around, demanding that he deal with it face-to-face.

She hefts Vua's baseball bat with a two-handed grip. Can she use it? Damn right she can. Just because she's never had to fight physically before doesn't mean she won't do it now.

For the first time in her very long life, Min has no song magic to protect her loved ones from danger. No way to enchant enemies and dissolve conflict.

The prospect of something like this freaked her out three months ago when the Hare wizard broke her voice in Quarter Square, and it sure as hell freaks her out now with a bunch of vengeful bikers threatening to do serious damage to her family.

A scream of frustration rises in her tender throat. Swallowing it hurts, almost as much as it would hurt to let it rip. She is her family's goddess. Their protector. It's her job to look after them. And the only weapon she has to hand is a bloody baseball bat.

She sits back, leans the bat handle against her inner thigh, and wipes her sweaty palms on her jeans. Right. So far, the thugs outside have only ridden aggressively and shouted insults from the road. Sticks and stones. No need to respond unless they actually break into the house.

Come on, Joe and Shad.

Tae takes up position on her left, Vua on her right, two powerful wolves sitting alert beside the chair and glaring at flitting shadows through the windows. Every time one of the motorbikes blasts past, they growl in unison.

Min lays her hands on their heads. They're quivering with anticipation, ready to explode into action at a moment's notice.

She's trembling too, but with fear.

The jeers outside are getting louder and braver. It sounds like they're coming from the front garden now.

Joe, where are you?

*

Everywhere hurts bad, but the shoulder feels serious. When I haul myself over the wall and drop to the other side, hot pain nearly turns my bowels to liquid. I pant hard and fast, and just about manage to keep everything under control.

Shad's bike is burning where it landed in the field. I can't see him.

I drag off my helmet and wipe my streaming eyes. My gloves are shredded. And my leathers. My boots have survived, but my helmet's face shield is cracked. Even outside of my whole-body internal pain, distinct from all of that, every bit of my skin throbs like a hundred fingers slammed in a hundred car doors all at once.

I limp to the burning bike.

My hearing has gone dull, but a quick backwards glance tells me all I need to know. The truck idles next to my dead bike and the shooter stands on the cab roof, watching me.

I limp faster.

Shad's landed on his back in a dry ditch fifty feet from his bike, out of sight of the pick-up. I drop to my knees. His clothing is charred and mostly gone. His skin doesn't look much better. Only his helmet and boots are intact. He smells like pork grilling on a barbecue.

He cracks open one bloodshot eye. "Get these clothes off me. I must shift quickly."

A breath I hadn't realised I was holding whooshes out of me. At least he's alive. The big man and I keep on saving each other's lives and I love him. We already lost his wonderful wife. Losing him would be too much to bear.

I haul off his boots as gently as I can and remove his helmet with great care. As far as I can tell, his skull isn't damaged, but the remaining scraps of clothing are stuck to his burned skin, so I leave them alone. My injuries hurt like hell. I can only imagine the agony he must be in. "You're good to go."

"I will remain wolf until after the full moon next week." He gasps in pain. "To heal. You understand?"

"Do it now. They're gonna come back for us, and we need to deal with this pair then get home quick. The rest of the gang is outside the farmhouse threatening our family."

His angry growl starts human and transforms into an animal snarl as he changes.

I've seen this happen at close quarters several times. He and his daughters shift on three or four nights either side of every full moon, whether or not they want to. But they can also choose to shift whenever they like, night or day, anytime during the rest of the month. The sounds of cracking bones and stretching muscles no longer appals me, although on this occasion I don't enjoy seeing his burned flesh tear.

Within a minute, he turns into the massive wolf we love and respect. He gets up a little stiffly, swings his head low a couple of times, then gives a vigorous grunting shake of his whole body from nose to tail. When he looks at me, his eyes are intelligent and clear.

The truck is reversing.

"They're coming."

His ears are already cocked in that direction. Yeah, like I need to tell him what *I'm* hearing.

"Wait until they go past. Then I'll walk along the road away from them. When they come after me, you take the driver. Okay?"

He butts my temple with his snout. I take it as a yes.

"If they don't go past, I don't know what the fuck we'll do."

He butts me again. I guess he doesn't care what they do or don't do. As far as he's concerned, they're dead men already.

The truck whines past in reverse and continues until it reaches the bit of road closest to Shad's burning bike, where it stops.

I roll back over the wall, fighting to stay conscious when my shoulder screams and the world threatens to go dark on me. Luckily, I manage to stay upright when my boots hit the tarmac.

A shout from back along the road tells me I've been seen, but I pretend to be stunned and stagger away in the other direction, the helmet dangling heavily from my left hand while I try to find the least agonising position for my right arm.

The truck engine starts in my direction, coming slowly in a low gear. I stumble along with my head down, and they keep coming until the vehicle's footbrake gives a dry squeal behind me.

About ten feet, I guess. Not close enough.

"Hey!" comes from above. The shooter must still be standing on the cab roof. "*Hey*!"

I pause and sway a bit, then shuffle back three steps. That should do it. My back muscles twitch in anticipation of a shotgun blast, but I grip the helmet's chin piece and wait. I'll only get one chance.

A savage snarl starts from my right and keeps going. I spin that way as Shad launches himself through the driver's open window, and the man's scream cuts off abruptly. I continue my spin and hurl my helmet at the startled shooter. One chance.

It hits him full in the face. He drops from sight behind the cab while his shotgun slides across the roof and clatters to the road.

I nearly faint when I stoop to pick it up. There's silence inside the cab, and everything is quiet behind on the flatbed too. But the shooter is waiting for me around there and nearly takes me out with my own helmet.

I rock back as it whistles past my face, then touch the barrels to his knee and pull both triggers. The blast blows him across the flatbed and slams him into the far side panel, where he curls up and starts shrieking.

Not for long, though. Shad jumps up and tears his throat out, then drags his body from the truck. I throw his lower leg down next to him. The driver's body is there too. Also missing its throat. The price of blowing up a werewolf's bike.

Some battles need to be fought.

We drag both bodies over the wall, climb into the cab, shunt my wrecked bike to the side of the road, and take off to help our family.

*

It's darker indoors than outside. Or maybe it only seems that way. In any case, Min's vision feels keener when she watches the men peering through windows at the front of the house and running past the kitchen window at the side. No one has tried the back door yet, but there have been several heavy thuds against the front one.

The sisters' hackles are up and they're growling constantly. When Min stands, they spring to all fours, glaring at the moving shapes with cold fury in their eyes.

Someone turns the back-door handle. It's locked, but it can only be a matter of time before they force their way in. She grips the baseball bat, takes a few test swipes through the air, and selects her position near the door.

Tae stands across from her, facing the edge of the door that will open, ready to greet anyone foolhardy enough to walk through it. Vua ghosts through the shadows in the passageway to the front door.

Min shudders. Something must have happened to Joe and Shad. They should have been here half an hour ago. Nothing would prevent them from coming home tonight, except...

No, she won't go there.

A booted foot smashes the small pane of glass above the back door's handle. A gloved hand thrusts through, rattling the handle and scrabbling around for the key.

Min's heart pounds urgent strength into her limbs, and she whips the bat as hard as she can against the hand. It connects with a loud crack.

The hand disappears and a cursing shadow lumbers away from the door, only to be replaced by another. The new one stoops to the broken pane and a bearded face leers in.

Tae hurls herself at him, snarling and snapping.

"Fuck!" He jumps away and bellows, "Dog! They've got a fucking big dog in here!"

Vua growls near the front door, where two fingers are poking through the letterbox and feeling around inside. She bites them, and they disappear fast. Whoever owns them howls in pain and kicks the door.

Min edges to the front room doorway, trying to see how many attackers are out there, but without standing at the window she can't see the full picture. And she isn't about to do that.

The only one who stays still long enough for her to see him properly is a big man sitting on a raised seat on the back of a trike. It's the idiot who picked a fight with Shad last week. From the way he keeps shouting commands at everyone, he must be their leader. He wears a neck brace and moves stiffly. In his right hand he holds a pump-action shotgun.

Min's blood runs cold.

The leader says something to the man below him, the trike rider, who fishes a phone from his chest pocket and thumbs a number. Seconds later, a shredding guitar ringtone sounds outside the back door. The trike rider passes the phone to his leader, who speaks into it briefly then hands it back.

What now?

Fire flares bright in the darkness outside the back door.

"Tae. Here." Min pulls the kitchen door after Tae as she trots into the passageway, but before the door finishes closing, the kitchen window is smashed, and flames explode in the room. She slams the door shut, turning from it as another petrol bomb smashes through the front room window.

Two more crashes come from upstairs, followed by a sound like a roaring wind. Within seconds, fire is raging through the house.

They have two options: face the bikers outside, or retreat into the basement. She discounts the basement immediately. They'd be trapped down there. So. Outside it will be.

She stands inside the front door, wielding her bat and looking at her friends.

They regard her calmly.

"Ready?"

*

A dancing red glow lights up the sky beyond the hilltop ahead of us. My stomach sinks. I know what we're going to see in a few seconds. Our temporary home stands alone in the valley, and only one thing would light up the sky like that.

I can't grind the pedal any deeper into the floor, but that doesn't stop me trying. Shad's struggling to keep his footing on the bench seat at my side as we bounce over the hilltop and hurtle down the road, but his gaze is pinned on the blazing farmhouse, and I know the rough ride will be the last thing on his mind.

The road outside the house is littered with abandoned bikes. Their riders are all on foot in our front garden, pacing around or jigging up and down. Waiting for our women to leave the burning building, I guess. All is silent from this distance, but I can imagine the din they'll be making.

A single figure sits aloof from the action, a big bloke high on a box seat behind the saddle of a chopped trike, silhouetted against the fierce flames.

I keep my boot jammed to the floor and we accelerate down the long shallow incline. My plan is to smash into the crowd of bikers in the garden, get Min and the sisters on board, and make our escape.

Too late. We're only a hundred yards away when the front door opens and three figures race from the house, Min swinging a baseball bat at every head within reach while Vua and Tae attack as a team. They savage one man then leave him in a heap and drag a second one down.

We're nearly there.

The bikers scatter from the wolves, Min running around taking swipes at heads with her bat. She's like an angry whirlwind with pink-streaked hair.

Fierce pride surges through me. *My woman.*

The bloke on the trike stands high above the scene and aims a shotgun at the nearest wolf, Tae.

I haul the steering wheel to the left with my good hand and aim for the trike.

He half turns to us, his movements restricted by a neck brace. It's the big bugger Shad hammered before we left his town. He turns all the way and swings his gun barrel in our direction.

I brace for impact and slam the trike into his trike as he fires. Our windscreen explodes in a shower of glass.

Shad's scrabbling at the door. I lean across and flick the lever to let him out, then roll out of the driver's door and stagger around behind the upturned trike.

The big man is lying on his back, legs trapped under his machine, bloody but still conscious and still gripping his pump-action shotgun.

KERCHEK! He reloads and aims it at Shad as the big wolf skitters around the spinning front wheel and charges at him.

I kick the barrel as he fires, sending his shot harmlessly into the air.

Shad rips off his neck brace and tears his throat out.

Bike engines bark into life all around us. Vua and Tae are savaging everything that moves, and Min is still swinging her bat hard at everything that doesn't move fast enough.

I pick up the pump-action and fire two more shots to encourage everyone to fuck off. Which they do, fast, leaving us standing in what looks like a war zone with four dead bikers on the lawn as well as Mister Personality at our feet.

The trike bursts into flames, and the pick-up tangled with it looks likely to follow suit, so we move away. Sirens sound in the distance. They're still a long way off but will be with us in a matter of minutes. It's time to go.

Shad stays in his wolf form. I explain why, while his daughters shift back and dress quickly in the spare clothes they keep in the tail packs of their bikes.

I consider taking one of the gang's abandoned bikes, but only for a moment. The adrenaline is subsiding, and my shoulder is agony. No way can I ride.

Min pulls her big Suzuki alongside me. I climb up behind her. Tae helps Shad to sit behind Vua, then flashes up her own bike.

The sirens are just over the hill. We wheel the other way and take off fast.

Licking wounds

MIN POINTS HER toes to ease the threat of leg cramps and stares up into the oak tree that fills what's left of the roofless derelict cottage. In the early light its leaves show the first yellowing hints of autumn.

She shuffles her shoulders up higher against the rough wall. Last night was cold, but the baby-blue dawn promises a warm sun today. It lights Joe's tanned face and paints his pain lines even deeper against the old, fissured tree bark.

His eyes are closed, but she doesn't think he slept any more than she did. As soon as they'd draped a camouflage sheet over the bikes and the wolves had melted away into the darkness to patrol the area, he lowered himself gingerly to sit propped against the tree, blended his injured shoulder into its soothing wood, and remained motionless for the rest of the night.

He's put on some weight during the summer, and it's all toned new muscle. He was tall and lean when they found each other, strong from his carpentry work but not packing any bulk. She didn't notice his body changing until one night while they were making love, when he held himself above her on powerful arms, muscles rippling across his back and shoulders under her fingertips.

It's from all the motorbike riding and the heavy manual work he and Shad take whenever they can find it. He's still her lovely shaggy-haired and bearded lover, but now with added oomph.

My beautiful man.

Always. But he's very different this time around. He's always tough, resolute, and obsessively protective of her, but in this life he's determined to do things his way.

He was like this in some of his previous lives, and they never ended well. Two in particular, consecutive lives when he went way past stubborn, took everything to extremes, and wrecked their relationship.

His two lion lives.

A shiver runs up her spine and gives her a shudder when it reaches her scalp. That dreadful time was three thousand years ago, in ancient Egypt, but there are too many similarities for comfort now.

There are also some new talents. Like his ability to detect thin places, even ancient paths between the Wild and the outside that haven't been used in centuries. He can sense them from a distance and follow his nose right up to and through them. Where has *that* come from?

Putting everything together, she can't deny the sensation that they're hurtling downhill to some unavoidable disaster. It terrifies her.

That's why she's lying to him, letting him think she's trying to recapture her song magic, when she isn't. She can still sing, although even her normal voice lacks its usual quality, but the magic is gone completely, and she's only pretending to try and get it back.

Because she loves him. Because she has to protect him from himself. Because while she's vulnerable like this, without her magic, his protective instinct is overriding his compulsion to confront Tyac.

He's staring at her.

She hides her guilty jump by shifting position. "How's your shoulder?"

His eyes focus, and she realises he was staring into the distance, not at her. "Someone's coming."

There's no one in sight. Not even the wolves. She strains to hear anything unusual, but the early morning birdsong continues undisturbed and nothing else seems amiss. He must be feeling the approaching stranger through his tree.

"Shad's bringing someone from the road." Joe lifts his free thumb towards the hill behind him. "Tae and Vua are still patrolling." He eases his shoulder out of the tree trunk and cups his right elbow with his left hand to take its weight.

"You need a sling."

"Yes."

"We should get it X-rayed."

"No." He rests his head back and groans as a wave of pain washes a grey pallor across his face. "Coming over the hill now."

Two figures come into view on the skyline, silhouetted by the rising sun, Shad padding alongside an old man who wears his grey hair long under a battered cowboy hat and walks with a familiar rolling gait.

"Looks like Andrew."

Joe raises an eyebrow.

Min squints. No doubt about it. "I wonder how he found us."

"I wonder *why* he found us." Joe closes his eyes. "He's nervous."

Min chuckles. "That'll be the Shad effect."

*

Yes, our friend is still nervous of Shad, but there's more going on than that. I can't put my finger on it, but something slippery lies beneath his healthy fear of the big wolf herding him down the hillside. Something sly. I stay put as he lengthens his stride when Min stands to greet him.

He throws his arms wide and accepts her hug with a grin. "It's good to see you."

"You too." Her voice is muffled in his shoulder.

I'm reminded of their hug before the battle for Quarter Square, three months ago. He'd been exposed as untrustworthy just then, too. Not intentionally so. I'll give him that. His heart was in the right place, so he hadn't considered the possibility that he might be betraying us. But Queen Fiona of Hare and her warrior wizard had tricked him. He was secretive, and his foolishness brought war into our home. We all lost loved ones that day.

"Joe." He holds Min's hand when he turns to face me.

"Andrew."

"What have you done to yourself?"

I don't bother to answer because his expression of concerned concentration suggests he's using his threading magic to see the damage for himself.

He winces. "You've broken your collarbone and two ribs. Hold still."

The sensation is soft, like gentle warmth spreading through my chest, easing the pain. It reaches my neck, and I relax into it.

"Stand by."

What for? The warmth turns into fierce heat and my collarbone hurts sharply as if someone is tweaking it hard. I lean into the sickening pain, moaning as the heat leaves me.

"I've set it."

"You could have warned me." It's hard not to sound like a whining child.

"I did. There are no punctures or any other internal injuries that I can see. The ribs are both in place. Just cracked. They should heal fine, but you'll need to keep that shoulder immobile for a few weeks."

Min roots around in her tail pack and produces a dark blue cotton headscarf. "Sling."

Andrew and I sit in the pale sunlight on a broken-down stone wall out front of the old cottage while she fixes her scarf to take the weight of my arm. It gives me some relief.

She drapes her denim jacket across my shoulders. "We need to get you and Shad some new leathers." She sits on the wall and swipes her phone screen.

Andrew glances at Shad, who is watching him steadily.

"What are you doing here, Andrew?"

He regards me for a minute, as if calculating all my possible responses to his answer. Finally, with a shrug, he says, "Your friendly Home Office man sent me to recruit you."

Min looks up from her phone and we raise eyebrows at each other.

Andrew rolls the turquoise stone plaited in his hair. The familiar gesture fills me with sadness for a way of life I grew to love during our brief summer in the square. "Sebastian Merritt's system is programmed to alert his department to reports of magical activity anywhere in the country. Incidents involving wolves or biker gangs are flagged automatically into the top-priority group. Last night's reported action had both wolves and bikers, and it bears so many similarities to the battle at Quarter Square that he reckons you had to be there. So he had me flown up to take you back to him in London."

"Well, you can fly back and tell him my answer is the same as last time he asked."

"It isn't as simple as that. The people who met me off the helicopter gave me a car and directions to this camp of yours, so I assume Merritt is watching us now." He looks at the empty sky from under his brows and murmurs, "Can they hear us with satellites, or just see us?"

"No idea. What did you want to get mixed up with him for, anyway?"

"He had me picked up in Totnes, two weeks after I left you. Said I'd been under observation since I walked out of the theatre that day. He offered me a job in his department."

"Doing what?"

"Not much. I'm their lab rat. They study me."

"Study your magic, you mean."

"Yes."

"Why did you accept his offer? Why would you want to let them study you?"

His haunted look is back. "When I left Quarter Square, I was beaten. You know that. He came along offering food and shelter, so I took it. I needed some peace and quiet, you know? To get over all that stuff."

He's been caught out before by trusting the wrong people, so that much at least rings true. Not that I think he'll lie to us. But I have to try and read Merritt's manoeuvres through the mist of Andrew's naivety.

"I hardly ever see Merritt, but he's been as good as his word. No one tries to make me do anything I'm not comfortable about. And they look after me okay. I'm free to do as I please when they're not running one of their exercises."

"Why did he send you after us?"

"After you, Joe." He drops his voice again. "As far as I'm aware, he doesn't know anything about Min. He hasn't asked about her and I haven't volunteered any information. We never even discussed you until I went to him with a request."

Here we go. "What request?"

He resumes his normal volume. "I met this man in the Wild. His name's Stone, and it's a bit like talking to myself in a mirror. Not looks-wise, but we're interested in the same things. Remember I told you how I've been searching my whole life for angels?"

"Yes."

"He knows where I can learn about them. Maybe even meet some." His eyes shine like a kid's on Christmas morning. "But it's a two-man job," he whispers, "and Stone says this will be the only chance I get, because something important is going to happen this year that might never happen again in my lifetime. He says the event will last one month and we need to be in place before the full moon. That's next week."

I nod to Shad. "Yeah, we know."

Andrew eyes Shad too.

"And Merritt wants to learn about these angels too?"

"No. He doesn't care about them. But when I asked him for four weeks leave to go and find them, he said I can have the time off on full pay if I bring you into his operation. I didn't have a clue where to find you and thought I was going to lose the chance to see my angels, until early this morning when he had me woken with orders to get on that helicopter and bring you in."

I snort.

He scans the skies again. "I don't know what you have against Merritt, but from what I've seen he's an okay employer."

Yeah. He's so okay that Andrew has half convinced himself he's listening to our conversation via an orbiting satellite.

Min stiffens. I wait for her to tell me what she's seen on the web, but she says nothing and continues reading her phone.

Andrew whispers so quietly I have to strain to catch his words. "I don't intend to take you back to him. I'm not here to sell you out. I figure your best bet is to come with me and we'll give Merritt's people the slip. Spend a month in the Wild with me to let your trail go cold. One thing's for sure. He's got your location now, and if you don't come with me, he'll continue tracking you. The next people he sends mightn't be so gentle. Come with me."

Not a chance. Apart from the ridiculous notion that I'll leave Min, I'm being asked to trust three dodgy people. Some stranger called Stone, Merritt the government arsehole, and Andrew, whose poor judgement of character recently caused the deaths of our friends and nearly destroyed our community.

"I'm sorry about your angels, but it's a no."

His shoulders droop. He stares at the ground.

Min catches my eye. "Walk with me." She offers a hand to help me up from my low seat.

We wander away from Andrew without speaking, walking among the scattered remains of the stone wall. A familiar shiver crawls over my skin, and I scan the horizon for a likely thin place. Up ahead on the skyline stands a weather-beaten clump of holly and hawthorn. I link my good arm with Min's to guide our stroll in that direction, and the shiver grows stronger with every step we take towards the ancient copse.

She looks over her shoulder before she speaks. "The police officers who interviewed you in London after Carole and Tony were murdered. What were their names?"

"Detective Chief Inspector Dawson and Detective Sergeant Smith. Why?"

"Jennifer Smith."

"That's the one."

She draws us to a stop and hands me her phone, watching as I read the Breaking News box on a tabloid newspaper's website.

Policewoman Murdered

The report is brief and shocking. A terribly mutilated body was found hanging from a plinth in Trafalgar Square an hour ago and the authorities were unable to prevent hundreds of early rush hour witnesses seeing the horror before they could screen it from the public gaze.

DS Smith's warrant card was clearly visible on a cord around her neck, and the Metropolitan Police, left with absolutely no choice in the matter, confirmed her identity at a hastily convened press conference.

The world swims around me. I swallow hard to fight down the bitter threat of vomit, while a pulse hammers in my throat and ears. The brief description of Smith's terrible injuries is too close to home. It's exactly how Carole and Tony died, torn apart by Tyac.

I pull myself together for Min's benefit. "She was nice to me. I mean, even when I was their only suspect, she was okay. And once they were satisfied I wasn't their killer, she was sympathetic and kind. It's horrible to think of her dying like that."

"It's Tyac."

"I know."

"He's trying to flush you out."

The bastard. My neck swells with fury and a growl grows inside me.

"Stop it!" She shakes my arm but lets go when I wince. "Sorry. I didn't mean to hurt you. But you have to drop this macho crap. We're not in any fit state to take him on right now. Either of us. Are we?"

My shoulder hurts too much to shrug.

"We need to get the hell away from here," she says. "Now. He's probably on his way. Who knows what information he got out of her before she died? And Merritt might have shared his intelligence with the police, with Tyac probably accessing it."

"That's a bit of a leap."

"But we don't know, do we?" Her voice is hoarse with all the talking and she's nearly rasping in frustration at me. "And in case it *did* happen that way and he *is* coming here, we need to be somewhere else bloody quick."

"Okay. We'll move."

"Not together."

"What?"

"We're vulnerable, my love." She scans the open land around us. Her face is drawn and tired. I haven't seen her so stressed for months. "Look at us. You're injured and I've got no magic. We're travelling with three wolves, and one of them is injured too. Merritt found us like that," she snaps her fingers, "and after last night I bet his won't be the only department interested in us. We need to split up and get away from here in opposite directions."

I stare at her.

"And you need to disappear into the Wild," she continues. "Somewhere nice and quiet and out of trouble, say for a month or so."

"With Andrew, you mean."

"Can you think of a better plan at short notice?"

I can't. But the realisation that this is the best way to protect her, maybe the only way in these circumstances, hits me like a kick in the stomach.

Tyac isn't after her. He never is. Not directly. It's always me he hunts. If I stay apart from her while he's on this current rampage, she won't get in harm's way. Not from him anyway.

It makes sense on that level, but it goes against my hardwired instinct to protect her and never leave her side.

She's my love. My soul mate. We belong together, no matter how difficult it might sometimes be to reconcile our different approaches to the problem of Tyac, and no matter how those differences are starting to affect our relationship.

But I can't deny that on this occasion she's right. Separating makes sense. "Where will you go? You'll keep Shad and the sisters with you, won't you?"

"Yes, we'll stick together. I think we should slip into the Wild too, until we've lost anyone who might be tracking us." Her eyes flicker upwards. "Then we'll go back to Manchester. We had a good set-up there."

That's a dig at me. I didn't like the Manchester set-up as much as she did. She sang in a club. She got Vua and Tae in there as cage dancers and fixed Shad and me up with jobs on the door. I hated it and persuaded her to leave after only two weeks. This is the nearest she'll come to saying, *I told you so.*

"I'm not comfortable with the idea of you being out in the open while I'm safely tucked up somewhere with Andrew."

"I'll have our wolves with me. And I have managed without you once or twice before, you know." She winks.

I shake my head in resignation. "Let's go and give Andrew the good news."

"We should ditch our phones. Merritt's probably had someone hack into them by now." She palms one into my hand. "Here's my spare. And here's its battery. Keep them separate and leave it turned off until you and Andrew can give Merritt's people the slip. I'll text you my new number when I get one."

I slip the phone into the slot inside my left boot, and the battery into the little key pocket in my jeans waistband. "How will I find you if we lose phone contact?"

"Let's meet in London. There are twenty-one havens in the city, so we can keep on the move and still find each other. We'll take them in alphabetical order. Andrew says his project will run from full moon to full moon. In five weeks from now, on the Saturday, I'll be in Abbey Wood. I'll stay there for week one, then move on to Broad Ford Bridge for week two, Cobbler's Walk for week three, and so on. Always Saturday to Saturday."

She has it all organised. Makes me wonder if she can't wait to be free of me. "I don't know the London havens."

"Andrew knows them. If you get separated from him, go to Abbey Wood and find the thin place. If I've already moved on, I'll tell the insiders there to look out for you and bring you to me."

Talk about a done deal. "Okay. By the way, if you're looking for the nearest thin place to get into the Wild after we've gone today, try that copse on the skyline behind us."

She looks back. "How do you *do* that?"

I wink. "It's a kind of magic."

She stops and gives me The Look.

I relent. "You know when you're bursting for a wee and finally get to let it go, how a shiver runs across your back and shoulders? It's like that."

She squints at me. "I don't get the back-and-shoulders shiver when I empty a full bladder. I get it from my chin up into my lower gum."

"You're weird."

"*I'm* weird? Ha!"

We hug. I feel like I'm about to have one of my limbs amputated, and the limb is eager to get the job done. Then I feel her sobbing and realise she feels as awful about this as I do. The lump in my throat is impossible to swallow.

I hold her until her shoulders stop heaving.

Then Shad's there, leaning heavily against my leg. He knows.

I press my forehead to his. "Heal well."

He returns the pressure and replies with a low rumble in his throat.

Min wipes her eyes and watches us with a brave smile.

Let's go

DON'T FORGET," ANDREW mutters as we walk to the car, "Merritt's people gave me this ride. I'll be amazed if it isn't bugged. Liverpool's an hour away, and it'll be best if you sleep the whole time. Just saying."

"We could leave their car and go through the Wild. There's a thin place here."

"You're gonna have to trust me, Joe. I know, I know, my track record sucks. But I need you to go along with my route plan for this first phase, okay?"

His fine-looking Native American flute is on the passenger seat. I put it on the back seat and ease myself in, making no promises. But the magical anaesthetic he supplies for my broken bones helps me to relax, and when he removes the warmth to wake me, I'm surprised to find I actually dropped off and slept properly.

"We're here."

"Where?" I peer groggily at substantial Georgian and Victorian neoclassical buildings all around.

"Liverpool." He points to a huge domed glass roof on our left. "This is Lime Street railway station. I'll dump the car, then we're going in there."

I try not to jerk my shoulder too much as I struggle upright in the seat. "What train are we catching?"

He's distracted by an impatient taxicab that swerves past with its horn blaring. "First one to London." He drives around behind the station and back down the other side of it, stopping outside the steel gates of a hotel car park. "This'll do. You want to get out now so you don't have to walk as far? I'll be with you as soon as I dump this."

I swing the door open and climb out, trying to protect my shoulder but still managing to bang it on the roof. I swear a bit and shuffle across to the opposite kerb while he drives on through the gates.

This is my first time in Liverpool. I like its big, solid, old-city feel. The muted hum of traffic from a busy road across the front of the railway station is pleasant, like bees going about their business on a summer day. This road I'm on is a quiet backwater, and somewhere down towards the main road, a thin place sends its faint shiver over my skin.

I walk that way, taking my time and guarding my shoulder. The shiver gets steadily stronger past the hotel entrance, past a service entrance to the railway station, across a deserted side road and on down, with the sensation creeping up my back and tickling my neck.

"Joe," Andrew calls as he jogs down.

I continue for a few more paces. The thin place is close.

There, in the soot-furred brick wall of a small warehouse. Two wooden doors inset a couple of feet from the building façade, painted dark red and bearing the message *Fire escape – Keep clear*. Strong shivers in waves.

Andrew has slowed to a walk and is crossing the side junction, his flute in its pouch strapped across his back.

I step into the alcove and grow my face through one of the wooden doors, focusing on the thin place shiver and intending to see the Wild on the other side.

It's beautiful. Clean, open scrubland slopes down for half a mile to a broad river glinting in the sunlight, with a headland of red sandstone cliffs on the opposite riverbank and tree-blanketed hills beyond that, then a faintly dark mountain range in the far distance. The air tastes salty and inviting. There isn't a human being in sight, but an elegant three-masted sailing ship sits at anchor by the near bank.

I pull my head back through the door in time to nod at Andrew as he draws level and raises a quizzical eyebrow. I lean against the wall and blow a weary sigh, grateful for the flood of soothing warmth he sends through my shoulder. “Thanks.”

“No problem. You good to go?”

We cross the road and continue down to the station entrance. It’s like walking into a cathedral of transport. Noises big and small from all over the cavernous building bounce around the curved glass roof high above and echo off hard surfaces everywhere. Hot food and drink smells assault me, chief of which is the delicious, bitter aroma of freshly brewed coffee.

A groan of longing escapes me.

He chuckles. “There’s time for breakfast.”

I aim straight for the coffee shop. “You got any money? I’d forgotten I don’t have a penny on me.”

He sits at one of the metal tables outside the shop and shoves a chair out for me. “I have some money.”

Our face-masked waitress’s friendly manner doesn’t slip at the prospect of serving an old Davy Crockett lookalike and a torn-up biker. Breakfast arrives quickly and Andrew grins when I moan with pleasure into my coffee cup.

“Eat, Joe.” He lowers his voice slightly, although the chances of us being overheard in the echoing racket are slim. “We’re going to need our strength.”

I pause with an egg-smeared sausage at my mouth.

“Don’t look around. Carry on as if I’m talking normal crap, okay?”

I bite the sausage and nod.

“We’re under surveillance. Have been by car since we left Min, and I think there’s a team of four on foot in here.”

“Merritt’s people?”

“I guess so. Who else would it be?”

I shrug without thinking and wince.

"We're not getting the London train," he says. "Or any other mainline train they can board to keep an eye on us. I never intended that. Merritt can go take a jump."

"So where are we heading?"

"We'll take the local Wirral line that goes under the River Mersey to Wallasey on the other side. I have a car hidden over there that Merritt doesn't know about. The escalator down to the Wirral line is diagonally across to your right." He watches while I locate its entrance. "Yeah?"

I take another bite of egged sausage and nod again.

"Thing is, we're going to have to run. I'll do what I can for your shoulder, but it's still gonna hurt like hell. Can you do it?"

"Yes."

"Good. The Wallasey trains run every few minutes, so we shouldn't have any problems once we're underground. I hope not, anyhow. I'm thinking our best bet will be to wait for one of those rushes when lots of people get off a train and emerge from the escalator, and go for it then."

"Okay." I drain my first coffee and take a long drink from the second cup. "But instead of running and drawing all that attention, how about we buy me some painkillers from the pharmacy over there, then wander along towards the escalator in the crowd as if we're killing time while we wait for our London train?"

"Much better. That's the plan." His eyes dart from stranger to stranger.

"Stop that. If you look jumpy, they'll watch harder. Take it easy."

"Okay." He takes a shaky breath. "You ready?"

I finish my coffee and wonder when I'll next get to enjoy one in peace. "Let's go."

Belle

I PRETEND TO COMPARE the shampoos and shower gels on a display stand inside the shop window, while Andrew buys me over-the-counter painkillers, and I catch his eye when he hands the box to me.

"Two watchers over by the ticket office. Military types. One ginger, one bald, both wearing green bomber jackets and earpieces."

"I see them."

"They're not even trying to hide."

"No reason why they should. Their job is to make sure we go where we're supposed to go. This is what Merritt's people are like. They want us to know they're here."

"Another two watching from the entrance to the Wirral line escalator." I study them in the convex mirror above our heads. "Same bomber jackets."

He follows my stare. "Shit."

"They all look fit and fast. Got a Plan B?"

His reply is a tired sigh.

I pretend to read the ingredients label on a shampoo bottle. "I've got one."

"What? I'm not getting on a mainline train. There's someone I have to see before we leave this region. And I reckon Merritt can have a train stopped any time he wants, no problem. So no mainline train."

"No train. We're going to walk out of the station the same way we came in."

He eyes me. "Ri-ight."

"And when we get to the entrance, I want you to drag all those tables and chairs from outside the café with your magic and dump them in a heap to block the way while we get out of sight."

"I can do that. Where are we going?"

"Back across the road to the fire escape doors where I waited for you after you parked the car. If you make enough mess with the café furniture, we'll get there before they break through."

"What'll we do when we get there?"

"Leave that to me."

He frowns.

"Trust me." I replace the shampoo bottle and palm my old phone onto the display shelf behind it. "Ready?"

It works like a charm. Andrew pauses in the station entrance to drag over a dozen metal tables and several dozen chairs. He also uproots the maze queue stanchions and their ribbons from outside the ticket office to wrap up our four chasing watchers with the complicated pile of shiny junk. The entire operation takes him only seconds, but the shouts and screams of alarmed bystanders last until we've sprinted up the street and out of hearing range.

My shoulder is agony. When we reach the fire escape doors, I take a moment to recover.

"They're coming." Andrew's fit for a man of his age. He isn't even breathing hard.

I haul him into the alcove and press us against the wooden doors. "Close your eyes and hold your breath."

"What?"

"Do it now." I hold his hand and grow us through the old timber.

I feel his fear. The process is quick and smooth, but for him, I guess it probably seems like an eternity. That's how Min describes it, anyway.

When we break free on the other side he falls to his hands and knees, shaking his head vigorously as if trying to clear his ears of buzzing insects. "What the fuck was that?"

I chuckle and remember not to shrug.

He stares at me. "What did you do?"

I gesture with my good arm. "Welcome to the Wild."

His eyes open as round as saucers as he shuffles his backside on the bare earth and takes in where we are. When he sees the ship down on the river, he gives a squeak of joy and leaps to his feet. "The *Belle*!"

He's nearly dancing with delight. He grabs my good hand and shakes it with such enthusiasm my other shoulder shrieks. I've never seen him so happy.

I retrieve my hand and dry swallow some painkillers. "You know that ship?"

"Hell yes. I hoped she might be in Liverpool, but you never know. She gets around."

He pauses in his merrymaking. "You know, if we'd made it across to Wallasey on the underground train," his expansive wave takes in the far side of the river, "I'd planned to go into the Wild anyway. I only know one thin place in this region and it's over there. But here's you slipping us through on this side of the river, and we get to see the *Belle* too. This couldn't have worked out any better."

He pauses to study the air that's this side's access to the thin place and throws me a shrewd look. "How did you know this is here? And how the hell did you take us through those wooden doors? And why didn't you warn me?"

"I did warn you." Maybe my grin is a bit cruel.

"You're not going to tell me, are you?"

Damn right I'm not. I'm not exactly comfortable with him even knowing I have this ability. I haven't stopped liking him, but I don't trust who he's talking to these days. "Come on. Let's go see your friends on the ship."

The bare scrubland gets sandier underfoot as we walk down to the river. I enjoy the clean, salty air, and before long we're shuffling over low dunes of fine white sand that sprout tussocks of sharp-edged marram grass, until we crest the final dune and look down the long sloping beach at the splendid ship.

I'd assumed from a distance that she is at anchor, but actually she's tied up to a long wooden jetty parallel to the shoreline, with her sharp nose pointing out to sea.

A ramshackle row of single-storey timber buildings huddle along the jetty, with smoke rising from a couple of rusting tin chimneys. Behind the ship's stern a two-hundred-yard diameter pool has been scooped out of the shoreline to form a small tidal dock. It looks like nothing in the world other than the beginnings of a port, and yet again I feel as if I'm walking back into an earlier time. This one sends a thrill of excitement through me, like a promise of something good.

Beneath the thrill, from somewhere over near the tidal dock, comes the strong and steady thrum across my skin of a regularly used thin place.

A small group of men are on the jetty, looking up into the masts and rigging of the ship where eight crew members are working in a row abreast while standing on ropes slung beneath one of the substantial horizontal spars a hundred feet above the deck.

The ship's line dips in a graceful shallow arc from her pointed bow to her middle, below her tallest mast, where it levels out and then lifts again on its way to her raised and rounded stern deck.

Multi-paned glass windows run all around the stern below that raised deck, which is enclosed by carved handrails and bears a steering wheel as tall as a man.

Forward of that position are secured two robust open boats, one on each side of the ship, and from there the deck is clear and clean other than behind the foremast, where something like the flat roof of a low wooden hut with a busily smoking chimney suggests the location of the ship's galley. I wonder if they serve coffee.

Finally, in the bow, stands a pair of miniature cranes and an arrangement of pulley blocks, thick ropes, and two big anchors. Everything speaks of sleek speed and efficiency.

"It's a beautiful ship."

"She's a barque." Andrew sounds proud of her.

"What's a barque?"

"Hell if I know. It's the name for this type of ship. Four years ago, I sailed in her to New York and back here to Liverpool by way of Martinique. We took Lancashire cloth over and brought Caribbean rum back. The weather was fine for most of the way, and the whole trip was like a dream. Mind you, I was a guest on board. I wouldn't want to crew one of these things. Long hours and hard work."

Raised voices come from the group on the jetty, drawing the attention of an officer on *Belle*'s stern deck. He crosses the gangplank, and they all shut up when he speaks quietly.

"That's Mister Samson," Andrew says. "Good man."

"Captain?"

"Second-in-command." He watches while the group disperses, and then the officer waves to us. "Let's go down and say hello."

Andrew introduces me as a friend, and we shake hands. Mister Samson is about the same age as him. His face and neck are suntanned to a deep mahogany, which is set off to startling effect by his open-necked white cotton shirt, and his accent sounds like a cultured blend of English West Country and east coast American.

"Where are you coming from this time?" Andrew wants to know.

"Same trip you did with us."

"Same cargo?"

Mister Samson's face crinkles when he smiles. "Come aboard. The captain will be glad to see you." He leads the way across the baton-ridged gangplank and murmurs something to a sailor, who nips away smartly.

Men and women are pretending to be busy around the deck while they cast surreptitious glances in our direction, but there's no hostility evident. Several of them return Andrew's friendly waves.

We stand with Mister Samson and wait, but not for long. Rapid footsteps announce the imminent arrival of someone running up a staircase on the other side of two lacquered doors beneath the raised stern deck. A moment's silence follows, before the doors open and a vision in polished leather knee boots steps out onto the deck.

If I had to guess her age, I'd put her somewhere between forty and fifty, but her beauty is ageless. She is tall and stunning. Striking in every way. Blue-black hair is brushed back from her brow and flows in loose curls around her shoulders, shining in the sunlight. Her dazzling white shirt is similar to Mister Samson's, wide open at the collar and setting off a dark tan. But her shirt is filled out in a far more spectacular fashion.

She has the build of a shapely superhero and walks with arresting self-confidence, thumbs hooked into the top of her wide leather belt and with the hint of an amused swagger.

"Well, now, look who's come to visit with us." Her low-pitched voice flows like sweet syrup on a slow Alabama afternoon, and her perfume fills the air like exotic flowers in the night.

Andrew sweeps the back of his hand close to the deck in an extravagant bow. When he straightens, his eyes are glittering, and he looks fit to burst with happiness. "My captain, you are a sight for sore eyes."

"There'll be plenty of time to look later. Come here and let me get a taste of you." She throws her arms around him, and they kiss deeply.

I step back in surprise, catching Mister Samson's eye. He's beaming.

Eventually the kissers come up for air, both of them flushed and slightly breathless.

"I've missed you, my wizard." She holds on to him and studies his face. "I've missed you bad."

He hugs her tight. "Me too." Then he notices me standing here like a lemon. "Allow me to introduce my friend, Joe Walker. Joe, meet Captain Lucinda Mercedes."

She dazzles me with a wide smile. "Welcome, Joe Walker."

"Thank you, Captain Mercedes."

"Please, call me Lucinda. Any friend of Andrew's is a friend of mine." Her gaze flickers between the two of us with an unspoken question for Andrew.

"A friend of like kind," he says. "Joe is a wizard too."

That too catches me unawares. I'm no wizard, but I suppose after the surprise I gave him an hour ago, it's natural for him to think I am.

"Tell me what you've been up to," Andrew says. "I want to hear it all."

She links arms with us, one to each side of her but considerate of my obviously injured shoulder, and walks us to the lacquered doors. "I'll tell you everything, but let's get you two freshened up first. My bathtub is at your disposal. Believe me, you need it."

I win first go in her bathroom without even knowing there was a contest.

While the substantial tub fills, I investigate four rows of walnut boxes on the wall, each with a hinged lid and inscribed brass plaque, and each containing a glass jar of scented bath salts. There are sixteen of them in alphabetical order, from anise to sandalwood. The frangipani jar smells like a lighter version of Lucinda's perfume. I sprinkle a handful of coconut-scented salts into my swirling water.

One-handed washing is awkward, but the heat soothes the pain of my broken bones and emerging big bruises. Once everything is scrubbed as thoroughly as possible, I lie back and let the soapy water float me along the edges of sleep.

Andrew and Lucinda whisper and giggle on the other side of her cabin's dividing screen while they wait for me to finish.

That's why they insisted I must go first, I realise. So they can share a leisurely bath together when I get out of their way. Their delight in each other is touching. They're clearly in love, and I'm still trying to get my head around this new side of Andrew.

Dark horse.

That would be a good Native American name for him, if the Navajo hadn't already given him one in his youth. He once mentioned what it was, back in Quarter Square before the shit hit the fan, but I can't remember it. Dark Horse will do for now, as far as I'm concerned.

I wish Min and I could enjoy a love as easy and uncomplicated as theirs.

My sigh sends clouds of steam billowing aside. I miss her already. This is the first time we've been apart since I met her in this incarnation of mine. Only three months ago but already it feels like a whole life. I wish we could be together. I want to see her, to breathe in the clean smell of her hair and the light fresh fruit scent she always wears. I want to hold her forever. My heart aches for her.

Lucinda taps on the screen. "When you're finished in there, Mister Samson says you're welcome to use his cabin to dress. It's next door."

"Thanks. I'll be done in a minute." I haul myself upright and stand dripping, looking at my torn, dirty clothes on the chair.

My boots are scuffed but undamaged. I don't fancy putting anything else back on.

Her voice floats over again. "Mister Samson says you and he are about the same size, and he's put out a set of his clothes for you in the cabin."

Good man.

From Mister Samson's perfectly neat cabin, it sounds like the lovers are getting down to enthusiastic business in the bathroom I vacated. I sing a Led Zeppelin medley while I dress to assist their privacy.

The black trousers are skinnier than I normally wear, but a snug fit is nothing to complain about and they tuck inside my biker boots as if designed to. The billowing white shirt and sapphire blue waistcoat fit comfortably. I assume the black silk headscarf is to make a new sling, but I can't manage it one-handed.

I enjoy my piratical image in the full-length mirror, but when Lucinda's gasps begin to crescendo next door, I leave to go up on deck.

A pair of knee-booted legs appear at the top of the nearly vertical ladder outside the cabin. I wait at the bottom and admire Mister Samson's balance and agility as he descends, facing away from the ladder and without using his hands, his fast feet hardly touching the steps.

"Thanks for lending me these clothes."

"You're welcome. I'm doing my midday rounds. Would you like to accompany me?"

We walk forward into a spacious area beneath the upper deck. It's quiet and peaceful. Noises from elsewhere on the ship carry through to us only as muffled thumps and bumps.

My eyes struggle with the darkness after the bright autumnal sunlight that flooded the stern cabins. Golden shafts shine through a few open hatches into this section, like broad diagonal bars filled with dancing dust motes.

Mister Samson walks confidently into the sudden gloom, as if he could make his way with his eyes closed.

"Have you been on this ship a long time?"

"I joined *Belle* as a boy and sailed with Lucinda's father for forty years. John Mercedes was a great man. He died six years ago, whereupon Lucinda took command."

"Is that unusual? Having a female captain?"

"It isn't common, but she's lived aboard all her life, and John trained her for the position, so the transfer of ownership and command was smooth. She's as good a captain as her father was, and that's saying something."

"I'm sure it is."

My eyes are adjusting to the dim light, and I stop in surprise when we come to a cannon pointing at the outer wall of the ship.

We're on a wide platform that runs around above the outside of an empty cargo hold. The platform bears sixteen cannons, eight each side. They're stubby affairs with wide barrels, all tilted down at a shallow angle.

"I thought you were a cargo ship."

"So we are. These are for defence, not attack."

"They're odd-looking things."

"Carronades. No good for long-range firing and not very accurate even at short range. But lighter than cannons, allowing us to mount a full broadside at close quarters."

"Why would you want to do that?"

"Pirates." He gives me a *Where have you been?* look.

"Pirates." I study the removable panel in the ship's wall six inches from the mouth of the nearest gun barrel. Good joinery.

"We prefer to run. We're fast enough to get away most times. But if they take us by surprise and come close enough to grapple, these are our last defence. A broadside will hole them along the waterline and sink them fast."

"You've done that?"

"Certainly we have. Five times while I've been aboard." He shrugs. "Would you prefer us to let them take our ship and murder us?"

"No." I shrug in reply without thinking and gasp in pain.

"Shall I tie that for you?" He fashions the headscarf into a sling around my neck.

"Thank you." The weight of my arm coming off my shoulder brings some relief, but I still feel sick from the sudden wave of pain, so I dry swallow more tablets. "I need fresh air."

He gives a sympathetic wince. "Go up top. I'll join you shortly. We're invited to lunch in the captain's cabin with Lucinda and Andrew in," he checks his pocket watch, "forty minutes."

I'm better in the open air, with a stiff sea breeze ruffling my beard and making me feel very nautical, if rather chilly. The narrow gangplank that was horizontal when we boarded is now tilted at a steep angle to the jetty. Shuffling down it carefully like a penguin with a damaged wing dents my salty seafarer self-image, but I want to get a closer look at those concealed gun ports from the outside.

It's excellent work. The seams are visible, but only because I know to look and can calculate where they are. I couldn't do a better job myself.

That isn't me being conceited. Even with my wood magic, I doubt I could conceal them more effectively while keeping them operational. Someone has done a superb job.

I wonder if I ever built a ship like this in a previous life. Or worked on one. Things feel familiar, but that might be because the vessel is made of beautiful wood. Min will know. I'll call her as soon as we're back in the outside.

A strong shiver turns me to the stern, and curiosity draws me towards the tidal dock. I glance up at Lucinda's cabin as I pass and see Andrew sitting in a window seat, playing his flute. He pauses and waves, and I nod back, but my attention is focused on the steady thrumming of a thin place.

The final building on the jetty is newly built, in marked contrast with its scruffy old neighbours, and the vibration comes from inside it. I check all around the strong, square construction of heavy tarred timbers. It's windowless. A tarred timber door appears to be its only access.

No one is looking, so I try the door. It's locked. The thrumming vibrates through my body. To give off such a powerful signal, it has to be either a big thoroughfare or a well-used one. There isn't enough space inside the building for a big one. Well-used, then. Someone is making regular trips.

Revenue officers

"WHAT DO YOU mean, no rum? You said you had a hold full of it." Andrew wipes his mouth and hands his plate of fish bones to Johnson, the captain's white-haired Jamaican steward, with a nod of appreciation.

"Yeah, I said we *had* it," Lucinda says. "Not that we *have* it." She smiles at Johnson as he lifts her plate. "Thank you. That was tasty."

The old man clicks his tongue. "It was more of the same, Cap'n, but you're a darling for saying so."

"We'll get fresh food soon," Mister Samson promises him.

My lightly fried cod steak was delicious, but if they've been eating the same thing every day, I can understand how it would get tedious. I hand my empty plate to Johnson. "Thank you."

"I have something for you." He takes my plate to the sideboard and returns with a tray containing a china cup and saucer, a jug of steaming hot water, an old tin with a tight-fitting lid, and a chipped bone china French press. He places it before me with a friendly grin. "Andrew says you like this."

"Coffee!" I sound like an excited child.

"My own personal store, all the way from home. No one else on board knows how to appreciate the best taste in the world." He winks at my expression when he pops the lid off the tin and the aroma of freshly ground beans fills the cabin. "Enjoy!" He beetles off to wash up our crockery.

The others watch me prepare my drink as if I'm performing strange magic. I motion an invitation to share, but they all decline.

Andrew sighs. "I could almost taste that rum too. What have you done with it?"

Lucinda nods across the river. "It's over in Wallasey."

"With Gully, I suppose."

It's her turn to look surprised. "You know Gully?"

"I do."

I don't know who this mutual acquaintance of theirs is, but I enjoy watching their affectionate sparring.

Andrew pours himself a second cup of tea. "So why has Gully got your rum, instead of one of the Liverpool buyers?"

"Revenue officers."

"What?" He stares at her. "Here? Since when?"

"Since this time last year. We tied up alongside and everything looked normal until suddenly they were swarming all over us and taking half our cargo."

"Half? That's not revenue. It's robbery. Who do these people claim to represent? There's no crown or government around here. What's their authority?"

Lucinda and Mister Samson exchange a look. "They are their own authority," he says. "They have guns."

"So do you."

"Their pistols spray many bullets at once with a sound like a sail tearing."

I lock stares with Andrew, who looks as concerned as I feel about automatic weapons from our world turning up in this one.

"These men are powerful," Lucinda says. "Six months ago, we encountered others like them in Bristol. For all we know, by now they might control every port on this western coast. I won't even try to bribe the local buyers, because it isn't greed that drives their obedience. It's fear."

"That's why we're still eating fish," Mister Samson explains. "The buyers expected to receive our cargo of rum today, and we expected a return cargo of cloth plus fresh stores. When we arrived empty, they refused to load us. They turned down the profit because they know we're defying the Revenue and they want no part of it."

Andrew shakes his head thoughtfully. "So what's your plan?"

"From now on, when we come to Liverpool, we'll deal with Gully. His connections from that side of the river are as good as the buyers on this side." Lucinda shrugs. "Shadier, yes, but equally profitable for us and no Revenue to pay."

"Watch out for the Wallasey wreckers."

"Doing business with Gully will protect us from the wreckers." She strokes the back of Andrew's hand. "Some of my crew is over there with him. We're crossing on the tide this afternoon to pick them up and see if Gully's influence extends to fresh food and water. Will you stay with us for a few days, until we sail?"

Mister Samson checks his pocket watch. "We leave in thirty minutes. I'll go check everything is ready up top."

"Joe and I must be in Cornwall before the full moon."

Cornwall, eh?

"Full moon in four days," Mister Samson says as he leaves the cabin.

"Yes, and we really should get there a day or two before then." Andrew squeezes Lucinda's hand. "We can stay one night, and I planned to see Gully before we head south anyway, but we need to be on the road tomorrow."

She gives a small sigh. "When will we have some time, my love?"

"Soon, I hope. Now that we have Gully in common, we can keep in touch more easily."

I sit back in my chair, luxuriating in a pleasant combination of being both energised and mellow from Johnson's fine Jamaican coffee, when a movement outside catches my eye.

The uneven thickness of the glass panes in the cabin windows plays tricks with light and shadows, so I'm not sure what I'm seeing at first. I move slightly to look through a clear bit, and all doubt is removed. The door to the new building on the jetty has opened inwards. A dark space exists now, where before there was only the solid timber door.

Someone steps out into the daylight. A man from my world, wearing a shiny green bomber jacket and holding a walkie-talkie to his ear.

A heavy pulse throbs in my throat.

It's Baldy, one of our watchers from Lime Street station.

Chase

"ANDREW."

The urgent warning in my voice jerks his head up. He follows my stare. "Shit."

The others are alerted too. Johnson holds up a stylish midnight-blue frock coat for Lucinda to slip her arms into, and hands her a long-barrelled pistol.

She checks the firearm and drops it into an open holster on the back of her wide trouser belt beneath the coat, which she leaves unbuttoned. "I'll deal with this. You two stay down here."

"It's the Liverpool crew," Andrew groans.

She gives him a quick frown. "It's the Revenue."

"*What?*" Andrew jolts back in his chair. "Luce, this is bad. He's one of the men who chased Joe and me in our world this morning. We know the organisation he works for. If that's what you call the Revenue then this whole thing just got so much worse it's off the scale."

"They're chasing you? Why?"

"Their boss wants Joe to work for him. But that's not the point. Well, it is a bit." He pauses and slows down. "The main thing is that while they're powerful in our world, in your world they'll be unstoppable. This is awkward for me and Joe right now but the bigger picture for everyone in your world is terrible."

"Stay out of sight down here. There's never only one of these men. I'll get rid of them." She sweeps from the cabin with Johnson in her wake.

Andrew's watching the jetty. "She's right. All four of them from this morning are here. They're coming on board. And a fifth man is staying on the jetty. Let's watch from the top of the ladder."

We stand in the shadows, back from the windows in the double doors below the stern platform. From there, we have a clear view of the main deck.

"Single up!" Mister Samson's shout comes from above us.

Sailors respond by unwinding thick ropes from bollards and running in one of the doubled mooring lines at each end of the ship.

Groups of other sailors stand around, ready to do whatever it is they do when the ship sets sail. They're all trying to look casual while watching the confrontation.

Lucinda meets the boarders at the head of the gangplank. She looks totally in command and very impressive in her dress coat, fists planted on her hips and a steady wind blowing her long hair back from her face.

The Liverpool crew don't look impressed. Baldy watches sailors hauling in dripping wet ropes and laying them down in long overlapping loops on the deck. He raises his voice above the wind whining through the rigging. "Going somewhere, Captain?"

"Yes."

"Where?"

"To sea. Our destination is none of your business."

"It is my business if you're trying to leave without paying Revenue."

"There's nothing to pay. We entered port empty, and our suppliers failed to provide our expected cargo, so we're leaving empty. We're going now." She nods up to Mister Samson on the stern deck.

"Remove the gangway lashings," he shouts.

"Don't." Baldy produces a machine pistol from inside his jacket. He levels it in Lucinda's face, while the three other thugs produce identical weapons and wave sailors away from the gangplank.

Johnson steps forward, as if to stand between Baldy and Lucinda, but she stops him with a gentle hand on his forearm.

"This is bad." Andrew's voice trembles.

"Think it will help if we give ourselves up?"

"They don't even know we're here. This is about money, not us."

"You've sailed into our port," Baldy says, "so you owe us Revenue That's the rule. If you've offloaded your cargo somewhere else to avoid giving us our share, I'll take it in money."

"We have no money on board."

"Rubbish. How were you planning to pay for your cargo without money? Don't piss me off, lady."

Lucinda sets her face firm. "No cargo. No money. You can have your share of fresh air and like it."

"Captain, you just lost your ship."

All around the deck, sailors tense. Some of them tool up with whatever's at hand, while Baldy's henchmen cover them all with their machine pistols.

"Gonna get nasty." Andrew rolls his shoulders. "You ready?"

"Yes. Can you stop their guns firing from here?"

"Not all at once. One or two of them. Depends how far apart they are. If they'd stop moving around..."

"Mister Samson." Lucinda's voice carries clearly. "Carry on, please." She glares daggers at Baldy. "Unless you go ashore now, you'll be coming to sea with us."

I crouch to peer through the bottom of the window and touch the wooden deck with my fingertips, ignoring Andrew's curious look and trusting him to do his thing with the guns.

"Nobody move!" Baldy is red-faced and wild-eyed. His arm wavers a bit and his pistol trembles.

Lucinda turns away from him. "Get off my ship."

Baldy shifts his aim a few inches and pulls his trigger, blasting Johnson across the deck in a three-second burst of bullets. The old man crashes down on his back and doesn't move again. A red stain blooms across his shirt from right chest to left shoulder.

Lucinda draws her long-barrelled pistol and shoots Baldy between the eyes.

Before his body hits the deck, I shape six nine-inch spikes from the deck oak beneath the other three thugs and send one ripping through each of their feet.

They scream in agony while blood oozes from their pierced boots, all pinned in place and neither knowing nor caring that their guns probably won't work.

Sailors move in and finish them off with knives. When I'm sure they're all dead, I retract the spikes and return the deck to its normal shape.

Andrew stares at me.

"What?" I pause my reach for the door handle.

"Remind me not to piss you off."

"Let's see what their mate on the jetty is up to."

Lucinda is sitting on the deck, cradling Johnson and rocking, her tears falling onto his face.

Andrew goes to her.

I climb up to the raised deck and look for the fifth man.

Mister Samson joins me at the stern rail. "There." He points at a green-clad elbow poking out from behind the new building.

The man's head follows his elbow as he peeps around the corner at us. He's talking urgently into a walkie-talkie.

"He's calling for reinforcements," I say. "We should leave now."

Mister Samson is already shouting as he strides to his place at the ship's compass. "Let go for'ard. Let go aft. Stand by all canvas. *Move*, lads and lasses!"

Sailors spring into action everywhere, including some who speed up the masts like monkeys.

The man on the jetty is staring away from us. I follow his gaze but don't see anything other than the broad brown river, its waves short and steep from the sea wind blowing against the fast-flowing tide, and green hills sloping down to the riverbanks on both sides of it.

But that doesn't mean nothing is coming. Muscles twitch behind my ears when a throaty marine engine growls at the outer range of my hearing. The noise grows, still quiet in the distance but definitely coming our way. It doesn't belong in this place any more than machine pistols do, and like them it promises nothing good.

"Mister Samson, can you hear that noise?"

"Yes. What is it?"

"I'm guessing it's a Revenue ship, and that it'll be built with the same kind of engineering as their weapons. We're not leaving fast enough."

He takes a deep breath and roars, "Cut and run! Cut and run!"

Lucinda jerks around to stare up at him. She's still holding Johnson, her shirt dark with his blood.

Mister Samson pays her no attention. "Let go inner and outer jibs! Stand by flying jib! Cut and run now!"

As far as I'm concerned, he may as well be shouting in a foreign language, but his orders produce an extraordinary response from the crew.

Two thumps come in quick succession, one from up near the front and the second from below our elevated position at the back, as a sailor on each station swings a big axe and severs our remaining shore lines.

A cascade of white canvas falls open above the bow, while tug-of-war lines of sailors run away from the mast with ropes in hand.

Two great triangular sails billow for seconds and crack like a double whiplash when they catch the wind. Then two more follow suit.

I stagger when the ship lurches beneath me.

Mister Samson grabs my good arm without sparing me a look.

I manage to stay on my feet and hold the polished timber handrail.

A ginger-haired giant with a wild beard stomps up and takes his place at the man-sized wheel, making it look almost dainty in his huge hands.

"Steer for that headland," Mister Samson tells him, pointing diagonally across the river to the final point of red cliffs before the open sea on the Wallasey side.

"Aye, Sir."

A middle-aged sailor in a blue jacket and salt-encrusted black cap takes position beside the brass compass and lifts a whistle to her lips.

"Let go flying jib, Bosun," Mister Samson says. "Stand by mizzen and topgallants."

I assume *bosun* is a rank, rather than the woman's name. She blows a brief series of high-pitched notes and sailors all over the ship respond to the code.

Lucinda runs up the steps as her ship creaks everywhere and takes flight across the oncoming wind, shuddering like a great straining beast.

The bosun plays another tune, and huge sails fall open above our heads. Sailors run their lines away and haul them hand-over-hand through pulley systems until all the sails are pulled taut across their surfaces.

Lucinda strides across the deck. "What's the hurry?"

I point to the dark-grey gunship emerging from a hidden backwater upstream, about two miles behind us on the other side of the broad river. Its sharp bow and the big gun mounted above it confirm my worst fear. The distant growl of its powerful engine is now clearly audible beneath the wind roaring across our sails.

Andrew arrives behind Lucinda and follows my pointing finger. "Oh, shit."

Lucinda leans on the handrail and shouts over the wind. "Morris, Smith, please take Johnson to my cabin." To Mister Samson she says, "Gun crews ready, I think."

He speaks to the bosun, whose new tune clears the upper deck in seconds, leaving only ten sailors tending sail lines and a similar number scattered around in the high rigging.

Mister Samson continues to issue incomprehensible orders like a puppet master, using words and whistles to make his sailors perform shows of strength on the deck below us and brave acrobatic feats above.

Belle churns through angry mud-coloured water, surging with the strong tide and smashing into choppy waves, driven by the wind in her sails. Rigging ropes hum all around. Every few seconds, spray lifts over the windward side of the bow and splatters across the upper deck, the final drops of each wave hitting our faces like gusts of salty rain. I hug myself and try not to shiver with the sudden drop in temperature out on the river.

The gunship's proud bow-wave indicates its power and speed. They're closing on us. And our diagonal route across the river isn't even taking us directly away from them.

"Ready about."

Three piercing notes inject renewed alertness into all the sailors.

"Hard a-starboard when I give the word, Red," Mister Samson tells the big helmsman and points to the Liverpool bank a mile downriver from us. "That clump of trees on the hill will be your mark."

"Aye, Sir."

"Hard-a-lee!"

The world goes crazy for a minute as we execute a ninety-degree turn, with people hauling ropes under the bosun's eagle eye and reacting instantly to her micromanaging whistles. Our sails flap like monstrous mad birds then slam across to the other side, where the wind catches them and shoots us forward again. The surface of the river rushes past just below deck level.

I hang on with my good hand, leaning my body into the rail, trying not to slide down the sloping and slippery deck and land in a heap in the corner. I'm soaked through and shivering in the cold wind, but at least I'm still upright. No one will have the time or inclination to laugh at a landlubber falling across a tilting deck right now, but I still don't want to be that clumsy fool.

Lucinda, Mister Samson, and the bosun don't hold on to anything, and Red needs only his light touch on the wheel to maintain his balance. They bend their left or right knees all at the same time, leaning into *Belle*'s violent movements like synchronised dancers.

The gunboat is heading straight for us again, adjusting its course by degrees as we hammer back across the river. Four figures are visible on the foredeck, getting busy around the big machine gun, and more men appear on the upper deck bearing firearms. Despite the extra speed our towering mainsail has given us, it looks like we'll be within their firing range soon.

"Can you stop them?" I ask Andrew.

Before he can answer, he gets a slap of spray in his face. He spits out salt water and wipes his eyes. "If I had help, I could stop them. On my own," he grips the handrail and glares at the gunboat, "I'll see if I can slow them down."

I try to get my shivering under control. No one else seems to be suffering from the chill apart from Andrew and me. The hardy seafaring types get on with their jobs as if it's a fine afternoon.

Which it is, actually. The sky is pale blue and the land stretching back away from the riverbanks is green and peaceful. Things look a bit dark and threatening out on the horizon at sea, but for now, everything on and around the river is calm and pleasant. Except for the steady wind whipping spray across the deck to soak us every time we slam into another wave and the gunboat chasing us.

Andrew studies the vessel with intense concentration, but as far as I can see it hasn't slowed down at all. Silhouetted figures are now visible behind the windows of its enclosed bridge, and I can distinguish different hair colours in the machine gun crew.

A new sort of shiver creeps up my back, like an old friend met in a hostile place. Until now, it's been hiding under the cold wet unpleasantness.

Instantly, I'm alert and casting my gaze around. There's no doubting what this familiar sensation indicates. It's weak and watery, but somewhere within my detection range, probably no more than a few hundred yards away, is a thin place.

It isn't on the Liverpool bank we're charging towards. And the Wallasey bank over our shoulders is too distant. But it's in that general direction.

I make it to the stern rail without falling on my arse, walking on the outer edges of my feet to aid my balance as if I'm on a rocking, speeding train. I make it to the back of the ship and concentrate on the shiver.

"Ready about."

Great. I hold on tight and press my hip against the rail.

"Hard-a-lee!"

The world goes mad again, but this time I know what to expect and cope with it better. When we settle on our new course, I return to my place at the front rail and try to locate my shiver.

"Harden up, Red." Mister Samson speaks quietly to the helmsman. "Two points into the wind."

"Aye, Sir." Red turns the wheel one big, polished spoke at a time.

"That'll do," Mister Samson says, watching the jibs and mainsail. "Good man."

Our latest turn is helping me to pinpoint the thin place, but the direction my instincts are leading me is a strange one. The source of my shiver seems diffuse, and big, as if spread across a wide area. I've never felt one like it before, but even stranger than its feeling is its location, slap bang in the middle of the river. It's definitely a new one on me.

Andrew staggers and nearly falls. His eyes have sunk into their dark sockets. "Gotta rest for a minute."

I grab his arm and help him sit on the deck with his back to the rail. His exhaustion is shocking. "Take it easy."

"No good," he groans. "Can't stop the boat so I've been jamming their gun. I hope they don't realise it can fire now while I get my strength back."

A prolonged metallic clatter in the distance and a line of spurts bursting from the water barely a hundred yards behind us sinks that hope.

He groans again. "Get me up."

I do so, and once he's in place at the rail his back trembles beneath my hand.

Everyone on deck is transfixed by the enemy boat's machine gun. Even Red peers over his shoulder instead of looking where we're going.

"Is there any chance we might outrun them?" I ask.

Mister Samson still looks calm, but his expression tells me the truth before he replies with a slight shake of his head.

I speak low. "I know how we might be able to make them lose sight of us for a minute or two, if that would help."

He pitches his voice to match mine. "Tell us."

Lucinda edges closer and bends her head to listen.

I plant my feet on the deck so I'm giving Andrew back-to-back support, and point my good arm to the thin place, several hundred yards over to our right and towards the river mouth. "There's a way out of your world and into mine. You won't see it, but I can feel it." I move my pointing finger to keep it at the centre of the shiver as we pass it by. "I can direct you and maybe we can sail through it."

Lucinda and Mister Samson stare at me.

"He can do it," Andrew growls through gritted teeth. "Trust him."

Now they both look at Andrew with concern.

"He's using his magic to prevent their gun from firing," I tell them, "but it's exhausting him, and I don't know how long he can hold out."

Lucinda calls a sailor to her. "Take over here. Support Andrew against the rail."

Once I'm released from that duty, she walks Mister Samson and me away from curious ears. "Will they be able to follow us through?"

"I expect so. This might be where they brought their vessel through from my world to yours, so they might know it. But even if they do, we'll be out of their sight for the period between us passing through and them following. Will that help?"

They exchange a thoughtful look, then Mister Samson nods. "Tell us exactly where it is."

The shivers are coming in regular waves now, although they're diminishing in strength as we sail farther away from their source. I point to their centre on the river surface.

"Is it wide enough for us to sail through?" Lucinda wants to know.

"I can't guarantee that, but do we have any alternative?"

"There's a bigger concern than its width," Mister Samson says. "You're pointing at a sandbank. Right now, we would clear it, just, but the depth of water is reducing by the minute on this fast ebb tide."

"Do you think the sandbank will exist in your world?" Lucinda asks.

"I don't know."

The machine gun sounds a short clatter. Heavy bullets spit over our heads, and everyone ducks low when the rear sail is shredded and several rigging lines part with a series of cracks.

"Sorry," Andrew calls. "I blinked. Got it again now."

"That settles it," Lucinda says. "If we try the sandbank route we *might* lose the ship, but if we don't try we *will* lose her. Joe, guide us to your passageway. Mister Samson, take us through."

Through a thin place

"WHERE ARE ITS outer edges?" Mister Samson's ability to sound calm, despite determined death chasing us and a possible calamity right ahead, impresses me all over again. "Can you detect them as we get closer?"

I estimate the left and right limits of the thin place and point to them.

"That's wider than I expected," he observes. "It should provide a narrow channel either side of the sandbank with the tide at this height. I'll take us through the starboard one. Please keep pointing to the far-right edge of it."

To Red he says, "Bear three points to starboard of where Joe is indicating, and prepare to head up into the wind when I give the word."

"Aye, Sir." Red gives me a confident wink.

The gunboat is only half a mile behind. I wonder when we'll be in range of their small-arms fire.

"They're catching us." Andrew's voice is weak.

Lucinda squeezes his shoulder. "We'll be through Joe's magical passageway in a few minutes."

"They'll follow us through," he wheezes. "We'll need to be ready for them."

"We will."

"Stand by to head up," Mister Samson tells the bosun, who relays the message by whistle.

Waves of shivers wash over me when we sail across the hundred-foot-wide front of the thin place. I lean into the rail and concentrate on pointing at the right-hand edge of it, aware that everyone except Andrew is watching my finger.

When my outstretched arm moves across my body, Mister Samson says, "Head up!"

"Andrew," Lucinda says as we turn into the wind, "will you tell us when they can't see us?"

He doesn't reply. He looks barely conscious.

She calls for a second sailor to help the first in supporting him.

"I'll tell you," I say.

When the noise of the wind in our sails dies, all my senses are numbed. Our momentum carries us through the thin place, and the only sound is a continuous, steady lap of water running past our hull.

The precise line of the thin place's threshold is apparent from frowns and quizzical glances sailors give one another when they pass through it. Andrew and I know to expect the muscle jump, but it always surprises first-timers. I watch its effect ripple through the crew, from the bow back towards us in the stern.

My muscles jump and I turn to watch the gunboat fade from view, as if a sudden mist has closed around it. I nod to Lucinda. "Now."

Andrew's legs give way. The sailors lower him carefully to the deck.

When the wind returns, it feels fresher in this world than in the one we've left. It's coming from the same direction, but noticeably stronger. Maybe that will be in our favour.

"Ready the kedge anchor to port," Mister Samson tells the bosun.

In response to her whistle, two sailors run a rope out beneath the guardrail behind the big main anchors in the bow, and then back inboard over it. They tie its end to a smaller anchor, which they balance across the rail and stand ready to drop it overboard.

"Two points to port," Mister Samson tells Red. To the bosun, he says, "Stand by to gybe into a dead run."

Lucinda lifts a slender canvas tube from the compass tower and calls into it, "Gun deck, this is the captain. All ready?" She holds the tube to her ear and listens. "Very good. Stand by."

Sailors all over the ship are staring across the water to the Wallasey riverbank three hundred yards away.

Where two minutes ago there were green hills sloping down to sheer red cliffs at the water's edge, what we see now is typical twenty-first-century seaside urban. Densely packed rows of house roofs step down from the highest point in the landscape to a promenade beside the river.

Cars pull over on that broad road and people get out to gawk at us.

Golden-red sands along the town's foreshore in *Belle's* world have been replaced by colossal flat slabs of bare, green-tinged, dark rock in mine. And at the far edge of land, where an uninhabited coastline had turned away from us as the river mouth gaped into open sea, there now stands an imposing fort. Square, squat, and solidly built of substantial sandstone blocks, it projects out from the headland into the river.

"Fort Perch Rock." Andrew tries to shuffle his back up against a rail post. He clears his throat when his voice cracks. "Not military anymore. Entertainment. Nothing to worry about." His eyes roll up and show white as he slumps over. His head hits the deck with a dull thump before the nearest sailor can get to him.

"There's no danger from that fort," Lucinda shouts. "Pay attention to the task in hand, people."

Mister Samson ignores the fort. He is studying the flapping foresails. As soon as they fill with wind, he tells Red, "Swing to port."

He watches and waits for some moments, and all the sailors appear to hold their breath with him.

Or maybe that's just me.

When we reach a point in our leisurely turn that seems to satisfy him, he calls, "Drop the kedge."

It goes in with a loud splash.

Another pause follows, and then all at once he issues a string of orders, and the bosun whistles a complicated tune, and sailors everywhere spring into action.

Belle jerks against the anchor rope and presses me to the rail as she pivots. Billowing white sails blot out the sky above. Then, in response to the bosun's whistle, a sailor in the bow swings an axe to cut the bar taut rope and we surge forward, thundering through the waves with the strong wind behind us.

"Gun deck, stand by," Lucinda calls into the canvas tube.

"We're fifty yards from the thin place when a dark shape blooms in its centre and the gunboat bursts through into plain sight, coming right for us at high speed. The sudden throaty roar of its engine makes me jump. A split second later, I throw myself to the deck, along with everyone else, when its machine gun opens fire.

It keeps firing nonstop, spraying the air over our heads with bullets for several seconds then firing hundreds of them into our bow. Heavy impacts shudder through *Belle* as if a murderous drummer is hammering her hull.

I peek through the carved rail and see the corresponding one around the bow getting shredded into deadly flying splinters. Foresails flap in tatters above the ruined rail and broken lengths of rigging hang everywhere, swinging uselessly to the vigorous motion of the ship.

The machine gun falls silent for a moment, and I risk raising my head.

"Collision course!" a sailor shouts from the mainmast high above. She clings to a rope with one hand and points directly forward over our bow with the other.

"Steer straight for that channel," Mister Samson tells Red. "The channel is *ours*."

"Aye, Sir." Red holds the wheel rock solid even though he's stretched out on the deck like all the rest of us.

A burst of small-arms fire into the rigging sends our sailors scurrying for safety behind the masts.

Then the machine gun opens up again. Sails and wooden spars disintegrate in a prolonged hail of hot destruction. Our sailors up there plaster themselves to the mast and hang on like grim death, while we crash through the waves with the strong wind behind us.

"They will break off," Mister Samson insists.

We're playing chicken with a modern warship firing its heavy machine gun at us.

During another brief pause in the hideous cacophony, a shout comes from our lookout above. "He's going down our port side!"

The terrible barrage starts again. Heavy impacts shudder through our hull and the rail explodes into smithereens, starting at the bow and continuing all down our left side.

"Gun deck, we will engage to port!" Lucinda shouts into the communication tube.

Two sailors fall from high aloft and crash to the deck, where they lie still. For an instant I'm relieved to see neither of them is our female lookout, but then it strikes me that two more men have died. Two more families who don't know it yet have loss and grief in their future.

"Hold her steady, Mister Argument," Mister Samson tells Red. "Good man."

The gunship powers down our side, close enough almost to reach out and touch, its machine gun ripping chunks out of our deserted deck.

Lucinda shouts down the tube, "Gun deck, broadside to port in three, two, one, fire!"

Belle jumps violently beneath me, followed immediately by a brain-jarring blast below and an explosion mere feet past the rail. A curtain of oily flames and black smoke rises forty feet above us. It scorches my face even as it slips astern. Then another explosion rips the air and screaming lumps of shrapnel carve deep scars in the woodwork all around us.

I bury my head in my good arm and wait for it to stop.

Which it does, instantly, when we sail back through the thin place and leave the fiercely burning hulk of the gunship in the other world.

Waleas Eig

HOURS LATER, MY hearing is still numbed from the explosions and gunfire, so the wide salt marsh is a quiet place inside my head.

I study the sandstone cliff that rises sheer from the wetland half a mile away. *Waleas Eig*, Mister Samson called it, which sounds similar enough to Wallasey. He said it was a Saxon name that translated as 'Island of Welshmen'.

It fills the horizon from its lowest point three miles to my right, where we left the River Mersey on a channel into the marsh, to a cliff where it meets the sea a mile away to my left.

If it was actually the monstrous reddish-brown whale it resembles, its blowhole would be opposite where *Belle* sits at anchor behind me.

I've seen the far side of that sandstone plateau twice today, from over on the Liverpool shore this morning and then at much closer range during our brief jump into my world this afternoon. The twenty-first-century residential town I saw then has gone now. It never existed here. This bleak, untamed landscape is all there is.

Red Argument unsticks his sea boots from the soggy ground, squelching them free one at a time and leaving six-inch-deep holes that water rushes into and fills quickly. His expression suggests he likes this place no more than I do.

A muffled clunk carries through the air. We turn to watch the sailor who dropped us off row back here on his second trip, to bring Andrew and Lucinda across from the *Belle*.

When the boat grates to a halt in the grassy shallows, I hold it steady while Red offers Lucinda his hand to help her splash ashore. He returns for Andrew, whose eyes barely flicker when the big man scoops him from the bottom of the boat, while Lucinda hugs her lover's flute and cowboy hat as if they're treasures.

Andrew's skin is waxy. His hair falls in thin strands over Red's arm. He doesn't look as deathly grey as he did right after the battle, but the small improvement isn't exactly encouraging. I've seen him tired from wielding his molecular magic before, but nothing like this. His determination saved us out there on the river. No question about it. I only hope it hasn't drained him beyond recovery.

Red carries him as if he's a child. He sets off for the highest point of the cliff in as direct a line as the treacherous terrain will allow, but before following him I pause to look back at *Belle*.

The bosun is sitting cross-legged on the deck near the galley roof, sewing Johnson and the two dead sailors into their canvas hammocks, ready for burials at sea.

I took some quiet minutes in Lucinda's cabin to say goodbye to Johnson before we left. His personality still fills my memories of our brief time on board. I'll miss him and can only imagine how Lucinda must feel after losing her lifelong friend.

Elsewhere on the upper deck, sailors are repairing torn sails, damaged rigging, and destroyed fittings. There's none of the boisterous banter we heard when we first arrived on the ship a few hours ago. Everyone is subdued. It's a time for private thoughts.

Mister Samson waves from the stern deck.

I wave back before turning to trudge through the marsh. "Where are we heading?"

Lucinda points to a line of trees along the top of the cliff. "Gully's Wood."

I estimate we'll be there in half an hour, but the strength-sapping slog takes us twice that time and we arrive at the edge of the marsh in the sudden darkness of a September evening. Dry ground slopes up to the cliff face another few hundred yards farther on, before we come to a winding but nearly vertical set of steps cut into the rock.

I glance back out over the marsh on our way up, but a heavy mist has rolled in from sea and it's like we're climbing out of a swirling cloud.

The rock surface is damp and gritty underfoot, making the grip of my boots uncertain and every step extra tiring. By the time we drag ourselves to the top, I'm soaked through with swamp water and sea mist from the outside, and sweat from the inside, and wearier than I've ever been before.

Trees grow right to the edge of the cliff. Lucinda leads us through the wood. Red walks in her footsteps with Andrew cradled in his arms. I take up the rear.

My broken shoulder aches horribly. I want nothing more than to grow it into one of these birch trunks and feel gentle healing sap flow through my pain, but the flickering promise of a friendly campfire through the trees keeps me trudging along behind the others.

Twelve of Lucinda's crewmen are huddled around the fire at the near side of an open space under the stars. At first sight, I take it for a clearing, but when we leave the tree cover and clamber down a rocky path, I realise it's a small quarry. The sailors look glum until they see their captain, when relieved smiles light up their faces.

She motions them to wait by the fire, directing Red to take Andrew to the far side of the quarry where another faint light flickers through the foliage. She takes us to a construction built of living trees woven into a shape like two-thirds of a big bell tent. A four-foot-high screen of saplings across its wide mouth completes the shelter.

I'm too tired to think, but I'm impressed at the skill on show.

Lucinda knocks on the outer frame.

A low drone comes from inside, like an angry person muttering.

She knocks again and calls, "Can we come in, Gully?"

A *do what you want* sort of grunt sounds, so we round the screen and enter. It's darker inside the hut than outside under the stars, despite a small fire that smokes beside a low bed of dead grasses. The guttural muttering resumes from a dense patch of shadow at the back of the hut.

Andrew groans when Red lays him on the bed. Red stretches his back and steps away. The occupant of the hut leans forward to look at Andrew.

When firelight illuminates his deeply lined face, my heart stutters for a moment, then thumps in fury.

Andrew's friend Gully is the old wizard who brought an army to Quarter Square, intending to murder us all and take the square for the Hare tribe.

I suppose it was nothing more than another battle for him and his men, but for me it was an attack on everyone and everything I love and cherish. The army he commanded killed my friends in that attack. He personally injured Min's throat and ruined her song magic.

He escaped then, but he's within my reach now, and it's time for him to die.

Gully's Wood

GULLY'S CLOAK OF feathers rustles like dry grass when he leans forward to hawk up phlegm and spit it into the flames. His greasy bald head glows red in the firelight. He glares at me with one eye wide while the other squints and waters in the smoke. "Don't be growling at me unless you want a fight, young man. You don't look too good for it right now."

Lucinda and Red are both staring at me, which probably confirms that I growled without knowing it.

And he's right. I'm too hurt to do him any damage. As well as that, once the fury clears from my mind, I realise the person who took away Min's magic is probably her best hope for getting it back.

Red looks troubled. He makes a move to stand between us and protect me.

Gully sneers up at him. "What's your name, big lump?"

"Argument." Red no longer looks uncertain. He bristles in the firelight, and his upper body seems to inflate. "You want one?"

"Red." Lucinda restrains him with a light touch on his arm.

Gully chuckles. "Sit." He flaps a vague wave around his hut and waits while we each find something in the shadows to perch upon. "What's Andrew done to himself?"

"We were attacked. He used a lot of magic defending us." Lucinda's tone is neutral. I wonder if she would rather the wizard remained unaware of her feelings for Andrew.

I don't really know any of these people and have no way of gauging their relationships with each other. I decide to sit back and observe for a while.

Gully shuffles his creaky wooden chair next to the bed and lays his hand on Andrew's brow. His muttering starts again, but this time it sounds different. It's as if the incomprehensible words are charged with purpose instead of just being a long string of complaint. It becomes almost a chant.

He closes his eyes, and Andrew's flicker open for the same interval, but then they both return to their previous states and neither mentions whatever is passing between them, although it's clear that something is happening because Andrew's face relaxes and spots of colour return to his cheeks.

Gully stops chanting but leaves his hand on Andrew's brow. "Your rum left for Chester this morning," he tells Lucinda.

"When will I get paid for it?"

"You can either collect the money when you make your next delivery here or take another cargo in full payment now."

"What cargo? Where from and to?" Lucinda sounds cool and efficient, which encourages me because I'd prefer not to think of her as a friend of the horrible old man.

"Three choices. First is Lancashire cloth from across the river. Same cargo for London you were due to load this morning. But if what I've heard about your adventure today is true, I don't expect you're keen to return to Liverpool. Second choice is slate for Dublin from Porthmadog, further down the Welsh coast. Third choice is wool from Skinburness, up in Cumbria, probably good for Iceland but you'll need to arrange your own buyer."

If word of our battle with the gunboat has reached him so quickly, he is well informed.

Lucinda stares out at the night sky.

"You know Porthmadog or Skinburness?"

She shakes her head.

"Nor do the Revenue men yet. They're small ports. But if you need more extensive repairs than your crew can make, there are skilled people in Porthmadog. Go around Ynys Mon, into Cardigan Bay and upriver from Harlech. Also, I have a buyer in

Dublin for the slate. And there's a consignment of Irish whiskey over there you could bring back to Porthmadog for me."

"You're very organised," Lucinda observes.

"I'm using my contacts to help us all along while we see how this Revenue business develops." He shrugs. "And making some commission."

"Very well. Porthmadog it is."

Andrew stirs. "Good choice." Although his voice hasn't returned to its normal strength, his eyes show intelligent awareness for the first time in hours.

Lucinda's on her feet and by his side in a flash. She takes his hand. "Are you going to be all right?"

"It'll take more than an angry gunboat to beat me."

"Quiet now." Gully keeps his hand on Andrew's forehead, but his tone seems more preoccupied than caring. He closes his eyes and tilts his head, as if listening for a tiny noise. His lips move soundlessly.

Red shrugs at me.

Gully's cloak shivers and he opens his eyes. "When do you intend to sail?"

"An hour past midnight," Lucinda says, "when the tide's flooded the marsh. Why?"

"I recommend you go *as* it floods, rather than waiting until the tide is high. And head across the moss directly out to sea. Don't go back into the River Mersey."

"Why?"

"They're waiting for you at the mouth of the pool. If you don't appear there, it's my guess they'll come looking. You'll want to be away at sea before that happens."

"We will." Lucinda bends to hug Andrew and whisper something in his ear.

Gully watches with interest. "Remember, you're not a smuggler anymore."

She straightens, still holding Andrew's hand, and raises a questioning eyebrow.

"Yesterday, you were a smuggler. Today, you're a pirate. There'll be no negotiating your way out of another encounter with the Revenue."

"I don't intend for us to have another encounter."

"Then you should leave now. My agent will be expecting you in Porthmadog."

Lucinda lays a warm palm against my cheek. "Thank you for your help. I hope we'll meet again in happier circumstances. Look after my man for me."

"I will."

She plants a kiss on Andrew's lips, then hurries out with Red in her wake.

Her perfume lingers in the air. Frangipani. I'll miss her.

Andrew drifts back into sleep. Gully stays with him, chanting his low, wordless tune and restoring strength to Andrew through the palm of his hand.

At least, that's what I assume he's doing. He doesn't explain it to me. He doesn't speak to me at all, and I certainly don't feel like making small talk with him.

The moon rises through the wood across the quarry. I rest back against the shelter wall to watch it lift above the trees and set sail into the night sky.

Gully's weaving style is different to mine. Where I would have grown the living plants together naturally, he's bent and broken them to his will. The structure looks good from outside, but its thousands of strands are brittle, bruised, and forced. I heal the ones nearest to me and extend the relieved area as the night passes. The process soothes my pain in return.

Around dawn, I wake from a light sleep to hear two voices. I keep my eyes shut and listen to their quiet conversation.

"I understand why you want me to stay close to Merritt," Andrew says. "I want to know what he's doing as bad as you do. But I'm not giving Joe up to him."

"I don't expect you to give him up."

"What, then?"

"Just tell Merritt you're still on board with his scheme. Contact him on your way down to Cornwall. Tell him you'll bring Joe in after your jaunt."

I crack open my eyelids and start to fashion a noose from the sapling above Gully's head.

"I'm not..."

"Look, I know you won't take him in. Well, probably not. You have a month to persuade him. But," he talks over Andrew's protest, "if you can't persuade Joe in that month, then you can go back to Merritt and tell him honestly that you tried. Maybe he'll still take you back, even without Joe."

Andrew remains silent.

"You said it yourself," Gully presses on. "It's important. We need to know what that bastard is planning next. What his big picture is. Especially now we know he's behind the Revenue."

For the first time, I hear the hint of a Welsh lilt in the old man's gravelly voice. And as much as I don't like the direction of his thoughts regarding me, he obviously believes what he's saying.

The noose is finished.

"This is bigger than you and Joe. Bigger than me." His cloak rustles, and he groans when he stands, then he stamps his feet a bit. "I've been alive a long time and this is bigger than anything I've ever seen. It's a dangerous time. It's bad, and it's going to get worse."

"I know it," Andrew says. "You know I'm with you all the way. But I won't betray Joe."

"I'm glad about that." I stand and stretch, nod to Andrew and give Gully a cold glare. "Because I'm not in the mood to be betrayed."

Gully shakes his head. "There you go, growling at me again. I could get the wrong idea about you."

"No, you have the right idea about me." He's shorter than I expect, and quite stooped. Bearing in mind the only previous time I've seen him vertical he was standing on the roof of my theatre and commanding the soldiers who were trying to kill my friends and me, I wouldn't feel guilty about stretching his scrawny neck until he decides to behave himself. He has it coming.

The quarry is filled with a cold, damp, swirling mist. I stamp my feet and roll my good shoulder, wishing I could grow the injured one into a tree but unwilling to do anything like that while Gully is watching.

I ignore the old bastard and ask Andrew, "When are we leaving?"

He tests the strength of his legs and rolls his neck a bit. "Now."

Gully drops back into his chair with a dry rustle.

I weave a thick strand from the sapling and grow the noose down towards his head.

Andrew stares at it.

Gully pokes the fire with a stick and releases a shower of sparks. "Look, Andrew's all excited about this thing you two are going to do. I understand that. He's been waiting a long time for something like this to happen. And I understand why he needs you with him. His contact said to bring along a seer."

What? I halt the noose's progress down from the roof.

Gully's gaze remains fixed on the glowing embers of his fire. "I understand all that. And I know you hate me. If I were you, after what happened in Quarter Square, I'd hate me too."

He lifts his eyes to mine. "But if I'm right, there's some shit coming like you wouldn't believe. If I'm right, some of us enemies are going to be fighting on the same side before long. So don't you go digging yourself a hole and refusing to get out of it. Okay? Because we're going to need each other."

I grow the sapling back into itself and release the noose.

Gully peers up at his roof and then at me with a curious expression.

Andrew blows a sigh of relief. "Come on. We've got a road to hit."

On the road

A THIN PLACE IN the trees behind Gully's hut takes us back to my world. I pick up a slender stick and strip its bark as we go. We walk down a footpath to a wide gap carved through the sandstone cliff and a busy junction of twenty-first-century roads lined with houses. The sun is up. The air is sharp.

I stop to take in the panoramic view. "What did Gully call that marsh?"

"The moss. Locals know it by that name here in the outside too."

We dodge brisk traffic across the junction to the top of a steep road. It takes a similar line to our tired route up the slope to the cliff face yesterday evening.

"Looks like dry land down there."

The bottom of our long road opens out to a wide expanse of grass marked up with several football pitches, on the far side of which are an embanked railway line and a busy motorway system of sweeping flyovers. Beyond that, modern housing estates stretch across the plain, punctuated here and there by supermarkets and warehouses.

"They reclaimed it," he says. "Maybe some parts of the original moss are still there."

A range of blue-grey mountains line the horizon to the southwest.

"Is that Wales?"

"Yes. Snowdonia. Luce is sailing around to the other side of those mountains in the Wild."

He nudges me across the steep road and into a lane that runs off it, with the rear gardens of some of those 1930s houses on our left and a row of private garages on our right. A hundred yards along, he fishes a set of keys from his trouser pocket and opens one of the up-and-over garage doors. A nondescript family car sits inside. He releases the handbrake and eases it out, then locks the garage door again.

I didn't know he could drive. "Yours?"

"Gully's. Get in."

And we're off. I let Andrew navigate the rush hour and get us onto the motorway before I interrogate him.

"Okay. No one's listening now, so tell me what we're going to be doing for this next month."

"Truth is, I don't know much more than I already told you. So far, Stone's told me enough to get us to a certain place by a certain date."

"What you're saying is you don't really know what you're getting us into."

He winces.

"Fuck's sake, Andrew."

He concentrates on the road ahead and says nothing.

I start whittling the stick. "Enough of this shit. Tell me what you do know. You can start with exactly where we're going."

"Tonight, we'll stay in a house in Looe, on Cornwall's south coast. Tomorrow, we'll walk into the Wild and go to the place Stone showed me, which is where you'll be living. It's a quiet spot in the woods, away from the Tin family's stamping ground on Bodmin Moor and the Hare stronghold in Dartmoor Forest. The war zone shifted from the River Tamar this summer anyway. As soon as Hare lost the battle in Quarter Square, Tin pushed hard, and the front line is right up on Dartmoor now. Queen Fiona is pretty much under siege at the moment. So the hostilities shouldn't come anywhere near you."

"Hang on. You say *I'll* be living in the woods. You won't be with me?"

"No, I'll be in the house in Looe."

I twist in my seat and stare at him while he watches the road. Is it my imagination, or does he look guilty? "Spill."

He sighs. "Here's the deal. We'll buy you some camping equipment today on the way down there. Not a tent. Stone said he'll put up a shelter before you move in, but you'll need a sleeping bag and stuff. I'm your support team. I'll bring you food and clean clothing every day, taking away your trash and dirty laundry."

"That's nice."

He glances at the figure I'm carving. "Is that me?"

"No. I can make it you if you want."

"No!"

I manage not to chuckle at his alarm. "Apart from living rough in the woods, I'll be doing what, exactly?"

"Watching. Listening. Observing, in whatever way your talent will enable you to study the angels."

He takes his eyes off the road for long seconds while he studies my face, until I nod twice at the road ahead to encourage him not to kill us.

"They're there," he says. "From the way Stone describes them, I'm convinced he's telling the truth. They sound exactly like the one I saw all those years ago."

If this Stone character is a con artist, Andrew might be the easiest mark he'll ever meet. "That's twice today you've referred to me as having some sort of seer talent. This is the first I've heard of it."

"Is it? He adopts his wise-old-teacher tone. The one that used to impress me. "Really?"

I wonder what he's heard about me. How much of it is gossip following the battle. How much is rumours from elsewhere. What does he actually know?

"Tara said you see things."

She did say that, but I haven't thought it means I'm a seer. "So, somehow, I'll be studying these angels. And you'll come in every day to bring me food. And what else? There must be more to it than that. What's in it for Stone?"

"He's a scholar. He wants to learn about the angels too."

"Then why can't he sit in the bloody woods for a month?"

"Because he can't bloody see them. Only by accident now and then, when he isn't expecting it. He's spent years pinning down where they live, but he can't study them because he isn't a seer."

I watch the scenery pass by while I wait for the next bit.

"And neither am I," he says.

There it is. "If Merritt hadn't found me, you'd have lost this chance."

"Yes. It was pure luck."

"Hm."

"I didn't betray you." His eyes are fierce. "I won't betray you."

"Watch the road. When do I get to meet Stone?"

"You don't. He's a private person."

"See, you're not selling this to me."

He crosses two lanes of traffic to pull of the motorway and sweeps up an access road to a service station, where he slides into the nearest empty space and stops the car with a jerk.

"There's nothing to sell. Either you'll do it or you won't. I really want this. You know that. And I can't do it without you. It's not dangerous. It's a month of observations. But if you won't come with me, there's fuck all I can do about it. I'll give you your train fare to wherever Min's hiding and we'll call it a day."

He climbs out, slams the door, and stomps off to the service building.

When he returns, he's bearing a peace offering in a cardboard cup. He passes it across, and I sniff it suspiciously while he climbs back in. It smells like coffee. Sort of.

"I know your intentions are good, Andrew, but I've seen how sometimes your character judgement sucks. You can't speak for Stone, and I'm not allowed to meet him. I don't like that."

"I understand."

"We'll see how it goes, eh?"

His grin stretches from ear to ear. "Yes."

"If Stone turns out to be a bad 'un, if it gets shitty, we'll deal with him. Just watch him, okay?"

"Okay."

I sip the so-called coffee and immediately replace its lid, open my door to put the cup of rancid liquid on the tarmac, and settle back in my seat. "Let's go."

"No more strong smells," he says as we re-join the motorway.

"Pardon?"

"Coffee, minty toothpaste, perfumed soap and deodorant, that sort of thing. You'll be sitting in one place in the Wild, and strong smells might attract unwanted attention. No campfires or metal either."

No coffee. "It's autumn. The nights will be cold."

"We'll buy you lots of layers."

"Why no metal?"

"When Stone showed me your camp, we felt the faint presence of fae in the area. He says he's never seen them in all the years he's been going there, but he'll send someone to keep an eye out for your safety. Anyway, in my experience they don't bother humans if we don't bother them. But iron pisses them off, so Stone said best not to take any in." He glances at my carving knife. "Sorry."

"Fae?"

"Yes, but it won't be a problem. We can get a sleeping bag with a plastic zip. I checked. And clothes. The only problem was your voice recorders. I could only find ones with metal cases. But I think I've fixed that with a pair of slim wooden boxes meant to hold business cards. We'll have to check your voice will come through the wood okay. What we don't want is the presence of metal escaping in the other direction, but I think they'll do fine."

"Fae."

"Yes."

"Fairies."

"Yes."

Welcome to my life. "Voice recorders?"

"For your daily reports. I got two. I'll collect one from you and give you the other one, all charged up each day, with your food and clothes."

"Who is Stone sending to keep an eye on me?"

"No idea. He says he hasn't found the right man yet, but he won't leave you unprotected."

"Anything else I should know?"

He thinks for a minute. "No, I reckon that's it."

"This house you'll be living in. Is it Stone's?"

"No. Nothing to do with him."

"Whose, then?"

The pause is brief, but it feels significant. "Gully's."

Gully again. Andrew is in thick with that old bastard, which is odd, considering they were enemies on the battlefield only three months ago. "You and he made friends quickly after Quarter Square."

"We knew each other before, but I wouldn't say we're friends. That day, I know you all thought I'd betrayed you, but he thought I'd betrayed him. I didn't betray anyone, actually, but the consequences were bad for him, and I expect he reckons he has reason to be pissed off at me more than anyone else."

"What bad consequences?"

"He fell out of favour with Queen Fiona, big time. That's never a good thing to happen, but especially when he was already in conflict with her home-grown wizards. As far as they were concerned, the moment she withdrew her protection he was dead meat."

"He's in hiding?"

"More like keeping a low profile. In the Wild, North Wales and Waleas Eig is his power base."

"So what was he doing down in the West Country?"

"Playing the long game."

"What does that mean?"

"I don't know. It's what he said when I asked. All I know is that for some reason, he was prepared to slum it as one of Queen Fiona's wizards. He wouldn't have done that unless he thought it was important. The way he's worked up about Merritt, I guess it had something to do with your Home Office man."

I let his tease pass. "It's fortunate for him, then, that you've infiltrated Merritt's operation."

"Gully found me right after I left Quarter Square and persuaded me to get myself captured by Merritt's people." Andrew gives a rueful laugh. "Coincidence is never a factor when Gully's around. It's like he plays chess against the universe."

"I suppose we're his pawns."

"Yep. And he always plays a long game, so his motivations can be as murky as his plans."

"Nice bloke."

Andrew taps the steering wheel. "Useful, though."

Hm.

I slip the phone from its pocket in my boot and put in the battery.

Andrew glances at it. "New phone?"

"Min's reserve one."

Her text arrives as soon as I turn it on.

Andrew cocks his head at the soft chiming noise.

"Min's new number."

He chuckles. "We're getting good at this tradecraft stuff, aren't we?"

I tap in her number. "Hello, love. You okay?" … "I'm fine. Guess who we met in Wallasey."

Thirteen thousand years of baggage

WE DIDN'T TALK for long. I was starting to feel guilty about why I've really accompanied Andrew on his silly jaunt, so saying goodbye and turning off the phone while filling my eyes with the open road under a wide sky ahead gives me a sense of freedom I wasn't even aware I've been missing.

It's time to face the truth. I let Min believe my only reason for hiding in the Wild for a month was to thwart Tyac in his hunt, but I hadn't needed too much persuasion to spend a month away from her.

There. I admit it.

She's trying her best not to control me. After Quarter Square we established that my freedom to make my own decisions isn't negotiable, that it isn't hers to allow or withhold depending on how she feels about an issue. But every time she deals with it, I see the struggle written all over her face.

I've even started to wonder if her song magic is really broken.

Would she lie to me about that? Would she endanger all our lives to keep us on the run and keep me in line?

My automatic response is: no. No way. But the worm of doubt makes my mind itch. It points to her unshakeable belief that the only way to deal with the threat of Tyac is to run away from him. The belief she's lived by for centuries. Millenia.

I still love her. I'm hardwired to love her and don't see that ever changing. But she brings thirteen thousand years of baggage to our relationship, and sometimes she's bloody hard work. Especially when her overriding instinct is always to whisk me away from any hint of danger.

So, I'd reached the stage where, when she suggested we should spend a month apart, the thought was immediately attractive. Guiltily so, and against all my instincts, but still attractive. I couldn't admit it even to myself at the time, but it's true. After only twenty-four hours away from her I've achieved sufficient clarity of thought to see through my own denial.

Life has been crazy this year, ever since we met. So much has happened. So many people have died. And still, no matter what she says or how hard she tries, I see her fighting the urge to control me at every turn.

A month of peace and quiet while studying some woodland community is just what the doctor ordered. We need a break from each other's pressures. It's innocent, and gentle, and no one will get hurt.

Lies of omission and commission

MIN CURLS UP in her armchair, cradling a mug of hot blackberry tea and staring out of the tall window. It's a pleasing view of one of the few remaining ungentrified spots along this part of the canal, but she isn't really seeing it.

Her mind is full of the image of poor Jennifer Smith's mutilated body, hung up in Trafalgar Square. Some idiot took a photograph and posted it on the web. It's everywhere. As fast as people take it down in one place, it springs up in ten others.

To make matters worse, someone has leaked a Scotland Yard internal email that draws attention to the marked similarities in Detective Smith's fatal injuries and those of Joe's wife and her lover, and the fact that Smith was on the team investigating that double murder.

Min knows in her bones that Tyac leaked that email.

The media are enjoying their *London Serial Killer* frenzy. The tight-lipped silence of the police is like fuel thrown on that fire.

Without doubt, some people in authority know these murders are the work of a crazed werewolf. They might not know his name is Tyac, but they're aware of his existence and his nature.

Merritt, for one. The secret Home Office department he leads exists to investigate precisely this sort of thing, and he told Joe point blank that he knows a werewolf committed the murders for which Joe was temporarily in the frame. But he isn't saying anything in public, and neither is anyone else who knows the truth.

As well as imagining Jennifer Smith's horrible death all the time, Min is also busy tracking dozens of detailed witness accounts of another incident that's been posted all over the web.

They tell of a pitched close-quarters battle on the River Mersey between a modern gunboat and an old-fashioned pirate ship. Both vessels appeared suddenly out of a bank of mist a few hundred yards off New Brighton beach in broad daylight and blasted hell out of each other, before the gunboat sank and the pirate ship disappeared back into the mist.

The Ministry of Defence issued a brief statement to explain that what members of the public saw was a practice run for a forthcoming Navy Days event, involving a single vessel and a projected hologram of a sea battle with a pirate ship in full sail. It said the staged rehearsal uncovered several glitches in the system and added that this sort of thing is what rehearsals are for. The Ministry apologised for any alarm the rehearsal may have caused onlookers and assured the public that no injuries were incurred, and no one was in any danger.

Despite this official statement, witnesses are talking online about dead bodies washing up on the beach before the military screened off a four-mile stretch of shoreline and imposed a strict no-go zone there for the rest of the day.

Mersey River Battle is trending on Twitter.

No one in authority is taking these claims seriously, and television news bulletins covering the story very briefly are repeating the government line.

Of course they are.

She hears that in Joe's voice and smiles.

But twenty-four hours later, the internet is still buzzing with the story. There's no doubt in her mind that something bad happened there.

Ships slipping in and out of sight through a mysterious mist smacks of thin places between the Wild and the outside.

She's seen the same sort of thing herself, many times, and no other explanation fits the reported facts so perfectly.

And New Brighton beach is in Wallasey, where Joe and Andrew spent that very day.

She sips her tea. Joe didn't mention a sea battle, but knowing him and Andrew, she'd be astonished if they weren't in the thick of it.

At least they survived. Although that doesn't make her feel any better about believing that Joe lied to her.

Like I've been lying to him. Lies of omission and of commission, chipping away at the cement of our trust.

Shad opens one eye when she reaches for her phone. She smiles at him and starts thumbing a message to Joe before she can think twice about it.

> I'm sitting by my favourite window in our old warehouse squat, looking down at the canal and remembering you teaching Shad the words to *Kashmir* in this room. I don't think he'll ever get the tune quite right, but I'm not convinced melodies matter too much with Led Zeppelin songs anyway.
>
> Joke! Don't shoot me!
>
> He's here with me, lying on a rug. He hasn't shifted back since the attack, and I expect he'll do as he told you and stay wolf until after the full moon this week. His burns don't seem to be troubling him. I can't even see them, but I'm sure he's healing under there.
>
> Tae and Vua are asleep after shifting at dawn.
>
> I started back at the club last night. Brian the manager wants the girls back too, and they'll be happy to dance again as soon as the full moon

passes. They'd feel perfectly natural walking around naked all day every day, so dancing in bikinis is no problem. But they look simply gorgeous when they're all oiled up in those gilded cages and Brian says his customers haven't stopped talking about them since we were here last month.

He asked about you and Shad too. Says he's never had better doormen. I told him you're both working away and will call him when you're back in town.

I know you hated that job, my love, but Shad was fine with it, so I imagine he'll want to start again next week.

Last night our wolves hung around outside the club until I finished my gig. Vua bought me a dog whistle that's soundless to humans. I don't feel in any danger there, but if something bad does happen, I'll give one blow on that thing, and they'll be inside the club terrifying everyone in seconds.

I explained my husky voice by saying I've had a cold. The musicians were kind to me.

Which brings me to my reason for this mega-text.

I got a bit upset when I realised you hid the truth from me about that pirate ship business in Wallasey. I've read about it on the web since we spoke, It's all over social media. Onion Layers is Tae's new favourite talkboard for conspiracy theories, and it has nine different threads going on the story.

You were there, weren't you? I can't imagine you and Andrew not being involved somehow. But you never mentioned it on the phone. And now all I get is your voicemail, so I suppose you've already gone into the Wild and we won't get to talk again for a whole month.

Anyway, your little deceit upset me. Until I got to thinking about it and realised we're both keeping secrets. For each other's benefit, probably. Maybe sometimes just for a quiet life.

You know what, my love? Lately, it feels like the only place I can be completely honest with you is inside my own head when you're not around.

Can you tell how difficult this is for me to admit? That's why I'm circling around what I really need to say.

Okay, here goes.

I've been lying to you. I've been letting you think I'm trying to heal the magic in my voice, but I haven't been trying at all.

I've lied to you because I love you and I'm scared for you, and I want to protect you from yourself. While I've been vulnerable like this, your protective instincts have had you looking after me instead of riding out to fight Tyac and die again.

I'm sorry for my deceit. But I'm still terrified.

That's why I persuaded you to go with Andrew for a month. I couldn't bear to see you injured and vulnerable when Tyac is on the hunt again. And I knew if you were around me, you'd be in more danger than you are while hiding away somewhere with Andrew.

I can't lose you again so soon, Joe. I can't take it! My love for you is bigger than anything. Bigger than the world. Bigger than history. I know you love me too, but you only get one life at a time for your love to grow in. Mine goes on and on, building forever without a break, except that every time you're torn out of my heart again, I have to live without you for years, sometimes decades. Sometimes centuries. But I don't stop loving you and the pain never goes away. Don't make me go through that again. Please.

I'm thumbing this like a woman possessed. If you were here, I'd be sobbing and screaming my fear aloud for you to hear. Or maybe I'd keep it bottled up the way I always do. Maybe I'd carry on telling lies to try and keep you safe.

I'll probably text you some more while you're away, to try and explain how I feel and why. I know I'm a control freak. I know I'm wrong to manipulate you. I see that clearly when I'm sitting here in the peace and quiet, and I can only imagine how frustrating it must be for you. Maybe it'll do me good to write it all out here, knowing you'll read it when you come home to me.

Stay safe my love. I can't describe how much I miss you. How it hurts that we can't be together. Stay safe. That's all that matters. I love you.

Oak and water

GULLY'S HOUSE STANDS apart from its neighbours in the River Looe valley, so we have to walk down into the little seaside town to cross its stone bridge then up the steep road that climbs the west valley side.

Andrew looks at me sideways. "New look."

"Yes." Before taking a long hot shower this morning, the last one I'll get for a month if everything goes according to plan, I shaved my head and beard down to bare shiny skin. It feels strange, but good hygiene will be important while living rough and there's no way I'll be able to keep long hair and a full beard clean. I'll wash my skin and stubble with scentless soap every day and it will soon grow back, but for now my warmth depends on my new woollen beanie hat and scarf.

"Suits you."

I eye his long grey locks and doubt he would ever shear them off. "No, it doesn't."

We walk a mile into gentle green countryside before he leads me off the road and along a sun-dappled woodland path. Autumn hasn't reached Cornwall quite yet, but its imminent arrival is in the air.

"Hell of a commotion last night," Andrew says over his shoulder. "Did you hear those cats?"

Ah. Yes. I remember now. The two stray cats Gully must feed when he's around bedded down with me in the back bedroom. All was peaceful purring until an unwelcome stranger cat investigated the open window at half past one and landed heavily on one of my sleeping new friends, at which point hell broke loose.

I remember waking in a state of high alert, already moving to the spitting, yowling chaos of torn fur and flashing claws even before I was fully conscious, and snarling "Get out!" in the intruder's face.

There was a moment of frozen awe before the stranger fled, then our two strays rubbed themselves against my legs, and we settled back down to sleep. The entire incident lasted probably no more than thirty seconds.

"I'd swear I heard a lion roar in the middle of it." Andrew gives me some side-eye. "Must have been a dream superimposing itself on my memory later in the night. Weird."

I give a noncommittal grunt and explore my coffee-deficiency brain pain. So far, it's only a dull ache. There's no knowing how bad it will get before it gets better.

Andrew has my new gear in a small haversack on his back, although there's precious little of it, leaving me to carry the short-handled plastic spade in my good hand and one of the recorders in my chest pocket behind the sling. I've pierced each of the wooden business card holders with a grid of tiny holes to correspond with the recorder's microphone at the front, and a slot on one thin edge to enable access to the plastic on/off slider button. It works.

Shivers across my skin have been building in strength for a couple of minutes. Now they wash through me in shallow waves. This isn't a well-used thin place. It gives me only a small muscle jump when we walk through.

Within minutes, our new track in the Wild meets a fast-flowing river, and soon we come to a line of stepping stones across it.

Andrew goes over it first. I follow carefully, mindful of my poor balance with a broken wing. The last thing I want is to be wet and cold and possibly injured even worse on my first day living out in the open.

We trek over wooded hills for a mile or two more, until Andrews stops in a flat clearing halfway up a rise, catches his breath, and spreads his arms wide. "Welcome to your new home."

It's a roughly circular small plateau, thirty feet across, hemmed in nearly all around by oak and elm trees with some ash, birch, holly, hazel, and hawthorn among them. Looks like elm disease was never a problem in the Wild. That's good news.

A fifteen-foot gap in the trees where we enter the clearing offers a pleasant view of thickly wooded and rounded hills to the east, some of which we've just climbed. Most of them look smaller than ours, but I get the impression they're similar sizes and the only difference is the land rising steadily away from the inlet at Looe.

At the back of the clearing, the magnificent trunk and strong boughs of an ancient oak dominates the whole space, its hefty canopy sheltering the carpet of grass and moss below.

A clear stream runs along one edge, beside a bank bound together by the oak's big roots, before tripping over a small rocky waterfall and disappearing into the undergrowth to continue its course down the hillside.

The shelter Stone promised consists of two lightweight branches arranged in an upside-down V shape and leaning against the old oak, with saplings woven around them loosely and leaves and tree bark stuffed into holes here and there.

"I'll tidy that up."

"I thought you might." Andrew stands with his head back, eyes closed, hands on his hips. "Can you feel it?"

"The peace and quiet?"

"The fae. It's the peace and quiet that lets me feel it. When I was here before, Stone talked the whole time, so I only felt snatches of it." He circles the clearing with a near-rapturous expression, almost dancing. "It's old. Very old. It hasn't been used for a long time, but there's no doubting this is a glade."

"As in, a druids-and-mistletoe sort of glade?"

"Yes, them too. Oak and water. But who do you think the ancient druids got their nature magic from?" His eyes glitter with excitement. "The fae, that's who. Magical people who were here long before any druids arrived and who stayed after the druid religion died out."

"People?"

He wrinkles his nose and rocks his hand. "Creatures."

"What sort of creatures?"

"All sorts."

"What I'm asking, Andrew, is should I be concerned about this?"

"Nah." He inhales deeply and holds it in before letting it go in a big whoosh. "They're long gone from here. It's just exciting, you know? It's holy, like finding an ancient cathedral no one knew even existed."

"I get it." I relive him of the haversack and sit on a thick log. My shoulder is sending stabbing pains through my whole upper body and all I want to do is grow it into a comfortable tree. The magnificent oak is looking good. "You're going to walk that six-mile round trip every day, then?

He tears himself away from his imaginings and drags his attention back to me. "Yes. I suppose I'd better be getting on. Have you thought of anything we've overlooked? Anything you want me to bring in tomorrow morning?"

I flick through my folded clothing, towel, wash gear, and paperback novels. "No. I'm still not sure what I'm supposed to be doing, mind."

"It'll come to you. I'm sure it will. Don't forget to make a recording every day, to tell us what you've seen and heard. Even stuff that might seem unimportant to you. Just say it. Okay?"

"Okay."

"I wonder where your protector is. Stone said someone will be here."

I shrug, and wince when a bolt of sharp pain in my collarbone reminds me not to do that.

He dithers about leaving. "Anything else you need?"

"Some of that peace and quiet you mentioned."

"Ha. Okay. See you tomorrow."

I follow the sounds of his departure until it disappears into the morning, then lower my aching body to the ground beside the old oak and grow my shoulder into it.

The relief is instant and so overwhelming I nearly fall asleep. I drift on a gentle wave of freedom from pain, tuning into the vibrations of the woodland, picking up Andrew's steady footsteps and following his progress until he crosses the river and passes through the thin place.

My next priority is to replace Stone's flimsy effort with a decent shelter. Maybe he only started it off to confirm where he wants me to stay, and the lean-to is his message to simply get on with it.

The shape of Gully's hut in Waleas Eig will work well, so I get to work copying that design while my shoulder is still nestled inside the oak.

I leave a seventy-degree gap at the front that corresponds with the open space between the trees across the clearing. It will be good to watch that wide view change from summer into autumn. Good to have the rising sun fill my home every morning.

The main structure is completed by early afternoon, so I take a break and open my food parcel for the day.

An apple, an orange, and a slice of cold toast smeared with chicken paste for lunch, with a cold bacon sandwich for later.

Tomorrow, Andrew and I will have words about my menu.

I dip my pint mug into the stream. Its water is cold, clear, and delicious. I fill the mug again and settle back down against the oak, growing my shoulder into its trunk seamlessly as if it's always lived there.

White cauliflower clouds drift in from the sea and bounce over the hills on their journey inland. I follow them until my eyelids droop and I surrender to sleep.

There's a lake below me. A long lake, cupped in a hollow between several thickly wooded hills, in the shape of a slender isosceles triangle with its short base the nearest side to me.

I'm not flying, or floating in the air, although neither of those things would seem strange if I were. I look down on the lake from a raised vantage point, as if I'm standing on a small hill above and back from one of the equal angles.

The water reflects a clear blue sky. Heavily leaved trees crowd down to its shores, from the pointed end away in the misty distance and nearly all the way along its two long edges towards us.

Us.

I'm not alone. Or, rather, I'm alone up on my hill, but there are other people in and around the lake below. A settlement of low conical huts fills a flat pad of land between the lakeside and the forest, and lightly clothed people walk about or sit and work among the huts. It's a quietly industrious scene.

There are three people in the water, except that on closer examination, they're not people. Not normal people. They're human-shaped but taller and broader of shoulder than any human I've ever seen. They stand naked, waist-deep in the lake, shining with a mellow golden glow. Not dazzling bright gold. It's deep, warm, and beautiful, like old rose gold.

One of them spreads his impressive golden wings wide, shakes water from them, and flies away. The powerful slow beat of his wings sings in my blood for a moment and takes him high into the sky, until he becomes a tiny dot and disappears from sight.

Shall I call you Wolf?

I AWAKE TO THE quiet reality of the forest. While I slept and dreamed, the bouncing cauliflower clouds have merged into a towering flat-bottomed bank of burned yellow and deep purple that sails majestically over the distant hills. It's beautiful.

I sip water and come around slowly, synapses still zinging from the vivid dream.

My sight seems clearer and my hearing sharper. Not by a significant degree, but enough for me to notice the difference. Enough for me to know, from a change in the air, that I'm being watched.

A chill runs through me and I ease my shoulder from the oak. I can't see who or what it is. I can't hear anyone. Strangely, and scarily under the circumstances, I didn't feel the intruder's approach through my tree. But the new presence is strong, and my skin crawls with the knowledge that someone is studying me.

I collect my haversack from the log and take the opportunity to peer into the dense, dark undergrowth. No one is visible. There's nothing I can do except stay alert and wait for the watcher to either appear or go away, so I get on with making the place my own.

I fashion a mattress of dry leaves and bark, lay my sleeping bag out upon it, and arrange my belongings either side. I'll be in the Wild for a month. Things will get icky fast if I don't keep the place neat and tidy. I crawl out of the shelter on hands and knees and come face-to-face with a big black wolf.

He occupies the middle of the clearing and glares at me.

Not black, I realise when my heart rate calms down a bit, and I get a decent look at him. His coat is heavy and dark in the shade of the trees, but he isn't totally black. There are deep browns in there too, and some strands of red. His eyes are grey.

We study each other.

I'm very grateful for the summer I've spent with Shad and his daughters. Before getting to know the Axe, I was morbidly terrified of wolves my whole life because of my recurring dreams of Tyac hunting me down and murdering me time after time. Without my recent experience, I don't know how I would have responded to meeting this big bugger.

There's no open aggression in his stare or his stance. I guess the angry glare is just part of who he is. He reminds me of Ban, the Axe pack's enforcer and Shad's trusted advisor. Anya's brother.

I only met Ban once, several months ago. For most of that day he was a man, an impressive figure with a powerful presence, and when he shifted into a big black wolf as night fell, I only saw him for a few minutes from a distance. Can this be him? If so, will he recognise me?

I sit on the log and watch the clouds, careful not to make further eye contact or any sudden moves, and hope he will just continue his journey and leave me to my solitude.

But when he settles down with his huge front paws stretched out, and maintains his steady stare, it dawns on me that he isn't planning to leave.

"Are you my protector?"

No reply.

I'm not expecting one, but I wanted to break the silence.

"Are you here to look after me for a man called Stone?"

A flick of his ears might have suggested some recognition of the name, but he gives me nothing. Just the same pissed off stare. His relaxed body language makes me think I've got this bit right, at least.

Eventually, as much to relieve my cramping muscles as anything, I stand, slowly, cautiously, and extend a nervous hand to him, palm down.

He doesn't move.

I take a tentative step, alert for the smallest sign of aggression, but still he makes no move. Not even a twitch of his tall, pointed ears. Two more steps take me almost within reach of him, where I stop, hands hanging loosely at my sides, trying my very best to appear unthreatening.

He gets calmly to his feet. His shoulders are at my waist level. When he lifts his enormous head, his serious grey eyes are level with my chest.

Without a sound, without any warning at all, he rears up on his hind legs and drops his heavy front paws onto my shoulders.

Pain hammers through my broken collarbone, and my knees nearly buckle under the agony. I manage to stay on my feet and remain silent, although I can only imagine what he'll make of my sudden sheen of sweat.

I'm not a small man, but he dwarfs me. He stands more than six and a half feet tall and must weigh three hundred pounds. And he isn't shy about leaning all his weight on me. There's dominance in that, which I'm not about to challenge. Right here and now, Ban or no Ban, he is the boss of me.

He nuzzles his snout all around my face, neck, ears, and the top of my head, sniffing and snorting vigorously in a curious, interested kind of way. His breath smells of raw meat, blood, and stomach. When he rasps his teeth across my face, the size and rough scrape of them makes me cringe inside.

Closing my eyes throws my balance nearly all the way off. I stagger back three paces under the unbearable pain of his weight.

He drops back to all fours, but my interrogation isn't finished yet. He shoves his snout into my crotch. I can't help yelping in surprise and fear. He takes a thorough sniff before lifting his head.

When he's had enough of me, he steps back and stares me in the eye. Then, finally, he settles down on the ground and regards me steadily as before.

"How do you do?" My voice breaks, and I chuckle to lighten the atmosphere, although that problem is clearly on my side only. He's perfectly comfortable. "My name is Joe."

He blinks slowly.

Is that understanding? Recognition? Just a blink? Who knows? Not me.

"Shall I call you Wolf?"

No reaction.

"Okay, Wolf."

My stomach rumbles. I collect the remains of my food from the shelter, sit on the log, and offer him half a cold bacon sandwich, but he turns his head away in haughty rejection. Fair enough. I eat both halves.

After that, the only place I want to be is sitting up against the oak with my shoulder grown into its trunk.

Wolf looks on dispassionately as I fix my pain relief, and he continues to watch all through the evening while I stay there and weave a three-foot-high removable screen panel for across the mouth of my shelter.

At dusk, noises out in the trees become sharper, more distinct, as if the changing light creates a channel at ground level that carries sound differently. I keep seeing faces in the foliage, but when I look at them directly, they're not there.

Wolf stays with me, and I start talking to him for comfort. He isn't bothered by the faces. If they're really there, he doesn't care.

Before I get my head down, I cross the stream to pee in the trees away from my camp. Wolf doesn't like that, but he settles in the clearing when I crawl back inside the shelter and struggle into my sleeping bag.

Night arrives without warning. I haven't seen the sun directly since I entered the Wild this morning, and my eyes have become accustomed to the gathering gloom beneath the trees. But one minute it's dusk and the next minute the world is plunged into deep darkness. Suddenly everything goes very quiet in the forest, except for the continuous trickling of the stream, and even that seems subdued.

The silence is intimidating, but brief.

The nocturnal world comes alive. Cracks of twigs, crackles of dry foliage, bumps and shuffles, quiet snorts and snuffles come from all around. I try not to let my ear muscles twitch every time a sudden noise occurs somewhere close outside the clearing.

I fish the recorder from my shirt pocket, make my first daily report, and try to get comfortable for the night.

A high-pitched dry fart sounds from somewhere, and I wonder what sort of creature produced the noise. I keep reminding myself that a fierce wolf is protecting me. I wish he was Shad.

I'm miserable, hurting, and lonely. I miss Min.

Visitors

DAWN CAN'T COME soon enough. After an uncomfortable night with little sleep, except for a few brief snatches of dream-haunted brain downtime, I'm cold, stiff, headachy, and eager to get some blood circulating in my limbs.

I crawl out of the shelter and ruffle the fur behind Wolf's ears like he's a dog, the way I often do with Shad.

But this isn't Shad. This is a strange wolf, as mighty and solid as Shad but nothing like him in temperament. This animal is not my friend. I jerk my hand away. Thankfully, he doesn't give any indication I've pissed him off. Maybe I imagine his long-suffering sigh.

Housekeeping warms me up as I stomp around tidying the camp and chewing a twig soggy to turn it into a toothbrush.

I'm wary of overdoing things after the mad activity of these past few days, not to mention my broken bones, so I stretch my tired and aching muscles to warm up while remembering my vivid dreams.

One of the golden angels in the lake smiled at me. I was awestruck, but my lack of response didn't affect her lovely smile, and once she'd acknowledged my presence, she went about her business.

What *is* their business, her and the other angels? They seem to live in the lake. Actually in the water. I've only seen one of them fly that one time, but they often flex their incredible wings. They swim beautifully, like supple, golden, winged dolphins gliding beneath the surface and playing together.

They live with the humans as part of the lakeside community. Humans go to the water's edge and talk with them.

On two occasions, an angel touched a human, once with fingertips to a boy's forehead and once when an old woman waded in deep for a hug. I got the impression then that there was healing going on; I added my thoughts to yesterday's recording.

No idea if Andrew and Stone will be interested in my dreams, but I have nothing else to tell them about.

I fetch my hand spade and head off to find a suitable place for a toilet. Again, Wolf isn't happy about me leaving the clearing. He keeps using his weight to deflect me from walking in whichever direction I choose, but I'm determined.

"Look, there's no way I'm going to foul my camp or the stream. That's my drinking water. Yours too, I expect. So I'm going, and you'll have to get used to it."

He growls a serious complaint but stops short of biting me, which is a relief, and eventually he follows me across the stream and into a small clearing thirty yards through the trees on the other side. He stays close throughout my awkward one-handed operation, and watches with interest when I bury my waste, then bars my way to stop me returning to camp.

"What now?"

He prowls around the toilet clearing with slow, deliberate attention to detail, sniffing, snuffling, peeing on bushes and trees, and then squatting to defecate over the place where I buried mine.

"Is this a domination thing, or are you covering my traces?"

He glares.

I look away to give him more privacy than he gave me.

The same thing happens at the little waterfall, where he watches out of the corner of his eye while I strip and wash, When I've dried off and dressed in today's clean clothing, he covers my scent with his own on the ground and nearby bushes. Then he catches a rabbit and eats it whole in a matter of minutes.

With my shoulder in the oak, I hear Andrew coming half an hour before Wolf does, which gives me a private smile. I get up to sit on the log before he walks into the clearing.

He nods hello, holding out my food bag in friendly offering, then jerks to a halt when he sees Wolf between us. "Holy shit!"

"It's okay. He's not dangerous."

Andrew circles the clearing, keeping an eye on Wolf, who ignores him. "What is it with you and wolves?"

"This one wasn't my idea."

"Stone sent him?"

"I think so. No one else has turned up."

"Hey, great house." He admires my shelter. "I recognise your inspiration."

He dumps my food bag and clean clothes in my lap, grabs my first recording, scrabbles to plug in his headphones, and listens to it straight away, ignoring Wolf and me for the next forty-five minutes.

When he opens his eyes, they're shining with tears. "You saw angels."

"I dreamed them. Not the same."

He jumps to his feet, very animated. "No, your dreams allowed you to see them. They're here, Joe. They're really here." He slips the device into his pocket and hands me its replacement. "Is there anything else you need?"

"Plasters and a new menu."

"Huh?"

"These boots have given me blisters. Never walked far in them before and they've rubbed my heels raw. Need some sticking plasters. And get yourself a cookery book. Find a bakery and bring me big Cornish pasties. Buy me cakes and chocolate to go with the fruit. Anything for a bit of variety. Just no more bloody paste sandwiches. Okay?"

"Okay." He shoots me a crooked grin. "But paste sandwiches is what you've got today. I never had to bother much in the kitchen before."

"Well, you do now. I'm in your care, so bring me some good food."

He squints. "What's a Cornish pasty?"

"It's a pie. Chunks of peppered beef with diced potatoes and vegetables cooked in a big, hand-sized parcel of golden pastry." My stomach rumbles. "Cornwall's national dish. You'll get them hot from the oven in any bakery down here. Follow your nose."

"Okay. Anything else?" He's almost hopping from foot to foot in his eagerness to get away. "Oh, how's your shoulder?"

I laugh. "Go on, piss off and listen to the recording again. Just don't concentrate so hard on it that you fall and break your bloody neck. I don't want to starve in here waiting for you to turn up again."

"You're a good man." He grabs my dirty laundry and is gone before I can reply.

My lunch is chicken paste sandwiches and a banana.

Faces appear in the foliage while I eat. Every time I focus on one, it isn't there anymore. But I keep seeing them in my peripheral vision. People, or things, are watching me. They're about child height. Their quick secretive movements remind me of the uglies who scared Min and me during my first journey through the Wild.

I'm not too concerned about them, because the atmosphere is very different to the cold threat I felt when Wolf stalked me yesterday, and he pays these creatures little attention. He registers them with a cool stare and then looks away. If he isn't worried, I'm not worried.

As I tidy up my lunch wrappings, I hear the unmistakable sounds of someone climbing the wooded hillside towards me. We listen to the noise and wait to see who's coming. I sit on the log behind Wolf to place him and his big, cocked ears between our visitor and me.

The first thing I see is a bowler hat. Not one like city types wear in London. This one is brown, and its curved brim gives it an old-fashioned style. Maybe it isn't a bowler at all. I'm not sure of anything right now, because the face beneath the hat pushes all other thoughts away.

It looks very old and quite youthful at the same time, in that his skin is weathered and deeply wrinkled while his bright, blue eyes glitter with interest and possibly a bit of mischief.

He stands as tall as my chest. He's climbed up one edge of the clear pathway and remains almost hidden behind foliage while he studies me.

I stare back. His approach wasn't stealthy and he's the first of these faces not to disappear the moment I glance in their direction.

Eventually, he moves the foliage aside, takes a single step into the clearing, and stops there. He's dressed neatly in old-fashioned brown and green country clothing, all corduroy and weathered leather, his right hand resting on a hefty blackthorn walking stick.

I assume he's stopped at the sight of Wolf, until I realise he is waiting courteously for me to invite him into my camp.

Is he a fairy? A pixie, maybe? I try not to smile at a notion that seemed silly only two days ago.

"Hello." I say it quietly, not wanting to frighten him away.

"Hello."

"Welcome to my home. Please come in."

He takes two steps into the clearing and cocks an eyebrow at Wolf. "Good dog."

Wolf ignores him.

"How do you do?" He addresses me over the animal's head. "What's your name?"

I have a vague idea that maybe I shouldn't tell someone like him my real name. But after hesitating briefly and wondering if I should be worried about this, I decide I'm more concerned about politeness than some daft rule half remembered from childhood fairy tales.

Maybe not my full name, though. "Joe. What's yours?"

"Thomas Appleleaf." He sits down with a grunt at the other end of my log. "People have been watching you."

"I know."

"They're interested."

"So it seems."

"I've cleared them off. They won't bother you again. What's that?"

"It's a sling. I hurt my shoulder." We study each other silently. "Are you a pixie?"

He shrugs. "I suppose you could say that."

"Does that mean you are or you aren't?"

"The word is *pisky*."

"Like a fairy?"

"No."

"An elf, then?"

He gives another of his enigmatic shrugs.

I guess this is as much information as I'll get out of him on that subject. "Is Thomas Appleleaf your real name?"

"It's *a* name."

"Right." I exchange a glance with Wolf.

"What is it you want to know?"

Where to start? "What are you, really?"

"I told you. I'm a pisky."

"That doesn't actually tell me any more than I already knew."

"Then you will be a happy man, for you already know what you want to know."

So that's how it's going to be. "Thanks for that." I start to get up.

"Where are you going?"

"I've got stuff to do. Nice meeting you." I step towards the shelter.

He gives a resigned sigh. "What is it you want to know?"

I sit back down. "What's a pisky?"

"What's it worth to you?"

"What do you want?"

He thinks seriously for a few moments. "The memory of your first love."

Ah, now there's a subject and a half. Does he know the enormity of what he's asking, or is it simply an innocent question with no hidden depths?

My thoughts flicker instantly to what Min's told me of my first life, and her tales of us together during my other lives all over the world since then.

I shy away from those images when it occurs to me that the little man might be able to read my mind. "Julie Andrews."

"Who's she?"

"An actress. My parents had her films on video when I was a boy, and I fell in love with two of her characters."

"What were the characters called?"

"Mary Poppins and Maria von Trapp."

He considers these names. "Tell me their stories."

So I do, all the way through.

"Thank you." He gives a sage nod as if I've bestowed some great favour upon him.

"You're welcome."

"We are fae. The Folk. Us piskies and elves, as your people call them."

"What do your people call elves?"

"Sylph is how they refer to themselves."

"Okay." I decide to appear as if I couldn't care less. It seems the best way to get information out of him.

We look at each other for a minute.

"What is it you want to know?"

"Will you tell me about the fae?" Maybe an open request will work better than the direct questions I've tried so far.

"Piskies and the Sylph are cousins from forever ago. We were here when your people came to these shores, and we were here when the people before your people came too. This is our home. It used to be *our* land, but it hasn't been so for a very long time. Your people have always driven the Folk back and forth between the Wilds and the outside. We never get to settle."

He gives me a forgiving smile. "I don't blame you personally. Our people have different natures, yours and mine, and the balances sway back and forth during different times."

"Wilds? There's more than one Wild?"

"There are two that I know of. The Wild and the deep Wild."

No one's mentioned this before. I wonder if Andrew knows there's a second Wild somewhere.

"Fae aren't human. Historically, we were equally at home in the Wilds and the outside."

He's well into his groove. I doubt I could stop him now if I wanted to.

"The outside became a difficult place for us during your twentieth century, and the priests have made the deep Wild almost impossible for us in your twenty-first. We've lived mostly in the Wild since then, but after they chased us from the deep Wild, the priests now hunt us in the Wild too."

He shakes his head sadly and stares at the grass beneath his boots. "I fear they won't stop until we're gone. *All* gone. The goldens have never hunted us. Even now, they don't tell the priests when we're around, although they know it well."

"Who are the priests? Who are the goldens?"

He grins. "Now we get to it. This is what you really want to know." He stands and gives me a funny little salute. "See you when I see you," he calls over his shoulder.

Wolf and I exchange another glance. When I look up, Thomas has gone.

I place the palm of my hand nonchalantly against a birch tree, but I can't feel his movements at all.

*

Sitting on the bank with my shoulder grown into the oak and my blistered heels dangling in the cool stream is my idea of heaven.

"Your feet look painful. May I heal them for you?"

My heart thumps. I twist to look around in all directions, even though I know the voice is inside my head.

Wolf wakes from his late afternoon snooze and squints at me.

"Don't be alarmed, Oak Man."

"Who are you?" I ease my shoulder from the tree and lean forward to peer upstream at the undergrowth that forms a living tunnel over the running water.

If the voice can be said to come from anywhere, other than my imagination, then that's the direction my internal compass tells me to look. There's even the suggestion of a distant thin place shiver about it.

"I'm Lael. We met yesterday, I think. I didn't see you, but I felt your presence on a track above the lake."

"You're the angel I saw in the water. I dreamed you."

"And you're the Oak Man."

"My name is Joe."

"Close your eyes and listen to my voice so that we may connect more fully."

I do so.

"It will be my pleasure to heal the skin of your feet. May I?"

"Yes." I wriggle my toes under the water. *"Please."*

A touch comes, an invisible caress as if someone's fingertips are smearing melted honey over the skin around and under my heels, and the soreness fades away. It takes seconds. Maybe not even that long.

When I lift my feet from the water, I'm not surprised to see clean, unbroken new skin where there had been torn white blisters. *"Thank you."*

"Close your eyes again. Let's see each other."

I'm on the hillside above the lake, disembodied as before but definitely not dreaming this time. Below, people of the village go about their day, undisturbed by or unaware of the ghost above them. A single angel stands in the shallows at the nearest end of the lake, waist deep in calm water, smiling up at me.

She waves and mouths, *"Hello."*

"Hello." I wave back and grin.

Her golden skin glows above and below the water's surface. Her straight, shoulder-length hair is like a sheet of deeply burnished copper. Great, heavy-looking wings of the same colour float on the water behind her in a way that looks both relaxed and potentially powerful.

She's naked and astonishingly beautiful, but it's so perfectly natural it hardly registers. On the face of it she looks about twenty years old, but her awesome radiance makes it impossible to guess her actual age.

"You have broken bones. May I heal them?"

"Yes, please."

"Is that why you embedded your side in the tree?"

"Yes."

Liquid warmth flows through my upper body, and the pain disappears completely. I groan with relief.

"I've never seen that form of healing before. Embedding in a tree. Your talent interests me."

"Your talent is wonderful. I've never felt such power. Thank you. Is there anything I can do for you in return?"

"We'll be friends, I think. It will be pleasant, and we'll learn from each other."

"We will." That grin is stretching my face again. The physical warmth from her healing my bones blossoms into emotional warmth and an overwhelming sense of well-being, like I've found a lifelong friend. Someone I can trust. And that she's looked inside me and finds the feeling mutual. I hope so.

She looks away to the trees beyond the village, and the sound of many bare feet walking on impacted soil reaches me. A young man leads a procession of children through the village to the lake.

"I must attend to these people now. My friend, Keni, is preparing to leave on a quest tonight. Let's talk again later."

Wolf gives my cheek a not-exactly-gentle nudge with his wet snout. Something about my state must have attracted his attention.

I scratch behind his ear absent-mindedly while watching the crowd of happy children gather on the lake shore and realise with a thrill that I'm using my right hand without even an echo of pain in my shoulder and ribs. *"I'd like that. Thank you, Lael."*

Her smile fills my mind as I stand up from the bank and our connection dissolves. Andrew is going to be so stoked at this. I'll probably have to hold him down when I tell him.

Wolf and I sit together to watch the day end. Our clearing gets dark early compared to the wooded hills to the east, which glow in warm colours and reflect the unseen sun back to us.

Sunset registers as a block of solid shadow rising steadily across the trees and subduing their colours, until all the land is grey. A broad, horizontal band of deep luminous blue divides the hilltops from the final minutes of pale daylight higher in the sky, and the yellow moon rises directly opposite us.

I jump nearly out of my skin when Wolf howls, but it's an awe-inspiring sound, and after the initial shock I close my eyes and revel in its lonely beauty.

When his evening song ends, our eyes meet. The tilt of his head and intelligence in his expression reminds me again of Ban, even more strongly than when we first met.

"I have some wolf friends."

He sits proud and regards me.

I take it as an invitation for me to continue. "They're werewolves of the Axe pack. Wonderful people. Strong, intense, and loyal. The bravest people I've ever known. I met the whole pack for the first time three months ago, over that way." I nod to the northeast. "There was a full moon like this, only silver, not yellow, and they scared the living shit out of me when they shifted that first night."

I wait for some response, some sort of body language hint that he understands my words, but he simply watches me.

"The tribal chiefs were Shad and Anya. They had a big family. The pack enforcer was Anya's younger brother, Ban."

No reaction.

"I knew him for just one day in his human form. Only saw him for a few minutes in his wolf shape from a distance. But I remember he looked a lot like you."

Wolf gives me nothing except that steady, unblinking stare.

"He was a big, black, disciplinarian wolf with grey eyes and an attitude of seriousness. A lot like you." I lean forward to look more obviously at him in the growing gloom. "I'd go as far as to say, exactly like you."

Nothing.

I raise my eyebrows.

Still nothing.

I sit upright on the log again. "Ban might think he has good reason to dislike me. Maybe even hate me. My lover, Min, is the Axe tribe's goddess. When we arrived in the camp that day, it was the beginning of the end for the tribe's ancient way of life. But it wasn't my fault. I didn't want things to happen the way they did."

I give him a steady look. "In fact, if Ban remembers clearly, he'll know I did everything I could to persuade the tribe to change their plans and avoid the terrible tragedy that was coming. Ban tried too. He knew the plan was dangerous."

I stare at the ground. "But I failed. We both failed, Ban and me. They wouldn't listen to us, and the tragedy hit. Many good Axe people lost their lives protecting Min and me from the monster Tyac, including Ban's lovely sister, Anya. So I'll understand if Ban hates me for my association with that terrible event."

We sit in silence while the moon sails high, the nocturnal world rustling and squeaking into life around us.

"Ban may remember that Anya and Shad invited Min and me to share their bed before we left for the run to Quarter Square. I'm sure Ban was aware of it. I want him to know I fell in love with Anya that day. I want him to know I grieve for her still."

He studies the moon.

"Ban left the tribe because of what happened. He walked into the Wild alone, and I haven't heard anything of him since. I wonder if he stayed wolf. I mean, if you are him, I wonder if remaining wolf is your way of dealing with your grief and anger."

Finally, he moves, rising to a half crouch to stalk slowly and silently to a bush at the edge of our clearing. He pauses for several seconds, then tears into the undergrowth. A shrill scream is cut off immediately and replaced by the sound of tearing flesh and furious snarling, chewing noises. He returns to his previous spot a short while later, licking his lips and cleaning his front paws industriously, ignoring me completely.

"Wolf."

No response.

I wait a minute then speak again at the same volume and in the same tone. "Ban."

His ears twitch. It's unmistakable. He doesn't look at me or give any other indication that he's heard me, but that ear twitch leaves me in no doubt.

"Hello again, Ban. I'm sorry for your loss. Anya was a magnificent woman and a magnificent wolf. The world is a poorer place without her. I know how much she loved you. I know how much you loved her. I'm sorry."

He turns his head and stares at me in the strong moonlight.

I stare back.

Then we exchange a nod of understanding, as we did that awful night before the world he loved was destroyed.

Keni's quest

I SIT WITH MY feet dangling above the stream, patting my bare soles on its splashing silver surface, and connect with Lael as effortlessly as just thinking about doing so. I can see through her eyes and hear her thoughts while she sits on her favourite flat-topped rock and swishes her feet gently in the lake water, watching with a mixture of pride and trepidation as Keni's skin turns from his normal colour to deep bronze.

Her childhood friend, lifelong love, and prospective husband has spent most of the past moon cycle in the lake while she and the other goldens prepared him for his quest.

He's ready. At dawn yesterday, his wing tips sprouted, only to shrink back into his flesh when he surfaced from his meditation and climbed out of the water.

Tonight, as he basks in the concentrated focus of the six living goldens and the throng of elder spirits who've passed on and now inhabit the water, he is reaching the point of climax. Water glows around him, and now his skin colour is changing to gold. At dawn, a few hours from now, his wings will grow fully, and he will fly.

She recalls how excited she was, a full turn of the seasons ago, standing where he is now, waiting for the moment she'd been preparing for her whole life. She's a turn younger than Keni in physical age, but having goldens for parents made a difference to her readiness.

It also gave her a fuller picture of what she might encounter on her quest. A moon cycle of preparation, no matter that the goldens always give every quester everything they have during it, can't compare with a lifetime of knowledge imbibed at the mother's breast and every day thereafter.

She slips into the water. "Are you ready, my love?"

His eyes shine with joy and excitement. "I am, my love."

The other living goldens silently acknowledge her feelings. They back away to give the couple some privacy, while maintaining their focus and imparting power to Keni.

The elder goldens stay where they are, where they always are, but she knows Keni can't see them and won't realise the glow in the water around him is from the spirits of those who've passed on.

She takes his hand. "There's something I want to say."

"Say it."

"I was always destined to become a golden. Myen was pregnant with me when she completed her quest. Lu completed his quest one moon later. I see now how unusual my childhood was, although at the time it didn't seem so strange to grow up the child of golden parents. It was the only life I knew, and it was a fine one." She squeezes his hand. "You were part of my wonderful childhood. You helped make it that way."

"You made mine wonderful too." He returns the squeeze.

"Keni." She catches and holds his gaze. "What I want to tell you is that even with my background and a whole lifetime of natural training, I still might not have survived my quest."

"But you did survive it."

"I was lucky."

"You were good."

"No." She shakes his hand urgently. "I was lucky. I slipped in and out without anyone seeing me. I never had to fight or escape from captivity. No one even knew I'd been there, so there were no angry hunters intent on dragging me back to the Mountain, where their priests would tear out my living heart and eat it raw in a religious frenzy. My quest was easy. Not everyone is so lucky."

He lowers his gaze to the gently swirling golden water.

"*You* might not be so lucky, Keni."

She lets him dwell on that. He will have considered it many times throughout his childhood, even as ambition burned within. Especially with the painfully crippled presence of his father, Mahu, to always remind him.

The first time he mentioned questing, when he was only a tender age, Mahu forbade him ever to think of it. But as the boy grew older, his determination developed into outright rebellion against his father, until Mahu disowned him in his early adulthood and forced his mother, Annam, to do the same.

The goldens have prepared him for the possibility of failure during this moon cycle. But he has only a short time left before he takes his one and only chance to become a golden. The quest he's dreamed of all his life is finally happening. Now he needs to face up to the possibility that things might go horribly, fatally wrong.

She won't insult him by voicing the thought that's sneaked into her mind, that his ambition might be tied too closely with his desire for her. The mix of motivations is always complicated and often shifting, and his purity of purpose has been examined to every golden's satisfaction during this cycle.

Warmth washes through her as the assembled goldens heal her anxiety.

Keni raises his gaze to hers. "I understand. And I'm ready."

"Come here."

They embrace for a long time. This might be the last time they will be together in any place other than her memory. While they hug, she faces that possibility, explores it, and puts it aside. This is a time for love and encouragement, not for rehearsing the possibility of grief.

She holds him at arm's length. "Which route will you take to the Mountain?"

The golden power imparted to him during the moon cycle of preparation is temporary. If he completes his quest and makes it home with gold from the Mountain, he will become a golden for the rest of his life. If he doesn't...well... She puts that thought aside again.

In any case, there are two routes he can choose from. A low-level flight directly to the Mountain will probably leave him some goldenness in reserve for his return journey. The risk involved in that route is that it's slow, and the men of the Mountain are more likely to notice his approach. A high-level outward flight will give him a fast approach and might allow him to enter the Mountain without alerting anyone to his presence. But it will exhaust his goldenness and leave him wingless, on foot for the entire return journey.

"I'll go high."

"That's what I did."

He grins. "I know."

Her heart swims in the rich new depths of his voice. This is how he'll sound forever when he comes home.

"But I didn't take one of the usual return routes."

"Oh?"

"I decided in advance that instead of running ahead of any possible pursuers through this world, I would travel back at least as far as Lake Sunrise through another world."

He frowns.

"There are several other worlds. Goldens act in all of them, not just this one. When it was time for my quest, Myen and Lu taught me how to hop between worlds. And now I'll teach you. If you want to know about this option, that is."

"I do."

"It won't be as simple as a straight line from the Mountain to Lake Sunrise in this world, but the journey should be a lot safer than running one step ahead of hunters if they're chasing you."

"Tell me."

"The shapes of land and water are broadly similar whichever world you are in, but people and creatures of the different worlds have settled in different places and made changes. So, for example, we can't rely on a track in this world existing in the corresponding place in another world. It might be there, but then again it might not."

He is paying close attention.

"There are places where the dividing fabric between two worlds is thin. These are the places you need to detect, so that even if you don't use every one, you'll always be aware of them if you need to slip through quickly. You'll feel them. They'll make you tremble inside. When you pass through one, you'll experience a little involuntary jump, as if you are asleep and dreaming of a sudden fall that wakes you up. Remember that sensation. Focus upon it the first time you feel it, and remember it. The memory of it will draw you to other thin places, and when you're near one you'll tremble inside."

"How will I find the first one, to experience this sensation?"

Myen and Lu join them, and with Lael they lay hands on his head and shoulders.

"We'll show you how to find it," Lael says. "When you reach the thin place, go through it with the deliberate intention to pass into another world, and you will do so."

She and her parents envisage the thin place near the Mountain that they all used on their quests, passing the image of its location to his mind.

"Can you see it?"

"Yes," he whispers.

"Can you see how to reach it from the Mountain?"

"Yes."

"And this is the route I took from that point." They maintain their powerful contact for some time to ensure the geographic memories are placed firmly in his mind.

"If you get into trouble in one world," Lael says, "you can hop into another one. I hopped back and forth a lot at first, but stopped when I remembered my father saying the men of the Mountain might have magicians who can find us when we do that too much."

"I don't know if they heard me or felt me," Lu says, "but my quest was difficult. Every time I hopped back into this world, I had hunters from the Mountain on my heels soon afterwards. So if you must hop, be ready to hop back quickly."

"I will. How many worlds are there?"

"There are many. They all occupy the same space at the same time. Your outward flight in this world will take you over an ocean and a continent, all the way to the coast of a different ocean. That's where the Mountain is. Your journey home will be across an almost identically shaped continent and ocean in another world. The one I hopped into, we call the loud world." She smiles. "You'll understand why when you get there. It's full of people, countless numbers of people who seldom stop moving or pause to see what's around them."

She stirs the water and creates spreading circles of ripples. "It's a tiring environment, but I hope it will be a good one for you. People in that world are unlikely to notice you if you travel quietly."

Owls call to one another across the lake as they hunt down through the long valley.

"Try to travel only at night. Your golden colour will fade slowly and even in that world people will notice it during daylight. My route avoided cities, which are places where many people live close together. Cities are lit up like daytime even at night. If you can follow the same route and avoid them the way I did, that will be good."

"Some people in the loud world see us for what we are," Myen says. "Some of them see us all the time, while others see us only occasionally. Some see us clearly when we are in flight. Don't assume you will be invisible."

"Thank you."

She kisses his forehead and floats away.

"Your normal colour will return by the time you've crossed the continent," Lu says. "Once that happens, you won't draw attention, but it won't help a great deal because by then your quest will be nearly over. Steal some clothing as soon as you can and dress like one of them until you reach Lake Sunrise. You'll need it immediately for warmth during the first part of your return journey, and it will serve you well to look like a native when you come down from the mountains and travel among people."

He stoops to kiss Keni's forehead. "Fly like the wind and come home safely. You are a son to us." He sends sympathetic warmth to Lael and wades away to join Myen.

"I'll follow your progress throughout your journey," Lael says. "You won't see or hear me, but I'll be watching you."

"Oh?"

"You'll know how I feel. During your quest, you'll be pulled in three directions at the same time, to all the places our people have lived since quests began. The Mountain, Lake Sunrise, and our home here on Golden Lake. Whichever one you're closest to will pull you the strongest. In fact, when you're inside the Mountain, it'll be so strong you'll have to force yourself to ignore it so you can leave again. But wherever you are, you'll be aware of all three places at varying strengths until you get home. You know about this, yes?"

"Yes. I'll use it to navigate from the Mountain to Lake Sunrise."

"Well, when you get those three pulls, I'll be experiencing the same sensation. I'll feel your direction, very strongly at first, and although it will reduce as your goldenness wears off it won't cease completely. Especially when you're near water.

So travel by river or lake whenever you can. That's the best way for you to follow the navigational pull for as long as possible, and it's also the best way for me to maintain watch over you."

"How will you do this?"

"This is what watching means. My parents were my watchers. I'll be yours. This will be my part in your quest."

The sky is heralding dawn. Soon the full moon will set.

She closes her eyes and remembers an overwhelming rush of emotion from her quest.

"When you reach the thin place to Lake Sunrise, you'll fall in love with the mermaid there. I did. Everyone does who encounters her. When she guides you through the loud world lake to Lake Sunrise in our world, remember me. Remember we love each other and that I'm here, waiting for you. You'll be able to leave her then. Remember me."

"I will." He kisses her.

She melts beneath his lips, fighting the strong urge to hold him and beg him not to go.

Loving warmth envelops them when all the living goldens lay hands upon them. The lake water shines golden. Keni shines golden. He sighs in ecstasy as his wings grow and spread wide into the air, and the tendons of his powerful neck stand proud when he throws back his head and utters a long, low, sonorous tone.

The goldens take up his song as he starts to beat his wings across the water surface, the sound drawing people from the village down to the lake.

Annam is there, on her knees at the water's edge, her tears of a mother falling. There is no sign of Mahu.

Keni extends his arms to embrace everyone, as if he would take the whole village and his life's history there with him.

Lael and the other goldens draw away when his wings beat the air powerfully, and more powerfully still, and finally lift him from the water.

His beautiful golden body drips a shower of shining water back into the lake. He draws his mighty wings back, and for an instant his bright eyes seem to burn when his gaze locks with Lael's. Then he soars into the pale morning sky like a golden bolt of lightning going home.

And he is gone.

*

At the apex of his high curved flight, when Keni passes over Lake Sunrise near the eastern coast of the huge continent far below, the three-way pull acts upon him for the first time.

Lael feels it with him, and through her I feel it too in a lucid dream, as if I'm a passive observer inside his head flying miles above the earth.

Dawn follows him as he descends and the land below rises to meet him, plains turning to desert, desert to mountains.

He flies directly to the Mountain, knowing instinctively which one it is from the strong tugging in his gut.

When he is almost directly above its peak, he locates the gaping hole he's been told to expect, and swallow-dives to it, plummeting vertically through the sleeping mouth and into the Mountain.

The sensation that he has arrived home and nothing exists outside of it nearly overwhelms him, but the goldens have prepared him well.

He lands lightly on a rocky ledge deep inside the silent Mountain and picks up the nearest two apple-sized nuggets of gold sitting there, one for Lake Sunrise and one for Golden Lake.

If luck stays on his side, he will fly straight back out of the Mountain and set off for home without attracting any attention.

But luck isn't on his side. Already, shouts echo around the mine cavern, accompanied by lights flickering in many places at once, including upon the ledged walkways high above him.

He's been seen, and he estimates his chances of flying straight back into the sky without being killed are negligible.

His insides ache as if they've turned to icy water. His instinct is to curl up on the rocky floor and beg for mercy. But he pushes through the fear and casts around for somewhere to hide.

He finds a small cave and hides in it while determined search parties pass by again and again. He remains as still and silent as stone, under a light covering of pebbles and shale, as the goldens taught him.

There's someone you should meet

THE BORDER BETWEEN my lucid dream and actual consciousness is blurred, but when I shuffle upright to sit against the oak and look out from my shelter to see great rivers of curling white mist making islands of all the hilltops, the early morning chill convinces me that I'm properly awake now.

My connection with Lael and Keni is instant and automatic. She shares her distress at his plight with the other goldens, and I leave them joined in meditation, drawing away to allow her privacy for her anxious thoughts.

Removing my back from against the oak's bark makes the withdrawal complete. I'm fairly sure my connection with Lael is via the stream water, especially after hearing her telling Keni that if he stays near water on his quest, it will assist in that purpose, and I suppose the tree's roots in the stream bed enable our connection when I lean against its trunk.

Could she just turn off my access to her thoughts and feelings if she wanted to? My guess is, yes, she could. I suppose the courteous thing will be for me to continue withdrawing whenever I feel she is struggling. The other goldens are her support. If she wants to discuss how she feels about Keni's quest with someone outside of that circle, perhaps, she need only ask, and I'll be there for her.

I wish Min and I could share a connection like this. Even better, one like Lael and Keni have. It would make it a lot easier to solve our relationship problems than by trying to talk around all the practical obstacles and emotional hurdles formed in our thirteen-thousand-year history together. Especially as I still don't remember most of it.

A brief commotion in the undergrowth signals Ban catching his breakfast. I follow his example by hunting through my haversack for the last remaining paste sandwich. Andrew had better bring me something more interesting to eat today.

He does. My second breakfast of the morning is an altogether more suitable vacuum-sealed tub of hot porridge oats and honey. Even better, for lunch and dinner, he produces two big Cornish pasties, a bar of chocolate, two cupcakes, a sugary energy drink, and a bunch of red grapes.

I no longer need the foot blister plasters he's brought, but the new menu is very welcome.

He isn't interested in discussing food or anything else. He sits on the log with his earbuds in and gazes out across the landscape with unseeing eyes, lost in concentration while he listens to my recording. Brief exclamations escape his lips twice, giving me some idea where he's got to in the narrative and how it's affecting him.

When it finishes, he shifts on the log and stares at me. "My angel in the Arizona desert, all those years ago. He was on a quest."

"I expect he was."

"I saw a sharp, bright light flying a parabolic arc high overhead. It took about ten seconds from horizon to horizon, east to west. That was him on his outward journey from Golden Lake."

"Probably."

"Then, when I met him on foot a few days later, all torn up, he was trying to get home from the Mountain. He was being hunted."

"Seems so."

"I wonder if he made it."

I guess we'll never know, but Andrew's musing isn't for me anyway. He's already on his feet and making for the clearing entrance before he remembers to ask if I need anything.

"Just your promise that what we're doing here won't harm the goldens or the people of Golden Lake village."

"Of course it won't."

"I hope not. What are you doing with these recordings?"

"I make two copies, one for me and one for Stone."

I don't like the feel of that. "What does he do with his copy? You don't know, do you? You don't know anything about him. This better not be another one of your fuck-ups."

"He's a scholar like me. We're learning about them." Pained by my lack of trust, he shakes his head as he leaves.

Thomas Appleleaf arrives shortly after my lunch. I've seen no faces in the foliage since his first visit, but my feeling of being watched hasn't gone away, and his polite appearance the moment I finish clearing up suggests my movements are being monitored.

His courtesy is helpful, mind, because Andrew only brings in enough food for me each day, and if Thomas appeared in my clearing during a mealtime, I'd feel obliged to share with him. It wouldn't surprise me to learn that he understands this situation.

I'm also completely over any embarrassment at the thought that piskies and whatever else are watching me when I leave the clearing to wash or go to the toilet. There's nothing I can do to change the situation. My options are simply to accept it or to agonise about it, so I accept it.

"Good day."

"Hello. I didn't hear you coming."

"No, you wouldn't."

Once again, I find myself conducting a seemingly innocent conversation while wondering what exactly he means by a simple phrase he drops into it like that.

My best guess is he's approached in another Wild and crossed into this one only when he reaches the clearing.

So why can't I feel that Wild's thin place? And how can I ask Thomas about it without revealing more of my own knowledge than I want to? I can't.

"Are you sleeping well?"

"Reasonably well, thank you."

"Dreaming?"

"Why do you ask?"

"Just wondering."

I drain my mug of clear cold water, aware that he's watching me and thinking he probably knows the stream water enables me to see the lake village and communicate with Lael.

Why doesn't he come out and say it?

I think he derives enjoyment from talking in circles rather than straight lines, saying things that sound clear on the surface but contain riddles and undercurrents. I'm sure he likes being in full knowledge of a situation while talking with someone who doesn't quite get what's going on. Someone like me.

If a human treated me this way, I would probably resent it. In fact, there's no probably about it. But every time my irritation threatens to surface, the little man's charming good humour smooths it away.

"There's someone you should meet." He produces a small porcelain bell, the size of a thimble, and shakes it daintily. No sound comes. Apparently, the bell has no clapper. "She won't be long."

"Who won't?"

"I won't." A little woman steps into the clearing. She's like a female version of Thomas, with a wrinkly, old, smiling face and dancing blue eyes. She wraps him in a hug and gives him a big smacking kiss on the lips. "Hello, lover."

Thomas introduces us. "This is Joe, He's a storyteller. This is my wife, Joan."

I'm a storyteller now? I suppose so. To him I am, anyway. He asked for the story of my first love, and I gave him *Mary Poppins* and *The Sound of Music*. Two for the price of one, although neither of them is really my first love. The story of Min and me is too precious to give away.

Joan tilts her head and regards me curiously. "Will you tell me a story?"

"What's it worth?"

She arches a quick eyebrow at Thomas.

He chuckles. "Joe learns fast."

"What do you want?" she asks.

"I don't think I want anything, thanks."

"What do you need?"

"I don't need anything at the moment."

"How about this then? When you need something, tell me what it is, and I'll see if I can give it to you."

"That sounds fair. What kind of story would you like to hear?"

"A true one. What other kind is there?"

So she and Thomas sit on my log, and I sit cross-legged in front of the shelter with one hand on Ban's neck, stroking behind his ear, and I tell them the story of Lael and Keni, or as much as I know of it so far. And as I talk, I try not to dwell privately on how I'm missing Min and wondering what she would think of these Wild people.

From time to time, they stop me to ask a question or discuss a point, and their interruptions become part of the narrative.

I'm touched by their evident delight in each other, which isn't dulled by their long-time-together realism and occasional knowing sharpness.

My throat is dry when I finish. I close my eyes as I drink deeply from my mug of stream water. When I open them, Thomas and Joan have disappeared as if they were never here.

But there's another presence. A big, greenish face that was among the ones I half saw before Thomas's first visit.

He's a very tall manlike creature whose features in my first days here blended into trees and bushes whenever I caught sight of him. Sometimes back then I stared hard at a tree, certain I'd seen him watching me and almost able to make out the lines of his face in a bark pattern. I think of him as the Green Man. He's never shown himself to me openly before. That he does so now is slightly unnerving.

We'll find him

Min makes a pot of coffee for Tae and Vua. She prefers to drink fruit teas and definitely isn't a fan of the rich black rocket fuel Joe loves, but he's converted the sisters to his love of coffee, so she's bought his favourite Italian Roast and brewed it his way for them. Its dark aroma rouses them from sleep, and they shuffle in to sit at the breakfast table.

Shad doesn't have a coffee in front of him and wouldn't touch it if she'd made him one, but he jumps up to sit on a chair and dips his head when they toast Joe. Then he returns to his rug and remains alert with his ears cocked, following their conversation.

Tae flashes up her laptop and scans the night's news. "Still nothing about Tyac. I don't understand why he made that big public threat to you and then disappeared again."

Min's been wondering the same thing.

Vua pours herself a second cup. "Any chance you and Joe might have got it wrong about who killed that policewoman?"

"No. His signature is too distinctive. He tears his victims apart, turns them nearly inside out, but leaves their faces and sufficient body skin intact to enable identification. I've seen or heard of exactly the same thing hundreds of times." She sighs. "Maybe thousands."

"Our legend says he shifts into a wolf every night, with no control over it. Is that true?"

"Yes."

The young women stare at each other.

"Every night," Vua repeats. "That would send me mad."

Min nods. "He's crazy mad in the dark and cleverly insane in the light."

"What does he do in the daytime?"

"He hunts us as a man."

They frown at that. Their high cheekbones, dark, watchful eyes, and thick, brown hair, brushed back and falling straight to their shoulders, reminds Min suddenly of Anya. Her strong warrior daughters will always bring honour to her memory.

"He works his way into positions of trust and power. Like a monarch's favoured advisor or a head of state security. His ideal situation is where he can live in the shadows and use his influence to have other people do his searching for him."

"What other occupations has he had?" Tae asks.

"Tax collector. Soldier. Spy. Powerful things like that. He's very intelligent." A wail rises unbidden and catches in her painful throat. "He'll tear us apart like he has every other time. He always wins. He'll find Joe and kill him. Again." Her fear and grief burst free.

Vua shuffles her chair around and hugs her. Shad nuzzles her hand and places one of his big front paws on her thigh.

A wave of guilt flows through Min's distress. It's only been twelve weeks since Tyac killed Anya. She wonders sometimes if Shad and the sisters think she's fortunate because Joe always comes back to her in a new incarnation, while their beloved wife and mother is dead and gone forever.

She melts into Vua's hug, remembers Anya's strong embrace, and dissolves in a fresh wave of tears.

Tae glares at her laptop screen and renews the search. "The bastard is out there somewhere. We'll find him."

On dying wings

THE HUNTERS BUILD a huge fire deep inside the Mountain and call to Keni. I feel his fear, and Lael's. It's like we're right there with him. Big black shadows flicker on rock walls everywhere in the red light from the fire far below, and the baying voices echo eerily.

The goldens warned him about this too. He can't understand the Mountain men's words, but the taunting tones make their meaning very clear.

Everyone knows this is the most dangerous thing a questor can face. If these men capture him, they'll hand him over to their priests, who will sacrifice him and eat his still-beating heart.

Daylight comes and goes far overhead. He has only tonight to fly free, he estimates, before his wings grow weak and wither away. His only option then would be to climb out, and a climbing escape from the Mountain is generally considered to be the most vulnerable part of anyone's quest.

The longer he leaves it, the shorter flight time his dying wings will allow. But the choice isn't his to make. He can only remain alert and wait for any opportunity to fly that his tormenters might offer him.

All day he's been surrounded by scuffling footfalls, disembodied muttering voices, and open flames burning on his hunters' smoking torches. Many times, when his hiding place was clearly illuminated, he wondered how they failed to see him.

Once, when he and Lael were children, Lu showed them how his goldenness can be absorbed in firelight, rendering him almost invisible in certain circumstances. It seems Keni's skin might have that advantage in his temporary condition.

At dusk, after the search teams all headed back up to the mouth of the Mountain, the silence below suggests they've left him alone inside.

He listens keenly before moving in tiny increments, careful to make no noise as he gradually dislodges his stony disguise. He creeps to the mouth of his little cave, freezing for long moments and alert for any sign that this is a trap, preparing to fly and hoping they won't see him and shoot him down.

He is about to fly when the small noise of a scraped pebble reaches his sensitive ears.

Someone is hiding nearby.

He concentrates his supercharged senses.

A rapid heartbeat thrums on the edge of his hearing. It narrows down his ambusher's position to behind one of the big rocks in a spill that stretches across the wide ledge outside the cave. Fast, shallow breathing accompanies the heartbeat.

Another pebble moves, and this one rolls into view down the shallow incline of the spill. Then a man's head appears above a big rock.

He looks young, about Keni's age, and his twitchy movements betray his anxiety as he peeks over the rock then drops out of sight again.

Has he seen his golden quarry? Or heard him, perhaps? Everything about the young man suggests he's in a state of nervous excitement. Maybe he thinks he's seen something but wants confirmation before he makes a fool of himself by raising a false alarm.

Whatever the case, Keni has to assume that discovery is imminent.

He has but two options. He can disable the man and fly clear. Or he can hope the man will give up and leave. If he chooses the second option, he might lose his wings, leaving him to climb out on foot and face unknown dangers on the Mountain's outer surface.

Lu said he'll be travelling a long way through snow in the mountains and that he'll need clothing. The young man preparing to spring a trap is wearing clothing.

He weighs one of the gold nuggets in his hand, steadies his breathing, and waits for the ambusher to show himself again.

His moment comes immediately, when the young Mountain man pokes his head above the rock in exactly the same place as before.

Keni steps from his hiding place and slings the dull, yellow rock. It hits the man square in the centre of his forehead, and he drops from sight in a slither of stones.

No further noise comes. There is deep silence inside the Mountain. Keni can't even hear the man's heartbeat anymore.

His own heart sinks. He hurries to the spill and tries to revive the man, but his skull is broken, and his life has ended. Unaccustomed to golden strength, Keni threw the nugget far harder than he intended.

He bows his head and apologises to the young man's spirit for his clumsy error, wishing him peace and good travels in the next place. Then he retrieves the gold nugget, strips the man of his clothing and thick animal skin boots, bundles the still warm textiles under one arm, and flies vertically, naked and glowing golden, beating his wings as powerfully as he can and heading for the sky.

Angry shouts sound as soon as he bursts from the mouth of the Mountain, and he swerves to avoid arrows shooting past him from different directions. He keeps flying straight up. His wing beats are already getting weaker, so as soon as he's climbed beyond the range of arrows, he tips to the north at a shallow angle and faces cold air on his gliding descent.

He coasts back to earth on dying wings and lands heavily on a rocky outcrop atop a different mountain, crunching both knees and losing skin from the heels of his hands, elbows, and chin.

*

"I'm glad Keni escaped from the Mountain."

"So am I." Lael's relief fills my mind like a glorious sunset. *"I've been terrified for him."*

Having said that, if my interpretation of what I saw overnight is correct, Keni is somewhere near the west coast of America in the Wild, so he still has a long haul ahead before he even reaches the Atlantic. And how he will cross the ocean to get back home, I have no idea.

Where is the Mountain? I imagine some old Western movie actor talking about there being gold in them there hills. California?

"Where are you, Joe?"

I visualise the footpath above the lake. Lael stands in the shallows below. The other goldens swim together some distance away. *"I'm here."*

"So you are." She smiles and waves. *"At least, your spirit is."*

That's interesting. *"What do I look like to you?"*

"Like water in the shape of a man. Similar to an elder golden, except you're transparent."

Fair enough. *"I'd like to visit your lake. Then you can see me properly."*

"We're always here. You will always be welcome."

"Thank you." Through the oak I feel Andrew's familiar footsteps approaching the bottom of my hill. He's late. *"I have to go now. See you later."*

She waves goodbye.

Andrew takes a seat on the log with barely a nod in my direction, staring out at tall sheets of rain walking in from the sea and across the distant hills.

"Good morning to you, too."

"Hm?" He glances up, but then returns his gaze to the horizon. "Oh. Yes. Morning." His body language says trouble.

I proffer the used recorder. "Something wrong?"

His shoulders slump, and he releases a long, burdened sigh. "Merritt."

"What about him?"

"His thugs were crawling all over Looe this morning. I saw them as soon as I walked into town, but it was too late. Two of the bastards hustled me into a back street, roughed me up, and gave me a fancy little device with a recorded message. I took it back to the house and transferred it to this." He swaps recorders with me, one for one.

"How did they find you?"

"I don't know."

"Andrew."

He holds eye contact for the first time. "I don't know." He nods at the recorder in my hand as he slips yesterday's one into a pocket. "You better listen to that. I'm sorry."

This doesn't sound good. I press play.

"Hello, Joe." It's my mother's voice. *"We're very worried about you. We heard about poor Carole and Tony being murdered in the summer. We only heard about it through the newspapers our friends sent over. We tried to call you, but you've disappeared off the face of the earth."*

My father mutters something in the background.

"Your father says you should have contacted us to put our minds at ease. Honestly, Joe, we're not sure we know who you are anymore. What's happening in your life? What's going on?"

Her voice threatens to crack, and she goes quiet for a moment with the recorder still running. A low-pitched machinery noise fills the pause. Air conditioning? Florida is probably still hot in late September.

"A policeman has come to see us. Detective Chief Inspector Dawson. He says you know him. He's a nice man. Apparently, there's been another murder in London and the police want to speak to you again. He says you're on the run!" She sobs and breaks off.

"Joe, this is Ian Dawson."

I recognise his soft Scottish accent. I respected him when he interviewed me in the summer. Even liked him, for a policeman. But I certainly don't like this new tactic of involving my parents. Upsetting them.

"I'm attached to the Home Office now, in Sebastian Merritt's department."

My heart sinks. There goes another good character assessment down the drain.

"You may have heard that my colleague, Detective Sergeant Smith, has been murdered. I'm sure you'll remember her. The investigation into her murder is running in parallel with our original investigation, which was never closed, so I know you'll understand that we need to talk with you again. To eliminate you from our enquiries. This isn't going away, Joe."

Obviously not, if he's flown all the way to bloody Florida to drag my parents into it. Devious bastard.

"This is your father."

Yes, I know.

"God only knows what you've got yourself mixed up in, but you need to sort it out. Do it for your mother's sake, even if you don't care about yourself anymore. DCI Lawson is staying over here for a few days, and we're all hoping you'll contact whoever it is you have to contact. Apparently," his disappointment in me oozes from every word, *"you know exactly who that is and what you have to do."*

His breathing tells me he's getting angry. I could have scripted his next speech for him.

"We all know responsibility isn't your strong suit. You walked away from everything that was good in your life two years ago. Including us. But now it's time for you to grow up and deal with this mess."

After some brief fumbling noises, my mother's voice comes again. *"DCI Lawson says his department will pay for us to fly over to England. He thinks it might help."*

I bet he does.

"So, if we haven't heard anything in a few days, that's what we'll do. Take care, Joe. We love you."

She's crying when the recording ends.

I sit on the log, stewing, tossing the recorder from hand to hand.

"Don't sling it," Andrew says. "We need it for today's recording."

"Fuck today's recording."

We sit in heavy silence for a while.

"Your dad isn't your number one fan."

"No."

He gives one of his infuriating sage-like nods. "It happens."

"More to the point, what are we going to do about this?"

"What do you want to do?"

"Stop the bastards from flying my parents over, for fuck's sake. I'm sure Dawson thinks this is all good and above board, but we know it's a threat. Merritt is telling me that unless I join his operation, he'll hurt my family. Isn't he?"

"Yes."

"So tell him I'll join."

"You sure?"

"You think I have a choice?"

He shakes his head.

"Which brings us back to how he found you in Looe."

"I told you, I don't know."

"Yeah."

He bristles. "You calling me a liar?"

"It wouldn't be the first time you've lied and betrayed people who trust you. And what about Min? Those bastards got to my parents easily enough. What's to stop them hunting Min down and using her as more leverage over me? I suppose now you'll tell me again that you've never mentioned her to Merritt, won't you?"

"Here's your fucking food." He throws today's haversack at me, snatches up the one holding yesterday's dirty clothing, and storms away down the hill.

I don't call him back.

Paths and patterns

I'M NOT IN the mood to talk to anyone, so I grow myself all the way into the great oak and let its immense gentle peace soothe me.

Thomas and Joan turn up, as I thought they would. Their sudden appearance without any warning confirms for me that they've arrived from another Wild.

I've searched my clearing's perimeter for thin places and found none, so evidently they have a different means of stepping between realities. I want to know how they do that. It'll be another string in my bow, and I look forward to surprising Min and Shad and the sisters with it. One day it might save our lives.

They call to me, Thomas and Joan, but I don't feel like responding. They're about to leave when the Green Man grows out of an elm at the edge of the tree break and points to my oak.

I don't know how long he's been there.

Thomas and Joan exchange a look, then thank the Green Man and leave. He stares pointedly in my direction before following them. None of them leave any kind of trail for me to track, even with my tree-enhanced senses.

The clearing hems me in. I don't feel trapped, exactly. I could walk out of here, out of Andrew's deal with Stone, any time I want. I don't even feel claustrophobic because that's only a word to me with my ability to exist inside a tree. Itchy is the best description. I'm emotionally itchy.

I stretch up with the oak, up to its highest leaves, and push my face into open air. Instant relief. I don't breathe inside a tree.

Couldn't, even if I wanted to, but the point is that I don't need to breathe air in a tree and I never miss it.

So, although I enjoy the taste of clean air at the top of my oak, the best thing is its mind-nourishing panoramic view and my feeling of freedom in boundless space. Three hundred and sixty degrees of shiny wet hills greet me beneath a misty sky.

Some trees are starting to turn yellow, some lime green, some are bursts of crimson, and a fan-stand of three tall aspens on a nearby hill to the north have already shed their lower leaves. But most trees still shine in the final days of their summer greenery. In three directions, they blanket hills rolling away with no interruptions to the horizon and no evidence of human activity. In the south, they slope down to the sea, only a mile away.

The coastline is abrupt, ending in sheer cliffs, and to my immediate south, a pretty little bay invites the mental image of sparkling blue water on a sunny day.

But not today, when clouds hang low, and my green siblings relish the moisture for their thirsty leaves.

A circular gap in the trees in the near southwest reveals a hill, bare of any vegetation except rough grass and topped by an outcrop of rock that's probably granite. The hill is unique among its heavily wooded neighbours and draws my attention to a pattern of tracks that appear to radiate from it.

They're rough and ragged, overgrown with late-summer exuberance. The only one wide enough to deserve the name *path* runs straight from the hill in my direction and passes close by the clearing below.

But if I let my eyes lose focus, the tracks combine to form a shape of some sort, almost familiar and yet not quite. A dragonfly, perhaps? I'd probably need to see it from the air to make any sense of it.

My lion is on the path.

The one who protected me in my boyhood dreams, and who showed himself to me briefly at Flo's funeral, which was my first ever experience of the Wild.

He isn't alone. Twenty or more lions of all ages and sizes emerge from the trees and stand behind him, including several other males with dark manes like his, although none are as fine. None are as imposing as he. There's no doubt that he leads the pride. He reigns as its king.

He looks directly at me. The others do too. The impact of their collective gaze is strong, but there's no threat in it. I'm supported. Protected. Safe.

My lion turns and leads his pride back into the trees. I can no longer see them, or even guess after a while where they are in the forest, but their existence encourages me.

I return to the base of my oak, refreshed and invigorated by my sightseeing trip, and decide that when the rain stops, I will walk the path.

Countless turns of the seasons ago

As I spend time in Lael's company, it dawns on me that her path is a spiritual one. She tells me this is unusual for a young golden.

Her parents and the three other living goldens are warrior protectors of the people. It's what questors always aspire to be, and what the successful ones always become. At least, they do at first. But eventually, some are drawn to a more spiritual life, and they are the ones likely to become active elders in the lake when they pass on.

Myen and Lu think Lael is being drawn to that life, but she isn't yet sure. She does know she's more comfortable with a peaceful existence than one of power and might. She's happiest spending time in the lake, absorbing her people's history from the elders and sharing it with those who want to hear, especially the children.

Today, many youngsters have come down to the lake, attracted by Keni's exciting departure and hoping to hear one of Lael's tales. I want to hear it too. The children range from babies in the arms of their older siblings to those who aren't much younger than Lael and Keni. The oldest among them is Awin, a quietly thoughtful girl who wants to quest and whose time will probably come during the next turn of seasons.

"Will you tell us the story of how our people got here?" she asks.

Lael smiles. "I already told that one."

The children protest. "You told it quickly," pipes up a boy, "and you promised to tell us the whole story another time."

"Tell us now," several children chorus.

"I will." Lael closes her eyes, as if thinking where to begin her story. But what she's doing is searching for a connection with someone else, or something else. It's like she's searching for the story so she can see it clearly while she relates it.

Her breathing slows and steadies.

Sitting in dappled afternoon sunlight on the bank of my stream, with my back grown into the oak and my feet dangling above the running water, my breathing slows with hers. We're swimming underwater. Not swimming exactly, more being pulled through the depths at speed, without feeling any motion, as might happen in a dream.

There are other beings down here, glimmering with flashes of gold. I can't see them properly. They're too faint and I'm moving too fast. Then I surface in an arid place, a desert under an incredibly deep blue sky and a baking hot sun.

Lael is ready. Her eyes are still closed.

I leave mine closed too and see the folk memories she has tuned into.

"Countless turns of the seasons ago, we came from the sea in canoes to live on a land of sand and sun and mountains. We lived there freely, in peace, mining the mountains for gold and using it to make beautiful things. Our priests led us. They were wise men who lived among us and taught us the mysteries of life."

"Like our priests," a boy says.

"Yes, like our priests. We lived there for a very long time, until a new nation of people arrived in the land and made life difficult for us."

"Did they come from the sea too?" a girl asks.

"No. They came by land, across the distant frozen wastes but spreading steadily down the coast towards us. There were only small numbers of them at first, but more and more came until there was no room in the land for them and us.

They were aggressive and wanted the land for themselves alone. Our priests did all they could to protect us, but we weren't warlike people like the newcomers.

"We had to leave, so the priests led us to a deeper place. We stayed on the same Mountain we always lived upon, but now our Mountain was in a new land, where the newcomers couldn't see us."

Some of the children frown, but I understand from Lael's description that their ancestors' priests led them into the Wild.

"Those priests of long ago found new mysteries in their new home, new magic, and a new way of ensuring the people's safety. They learned to fly and marked the land with the patterns of their flight. Yes, patterns like our priests have made here. It's a symbolic part of our tradition.

"But the ancient priests used the patterns to protect the people. They patrolled them and were as aggressive and territorial as the newcomers who forced us off our original land. The priests went out in the night and returned to the old homeland. They attacked the newcomers, stealing individuals back to sacrifice them on the Mountain and eat their hearts."

The children gasp in dismay and shock.

"Why?" Awin asks.

"Why did they eat the hearts?"

Awin nods.

"It became an important part of their religion. The priests gained strength and power from the magic of those sacrificial ceremonies, which they used to protect the people."

She pauses while the children digest this information.

"We lived for a very long time in this new place, mining gold from the Mountain and living peacefully again. Descendants of those who stayed still live there today. But after many turns of the seasons, a group of people decided to venture out farther into the land. They wanted to explore, away from the ocean, to see if there was somewhere else they might live."

"Why did they want to do that?" someone asks.

"They disagreed with some of the things the priests were doing. Particularly the sacrifices. They wanted to live their own way."

I don't blame them. Those ancient priests sound like something out of a nightmare.

"Did they fight?" a young boy asks.

"No, there was no fight. They parted peacefully and promised to keep in touch. They simply wanted to live in a different way, to walk different paths. And they did keep in touch. People from the split-off group returned to the Mountain regularly. They took gifts with them and stories of new experiences, and the Mountain people gave them gold to take back. The split-off group travelled across a great land, living in different places as they went but never settling anywhere for long, until after many turns, they reached the coast of another ocean. There they settled around a lake, which they called Lake Sunrise."

"Like our Golden Lake," a child says.

"Yes, very like our lake. And the descendants of that group of people still live there, many, many, *many* turns later. But after a time, things between them and the Mountain people became unfriendly. They were like two different peoples. The priests remained strong in their leadership of the Mountain people, while some of the Lake Sunrise people became goldens."

"Like you," an excited little voice shouts.

"Like me. But to become goldens, the people of Lake Sunrise needed gold from the Mountain, and the Mountain people didn't want to give it to them anymore. They protected it fiercely. Whenever young people flew to the Mountain on a quest, the Mountain men tried to capture them. If they caught one, the priests sacrificed the captive and ate his or her heart, like they'd done to the invaders on those far-off days of old.

"After many more turns, another split-off group of the Lake Sunrise people left to travel across the ocean. That group were our ancestors, who settled here in Golden Lake."

"But you still have to fly back to the Mountain for gold," a young boy says.

"Yes. Each questor brings back a small piece of gold as a magical token of the journey. Our ancestors hoped to find the same sort of power in other sources of gold, but they never did. There's a magical process in the act of getting the gold from the Mountain that doesn't exist anywhere else. So those who wish to become goldens must go to the Mountain and back for their transformation to take place. That's the quest. That's where Keni has gone now."

"Fool that he is," cuts in an adult male voice.

Lael's eyes open, and through them I see a young man dressed in a dark robe. His cheeks are covered in an intricate pattern of branding that's been dyed coal black.

"We shouldn't waste our young people," he tells Lael. "We don't need any more goldens."

The children lower their eyes. They don't look frightened of the young man, whom I assume is one of their priests. It's more like they respect both him and Lael and want no part of an argument between them.

"Greetings, Noala," Lael says.

"We don't need you," he insists, his eyes glinting with youthful fervour. I recognise a firebrand when I see one, and this young man looks like trouble.

"It's for the people to decide who they need," Lael says. Her voice is calm. "Not for you or me. Priests and goldens have existed side by side for many turns. It works. There's no need for conflict between us. We both bring value to the community. The people need your strengths and our strengths."

I think about that. Goldens give the people healing and protection. Maybe more, but that's what I know they bring to the relationship. What do the priests bring? Wisdom and leadership? And what do the people give back as their part of the bargain? Status and respect for the priests, probably. What do they give the goldens?

Love. Lael's emotion fills me and explains it more completely than words could.

I understand.

Noala tosses his head. "We don't need you."

Lael looks at the children, who raise their eyes to her.

Awin watches Noala stalk away. "Why is he so angry?"

"I don't know. He and Keni and I were friends when we were children."

Awin looks troubled. "Does he hate me because I want to be a golden?"

"No. I don't think he hates me either. He isn't a bad man. He wants to protect our people and he believes the priests' way is the only way."

"It's sad," Awin says.

Privately, Lael agrees.

Quests new and old

HUNTERS ARE ON Keni's trail. Their hounds started baying in the distance as soon as he landed, and I share his gut-wrenching terror of them. The baying reminds me of Tyac howling for my destruction. I have to work hard to keep putting that association aside and focus on Keni's plight.

He runs with the pull from the Mountain behind him, the taste of the ocean wind to his weak hand, and the pulls from Lake Sunrise and Golden Lake to his strong hand. Every time he pauses to listen, he fears the dogs sound closer, but he runs at a steady pace and eventually thinks they're falling behind. For now, at least.

His wings are useless burdens, shedding themselves in dull strips as he runs and shrivelling on the bare rock path. He stopped at his landing spot for only as long as it took to haul on the Mountain man's trousers and strap the stiffened hide boots to his feet, and he's grateful for them now. When the remnants of his wings finally fall away, he puts on the shirt too.

His borrowed golden strength and energy will last some days more. Lael had urged him to make the best use of it, to head into the snow and put as much distance as possible between him and the hunters before he hops into the loud world.

He'll need food soon. He could continue running at this pace for several days without it, but unless he takes on fuel as he goes, he will pay dearly for such excess once the golden strength leaves him.

He expects to reach the first thin place by sunset. Its image burns in his mind as if he's actually been there himself instead of seeing it the memories Lael and her parents planted in him.

Once through the thin place, he expects to find food in one of the shelters people in this mountainous part of the loud world build to assist strangers. He intends to eat well there before continuing his run farther into the north.

As he runs, he grieves for the man he killed. For the life he ended so stupidly. For the loss of his own innocence.

There are moments when he regrets following the quest. Despite wanting this more than anything since he was a child, he wonders if it's worth the cost. It's the tragedy that sours the experience, rather than the danger. He's always known there will be danger for him. He never considered that it might harm someone else.

Questing has already affected his family. He's lived with his father's bitterness and his mother's silent sorrow his whole life. But he forged ahead in his ambition, regardless of their feelings.

His love for Lael grew alongside their shared desire to become goldens. He misses those far-off days of sunny childhood innocence. He misses Lael and his mother, and even his emotionally remote father. He misses Golden Lake and wonders if he will ever see it again.

Even with golden memories of the thin place planted firmly in him, he's so upset by the young man's death, he nearly runs past the place at dusk. It's the sound of a high vertical waterfall from the other side of a ravine that alerts him to its presence, and he stutters his pounding feet to a halt.

On his side of the sheer drop, five man-lengths ahead of him, a sharp slot two man-lengths deep and half a length wide is cut into the valley wall.

This is it. In the absence of knowledge from his golden friends he would have veered away from the edge and jogged around the slot, bit he knows now what exists in the air above it.

He runs at it as fast as he can and leaps across, seeing in his mind's eye not only the bare rain-polished rock of his world but also a shimmering slender passage in mid-air that will take him into a new world.

A shiver crawls over his skin as his feet leave solid ground, and as he passes through the thin place every muscle in his body jumps at once. He lands on the other side and continues running, feeling taller and stronger and experiencing little echoes of the shiver across his shoulders as he leaves the thin place behind.

He's in the loud world. It doesn't look any different at first glance. Certainly doesn't sound any different. But the air is colder on his face, and something about it tastes odd. He pounds along the slender path that he knows in advance will run down the valley face, until he arrives at the sturdy little log cabin he expects to find there.

It's unoccupied but well-stocked by the generous mountain people of the loud world with food and dry clothing for strangers in need. He eats and drinks, changes into dry trousers and shirt, and puts on a thick quilted jacket with deep pockets that hold the two golden nuggets easily, one to secure his flight back across the ocean by a Lake Sunrise golden, and one to put into Lake Golden when he gets home.

If he gets home.

He shoulders a backpack full of food and continues on his way.

*

An old man in a dark cloak shuffles across the wide foreshore to the edge of the lake, where Lael sits in meditation.

She bows her head to him respectfully, and he returns the greeting before lowering himself awkwardly to sit on a rock.

"Good evening, Mahu."

"Good evening." He scans the clear sky. "It's a pleasant one."

"It is." Lael looks out over the lake to avoid making eye contact and putting him under any more pressure than he must already be feeling.

Eventually, he says, "I assume you're his watcher."

"Yes."

"How is he faring?"

"He escaped the Mountain and is running far ahead of his hunters."

"Hunters?"

"While making his escape, he killed one of the Mountain men."

The old priest's sigh seems to last forever.

"He didn't intend to take the man's life. He is grieving for his action."

"Of course he is." Mahu's gaze is fixed on the waters below his feet. "But that won't prevent them from hunting him until they catch him. Nothing will stop them now. He is lost."

"He's running strong and has every chance of evading them."

"In the circumstances, that is unlikely."

"You did it."

"He's only a boy."

"How old were you when you ran your quest?"

The answer stays inside his mind, and when Lael looks up, his rheumy eyes are fixed on the yellow moon. "I heard about a new conflict between you and Noala today."

"As far as I'm concerned, there's no conflict."

"I understand that. I will try to calm things down among the young priests. The people don't need to be made anxious by disharmony between us."

"I agree. Thank you."

He stands with a pained wince and bids her goodnight.

"Keni's father?" I ask.

"Yes. Mahu is the high priest of the people. He's our most honoured person alive. Many turns ago, he came back from the dead. Now he leads the people with wisdom."

"How did he come back from the dead?"

"In his youth, he was the strongest and fastest of all his friends. There was never any doubt that he would become a golden. As soon as he was old enough, he trained for the quest."

"Were you a child then?"

She laughs. *"This all happened many turns before I was born. How old do you think I am?"*

"I've no idea."

"I'm as old as I look. We're all as old as we look."

I give an embarrassed chuckle. *"I didn't realise. But I haven't seen any old goldens."*

"We usually pass on before we get old. Although some of us don't go very far but become one with the lake as elders."

"So, tell me about Mahu."

"He flew away on his quest and his outward journey went well, but he was caught inside the Mountain, and their priests tortured him. When a questor's wings fall away on the return journey, it's natural. It doesn't hurt. But they ripped Mahu's out of his back. It must have been agony.

"Once his goldenness left, his watcher lost him completely. All the people knew was that he was captured. They thought him dead, but the Mountain men kept him in a cage underground and brought him out to be tortured night after night. Only his courage kept him alive through it all."

"Why did they do that? I thought their priests ate hearts for their magic. Why torture too?"

"They hate us. What used to be a quick death in the time of our ancestors has become an extended period of torture, during which they keep their captives alive for as long as possible before the final ceremony. Mahu's terrible experience was the first we knew of this development. He's the only one who ever came back to tell us."

This is what Keni will face if they catch him. My respect for his and Lael's and the other goldens' courage climbs even higher.

"Three cycles of the moon later, Mahu's childhood friend, Sona, flew out on his quest. Unfortunately, the men saw him and shot him with many arrows before he could enter the Mountain. He fell from the sky and died. In the confusion, Mahu killed one of his guards and escaped.

The Mountain men chased him. Incensed at the death of their man, they hunted him right across that wide land. He was weak, starved, and in terrible pain. He was dying, but he refused to die many times over the following cycles. Hunting dogs from the Mountain caught up with him more than once, but he escaped their jaws every time, although with new injuries and pain to carry. By the time he reached the coast, he was like a shadow."

"So he went to Lake Sunrise," I say. *"And they looked after him."*

"No. He didn't have gold to pay them for the journey home."

I'm appalled. *"They refused him?"*

"They didn't refuse him. He didn't go to them because he assumed they would."

"Would they have? Really?"

"I don't believe so. Even before I met them, I've never thought they would do that to any of us. Mahu was young, and I believe he misunderstood the dynamic. I believe if he'd arrived at Lake Sunrise, they would have taken him in, cared for him, healed him, and brought him home."

She slips into the water and ducks her head under and out in a single smooth movement, rising with her copper hair shining in the moonlight. *"He and I have talked of this, and he agrees. He says in his youth, he saw things only in terms of day or night. Now, with age and experience, he sees many shades of dawn and dusk between the two extremes.*

"Still, his courage didn't desert him, even though his physical strength had. He made a boat for himself and sailed it across the ocean to us. People couldn't believe what they were seeing when he walked into the village. They'd given him up for dead

more than a full turn of the seasons earlier. They'd mourned his passing and honoured his memory. But there he was, like a spirit among them.

"They say it took many more cycles to heal him than it had taken him to journey to the Mountain and back. Sona's sister, Annam, nursed him back to health, and later they became husband and wife. Mahu's strength of body never returned, but the purposeful mind that brought him back to us has never left him.

"We honour his courage, experience, and wisdom. He's a peacemaker among us. Were it not for him, there have been many times when conflict between young priests and goldens might have torn the people apart. But Mahu is always there to calm thing down and bring us together in understanding."

This heroic description doesn't tally with what I heard earlier. *"You said Mahu was mean and horrible to Keni all through his childhood because he wanted to become a golden. He even stopped the boy's mother from talking to him. That doesn't sound to me like someone who respects goldens. Or even likes you. It certainly doesn't sound like a peacemaker."*

"His problems with Keni's questing are rooted in his own terrible experience. He feared his son would be hurt the same way he was, and he tried everything possible to dissuade him from pursuing his dream."

"Even withholding his love."

"Yes, even that. But the problems in his family life have never distracted him from his wider duties. He's a wise and gentle peacemaker. We love him."

Fair enough. To me, the old man sounds like a weapons-grade arsehole, but I haven't grown up in their culture, and I suppose they know him better than I do. Also, I acknowledge my own emotional baggage.

House of Ramesses

THE SEARING SUN beats down without mercy. The Procession of Preparation won't begin for some hours yet, but already crowds are gathering on both sides of the broad avenue, from the banks of the Nile through the great city to the shining new temple that will be dedicated this day to the lion god, Maahes.

Min crouches in a closed doorway to shelter from the relentless sun, and to avoid the stares of those who would pity or scorn her.

Knowledge of his dismissal of her has spread quickly, and, although the facts as reported are untrue, the effect of it isn't. When he turned his back on her advice, and she walked away, expecting him to follow, he hadn't.

It's quite possibly her worst error of judgement ever, and her enemies, *their* enemies if only he would see the truth, have pounced on the incident publicly and driven a wedge too deep to heal easily. Given his pride and determination, it might be too deep to heal in this life.

Her last hope is that he'll see her from the head of the procession and his heart will soften. If it doesn't happen, she will leave the city and watch his life from afar. She's already wounded, and it will hurt horribly to walk away, but she can't stay and see him race to his terrible death again. Not so soon. Not in two consecutive lifetimes.

She settles into her crouch with her back pressed flat against the shadowed wall.

The cheering crowd restores her to full awareness before he comes into view. He stands proud in his chariot, bare-chested and muscular, with scars old and new decorating his skin and his braided mane of red hair framing his strong face.

Pharaoh's Spear. The Scarlet Lord. Lion of Egypt. The names he inherited from his predecessor fit him like a skin, and well they should, for it was he who wore them in his last life when he was born to a different royal mother but the same father, the Great Ramesses.

Only he and she know that he lives again as his own younger brother. Unusually, this time he remembers his recent past existence as clearly as she does.

His first life as a prince of Egypt was glorious but brief, as is so horribly often the case when the lion grows strong in him. He died at the age of twenty-four years, and his living even so long had been a surprise to her. He hunted Tyac across the wide Nile delta for three years before finding success and fatal failure in the same catastrophic moment.

And now he's doing it again, embarking on the same course that will lead inevitably to the same tragic end. She has no doubt that Tyac already knows about him, and she expects this life to be even briefer than the last one.

He's here, his war chariot leading the procession. Her heart thumps so, she's sure her neighbours must hear it over their cheering. But no matter, because he's seen her.

He looks directly into her eyes, and she cries out in the delicious pain of love and hope.

Then he looks away, turns his face to the road and leaves her in the dust of a hundred horse chariots and a thousand foot soldiers.

Those around her still jump up and down and cheer madly, but in the midst of them, her world stands silent and still, except for her tears flowing unchecked.

In Manchester, she sobs herself awake as sunrise illuminates the yellow brown bricks outside her bedroom window.

Her pillowcase is damp. Her head aches as if someone's brained her with a sledgehammer.

This is the fourth time since Joe left with Andrew that she's dreamed the same vivid memory of that day in ancient Per-Ramessu.

It scares her, more than anything has in a very long time.

Jhed

KENI FEARS HE is being tracked closely, but he can't locate his stalker. He doesn't think it's the Mountain men. Their stealthy but rapid movements make distinctive noises, which he last heard two days ago when a small hunting party passed within calling distance while he rested beneath the roots of a great fallen tree. If they hadn't been so intent on speed, they might have caught him.

The incident taught him to value his own stealth over speed. There's no knowing when another fast-moving party might appear. He doesn't even know if the main pack he left behind in the mountains four days ago is still following his trail.

I can relate to his caution. It reminds me of running through the Wild with Min when Tyac first located our trail in the early summer, before memories and skills from my previous lives started to awake. Despite our terror, and my desperate need to put as much space as possible between him and us, Min insisted we backtrack frequently and lay false trails for the pursuing monster to follow.

I miss her. Our uninhibited closeness. The way we finish each other's thoughts. Laugh at unspoken jokes. Always know when the other needs a hug. I even miss the brittleness that started to grow between us on that first terrified flight and has now become an unacknowledged barrier that makes conversation awkward and leaves too much unsaid.

I miss her badly. There's a Min-shaped emptiness in the middle of my existence.

When we get back together, I'll talk with her about this communication thing. We'll find a way to fix it. Our love is too big for us to endanger it over stupid things like different approaches and competing egos.

We'll make it right again.

Keni's near miss persuades him to travel mostly in the loud world, despite its unknown dangers and the bitter taste of iron in its air when he came down from the mountains. He's become accustomed to that while he runs anyway, and its strength is reduced now in the majestic forest of towering trees.

Whoo. A low-pitched call carries through the morning mist.

He stands still. It's impossible to know where the sound came from, or even how close it is. Water drips from saturated trees, and mist swirls everywhere in strange shapes and shadows.

His heightened senses are attuned for whatever might be out there. The call isn't repeated immediately, so he picks up his pace and is soon running through the forest again. He feels vulnerable, sure that he's being watched.

Whoo.

It comes from somewhere on his strong-hand side and sounds closer than the first call. He freezes in place and waits for more, cupping his hands behind his ears to aid his already enhanced hearing.

No more mysterious calls come, and nothing moves except a light breath of breeze that washes the ground mist around.

He crouches low, squinting up a shallow rise to the near skyline in the direction of the last call. Trees and ground plants stand silhouetted in stark contrast against the milky-white sky, but no creature moves in his line of sight.

As he places his foot quietly to continue walking, a sharp snap sounds just ahead, like a strong tree branch cracking in a storm. Silence holds for tense moments, until an agonised low moan comes from the same direction.

A disgusting smell hits Keni in the face, like rotten meat and faeces and vomit all mixed together and stirred in a pot over hot embers. He gags and turns to flee, filled with unreasoning terror.

But he doesn't run, and he doesn't know why when every fibre in his body is screaming at him to escape. Something makes him pause and consider, although he filters the air with a hand over his nose and mouth.

The agonised moan comes again, but quieter this time. It ends in a sob.

Something is hurt. Its voice suggests it's something big. Even with the best of intentions, trying to help an injured creature can be a dangerous undertaking.

There's also that repulsive smell. And the still-strong instinct to be somewhere else, anywhere else, as soon as possible.

But his other instincts tell him this creature means him no harm. It's watched him all morning, he thinks. It could have attacked any time it wanted to, but it didn't even threaten him.

He approaches cautiously, peering ahead, listening hard, until the breeze lifts a patch of mist, and he sees a gigantic bear-like animal curled up on the ground.

One of its legs is trapped in a vicious device that's chained to a tree trunk and must have been hidden in the grass. The creature is trying to prise the trap apart. Blood shines on its fur and on the trap's iron teeth. It falls back with another distressed moan, and tears squeeze from the corners of its tightly closed eyes.

The smell is more terrible than ever, but Keni's instincts to help the poor creature override the blind fear impulse. He takes a tentative step forward.

Its eyes jerk open, and it utters a gasp of alarm.

"Let me help." Keni slips off his backpack and lowers it to the ground in small, smooth, unthreatening movements. "I won't hurt you."

The creature gives a trembling sigh, and the horrible smell fades away as if it never existed.

Keni seizes the trap and opens its jaws a bit. They're very strong. He manages to ease their teeth away from the creature's leg for a moment, but the jaws force themselves back together, and the animal gasps in terrible pain.

Only golden strength will open the trap far enough to release its captive. Keni's reservoir of golden strength is nearly gone, and what he wants to do might empty it completely, but he doesn't give it a second thought. He takes a great breath, grips the trap jaws again, and forces them wide apart.

The animal drags its torn leg clear and holds it, whimpering.

Keni lets the trap snap shut and touches the creature's ankle, trying to ask permission without words.

Its hairy feet are shaped like a man's, but they are as broad as Keni's thigh and as long as his lower leg.

It studies him through big, brown, liquid eyes for some beats, before lying back to let him examine its bloody wounds.

Keni smooths thick, shaggy hair away from the jagged rips on both inner and outer sides of its enormous calf muscle. Dark blood fills the puncture holes, running freely.

Goldens heal hurt and sick villagers. Lael's father, Lu, fixed Keni's arm when he broke it playing hockey as a boy, and during this past turn since Lael became a golden, he's watched her heal many children with bumps and scratches, and some adults with more serious injuries and illnesses.

He has no idea how it works or even how to summon it, but he doesn't doubt that his borrowed goldenness contains the ability to heal. His aching tiredness tells him the goldenness is all but exhausted, so he doesn't know if he can repair the creature's wound until it's as good as new, but he's determined to at least make a start on it.

He folds his hands around the calf muscle and holds his palms to the wounds, closes his eyes the way he's seen goldens close theirs when healing someone, and envisions the creature's leg whole again.

Warmth blossoms in his hands, reminding him of Lu's warm healing touch on his arm. It took several sessions to knit his bone back together. He hopes this damaged muscle and flesh will be quicker to heal.

The creature releases a grateful moan and relaxes visibly. It taps a broad brown fingernail to its huge chest and says, "Jhed."

"Jed?"

He repeats his name, emphasising the soft *J* sound, and Keni corrects his pronunciation.

Jhed rewards him with a wide smile. He taps his chest again, "Jhed," then points to Keni.

"Keni."

Jhed strokes Keni's warm hand with his leathery fingertips. "Keni. Whoo."

His breath is fresh and pleasant. Nothing about him smells like the disgusting odour he exuded earlier, which Keni assumes must be some sort of automatic defence under stress.

Does *whoo* mean hello? Probably. It's what Jhed called in the mist before he stepped into the trap.

"Whoo." Tiredness overwhelms Keni. He lies down beside Jhed's leg and holds on to maintain the healing contact while he sleeps. His new friend wraps his powerful body and comforting, earthy smell around him.

When Jhed shakes him awake gently, the midday sun is lighting treetops high above and the ground mist has gone. For a few beats, Keni struggles to remember where he is and what happened.

He aches everywhere and wants only to snuggle back into Jhed's arms and sleep for a whole cycle, but the truth filters through his exhaustion. He must deposit his nugget in Golden Lake by the night of the next full moon, and a quarter-cycle has already passed since the last one. Comforting sleep isn't an option.

Jhed lifts and folds him into a hairy hug, one broad hand resting on the top of Keni's head, holding him close while he murmurs low tones that sound like a softly struck drum inside his deep chest. Then he holds him at arm's length and speaks some intense words.

Keni thinks he's probably expressing gratitude. He feels blessed, and somewhat restored by his sleep, although he knows he's used the last of his goldenness. From now on, he has only his own strength and stamina to take him home.

Jhed stiffens and cocks his head, staring back in the direction they came from before his injury. He says something urgent and pulls Keni into a run, away from whatever he's heard.

A short jog brings them to a long corridor formed by a natural break between two lines of towering evergreen trees.

The moment they enter the corridor, shivers across his skin tell Keni they're approaching a thin place. Jhed heads straight for the end of the corridor, obviously intending to hop through, but Keni slows his pace.

Jhed grunts and pulls his arm, urging speed while casting anxious glances back over his shoulder.

Keni doesn't want to hop back into his world. Hunting parties of Mountain men are there.

He slows to a walk and pats his friend's hand. "Go on. I know you have to, but I'll be safer this side. You go." He stops walking and hopes he can find his way back to his backpack.

Jhed is horrified.

"Go, friend." Keni gives him a gentle shove.

Jhed sighs, pulls him into a brief hug, and then steps through the thin place and disappears.

Keni wastes no time. Something unpleasant enough to scare Jhed is coming, and Keni doesn't want to meet it. He runs back to the corridor entrance and stops.

They're close. He doesn't need golden senses to hear men coming from several directions, to see glimpses of movement through the trees and get whiffs of the sharp, smoky odour he associates with the iron trap.

He doubts Mountain men will have followed him into the loud world, but these people move like hunters just the same.

His retreat is cut off. He has nowhere to go but back into the corridor, so he turns and runs the way he came.

A sharp crack sounds from somewhere behind, and in the same heartbeat a white scar tears in a tree trunk beside his shoulder. He jerks away from it as another scar gouges itself in the next tree at his head height.

He doesn't want one of those gouges in his flesh. He sprints for the thin place and runs through it.

The clean air of his world makes him feel taller and broader, as if his lungs have grown bigger to fill with strength-giving goodness. He keeps running, desperate to get as far away as possible from the thin place in case Lu's suspicion is correct and Mountain men really do have magicians who can detect people hopping in and out of the world.

And he's glad he kept running, because his pursuers follow him through the thin place and come charging after him. Since they caught sight of him, they've cast stealth away. Their heavy boots pound the ground, and they rip through undergrowth rather than stepping around it.

He can't outrun them. He's still missing the energy he drained to heal Jhed. His only chance is to find somewhere to hide. As he sprints, his eyes dart about for likely places.

An old memory flashes through his mind, of a golden telling the legend of his father's quest.

Mahu never speaks of it nowadays, but like all of his age group, it's the first story Keni can remember ever hearing. On his return from the dead, Mahu told the people he'd sometimes climbed trees to evade his hunters, having discovered that they rarely look up when searching for a ground-dweller like themselves.

A suitable tree presents itself in Keni's path, and he takes the chance. By the time his hunters reach the tree, he is settled in its branches, made nearly invisible by its foliage to anyone on the ground unless they stand below it and stare right up at him.

They run past.

But his relief is brief. They return, moving in a line abreast and beating the undergrowth. There are five of them. They wear quilted clothing of woodland colours, carry gleaming black iron sticks, and move with an air of deadly purpose.

Again, they pass beneath his hiding place, and again they return to it.

He breathes through his mouth and remains silent, wishing his golden glow had already faded and convinced the men murmuring at the bottom of his tree must surely look up.

One of them does.

Keni's stomach flips and plummets.

The man has seen him. He raises his iron stick to shoulder height and points one end of it at him.

Keni stares back, trapped, expecting to feel a gouge ripped in his body and knowing he won't survive it.

A heavy thump sounds, and the man pointing the iron stick spins and staggers and falls to the ground with a thick arrow shaft sticking out of his back.

Arrows thump into two more of the hunters before they can react, and they drop dead.

One of the remaining two points his iron stick and cracks invisible gouge missiles at the surrounding trees until he, too, falls dead with an arrow in his throat and two more in his chest.

The single survivor flees back towards the thin place and is allowed to escape.

Mountain men. Keni is under no illusion about why they've saved him. He is theirs now. They step into the open all around to prevent his escape as they approach his tree.

Their guttural commands are demanding he climb down, and when he doesn't comply one of them shoots an arrow into the tree trunk right beside his head.

He slides down and stands, waiting to die, but instead of finishing him off they knock him to the ground and kick him, kick him, kick him for what seems like an eternity until he hurts everywhere.

Then one of them shoulders the other aside, rolls Keni onto his back, and draws a bright metal dagger.

His friends won't let him drive it into Keni's chest. He lashes out at them, and Keni knows his heart's blood will be dripping from the man's hand in a moment if he has his way, but he is overpowered.

His features are familiar, like those of the young man Keni killed inside the Mountain, but older. His father, probably. He is held back by strong arms and not allowed to kill his son's killer, but hot hatred lives in his eyes.

Again, Keni knows the others are saving him only to take him back to their priests on the Mountain, who will torture and kill him.

All hope is gone.

They haul him to his feet, tie his hands behind his back, and set off at a determined pace. He is surrounded at all times and still so dazed from the kicking he can't even think of trying to escape.

When they stop for the night, all he can do is curl up and wait for unconsciousness to release him from pain and fear.

The moon is high over the treetops when he wakes to a stench in the air and incomprehensible, alarmed jabbering from the Mountain men. His reaction to the stink is blind terror, until his waking mind remembers, and he realises what the familiar smell must mean.

Mountain men shoot arrows off in all directions. Clearly, they have no idea where their target is. All they know is the appalling smell and the cringing fear that grows stronger by the heartbeat. They mill about in panic, staring into the darkness with wild eyes, until the first one breaks and runs with the others following fast on his heels.

Keni lies quietly, still tied up but enormously relieved, until a pair of animal-skin-booted feet appears before his eyes. He cranes his neck to see the young man's father glaring at him with raw hatred in his face and the gleaming dagger in his hand.

He steps forward with a snarl and stoops to plunge the blade into Keni's chest.

A big, dark blur sweeps the man aside and hurls him away, where he hits his head on a rock and lies unmoving. When Jhed prods his body, his head rolls on a broken neck.

Dead. A son and his father are both dead because of him. Keni closes his eyes and apologises to the man's spirit.

Jhed uses the dead man's dagger to cut Keni's hands free. When he helps him to his feet, stars flow in rapid circles above. His blood roars like a winter wind inside his head, and the world flies away from him.

He comes around when a thin place jumps his muscles. He's being carried like a child while his friend jogs through the night. He snuggles against Jhed's warm hairy chest and lets the regular motion lull him to sleep.

Whoo.

Jhed stops.

Keni wakes and listens intently.

Whoo. It comes from somewhere in the pale night mist curling like a sea around the bases of huge trees everywhere.

"Whoo," Jhed calls.

Dark shapes emerge from the mist. Great, dark shapes. One heartbeat, there is only trees. The next, others like Jhed step into view.

Two of the smaller ones run to hug Jhed's thighs. He places Keni on his own feet and hugs the little ones, then stands upright to include in his embrace a breasted one his own size. The four of them make soft whimpers of affection and relief.

Keni watches Jhed with his family, his mate and their two young ones, while all around many others like them stand watching on and echoing their whimpers.

Jhed's mate is crying silently. The wet fur on her cheeks shines in the delicate before-dawn light.

Jhed kisses the top of her head and murmurs something soothing.

I'm safe, Keni imagines him telling her. *It was frightening, but I'm safe now.*

He draws Keni into the conversation, obviously talking about him, showing his healed calf wound and telling the story of their escapes overnight. His extended family listens with close attention.

Finally, he kisses his mate and children once more, and in a heartbeat, his family disappear back into the mist. Jhed scoops Keni up again and they continue their steady run.

The day is dawning when he stops and puts Keni down, waiting until he has his balance before he lets go.

They're back in the loud world, on a tree line at the very edge of Jhed's great forest. Below them is a wide slope down to a plain, upon which Keni sees in the distance what must be one of the glittering cities Lael described. To the north, a river flows out of the forest, down the slope, and across the plain. That will be his route.

Jhed holds him and murmurs soft words that boom low in his chest against Keni's head.

Keni hugs him back, wishing he could stay here so they could learn everything about each other. He wishes it dearly. But his quest won't allow any further delay. He can't stay in the forest, and Jhed can't leave it.

He squeezes his friend, then releases him and walks away to meet the river at the bottom of the wide slope.

"Whoo." Jhed is still where he left him, barely visible in the trees until he waves.

"Whoo." Keni waves back, then turns for the final time and walks away with tears running down his cheeks.

Precious time

THE DAY THE heavy rain stops is my first full one out of the tree. I've waited on the log to meet Andrew each morning, but the rest of my time I've been quite comfortable living inside the oak, feeling life all around me slowing and settling into its autumnal rest.

It got me through the irritating few days at the two-week point where a new beard always makes my skin sore and itchy. I did wonder if being in the tree might arrest its growth and only postpone the scratchiness, but it worked the other way and soothed the soreness while speeding the growth. No wonder the Green Man wears such a luxurious beard.

He's visited me a few times, and the more I relax the easier it is to sense his approach through the wood, as if someone's breath is misting the surface of my mind. He moves like sunlight and shadows across the bark of trees as he passes them by, silently, with very little vibration, until he decides to make himself visible. Then he simply stares at me.

I feel no threat, or even the disapproval his expression suggested at first. He doesn't speak, but the deep calm of his presence reaches me, and I interpret his silence as acceptance.

It's been invigorating to spend several quiet days of rain the way a tree does, drinking deep while watching the hills around me fade from vivid green into paler and paler shades of grey until they merge with the sky. It's definitely more comfortable than sitting inside a dripping shelter.

And I had a lot of thinking to do.

My anger at Andrew has evaporated. At least, I no longer wish someone would fire him into the heart of the sun. Our morning meetings are still brief and frosty, but only because his feelings are bruised. I don't know if he understands that it's his associations I mistrust, not his integrity.

After all, he and Stone might be harmless old academics, but he can't make the same claim for Merritt or Gully. And now, through his association with those two sinister bastards, my parents have been dragged into this mess when they should be enjoying a peaceful retirement in blissful ignorance of what their wayward son is getting up to.

When I finally rebelled against their ambition for me to take over the business, they took it as a personal betrayal. I understand why. They've spent their entire lives working hard to provide that future for me, and they can't see my rejection of it as anything other than a rejection of them.

It really isn't, but I couldn't persuade them around to my point of view.

And if they can't get their heads around me following my lifelong dream of working in wood, they sure as hell won't accept the concept of me living in different magical realities that occupy the same space and time.

Not to mention my hundreds of reincarnations and my immortal lover.

And werewolves.

By using my parents, Merritt has successfully dragged me into his nasty web. I dread to think what he really wants me for. I'll just have to trust in my own ability to avoid harming innocent parties and escape his clutch as soon as possible.

Andrew passed the message that I will return with him after our jaunt in Cornwall. He's received word back that DCI Lawson will stay in Florida in case I change my mind and he needs to bring my parents back to London.

Merritt is ruthless. I knew it the first time I met him, but his ruthlessness and corruption were confirmed beyond all doubt when we discovered his Revenue operations in the Wild.

I don't get the same feeling about Lawson. He's probably a good detective and maybe even a decent man, but he's in Merritt's employ now, and I wouldn't put it past that nasty bastard to have a second, far less pleasant employee over there in America keeping an eye on Lawson and my parents.

So, I'm stuck with it. At the end of our month here in Wild Cornwall, I'll have to return with Andrew to London and join Merritt's department.

Which makes this quiet period all the more precious. For the first time, I'm grateful for the arbitrary timeline Stone and Andrew insisted upon, which I now understand is linked to the single moon cycle Keni has to complete his quest.

My motives for coming on Andrew's gig were a mixed bag, but I've quickly fallen under the spell of the goldens.

The villagers are interesting too. Especially as their highest art form is woodcarving. Timber statues stand at the outskirts of the village and all around the lake, most of them in the form of tree trunks fashioned into totem poles, carved with geometric pattern shapes and painted in many colours on a base of earthy red.

They're all topped with white faces bearing red lips and big, square teeth. I notice three of them show human body parts disappearing between those teeth, two of feet and one a hand with splayed fingers, and a fourth that grips what appears to be a lump of bloody meat below its gaping mouth. A human heart, possibly.

They're a peaceful people, but their priestly religion harks back to a time of dark practices and savagery.

Gold leaf highlights decorate the tallest totems and many smaller wooden items, like brightly painted dolls and white masks. Maybe it has a ceremonial function. Probably a religious significance. As far as I can see, it's the only metal they use. They carve wood with stone tools, which makes their finely chiselled results all the more impressive.

Clay sculpture is also well developed in the village, but this craft seems more utilitarian than their decorative wood art.

Another spectacular woodworking talent they have is building the graceful lightweight canoes everyone paddles skilfully. Kids race them on the lake, and on land they play ferocious games of hockey with strong, polished sticks. Theirs is a happy childhood in idyllic surroundings.

Apart from occasional flare-ups by angry young priests, the relationship between villagers and goldens seems harmonious. People live in huts grouped around one end of the lake, and they play and hunt *on* the lake, while goldens are sort of ex-villagers who now live *in* the lake. They share the water with no social friction that I can see.

Studying their way of life is like a healing process for me, although I'm not sure exactly what's being healed. It's like living in a tree, but more active than that. It certainly encouraged me to spend some days and nights in the oak, and I can't remember ever feeling so completely in tune with the world.

My mind becomes quieter as my senses get sharper. The process is like a cool bandage of peace, easing anger or resentment that was so deep-seated I wasn't even aware of it until its removal leaves me feeling cleansed.

In a way, it removes me from the growing global catastrophe that so often occupies my thoughts.

No, not removes. It lifts me to a place of understanding and clarity.

I don't forget the war waged by disaster capitalists against my world and its billions of people.

In two, nearly three years of pandemic waves, the capitalist elite and the politicians they own have taken advantage of global confusion and have recklessly set the world back a hundred years in terms of public health, education, and food poverty.

Our western media monoliths never mention this fact. Never look at it, even sideways.

The war is undeclared and unrecognised by so many of the people already being hurt by it, people and their entire communities destined to be destroyed if it isn't stopped.

It's a war people like me are dedicated to fighting, because some battles need to be fought. We'll continue to fight by peaceful means against an enemy whose violence is instinctive and vicious. Our weapons are community, cooperation, and love. Hopepunk.

The war against evil will never end, because evil never stops. People think fascism was beaten in 1945, until it emerged again from underground in the twenty-first century, as evil and determined as ever.

We just have to keep on fighting it. On our terms, not its. Some wars have to be fought, but even when violence is needed to defend the innocent, violence itself is never the answer.

I don't forget any of that, but in my peaceful place, I see it clearly for what it is and come to terms with my possible new role in the fight. A role I don't understand yet. I don't know what it might be. Just feel that something is coming, and I'm peaceful about it.

The most significant change is when I stop thinking of my world as being distinct from the Wild. It's all one world, the outside and the Wild and the deep Wild. All of it is my world.

Also, without trying for it or even thinking of it, my impatience with Min's controlling ways has dissolved. I understand her. How can I not? I accept she carries the experience of many long centuries, and it isn't something she can just shrug off in a moment, or on a whim. Perhaps ever.

Her instinct to protect me is no more deserving of criticism than my instinct to protect her. Maybe they show in different ways, but the essence of them both is the safety and well-being of the other. Because we love each other, and that's all that matters.

Bumps in the fabric of the dynamic are just that. Bumps. We can smooth them out, gently, with mutual understanding.

Now I feel mean about how I've been treating her. I want only to finish this task I've committed to and get home to her. Home being wherever we are together.

"*You miss Min as I miss Keni.*" Sadness and anxiety fill Lael's words in my mind.

"*Yes. Although at least I know she'll be safe while I'm away. Our friends will protect her against anyone who might threaten her. I hope Keni comes home soon so you can be together. You don't say anything about your pain when we're listening to his thoughts, but I feel it.*"

"*There is much I want to say, but he won't hear my words. I was in agony when the Mountain men captured him.*"

"*I know.*"

"*He would feel my fear if I released it, and that wouldn't help at all. It might dispirit him. It would certainly distract him. The best thing I can do is live his quest with him and keep him in my heart.*"

"*He's in mine too.*"

"*I feel that, whenever you follow his journey with me. I'm grateful for your compassion. You once asked if there is anything you can do in return for the healing I gave you. You're giving me company and support when I'm frightened. Thank you.*"

I nearly say, "*It's nothing,*" but of course it isn't nothing. It's important for her, and I don't want to cheapen it with an automatic and meaningless phrase from my everyday life on the outside that she might misinterpret. So I leave it unsaid and settle for knowing she feels my sincerity.

"You and Min have led an amazing life. Lives. I've never heard of such a thing before."

I wince. The reciprocity of this mind-reading stuff can have unexpected complications.

"Your secrets are safe with me, Joe. As are Min's. Anything I learn from your thoughts and feelings while we're connected will remain private, as if they'd never been thought or felt by anyone except you."

"Thank you."

"It's nothing." She giggles at my embarrassment, then continues seriously. *"You and she are strong people. You have a long history that bonds you together, but still you both know your own minds. Often that can cause problems within a relationship, and I think you and Min are experiencing it more than ever in this life of yours."*

She certainly has us pegged.

"Life is changing fast in and around you. All the worlds are changing at once, although not all at the same pace. But trouble and danger are growing everywhere, and I can't help but think it's all linked. You and Min are part of this change. Your lives are caught up in the turmoil. There's a strong sense of destiny in events surrounding you. I'm not surprised she shies away from danger and wants to cling to what her experience says is the straightest route to safety."

"You're right."

"Min loves you more than life itself. She wants only to protect you and keep you alive. I know how she feels. If I'd thought I could persuade Keni to abandon his quest and stay here with me, I would have done so. My heart shrinks from the dangers he faces. Min and I are no different in this. Don't hold it against her."

"I don't." I have done so for months, actually. But my time in the forest is changing me, and Lael's insights are helping me to clarify the truth.

"Good, because Min is many wonderful things. She's a miracle. She's a brave person who fights fear every day of her life. And she's in love with you."

Trouble

"MIN." TAE WAVES to get her attention.

Min's on YouTube, memorising Melody Gardot's 'If Ever I Recall Your Face' for tonight's performance and making mental links in the lyrics that relate to her relationship with Joe. She pauses the video on her phone and takes out her earphones.

Tae nods to her laptop screen. "Trouble."

Min is instantly alert. "Tyac?"

"Not yet, but this will get his attention."

"Where are you?"

"Onion Layers."

Of course. Tae spends most of her computer time in conspiracy theory forums. While the mainstream news media has moved on from the vanishing pirate ship story, the sites where Tae lurks are still excited about it and she's monitoring a lot of online activity in her search for mentions of Tyac.

Min swipes out of YouTube and into Onion Layers. "Where am I looking?"

"The 'Golden Running Man' thread."

It's a busy thread, only a few days old but with seven thousand posts already. Min opens it while Tae gives a quick summary.

"It started last week when someone on the forum linked to two separate local news items containing reports of a golden man seen running south to north in the mountains of California. Mainstream media discounted the first sighting as a fantasy and the second as a copycat report, but you know what the Onion Layers people are like."

"No smoke without fire."

"Exactly. They came up with all sorts of theories, but once everyone said their piece the thread dropped down the front page a bit. Until two days later when he was seen again, in Oregon, still running in the mountains and still heading north. This third report was more detailed. He wore quilted mountain clothing, carried a small backpack, and ran with steady concentration like an endurance athlete. The only strange thing about him was his glowing golden face and hands."

What's this got to do with us? Min scans the thread, pausing at posts here and there.

"Someone linked to a fourth report last night," Tae continues, "which set the story off at full speed again. A hunter staggered out of the Oregon forest and reported the murder of his friends. He claims they tracked a golden man through a portal into another world."

"Uh-oh."

"Yes. His description of muscle jumps when he stepped through each way is clear and unmistakable. There's no doubt he's been in the Wild. The local media know nothing about that, of course, but they're taking the Golden Running Man story seriously now because it involves multiple deaths. America's national television networks picked it up overnight."

Min scrolls down through the thread. "Where is it on here?"

"Page twenty-three. But that isn't the bad thing. Go to page thirty-five and click the link in post six-oh-two-six. Unplug your earbuds."

The link takes Min to a website called Golden Triangle. There's no *About Us* page or introduction. The entire site appears to be a simple platform for a series of daily podcasts identified only by consecutive numbers. She clicks the last one, and seconds later, Joe's voice comes from her phone.

"The totems do serve a religious purpose, but I don't know what exactly because my conversation with Lael took a serious turn when I raised the subject."

Shad and Vua come from their bedrooms and stand by the dining table, staring at the phone while Joe's voice continues.

"The villagers are led by the priestly caste, and the totems and masks have significance in their religion. It's very old. If I've interpreted their legends correctly, these are the descendants of people who canoed across the Pacific Ocean to make their home in the American southwest before the people we now know as Native Americans arrived from the north a few thousand years later and ousted them. At which point, the villagers' ancestors migrated into the Wild. Some moved east across the continent, while others stayed put.

"Parts of their religion probably come all the way from that time. It certainly includes dark symbolism that suggests human sacrifice and cannibalism. The split occurred when some people rejected those horrible rituals and left the Mountain."

"What is Joe thinking to broadcast this?" Vua speaks their shared horror aloud.

"I don't imagine he knows it's being broadcast." Min clenches her fists hard, fingernails digging into her palms. "This will be bloody Andrew's work. But why has someone linked to it on the Golden Running Man thread in Onion Layers?"

"There's tension between this old official religion and the magical power of the goldens," Joe says. "The villagers know this power comes from the lake, but they don't understand how it happens. They think it's from the gold in the water, but the goldens believe it comes more from the collective power of the life-after-death elders who've stayed in the lake through many centuries, boosted from time to time by the personal sacrifices new golden candidates make when they bring Californian gold to the lake, as Keni is trying to do on his quest right now."

Min heart sinks. "How long has this been going on?"

"A new podcast has appeared on the site every day for the past two weeks."

"Since Joe left with Andrew."

"Since three days after you last spoke with him," Tae confirms. "I think few people knew about it until last night, but this morning, it's gone viral. Facebook and Twitter are on fire with it. Thousands of blogs and talkboards are linking to Golden Triangle and Onion Layers. By this evening the story will be on television news in America, for sure, and probably over here too because Joe's English accent points to a British connection."

Joe's voice continues. "The dynamic between goldens and villagers feels one-sided. Goldens help the people by healing them and protecting them from harm, but I can't see what the villagers bring to the relationship. Respect and gratitude? Whatever it is, the goldens seem content with it. Lael says the villagers bring them love. Maybe goldens really are as pure as they seem."

The podcast ends there.

Min's head is in her hands. "Tyac will hear this."

"Will he connect it?" Shad asks. "Has he ever heard Joe's voice in this life?"

Min stands up. "I don't know, but I'm not prepared to take that risk. Joe's somewhere in Cornwall, and the best chance of recovering my song magic to protect him will be with the help of my friend down there. Tara's the healer in Quarter Square, which is also our best way into the Cornish Wild. We need to get back down to the West Country fast."

In a minute, everyone is packed and ready to leave.

Min studies Shad, who shifted back to human form only yesterday after three weeks recovering from his terrible burns. "Can you ride?"

"Try and stop me."

River rescue

KENI LIES STILL as a stone in the undergrowth and watches a father and his two small children fishing from the riverbank nearby.

He stopped paddling well before dawn and lifted his stolen canoe from the water when he found a suitable place to hide it for the day.

He's comfortable with this routine and confident he is travelling unobserved but remains alert despite the lack of incident and his overwhelming tiredness. He can't allow himself the long sleep he needs.

Although the bright shine has faded, his skin colour is still too unusual to risk having it noticed. He's seen many people on his journey, of all sizes and shapes and several different colours, but no one in this loud world has golden skin.

By moving only at night and keeping his hood up even in the darkness, he's managed to paddle halfway across the continent and the moon has reached half full without anyone challenging him on his appearance.

He breathes silent thanks to Lael for her advice and holds her close in his mind. He can almost smell her warm presence.

This great river has grown as wide as Golden Lake is long. Details on its far bank are only visible if he squints. And it's busy with traffic, in both directions, big vessels chugging past him all day and all night. He doesn't know how much farther his canoe can take him safely. Already he is searching for an opportunity to climb aboard one of the big vessels and continue downriver in hidden comfort. He looks forward to getting some sleep then.

The fishing family seems to have settled in for the afternoon. The girl, who looks to have seven or eight turns of the seasons behind her, copies her father's movements with determined concentration and obvious adoration.

Her brother is a boy of about three turns who isn't interested in fishing. His father keeps an eye on him while he explores the insect life of the riverbank, calling out a warning whenever the little boy ventures too close to the water's edge.

Their language is unintelligible to Keni, but their mutual affection is evident. He envies the quiet closeness they share and wishes he and Mahu knew such an uncomplicated, undemanding love.

He dozes off in the peaceful warmth beside his canoe, beneath a tangle of tall grass. The late-afternoon sun beats down and sweeps him gently into a dream of home, where Lael and he are children again, they and their friends playing together in the lake without a care in the world.

How long he's slept, he doesn't know, but he awakes with a start and stares directly into the innocent eyes of the small boy, who has crawled into the grass and is sitting within his reach, smiling at him.

The father calls to his son, and again, and the boy leaves reluctantly, glancing over his shoulder at Keni as he returns to the riverbank.

Keni watches to see if he communicates his strange discovery to his father, but the boy keeps his secret, although he does send Keni a shy smile every now and then when no one else is looking.

The sun sails slowly through the deep blue sky. Keni wonders how long the family will remain. He needs to continue his journey.

Eventually, when shadows are growing long and everything glows magically, when certain individual sounds carry across the water as if they come from closer than they do, the father and daughter reel in their lines and pack away their things.

Keni prepares mentally to stretch his aching body and resume his nightly paddle.

The little boy falls into the river. He's standing with his back to the water, watching his father and sister packing away their fishing equipment, when the edge of the bank crumbles beneath his feet and he slips soundlessly from sight.

Keni nearly rushes from his hiding place but forces himself to remain still and silent. The boy's father will rescue him. There's no need for Keni to expose himself to the danger of discovery.

But the man hasn't seen his son fall. Nor has the girl. They're facing upriver and talking. They still don't know what's happened. And the current is strong. Already the boy will have been swept almost beyond rescue. Whether he lives or dies will be decided in the next few heartbeats.

Keni bursts from the grass and sprints along the riverbank. The man shouts something behind him, but he pays no heed. All his attention is on the water while he runs.

There! The boy surfaces and coughs water as he rolls once before disappearing again. The current is carrying him fast.

Keni runs past that point and dives in, stroking with the current underwater and searching for the boy's light-coloured clothing in the shadowy depths. He sees him just ahead, grabs him, kicks for the surface, and gasps when he bursts into the air.

The man and girl are running along the bank, reaching out to him and shouting incomprehensible words.

Keni treads water against the strong pull of the river and holds the boy's limp body up to them. His hands shine golden in the wet evening light. His face must be shining too. The man and girl stare at him for an awestruck beat before hauling the boy from the water.

The father presses his son's chest several times in rapid succession then blows life back into his mouth.

After a brief silence, the little boy convulses into a coughing fit and starts to breathe again, while his father and sister cry out in relief.

Keni sinks below the surface while their attention is distracted and lets the fast current carry him away.

The bad roads

THE MORNING SUN burns off the sea mist quickly and promises a fine day, maybe the last one of this year. So, once Andrew's trudged away with yesterday's recording, I explore the nearby path I saw from the treetop last week.

Ban isn't happy. He presses his weight against me, and if I'd been trying to get more than twenty feet from the clearing through nearly impenetrable undergrowth, I think he would have stopped me altogether. As it is, he's ill at ease but seems grudgingly accepting when I stop and sit down on the broad grass track.

The granite-topped hill sits at the southwest end of the straight avenue, but Ban blocks my view of it and glares at me. Okay, I get the message. I don't like the implication that he's my guard as well as my guardian, but his demeanour doesn't invite debate.

I roll up my shirt to make a pillow and stretch out to enjoy the sun on my chest. A light breeze caresses my skin. Sweet birdsong carries me away. I fall asleep.

A shadow flashes across my eyelids and my bare skin registers a momentary chill, sufficient to start waking me up.

Ban growls low in his throat and finishes the job.

I peer into the sky. It's empty. The birds are silent. Did I dream a slow, strong wing beat? Or did something like a golden really just pass overhead?

Whatever it was, Ban wastes no time in herding me back to our perpetually shaded clearing.

Thomas is waiting patiently on my log. "Hello, Doggy."

Ban ignores him, as he always does.

"Hello, Joe. It's good to see you out and about."

Out of the tree, he means. I'm sure the Green Man reports my movements to him.

I sprawl on the ground and roll my head, trying to ease a slight stiffness in my neck and wishing I could get some more of that sun. The clearing is chilly today. "Good morning, Thomas. No Joan today?"

"She's working." He looks at my right foot. "Do you know there's an iron nail embedded in the sole of your boot?"

I sit up and take a look. So there is. My fingernails are too short to prise it out.

"I'd leave it there if I was you."

"Oh? I thought your people hate iron."

"It makes me a bit uncomfortable, like an itch, but no more than that. I noticed your iron nail the first day we met and wondered if you put it there on purpose."

"No."

"Well, like I say, I'd leave it. It won't do me or mine any harm, and it might help protect you from those it does affect who might not mean you well."

"Such as?"

"Well, sylphs are badly affected by iron. They hate it. It weakens them and stops them making magic. I'm not saying they'd do you any harm, though. Or even wish you any."

He raises his voice. "I'm not saying that."

After listening for a moment, during which no response comes, he returns to his normal volume. "But sylphs aren't the only creatures that iron can hurt, and some of those others might be dangerous."

"Okay."

"The speaking things you carry. Your little iron boxes in their cases of wood. If I were you, I'd let the iron in them breathe too."

Why not? Today feels like a day when he's giving me genuinely helpful knowledge. I tap the recorder out from its wooden sleeve and return it to my chest pocket.

"You've been for a walk this morning?"

Like he doesn't know exactly where I've been and what I've been doing.

"You found that road." He looks through the trees in the direction of my sunbathing spot.

"Yes."

"They're the bad roads."

"How so?"

"The one you found is part of a big pattern."

I saw it from the top of my oak, but I keep the information to myself and let him continue his explanation.

"The pattern in this Wild is the same as the system of roadways in the deep Wild, where the goldens and their people live. Their priests cut the roads through the forest. They use them to hunt us."

So the villagers and goldens I'm studying live in what Thomas calls the deep Wild. That might explain my easy connection with Lael. We're probably in the same place, or very near to the same place, but in two different realities.

Communicating across realities will be a talent of the goldens, I guess. Certainly not something I expect to achieve without Lael on the other side.

Hang on. What? "They hunt piskies?"

"Sylphs first. The priests killed many of them and drove all the others away, then they turned on us. We didn't sit around waiting for near extinction like the sylphs did. We left."

"Into this Wild?"

"Yes, but even here we're not safe. Those roads are here too, and so are the priests sometimes."

"You've moved to the outside then?"

"You don't really think we'd be welcome there, do you?" He winks. "We visit now and then, maybe. But the outside isn't for us."

"Where, then?"

"Here and there."

His clever expression is back, and I've learned not to bother pushing for straightforward information when I see that. It's a waste of breath.

I study the trees across the valley. They're all turning now, but at different speeds and into different colours of autumn. Only the tall aspens are bare. Everything else glows like a mellow crowd of multicoloured cauliflowers spread over the hill.

"You could see the roads for yourself if you went into their Wild."

I continue my study of the panoramic view for a few moments before returning my attention to him. "Hm?"

"The road system the priests cut. You could see it from the hills above Golden Lake."

"Why would I want to do that?" I hope my bored tone of voice masks the sudden flame of intense interest his suggestion ignites in me. I can visit the lake?

He shrugs. "I don't know. Just thought you might be interested."

He leaves it hanging in the air, playing me at my own game. I should have known he'd be a master at it.

I break first, as we both knew I would. "How would I get there?"

"How do you normally step between worlds? Through thin places?"

"Yes."

"There's one of them up that stream." He nods at the steep hillside beyond my oak.

"Thanks." I glance at Ban. "But not everyone will be happy about me leaving here."

He watches the wolf snuffling about in undergrowth on the edge of the clearing. "We thought as much. Let's see what we can do about that." He gives his porcelain bell a silent shake.

We wait.

"What's up, lover?" Joan strolls into the clearing and bends to kiss Thomas full on the lips, then shoots me a friendly smile as she sits on the log. "Good day, Joe."

Thomas tilts his head in Ban's direction. "We need to keep someone occupied while Joe goes off to look at something interesting."

"Okay." Joan rummages about inside her coat and produces a tiny lantern.

Thomas stands to block her from my view. "Don't look."

"Why not?" I peer around him.

Joan's lamp is beautiful. The most beautiful light I've ever seen. All I want to do is watch as she sways it back and forth, back and forth. It draws me in.

Thomas steps between us again and snaps his fingers in front of my eyes. "Back to me, Joe."

What's all the fuss about? The old girl has a lantern. So what?

It certainly has Ban's full attention. He stares at it, his head rocking in a steady rhythm as he follows its motion from side to side.

Thomas turns me to the stream. "That's where you want to go."

Yes. Except that when I glance over my shoulder and see Joan's light, I only want to stay and gaze at it. It's so beautiful. The most beautiful light I've ever seen. Its lovely warmth spreads through me and invites me to step closer. It whispers to me of home, peace, safety, friendship, and love.

Thomas snaps his fingers in front of my eyes again. “Back to me, Joe.” He guides me past the tree. “That’s where you want to go.”

I step down to a shallow spot where a bed of gravel rises to the bank and the rippling water only washes over the soles of my boots.

“Good lad. That’s where you’re going, up the stream. Don’t look back.” He gives me a little shove to get me moving.

I leave my clearing behind and try to climb without getting too wet, but the incline grows steeper until the stream is a forty-five-degree waterfall. I clamber from rock to rock rather than trying to scramble through the rushing water.

A familiar shiver draws me up the hill and gets stronger as I approach it. There’s no missing this one. It’s concentrated over the stream in the only clear spot possible, a narrow avenue of access with densely wooded steep slopes rising from it on both sides.

The muscle jump is powerful, but more powerful still is the refreshing change in atmosphere when I step into the deep Wild. It’s like breathing pure fresh air after surviving on a stale canned imposter. Its taste is sweeter even than the clean air I’ve been enjoying in the Wild.

When the ground levels off, I turn to marvel at spectacular views all around. Everything shines. Everything flourishes. All the rich colours of autumn crowd together and sparkle in a fine misty rain.

My guess is that all the realities of any specific location will share the same climate but possibly different weather conditions. It makes sense, particularly when comparing the industrialised and polluted outside with the clean environment I just left and the even cleaner one I’m walking through towards Golden Lake.

My customary observation spot is here, on the track above the village.

It's quiet. Old people sit carving wood or weaving outside their huts, chatting contentedly, while in the distance the voices of children at play ring through the trees. Below that happy noise, other more regular sounds suggest light horticulture and woodland management activities.

The lake's quiet too. Lael is the only golden in sight, sitting on her favourite rock so silently she seems almost part of it.

She's with Keni. While he moves through the loud world, she sees it with his eyes and tastes its sounds and smells with his senses. I do too, connected to him still, here, through my link with her.

He's on a big boat, in the dusty darkness below decks, lying still beneath layers of heavy textile sheets. The quilted coat that nearly drowned him in the river is ruined. He removed his trousers and put a gold nugget in each of the deep pockets, then knotted the pocket material to keep the gold safe in case he has to swim again. He's hot and itchy, but the vessel is moving in the direction he needs to go and he's safe in his hiding place. At long last, he feels secure enough to drift into sleep.

"Have you seen the temple?"

My heart hammers. I had no warning whatsoever of Thomas's approach.

He nods past the far end of the lake to a substantially built squat red pyramid on top of a conical hill. The hill looks as symmetrical and manmade as the temple. Two parallel fights of steps are cut into its eastern face. At the bottom of the hill, the steps join a wide, grassed avenue that forms the central stem of a series of other avenues cut through the forest in an elaborate pattern.

One of those avenues will correspond to the grassy path where I sunbathed today. The one that runs from the granite topped hill directly past my clearing. But there are many avenues in the pattern here and I can't work out which one it is.

Everything is linked. The granite outcrop on top of a natural hill in the Wild where my clearing exists becomes a pyramid of red painted blocks in this deep Wild. And the pattern of paths I saw from the top of my oak is probably the same shape as the formal system of roads that radiates from the base of the temple hill here.

"Hello, Joe. I'm glad you've come to visit us." Lael's welcoming smile warms the inside of my mind, and she waves from the lake, where she's floating on her back and kicking away from the shore. *"You look how I imagined you would, except I thought you'd have a full mane of hair. Did I see you talking with Thomas Appleleaf?"*

He's gone. I didn't notice him arrive and now I haven't noticed him leaving. That's pretty impressive, considering the empathetic link I'm enjoying right now with every living thing in this vibrant place.

"Yes. Do you know him?"

Her chuckle is like silver water tinkling over pebbles. *"Everyone knows Thomas Appleleaf and his queen."*

"Queen?"

"Joan the Wad is queen of the Cornish piskies, and Thomas is their king. Didn't you know you were talking to royalty?"

I'll be more careful what I say to that pair in future. Why didn't they tell me who they are? Are they setting me up for something? It feels like they're moving me like a pawn on a chessboard. Their secretive manner that seemed quaint and comical before takes on a more sinister shade now.

"I'm sure they mean you neither harm nor embarrassment. Life has taught them to be cautious."

"According to Thomas, it's your murderous priests who've taught them caution."

"We've heard that claim before but have seen no evidence that our people are responsible for the suffering of sylphs and

piskies. We know they are suffering, but no one knows who is persecuting them."

"What's the name of that young priest? The one who came down to the lake, shouting at you and upsetting the children?"

"Noala."

"He's an angry man."

"He thinks our people should follow the guidance of the priests and not come to goldens for help. You're right. He's angry. And I disagree with him on the issue he's most passionate about. But that doesn't make him a killer of sylphs and piskies."

"How influential is he among the other priests?"

"He's the most vocal of our critics and is expected to become Mahu's successor one day. We anticipate the tension between goldens and priests will get worse when Mahu dies, unless we can resolve our differences before that day arrives."

"But you don't think Noala would hurt anyone?"

"No."

Hm. *"The piskies say your priests can fly."*

"They can't."

"Along those avenues cut through the forest."

"The avenues are purely ceremonial. They're cut in the same pattern our ancestors made around the Mountain in the old days. Our priests use them to remember our origins."

"Thomas says the priests hunted sylphs almost to extinction, and when the sylphs left for another place the priests turned to hunting piskies. Is he lying?"

"He's mistaken." Lael treads water and flexes her powerful wings, her golden glow lighting up the depths all around. The intensity of her conviction hits me from a hundred yards away. *"Something or someone did that, but it wasn't our priests. I've known these people since I was born. Noala and Keni and I were children together. We may have taken different paths, but he would never do that."*

Keni's mother walks down to the lake and stands alone, staring into the water. Her body language cries of suppressed fear and grief.

"I must tell Annam of Keni's progress." Lael swims to her.

"Give her a hug for me." I follow my track back to the thin place and return to my clearing.

"Here he comes." Thomas's voice carries before I see him. "Put your light away, lover."

I climb from the stream, untie my boots, and hang them from a branch to dry, pretending not to notice Ban's unsteady stance and confused expression.

Joan stands as I join Thomas on the log. "I'll leave you to it." She's gone in an instant.

How do they do that appearing and disappearing trick?

Thomas ignores my frown. "You saw the temple, then?"

Why is the temple so important to him? Before I get the chance to ask, an invisible presence fills my consciousness, and a dazzling light blossoms in the clearing entrance.

The light dims to reveal two magnificent men standing in the opening. They are tall and slender, dressed in flowing velvet outfits of rich, dark colours. Their shoulder length hair shines like the sea under a yellow moon. Their skin is like polished marble. They exude power and authority, staring down at us with an air of righteous judgement.

"Thomas Appleleaf."

Thomas clicks his tongue. "You boys do love your dramatic entrances."

One of them raises a perfect eyebrow. "Who are your companions?"

"This is Joe." Thomas's tone is dismissive, as if neither his questioner nor I matter to him.

"Joe." The speaker rolls my name around in his mouth, and I get the distinct impression he can taste my character through it.

The other one studies first me, particularly and with some hostility my shirt pocket and right boot, and then more benevolently my ancient oak.

Thomas nudges me and mutters, "Sylphs."

Oh. Elves. Yes, that feels right.

"And the wolf?"

Ban regards the newcomers with calm interest.

Still, I don't think he would appreciate me giving his name to just anyone. "He's a wolf."

The second sylph speaks. "You appear to be engaged in dangerous work, Thomas."

"If I was, it'd be my business."

"We are concerned not for your safety, but for the balance as it might affect our people."

I feel his shrug. "As I said, sonny, my business is my business. How's my lovely cousin Elane? I haven't seen her in ages."

"Queen Elane is well, but uneasy about the possible ramifications of your actions here."

"I'm glad she's well. Please give her my regards, and tell her Joan and I are fine. Thanks for coming." He turns to me and dismisses them from his presence with a casual wave.

The sylphs hold my stare. I can't drag my attention away from their suddenly increased shining splendour, until the dazzling light blooms again for a second and they disappear with it.

Thomas utters a scornful grunt. "Flashing lights and farts. Pay them no attention."

"What's dangerous?"

"Nothing. They like to think they're in charge of everything, is all. Hey, but them turning up might help us. Am I right in thinking you get a feel for living things you come into contact with?"

I raise an eyebrow at him. It won't be nearly as elegant as the elven one we just saw arch, but I expect it conveys my message.

"Jack says he thinks you do. And generally he doesn't bother to speak unless he knows what he's talking about."

Jack? Oh, the Green Man. I say nothing.

"Right. Well, I'm going to assume you do. So you'll have a feel for Joan and me, and those two sylphs, which will do fine. Stand up and close your eyes."

What now?

He sighs. "Just do it, will you? I'm not going to hurt you."

I stand, close my eyes, and wait.

"Going to check it's safe." A breath of air gives me the impression he's left, but before I can open my eyes a second breath suggests he's back. He touches my arm. "Remember the temple? Here we go."

I picture the temple without intending to. The little bugger's practising auto-suggestion on me.

"Open your eyes."

I'm astonished to discover we're standing on the pyramid, on a broad, inset platform near the top. Its building blocks are painted earthy red, as are two table-sized altars hewn from massive rocks and a smoothed stone conical dish on a waist-high pedestal.

All the avenues are spread out below us, and the pattern is easy to see. It's a huge, stylised hawk with a wingspan wider than its body is long.

"We can't stay long." He tugs me to the stone dish and licks his fingertips. "Do this." He wipes his fingers quickly across its surface.

I copy him.

"Close your eyes and taste them." He sticks his fingers in his mouth.

I do that too.

Pain. Fear. Darkness.

Impressions flash across my mind's eye so rapidly I barely register them. Black night and bright fire. Terror. Sharp, hot, slicing agony. Blood. Blood everywhere, pumping, spreading, pooling. Sinking, falling into darkness. Drinking warm blood. Eating a warm living heart. Strength. Life transferred. Incredible strength and power. Flying. Treetops spinning away below…

I force my eyes open and stagger away from the dish, my heart thumping fit to burst and pulses throbbing all over my body. The world swims. I have to remind myself to breathe, to make myself breathe.

Thomas grips my arm. "Don't let it go. Tell me if you feel anything familiar."

I do. I already know what he means.

"Tell me," he urges. "Say it."

"Piskies and sylphs."

"Our blood."

"Yes."

"Sacrificed here."

"Yes."

Return to Quarter Square

MIN KEEPS HER earphones in for the four-hour ride down to Plymouth. By the time they arrive outside Quarter Square, she's heard all Joe's podcasts on the Golden Triangle site. Now she's even more scared and angry than she was before they left Manchester.

Obviously, he has no idea his recordings are being broadcast online and listened to by thousands of people all over the world. He believes they're for Andrew's ears only, so he speaks freely of things Andrew knows about. Things he would never say openly in public. Things guaranteed to bring Tyac to him.

Andrew is betraying him. With every day that passes, with the publication of every new podcast, this so-called friend of theirs is sinking him deeper and deeper into trouble that might prove fatal. Joe is like an unsuspecting insect trapped in an invisible spider's web he doesn't even know exists.

Min hasn't wanted to kill anyone in a very long time, but if Andrew was here right now, she'd turn him over to Shad for instant destruction.

She climbs off her bike, stretches her back, and tries to stamp feeling back into her feet as she crosses the cobbled lane to knock on the theatre door.

No one answers.

That's okay, everyone will be out working. She steps back off the pavement. They'll have to trawl the streets and find someone out performing who'll come back and let them in. She wanders back over to the bikes, where Tae has her laptop open and is catching up with the news.

"Not good." Tae shakes her head as she reads. "Worse than this morning. I'll be surprised if that golden man stays free for long. Onion Layers posters are linking to hundreds of sightings all across North America. People have seen him canoeing at night, always heading east, and a Portland shopkeeper has been interviewed on four tv channels about a stolen canoe. There are two separate reports of the golden man carrying his canoe down through steep woodland from beside a dam wall to the river below, and several pairs of teenagers saw him from a lovers' parking spot in the middle of the night, navigating whitewater rapids like an Olympic champion. A firefighter in Kansas City says his little boy fell into the river when they were fishing yesterday and was saved from drowning by the golden runner."

Min rubs her tired eyes and tries to blink some moisture back into them.

"Someone mapped the reports," Tae continues. "Even allowing for genuine mistakes and stupid people seeking attention, they plot a west-to-east line that follows rivers across the country. Just as Joe's podcast predicted."

Vua looks over her sister's shoulder. "Any official interest?"

"Lots. Look, there's a new thread in Onion Layers dedicated to law enforcement and government activity related to the running man. Today, police are searching river freight traffic on the Missouri and Mississippi Rivers east of Kansas City."

"Poor boy." Min drains her bottle of now tepid water. "Still nothing that might be Tyac?"

"Nothing. Since this story broke, Onion Layers has become the central hub for all the conspiracy theory blogs and forums in this country. As well as a surge of interest in thin places and several groups planning to sleep inside stone circles in Britain and Ireland this week, posters over here are trying to work out where Joe is. No one knows, but that won't stop them thinking and talking about him. They're on high alert. If anyone sees anything like Tyac, Onion Layers is where we'll hear about him."

It won't be long now. Min feels it in her marrow. She *must* get her song magic back.

Tae frowns. "There's a lot of other stuff over in America too. Unusually high numbers of sightings."

"Of what?" Shad folds his neck scarf into his upturned helmet on his fuel tank, shakes out his long hair, and rolls his neck.

"Mythical creatures and urban legends. The sort of thing Onion Layers specialises in, but far higher numbers than normal. Ever since the Oregon hunter said he saw a bigfoot. He's in jail while the police search for his missing friends, by the way. But other people are claiming they've entered the Wild, and from these reported sightings it sounds like some Wild creatures have followed them back into the outside."

They all share a look.

"Not good," Min says. "Is this happening only near where that hunter lives?"

"All over America." Tae scrolls through thread titles. "Bigfoot from California to British Columbia, red weredogs in Alaska, wendigo in Quebec, trolls around Niagara Falls, something called a baykok in Minnesota, a mothman in West Virginia, werewolves and vampires and all manner of swamp beasts across the southern states, man-eating otters in Mexico, goat-sucking monsters in Chile," she looks up, "and many more."

Vua pulls a face. *"Vampires?"*

Min shrugs. "People are frightened. They'll see what they expect to see."

Light footsteps sound on the cobbles up the lane, and a young woman wearing a hooded tan duffel coat walks around the corner.

Min watches her. The walk is familiar.

The woman notices them without obviously looking. She hesitates for a second, then continues past the theatre door, keeping her face hidden inside the hood.

Considering the insiders' experience with bikers this summer, Min isn't surprised. "Tara?"

She stops and stares.

It *is* her. Min runs across the road.

"Min!" Tara gasps in delight.

They throw their arms around each other and twirl in the road, laughing and talking at the same time.

"I've missed you so much."

"Where have you been?"

Min holds her at arm's length and searches her face. "Are you okay? Is everyone in the square okay? No more attacks?"

"I'm fine. We're all fine. Come in." She looks up and down the lane before turning to the blank wall and snapping her fingers.

A wide door appears.

Min is impressed. "That's new."

"We've had snoops ever since the battle, so we strengthened our locks on the main door and always check no one's looking before we use this one."

The back of Min's neck prickles a warning. "Who are these snoops?"

"No idea. Jimmy thinks it's the government." She laughs. "But he always thinks that."

Min chuckles too, but she makes a mental note.

"Anyway, let's get you in." Tara holds the door open for them to wheel their bikes into the building.

Min walks down the dark corridor to the foyer, averting her eyes from the swing doors to the main arena and the stage where she and Joe spent happy hours working together in the summer.

Tara snaps her fingers at the foyer wall and holds the second magic door open for them to file out into the mellow afternoon sunlight.

Quarter Square.

Min inhales the rush of warm memories. Home. Friendship. Happiness. Safety. Peace. This place has meant all these things and more to her for a very long time.

Now different emotions crowd those good things out. Mostly grief and regret. Last time she was here, they had to defend their home in a terrible battle. They all lost loved ones.

If Joe is to be believed, many of those losses were her fault. He said if she wasn't so determined to protect him at any cost, many who died would still be alive.

She can't disagree.

No, it's stronger than that. She accepts the truth of what he said that day. If not for her series of stubborn judgement failures three months ago, the friends and family they all lost would still be alive.

Joe's right. It's her fault.

She wishes he was here right now so she could hold him and beg his forgiveness. She misses him so much it hurts like a raw wound open to the elements.

"Min!"

She doesn't know who called her name, but in seconds a crowd of old friends is hugging her and crying, and so is she.

Sick

PAINFUL FEVERISH SHIVERS shake me. My joints and muscles ached all night and complained no matter what position I tried them in. No real sleep came, but I got lots of incomprehensible images repeating at random on a nightmarish loop running through my brain.

Dawn spreads across the sky. I'm cold, inside and out. The world is cold. It's the first taste of winter, which is a time I normally enjoy, but today it brings me only dread because I've come down with something and still have six days of this trial to go.

I could pack it in. Probably should swallow some of the hot breakfast Andrew will bring in soon then borrow his arm to help me walk out of the Wild. I'd be in a warm bed by midday.

Keni and Lael will get on fine without me. The whole world will get on fine without me.

Crawling out of my shelter is bad enough, but when I drag myself upright the world tips drunkenly and sends me nearly sprawling. The mug of stream water I scoop up chills my stomach into a sudden cramp that doubles me over. I lurch to the toilet clearing and make it there only just in time.

Ban watches my antics without lifting his head from the ground. His eyes bear an expression of dull pain and I get the notion he's come down with the same thing.

Can wolves and humans catch the same bugs? Who knows? Maybe werewolves can. No reason why they shouldn't. Ban isn't less than human. He's more. It would probably have to be a superbug to lay him low, but that's what it feels like in me anyway.

"You want some water?"

He doesn't respond but watches me.

"I suppose you'll get some if you want some." I crawl back inside my shelter and grow into the oak. Not feeling my body at all is better than feeling it with a raging sickness.

Flo

MIN HOLDS A whippy branch back for Tara to follow her through a narrow gap between two tall bushes, then walks beside her when the path widens again. "The square was quiet last night."

Tara nods. "Winter in the air."

"It's more than that. Even with all the insiders coming out to see me, and the Axe people welcoming Shad, Vua, and Tae back, the place feels sad."

"Yes."

Min's never heard Tara sound so subdued before. They scramble over a fallen tree. "Is that how things are now?"

"We haven't had a party since June. No music. We haven't recovered from the battle. We saved Quarter Square, but we lost something vital. Our innocence. As well as the people we loved. Everyone's nice to everyone else. Helpful. Caring. More than before, even. We worry about each other, but I can't get anyone to talk about it."

Min studies the ground on the path before them. "Feels like people are walking on eggshells."

"That's exactly how it is. I don't know how to break the spell."

"Spell?"

"Figure of speech. Not an actual spell."

"More like a communal depression."

"Yes. And our new Axe friends are wonderful, but they lost half of their pack that night. They're grieving even more than we are."

Shad and the sisters have remained in human form. He's scouting ahead, pausing every few minutes for further directions from Tara. Tae trails about the same distance behind, and Min catches glimpses of Vua ghosting through the trees off to one side or the other. She doesn't once see or hear the Axe warriors who've shifted to wolf form and are escorting them through the Wild, but they're out there.

She lowers her voice. "Is the war situation in this region really as bad as the Axe made out last night?"

"At least as bad. Maybe worse. I think they wanted to get the seriousness of it across to Shad and his daughters without scaring any children who might be listening." Tara notices Shad waiting and points him on. "That's weighing on our minds too. And of course it's linked to our battle, so we can't ever forget it."

"If Tin has Queen Fiona besieged at the main Hare camp up on Wild Dartmoor, how come things are so bad this far south?"

"Many Hare soldiers weren't there when the Tin army surrounded their camp. Now they couldn't get in if they wanted to. They're living rough in the forest, attacking Tin supply lines and outposts. Tin sends patrols out, and they clash often, even down here near Plymouth. The Axe wolves are keeping a close eye on events. They say Tin has complete control of their home ground in Cornwall, and is maintaining the siege on Dartmoor, but that their army is losing more skirmishes than they win elsewhere in Devon."

Shad hasn't gone ahead when Tara waved him on. He puts a finger to his lips.

Min can't see or hear anything threatening, but she wouldn't expect her senses to compete with his. "What is it?" she whispers.

He squints, as if trying to put an unusual feeling into words. "Something's wrong." He pulls a face. "Maybe not wrong. Different."

Min and Tara wait for him to explain, while Tae and Vua hold their positions.

"You know how a thin place feels? This gives off the same sort of vibration, but instead of thin it feels thick."

Tara smiles. "It's okay. What you're feeling is a magical protection around the place we're coming to." She tilts her head and regards him. "You're *good.*"

She leads them through a narrow winding path to a grassy clearing surrounded by holly trees. Shiny, dark-green, prickly leaves and red berries form a circular physical barrier all around them, while an unbroken hedge of ferns within provides the strong magical protection Shad felt from a distance.

Tara sits cross-legged on the ground and gestures the others to follow suit.

Min glances around. "How will Flo know we've come to see her?"

Tara shrugs and grins. "She'll know."

"The wolves are guarding us. They're all around."

"They won't harm Flo. She's probably out there cuddling them right now."

A big blackbird flaps through the trees and lands delicately on a holly bush.

Min's heart leaps. "Is that Ouzel?"

The bird caws and hops down to perch on the shoulder of the young girl who steps into view.

Flo appears to be the same age as when she came back to life after her funeral. About twelve, which is seventy years younger than she was when she died.

She looks at each of them in turn, nods to Tara, and pauses when she gets to Min. "I know you."

"I'm Min. We were friends in Quarter Square."

Flo's bright-blue eyes lose focus, as if she's searching old images in her memories. Then they flash back to clarity. "You're the one who's cursed to be immortal." She drops to the ground and crosses her legs. "Why have you come to me?"

"I need to get my song magic back. I need it to protect someone who's in terrible danger. I hope you will help me."

"Who do you want to protect?"

"Joe Walker."

Flo goes unfocused again, but only for a moment. "The Oak Man. He's a good one." She turns to Tara. "What have you tried?"

"Lemon and lavender, last night and again this morning."

"Good." She asks Shad, "Want to get a fire going here?" then her bright attention returns to Tara. "We'll use garlic, cinnamon, camomile, basil, angelica, eucalyptus, and hyssop. Got them?"

Tara checks the contents of her woven medicine bag. "All except the eucalyptus."

"I remember there's a tree in Quarter Square."

"That's why I don't carry it."

"You can augment her treatment with eucalyptus later if need be. The rest will do for now." She sits perfectly still as if meditating, while Shad and the sisters build a campfire and Tara prepares her herbs. Without opening her eyes, she asks, "How did you lose your song magic?"

"A wizard took it from me in battle."

Her pointed little chin juts in surprise. "Battle? That doesn't sound like the you I remember."

Tara interrupts. "I told you about the attack on Quarter Square."

Flo pins Min with her startling blue stare. "You were using your song magic to help defend the haven against those Hare soldiers?"

"Yes."

"And it was the Hare wizard who took it from you?"

"Yes."

Flo studies the ground in front of her. It's like she's reading some invisible document there.

Nothing visible remains of the gentle old wise woman Min remembers. This new Flo is intense, like a force of nature brooding before it performs some powerful action or other. There's an almost frightening purity in her concentration, as if her mind is engaged with something at a cosmic level and she has to keep reminding herself that everyday matters are important to normal people.

Shad produces a cold beef sandwich from his pocket and tries to tempt Ouzel with a piece of it. The blackbird watches him but doesn't move. Shad shrugs and eats the sandwich.

Flo nods Tara to the fire and closes her eyes again, while her former apprentice prepares the potion in a kettle of stream water hanging from a makeshift tripod over the flames.

It smells delicious. Min inhales the scented air, tension melting away from her neck and shoulder muscles that have been bunched for months. She soars, and sees the land of her birth far below, bathed in sunlight and surrounded by the sapphire-blue ocean. Deep peace fills her.

Time passes.

Someone drapes a coat around her shoulders. The cold air on her back hasn't registered until now when it disappears. She continues to breathe slowly and enjoy the warmth of the fire on her face while sweeping forward through visions of her life.

Finally, she knows only the boundless deep peace.

"How do you feel?" The voice comes from a million years away.

She has to concentrate hard to recognise it as Flo's, then harder still to understand the question and explore some possible answers. There doesn't seem to be any urgency. "Peaceful."

"I'm not surprised you're holding on to the peace. The life you lead would be enough to make anyone a bit crazy."

Min frowns. Flo's making her think and lifting her from the peaceful place. Some of it is coming back with her into her normal thoughts, but she hasn't felt this calm in a long time and suspects it won't happen again in a hurry.

She opens her eyes. The day has passed while she travelled through her memories. Dusk fills the forest, and the light from their campfire flickers in the canopy of trees high above. A mug of cold herbal water sits by her knee. She drains it in one long drink.

Across the fire, Flo's gaze catches and holds hers. The girl's irises reflect the flames. "What are you scared of?"

"A werewolf monster called Tyac."

"Why?"

"He's insane. He kills Joe every time he finds us."

Flo watches a glowing spark rise away into the night. "Is that it?"

"What more do you want? He hates us. It's his only emotion. He blames us for my mother cursing him the first time he murdered Joe. He's hunted us for thousands of years since then. He never stops. He lives to murder my Joe and break my heart again and again."

Flo's powerful stare burns bright.

Min closes her eyes and slips back into the comfortable peace for another slice of eternity.

"What are you scared of?"

She returns slowly and brings a bigger truth with her. "Joe. When he's determined to hunt Tyac down and kill him, he scares me nearly as much as Tyac does."

Tara refills her mug and replaces it beside her knee.

"He scares me more, really. I deal with Tyac by running from him. Escaping from him. Lying low. I can't run from Joe, but when he confronts Tyac, he'll die another horrible early death and I can't bear to lose him again. Not so soon." A wave of pain swells in her chest. Her voice cracks. "All I want is to be with him, but the things I love most about him are the very things that will destroy him. Again."

The wave breaks. She buries her face in her hands and sobs. She's so alone. Her loved ones sit only a few feet away, sharing the warmth of the same fire, but they can't help her. She's lonely and afraid.

"I sent him away to keep him from harm, but I miss him so much. It's like someone's torn my heart out of my chest and keeps squeezing it to remind me Joe isn't here."

Her voice rasps as her pent-up pain pours out. "I ache for his touch, his smell, his warmth next to me in the night. I need to hear his thoughts and feel his laughter inside me. All I have are memories, and I have an eternal lifetime full of them already. I've spent entire centuries living on them, but they're thin compensation for his real presence. I don't want only the memory of him to keep him alive in my mind. I want *him*." She deflates into a sobbing lump of misery.

Flo waits until her shoulders stop shaking and her sore, swollen eyes are dry again. "What are you scared of?"

Min's protest dies in her throat when the young girl's stare pierces her again and carries her back to the comfortable place, where the world is warm and dark and velvety.

It feels like weeks later when the relentless voice reaches her there. "What are you scared of?"

She explores her answer in the friendly darkness. It isn't something she considers often. Maybe once in each of Joe's lives, and she always suppresses it for the common good. And because it isn't something she's proud of.

"Min." Flo's blue eyes wait for her. She already knows the truth, Min thinks, but she wants her to say it for herself. "What are you scared of?"

She sips herbal water. "I'm scared of losing control."

Flo tilts her head and opens her hands in a small questioning gesture. She wants more. She wants it all.

"Losing control of everything. Joe. Me. Everything." Min's heart thumps as if she's running from her fear. "I have to hold it all together. Joe's always so innocent at first. He never knows anything about us or Tyac. I have to teach him how to remember his previous lives. At the same time, I have to keep him alive and teach him how to survive in his present life. Because nine times out of ten, Tyac is already on his trail before we even meet again."

She shakes her head in irritation. "I'm no good at it. The survival thing. I'm rubbish. Joe's brilliant at it, but I have to keep him alive until he remembers how. Every time. And I never do it well. I have to protect him, and the only way I can do that is by holding everything tight. Very tight."

She wants Flo to agree. To say she understands. She begs her with her eyes. But this Flo isn't the kindly old woman who four months ago would have hugged her and murmured soothing words into her hair.

"I'm frightened of losing control. And I feel guilty for all the times I've failed to protect him." Min slumps.

That's it. I'm drained. And my throat hurts worse than it has in months. Some good this is doing. Who the hell said it should turn into a therapy session anyway?

Flo stares into the fire.

Min looks around and sends her family an uncertain smile. Her bottom lip is still wobbly, and she nearly crumples into tears again.

"What else makes you feel guilty?"

No. I'm not doing this anymore.

Flo leans forward and enchants her again.

Min sinks into the soft, velvet pillowed darkness. Should she support him or thwart him? Thwarting him is easy. She's been doing it subtly since they ran from Quarter Square and went into hiding. She's done it many times before, in nearly every life when he gets the mad idea that he can take Tyac. She could do it again this time too, as easily as breathing.

But it would be wrong. *She* would be wrong. She can't do it to him again. She has to let the control go.

It hurts. Just thinking about it makes her uncomfortable, even in this place of delicious security.

The control isn't all for Joe's benefit. It's as much for her as for him. Maybe more, because it frightens her to lose it, because for thousands of years she's been accustomed to always getting her own way.

So that's another thing she's scared of, and it's also something that makes her feel guilty.

It's time to put it right. She flirted with the notion when she confessed in the text he won't have seen yet how she's been lying to him. But that was only with her mind. Now she promises it with her heart.

No more thwarting him. No matter how tempting it gets or how easy it might be. He's chosen to take a hard road in this life, and she will walk it beside him.

Acceptance. And peace. But not for long, because there is more guilt. She might as well face the whole thing now or Flo will only send her back to finish the job.

Joe accused her of this when he was distraught over the loss of so many of the Axe people. He said their deaths were unnecessary. And he was right. If they'd listened to him, if *she'd* listened to him, those people would be alive today.

It's time to face her guilt.

Flo is watching her steadily when she comes back from the darkness.

Min looks at Shad, Tae, and Vua. Then she looks to Flo for strength.

The girl blinks her understanding.

"I feel guilty for sacrificing so many Axe people. I've done it many times over hundreds of generations. You've always been so faithful to me and have never faltered. You're the bravest, most wonderful people I've ever known. And still, I've let so many of you lose your lives protecting Joe and me."

She wells up as she regards her family. "This year, I did it again. Joe fought against it, and I think he hated me for a while after it happened exactly the way he feared it would. All your loved ones who died that night, I'm sorry, it was my fault. Vua and Tae, your lovely mother. Shad, your magnificent wife. Anya's brave death and the deaths of all the others are in my heart and on my head. I love you and I'm sorry."

Shad leans over and puts his big warm hand on hers. "We chose to protect you. We would do it again. Anya would do it again. You know that. We have free will and we make our own choices."

"Yes, but that night, there was another way. A different way. Joe said it. He needed me to support him in order to persuade you to change your plans, but I refused. If I'd done what he wanted, we would still have Anya and all the others here with us now.

The sisters kneel and hug her. "It's easy to see a thing clearly afterwards," Vua says, and Tae murmurs her agreement.

"Joe saw it clearly beforehand, but I didn't let him lead. That's a guilt I have to carry. Let me carry it, because its weight will remind me not to make the same mistake again."

Shad squeezes her hand. "You and me both."

Flo squints up at Ouzel, who's remained perched on her shoulder this whole time. "She's ready. Help me now."

The blackbird caws softly, and they both stare intently at Min. Their eyes reflect the flames, fierce red lights that grow and bore into her vision until only they exist in a sea of dense blackness.

Her body floats, as if she is filled with all kinds of birds, feathers, wings, clean air, thermal currents rising and swooping, rising and swooping through cool cleansing air, then landing gently back in the circle.

The fire crackles. Its smoke rises to filter through the branches and foliage high above. Her family and friends sit in the warm glow of it, watching her return with welcoming smiles.

Tara hands her another mug of herbal water.

"Thank you." Min needs it. "My throat feels ragged, by the way. Is this one of those treatments where it'll get worse before it gets better?"

"We haven't really touched your throat," Flo says.

Min's mouth drops open. "What was all that for then?"

"You needed healing in places more vital than any body part. We helped you heal those wounds. When you get your magic back, you'll use it more powerfully because of what you've achieved here today."

"So when will you do my throat?"

"We can soothe it," Flo says, "but we can't bring back your magic. Only the wizard who took it away can return it."

"Gully."

It's Flo's turn to look surprised. "You know my brother's name?"

"Your *brother*?"

Flo chuckles. "Yes, my little brother. I never liked him working for that awful Hare woman. He tried to persuade me to leave Quarter Square before I died, but I refused. He must have been delaying the attack while he tried to get me out. Once I died, he probably saw no reason to delay any longer. Don't worry. When I've given him a piece of my mind, he'll restore your song magic. We'll go to see him in the Hare camp tomorrow."

"He isn't there. At least, he wasn't three weeks ago."

"How do you know?"

"Joe met him in the Wild of a town called Wallasey, on the River Mersey."

"Excellent. That means he's no longer Fiona's puppy dog." Flo's smile is happy. "My brother has gone home to Waleas Eig, the place he loves best. We'll leave at dawn. You'll have your song magic back by tomorrow night."

Escape by river

KENI WAITS UNTIL long after the broad cargo vessel is tied up to the jetty and all movement aboard has ceased before he takes a risk and pokes his head over the weather deck.

Another night. Another city. The three-quarter moon rides high above thinly stretched clouds sailing on a brisk wind. He glimpses a wide, star-filled sky in gaps between bulky unlit buildings that line the river. It wakes again the yearning for open spaces that's been clawing at his insides for the quarter cycle he's spent hiding on boat, after boat, after boat.

Gangs of uniformed men search the vessels at every stop. Between the stuffy heat and fumes below decks, and his forced inactivity, he worries about getting careless if he can't find a different way to travel.

A canoe. He climbs out of the hatch and crouches on deck, horribly exposed and vulnerable but needing to check his first impression of the shape in the darkness. No doubt about it, there's a canoe lashed upside down to the wheelhouse roof of the boat in front.

He looks around and listens, wary of crossing open spaces with no chance of finding cover if anyone comes along.

Nothing. Apart from the gusting wind, all is still.

He stays stooped to run across the deck and over the lightweight metal walkway that shakes and rattles, sprints along the stone jetty to the next boat, pads over its sturdier timber walkway, and darts into a pocket of shadow behind the wheelhouse, where he crouches and waits for his heart to stop hammering.

Still no indication that anyone has seen him. No suggestion of any other living thing in his little part of the loud world.

He reaches up to untie the canoe's lashings.

Powerful lights flare into life along the jetty, blinding him in their bright glares and leaving him no place to hide. He freezes and squeezes his eyes shut, wishing the dancing violet images would fade from his eyelids and hoping against hope that the lights are nothing to do with him.

A distorted human voice shouts words he can't understand. From the jetty, the sound of many booted feet running in his direction tell him to get away fast.

Something slams into the guardrail as he reaches it. A red-feathered hunting dart is embedded in the timber, close enough for him to touch.

He leaps over the guardrail, hits the dark surface with a big slapping splash, and strokes underwater as hard as he can to the deep channel in the middle of the river.

His breath gives out before he gets there, but he doesn't surrender to the expanding pain and panic. Only when the strong current clutches him like he's a twig and bowls him along does he kick upwards into the night and fill his lungs.

He's already a long way downriver from the boat. The men crowding its guardrail look small in the cold glare of the lights behind them, but their shouts of alarm carry across the water when he breaks its surface.

A new throbbing sound drowns their cries. The curved front of a big vessel towers above him. Its bow wave lifts him and spins him helplessly. It pushes him up and aside, then pulls him back down and in. He swims hard to get away, but he isn't strong enough to escape the force that slams him along the hard side of the vessel towards its churning propeller.

Something coarse brushes his face, a thick rope with the broken remains of a fender bouncing from wave to wave.

He grabs it and holds on, swallowing water as he fights to pull himself clear of the immense strength-sapping drag.

He climbs high enough to clamp the soles of his feet around the rope at the top of the ruined fender. That allows him to relax his arms, cough up some river water, and recover his breath. But his limbs are too weak and shaky to stay there for long. He hauls his exhausted body up the rope, flops over the boat's solid timber side railing, and falls to the deck in a trembling heap.

The outer deck area is softly lit. Fortunately, no one is around. He drags himself through the nearest door into the vessel's humming interior and staggers down a flight of stairs, then another, and another, until he reaches the deserted, fume-filled engine room.

The gold nuggets are still safe in his knotted pockets.

He curls up in a dark corner and lets consciousness float away.

*

"Are you all right, Lael?"

Her tears are silent. *"No, I'm scared I'll never see him again."* She's swimming underwater to hide her distress from the villagers. Two fine lines of golden tears stream behind her before they blend with the lake water.

"I believe you'll see him again." I hug her with my mind. *"His instinct for survival is amazing."*

"No golden has ever returned to us after a quest so difficult, so dangerous. The only similar quest was Mahu's, and you know how that ended. He nearly died and has been crippled and sick ever since."

"Keni's still ahead of his hunters."

"Barely. How long can he evade them? And where are all these other hunters coming from? The loud world people. The worst any of us has had to deal with before is Mountain men.

They're bad enough, but Keni isn't safe no matter which world he's in." She weeps.

I hold her close in my mind. It's all I can do. I have no words that won't be useless platitudes.

She makes a determined effort to get herself together, surfacing near the village shore and stretching her powerful wings. *"You're sick. I'm sorry I failed to notice until now. Let me heal you."*

"Thank you." I shiver as her warmth flows through me and banishes the horrible aches and cramps from my muscles, but the trembling exhaustion remains.

"Better?"

"Yes, thank you."

"I'll look in on you regularly. Call me if you need me. I'll hear you."

"I will. Thank you." I drift off into sleep like a baby in her arms. My last waking thought feels like a promise. *"I'm sure Keni will come home to you."*

It's a curse

BAN RECOVERS FROM the bug overnight, but by dawn, I'm in an even worse state. The first frost of the year paints the forest sparkling white. It would be pretty if I didn't feel like death. The sharp cold is an iron band tightening around my head, and every muscle aches like I'm being beaten with heavy hockey sticks. I'm so exhausted I can't even grow into the oak anymore, so there's no relief anywhere.

If I move at all, it's only ever a groaning crawl on hands and knees to the toilet clearing, but otherwise I stay in my shelter.

Ban doesn't come near me. He barely looks at me.

Lael heals my pain when we communicate telepathically, but the exhaustion never lifts, and the sickening cramps invade my muscles as soon as I'm alone in my head again. I don't consider trying to return to the lake and see her in person. Even that short climb up the stream would be impossible.

Andrew's grateful that I'm staying on to see the project through, despite my condition. He doesn't argue one way or the other but doesn't try to disguise his relief when I make my decision.

Part of that is my desire to see Keni get home safely, but mainly I'm simply too weak to walk out of the Wild.

"I brought you blankets and more painkillers." Andrew wraps a woollen blanket around my shivering shoulders while I swallow two tablets with a mouthful of water.

The warmth is welcome but slight because the cold is mainly coming from inside me. I hand him yesterday's recording with clumsy fingers and wonder how long he'll hang around.

All I want is to crawl back into my shelter and curl up with my misery.

"Chicken soup." He pours a thermos cup and holds it under my nose.

It smells delicious. Too hot to drink and too heavy for me to hold, but delicious. I remember my mum nursing me through childhood mumps and measles. Min looms large in my thoughts, and I can almost feel her arms around me. I blink tears away, pretending it's steam from the soup.

I don't think Andrew is fooled. He puts a steadying arm around my back and holds the soup for me to sip.

We sit in silence. I drink the first cup, then a second, and feel a little better with its heat in my belly. By the third cup, I'm strong enough to hold it myself and dunk chunks of fresh bread in it. But then my stomach rebels, and I have to stagger urgently to the toilet clearing, waving Andrew back when he makes a move to accompany me.

When I'm done, he's still on the log. "I feel bad about leaving you here alone," he says.

"Stay if you want." I hope he doesn't.

"Do you want me to?" He doesn't sound keen, but I appreciate his sense of duty.

"Nah, I'll be okay. Only a few more days, and by the time we're done here I'll be over this bug."

"If you're sure."

"Go on." My attempt at bravery probably looks pathetic, and the light hurts my eyes too much to look up. "Bugger off and let me rest."

I stay on the log and listen to his progress down the hill, preparing to crawl back into my hole and try to sleep.

"Good morning, Joe. Hello, Doggy."

Apparently, peace is postponed. "Hello, Thomas."

He sits on the log and studies me. "You look dreadful."

"Thank you."

"Don't mention it." He shakes his silent bell. "We're going to fix you."

I'm not sure I like the sound of that. But before I can question his intentions, Joan leads a small procession into the clearing.

Two biggish piskies strain under the weight of an old-fashioned tin bathtub. Joan guides them to the middle of the open space and sends four smaller bucket-bearing piskies to the stream. Within seconds, my normally quiet home is buzzing with activity. A few minutes later, the bathtub is filled with cold stream water and twenty-odd little people turn their full attention to me.

Thomas gives me a happy thumbs-up.

"No way."

His face falls. "What's wrong?"

"It's freezing. I'm ill. You think I'm getting into a bath of cold water? Dream on."

"Is that all you're worried about?" He chuckles and strolls over to stand next to his wife.

They join hands over the bathwater. The other piskies maintain a respectful silence, although they all keep glancing at me from beneath lowered lashes while their king and queen do whatever it is they're doing.

I sit in a dull mind funk and stare at the ground between my feet. Next time I look up, thin wisps of steam are wafting from the water's surface. I stop my jaw from dropping open. Maybe I'm at death's door, but I want to maintain a bit of dignity.

A matronly pisky pours glittering salts into the water and stirs them while Thomas and Joan continue making their magic. The surface swirls and steams. The pink-cheeked matron watches for a while, then tests it with a finger and taps Joan's arm. "Ready."

Piskies try to lift the blanket from my shoulders.

I hold on tight.

"Stand up." Joan watches from near the bathtub. "We know you're feeling awful poorly. Let us help you."

"A hot bath will be lovely," I mumble. "Thank you, but you can leave me to it now."

They're having none of it, and I surrender. When I stand, the world goes dark and slides almost out of my reach.

Strong hands grip me, helping me to stay upright and walking me forward. Other nimble fingers unfasten and remove my clothing as we go. By the time we reach the steaming bathtub, I stand shivering in only my thermal long johns.

Joan nods at someone behind me. The thermals are whipped down to my ankles and a cold breeze strokes my painful body.

Joan's eyes widen. "Hello, pretty." She gives a coarse cackle, which the other piskies echo.

Except Thomas, who frowns at his wife and stomps back to sit on the log, where he opens a leather-bound book and studies it.

Joan sidles alongside him and cuddles up with a coy smile until he slips the book into a pocket. He wrinkles his nose and looks happy again when she kisses his cheek.

I turn back to the bath. I'm shivering violently and close to collapse. I don't care if I have an audience or not. Getting warm is the only thing on my mind. Strong pisky hands support me while I step out of my thermals, climb into the tub, and slide down until the water reaches my chin.

It's perfect. Heat soaking into my muscles melts all the aches away. Their sudden absence leaves me even more exhausted as tension drains from my neck and shoulders, but it's a pleasant exhaustion replacing the deathly one, and it's lovely.

Hands wash me. Lots of hands at once, all over. Then they give my muscles a light massage. I sink into it and enjoy the wonderful relief from pain and sickness, as well as the luxury of a hot bath and complete cleanliness for the first time in nearly a month. I groan with deep contentment.

"How do you feel now?" Thomas is standing at the foot end of the tub.

"Lovely." I crank an eye open for long enough to scan my circle of enthusiastic helpers. "Thank you, everyone. You're wonderful. I feel a lot better."

"Good. We'll come in and give you a bath every day until it lifts."

"The bug, you mean?"

"Bug?"

I try to peer at him for longer this time. It seems rude not to. "Virus. Chill. Whatever it is that's poleaxed me."

"It's a curse."

That jolts my eyes open. I fight their determination to close again. "What?"

"It's a spell. A powerful one. We can ease some of its effects, but it's too strong for us to break it."

"Who cursed me? Sylph? The wolf had it too yesterday."

Thomas exchanges a look with my hostile campmate. "Interesting. Not the Sylph. This isn't their style. They're too pompous and arrogant to play a sneaky trick like this. If they wanted to knock you down, they'd turn up in person and make a song and dance about it. No, someone's making you too sick to leave this clearing." He steals another look at Ban. "And that same someone punished your guard for allowing you to leave here the other day. Make sense?"

My mental exhaustion is lifting while we talk. It's that fast. I try to sit up, but the recovery hasn't reached my limbs. My arms are too weak to pull me up and the water is too inviting to fight it. "Who?"

"I guess it's someone who's angry about you visiting the red temple and doesn't want you to go back there. Wouldn't you say?"

Ride north, sail south

THAT WAS FUN!" Flo's eyes shine beneath the visor of her child-sized crash helmet.

"It's the fastest way to get around." Min holds the bike steady for Flo to jump down, then stretches her stiff back and studies the place Flo has directed them to after five hours in the saddle.

They've pulled off a busy main road into a lay-by. Twenty feet behind them is a gate to an old sandstone schoolhouse someone has converted into a pretty home. Ahead, a path leads to worn stone steps rising through trees to a ridge of rough ground above. Lanes slope away down a steep hill on the other side of the busy road, and through gaps between rows of houses Min sees low-lying land stretching into the distance. "This is your home?"

Flo gives a piercing whistle to Ouzel, who swoops down and lands on her shoulder. She kisses his beak. "It's Gully's home. Ours is the old western uplands, everywhere in it, all of it, but lately he's got attached to this place."

"The old western uplands?"

She gestures at the grey mountains blending with a dull, slate-coloured sky on the southwest horizon. "Cornwall, Wales, Cumbria, the Grampians, and the Northwest Highlands. This here is Wallasey, which they say is in England now, but in the old days before they reclaimed the marshes, it was a rocky island off the coast of North Wales. People here are descended from the ones who defended Wales against Romans, Saxons, and Vikings."

Min studies her. "You and Gully were around then, weren't you?"

"And Ouzel." Flo winks. "And you."

"How come I haven't heard of you until now?"

"We don't advertise ourselves."

Shad chuckles. "Come on, ancient people. I need food."

Tae opens her laptop, and Vua wheels her heavy machine alongside to read too. "We'll stay with the bikes. If there's food, will you bring us some?"

"Of course." Min looks around. "Where can we get into the Wild?"

Flo points back up the road to the crown of a hill they rode over. "Up there and double back into a footpath up to the woods."

"Why bother going all that way when there's a thin place just here?" Shad points up the stone steps.

Flo frowns. "Must be small. I can't feel it." She glances at Min. "Can you?"

Min can't.

"It's a way up. Come on." Shad strides to the steps.

Min catches up with him. "Did you teach Joe how to locate thin places? I wondered where he got that from."

Shad grins and winks.

"Wait," Tae calls. "People on Onion Layers are saying Joe's sick."

"I know. I listened to his latest podcast on the way here. The piskies are looking after him, but I want to find him quickly. As soon as I get my magic back."

"There's more," Vua says. "Keni thought he'd be safe for a while on the riverboat that nearly ran him down, but next day, Joe's podcast gave his hiding place away. A private company called Safe Combination Security has bought permission from the American government to hunt and capture him. SCS. They stopped and searched the riverboat in Pittsburgh, where several people reported seeing him escape over the side and swim away underwater."

Min hurts for him. "That poor boy."

Vua continues reading from the screen. "People are saying SCS is a dangerous company. There's a new Onion Layers thread dedicated to it. In the past twenty-four hours, groups of heavily armed SCS operatives have been sighted in Pennsylvania, New Jersey, New York, and California. And an hour ago, sixteen of them got off a plane at Heathrow."

Min's heart sinks. "They're in London. They're listening to Joe's podcasts and trying to find him."

Vua's nod is grim. "They'll lead Tyac to him."

Everyone stares at one another.

"Come on." Shad runs up the steps.

*

"I can't do it." Gully struggles to speak with Shad squeezing his throat. His words come out in a painful squeak.

"Shad," Flo says, "put him down. I know how you feel, but he's still my kin."

Shad releases the old man's throat with a growl and shoves him back into his chair.

"You've forgotten so much," Flo tells her brother. "It's time you came home."

Gully rubs his throat and works his jaw while he peers at her in the gloom. "I haven't forgotten."

"Then why can't you give Min her magic back?"

He stares into the fire with a glum expression on his craggy face.

"This is important," Flo says. "You remember Joe? He was here with your friend Andrew a few weeks ago. He's in terrible danger, and we need Min's magic to protect him. Magic you stole from her when you were working for that awful Hare woman."

"I understand."

"So give it back!"

Finally, he raises his eyes and stares at his sister across the smoking fire. "You know how it is. I can't remember as much as you do now, but I haven't lost everything. What I *have* lost is my staff. I used it to silence her magic, and I can't make her sing again without it."

Flo clicks her tongue. "Nonsense. That staff is only a prop, like your silly cloak of feathers. You don't need them. They're symbols of power, not the power itself."

He doesn't answer.

Flo taps her foot on the dirt floor. "So where is it?"

Gully stares at her for a moment then screws his eyes up as if in pain. "Queen Fiona's pet wizards took it after the Quarter Square fiasco. I was lucky to get out of her camp alive. If I go back, she'll kill me."

Flo lets fly an angry string of words in a language Min doesn't know.

"You don't know that," Gully snaps back, in English but just as angrily. "You're reborn and living in big-picture land. Well, good for you. Wasn't so long ago you were where I am now, so don't you go talking to me like I'm a fool. I did what I did for good reasons. Just because I failed doesn't make the cause any less important. So you can stop your bloody lecture right now."

Shad grabs him by his throat again and slams him into the wall so hard the entire construction shakes. "I don't care what you and your sister are arguing about. Joe's my friend and you're going to help us save him. If it costs you your life, you're going to help us. Do you understand?" His knuckles turn white as he squeezes.

Gully turns puce.

"Shad." Flo sighs. "Will you please put him down?"

Shad glares into Gully's bulging eyes for long moments before he releases him again.

Min tries a new tack. "Do you know where Joe and Andrew are?"

Gully's voice cracks the first time he tries to speak. He glowers at Shad, swallows with a wince, and tries again. "They're in the Wild, in the woods above Talland Bay, near Looe in Cornwall." He stares at the ground.

It's a start. She holds his hand. "I forgive you for taking my magic. We were fighting on opposing sides in a battle, and you did what you had to do in the circumstances. I don't take it personally." She dips her head and tries to make eye contact.

He meets her stare.

"Can you give it back to me, please?"

"I'm telling you the truth. I can't do it without my staff."

Flo springs to her feet with an air of command. "So we'll go and get it."

Gully gives a weary nod of resignation. "One of my ships is unloading cargo in Porthmadog today. Her crew and firepower might come in handy. We'll go by sea."

"We will not." Min has a long lifetime of bad experiences on ships. "We've got fast motorbikes."

"I won't travel long distances in the outside. And neither will you if you have any sense. These things happening in the Wild are worrying, but they're nothing compared to the danger we're all in from this country's government in the outside. You have no conception of the terrible events they're putting into place. And there's a dangerous government man called Sebastian Merritt who would love to get his hands on me." He glares at Shad. "Kill me if you want, but I'm sailing to the West Country in the Wild and that's my final word."

When they return to the bikes, Vua scans their faces and takes note of the new addition to their number. "No food?"

"We'll get some on the way." Min points to the distant horizon. "We're riding over those mountains to get on a ship."

"Okay." Vua starts her engine and Tae closes her laptop.

Min loves the unruffled way her werewolf friends accept whatever comes along.

Ten minutes later, they are thundering along the motorway to Wales.

*

Min feels like death. Her stomach lurched the moment *Belle* set sail on a stiff wind, and after two days on the wooden ship fighting an angry Irish Sea, she wonders if her insides will ever be trustworthy again.

It might help if she could throw up. She's spent hours hanging over the side, soaked to the skin from the relentless spray and shivering violently. She wills it to happen, but it doesn't, so she keeps stumbling back down to collapse into a hammock in the captain's cabin, where she sweats a greasy film all over and groans every time the ship slides down another wave or slams into another solid wall of water.

Lucinda Mercedes leaves her pretty much to herself. Min doesn't know if this is a kindness, or if the captain's duties keep her on deck through the rough weather.

A hurried conversation before they left harbour confirmed that Gully's claim about Lucinda's affection for Andrew is true. Nevertheless, she comes across as a capable woman.

She also mentioned that Joe spent a day aboard *Belle* and made a big impression. Apparently, his exploits led the crew to believe he's a powerful wizard.

Mister Samson moved into the crew's quarters with Shad and Gully so the sisters and Flo can sleep in his cabin next door to Min. They check on her frequently and encourage her to try a few bites of bland food. It seems she's the only one suffering from seasickness.

It's always been the same, even before she became immortal. Anything more than a ripple on flat water turns her into a groaning heap of woe.

Footsteps clatter down the ladder outside the cabin. She realises she's been asleep and that the ship's motion has changed. It's almost comfortable now, for the first time since they left Porthmadog.

Vua's voice comes through the cabin door, followed by some words in a man's deep tone. Then comes Vua's again, thanking someone for something. When the sisters enter the cabin, one is grinning widely and the other blushing.

Vua glares at Tae, but there's no real anger in her expression, even when Tae bumps shoulders playfully and nearly sends her sprawling in the ship's still-uncertain motion.

Min raises an eyebrow and waits for the explanation she senses is coming.

"Vua has a suitor."

Vua stares open-mouthed at her sister. "*Stop* it!"

"Why should I? It's a lovely thing." Tae winks at Min.

Min's mouth is so dry she has to try twice before the word comes out. "Who?" She sips water.

"One of the sailors," Vua replies.

"His name's Red Argument," Tae says. "He's a quiet mountain of a man who's lost his heart to my beautiful sister."

Vua's deepening blush suggests the attraction might be mutual.

Min feels better for her nap, especially now the sea is coming from behind the ship. There's still an unpleasant lifting sensation at intervals, followed every time by a downhill rush that prevents her stomach from settling, but it no longer threatens to leave her body. She rolls cautiously out of the hammock and tests her rubbery legs. "I'm happy for you."

Vua grabs her when the deck tilts sharply as the ship starts a prolonged, shuddering turn.

Min hugs her. "Really happy." Over Vua's shoulder, she smiles at Tae, who gives her a delighted thumbs-up. "So, where are we now?"

Vua lets her stand upright when the deck levels again. "Anchoring in Widemouth Bay." She shrugs in response to Min's unspoken question. "Somewhere. I don't know. It's the closest they can get us to the Hare camp. We have a night run ahead, with us carrying Flo and Gully."

"And me."

"Are you well enough?"

"I'll be fine when we get back on dry land. I'm coming."

Tae produces a plate of toasted bread slices and a jar of orange marmalade from behind her back. "You'll need fuel for strength."

She's right. Min's body rebels at the thought, but she forces it into submission and eats her toast while they prepare to leave the ship.

The coast is deserted in the early evening gloom when six sailors row them to a broad crescent of sandy beach. Vua's big redheaded sailor stands shoulder to impressive shoulder with Shad in the pounding surf to hold the boat steady while they climb out and splash ashore.

Shad and Tae go off in search of a thin place, while Min waits in the fine drizzle with Flo and Gully. Vua and Red move away along the beach for a private conversation until good-natured jeers from the other sailors bring them back to the main group. Then the boat rows out into the surf and back to *Belle*.

Gully complains about having to ride on a wolf's back.

Flo tells him to shut up.

"Before we go, you need to hear this." Tae and Shad have returned quickly, and Tae taps the closed lid of her laptop.

"What now?" Gully demands.

"Keni's left the Delaware Forest and is running to the coast. Bookmakers are offering odds on which lake in the outside will correspond with Lake Sunrise in the Wild. SCS operatives are all over New Jersey and upstate New York, roughing people up. There's a lot of bad feeling about them. People are finding thin places everywhere. Several creatures have crossed from the Wild and been shot dead. Keni keeps giving SCS teams the slip, but Joe's podcasts keep revealing his location. So everyone's talking about the podcasts." Tae catches Min's eye. "And that's very bad, because now the whole world knows where Joe is too."

Min's heart sinks so fast she nearly collapses.

"It hit Onion Layers today. A boy in Looe has been following Andrew from the town into nearby woods and back again for days. He recognised Andrew from things Joe's said on the podcast. When he posted about it, the forum went from nought to sixty in ten seconds flat."

"Joe," Min breathes.

"Tyac will hear about this." Shad pulls off his T-shirt as the moon rises over the headland.

Tae and Vua are already naked and crouching in their preferred shifting positions.

Shad hauls off his sea-sodden boots and jeans. "We must find Joe quickly."

"I need my magic to stop Tyac." Min's voice is hoarse with pain and fear.

Flo squeezes her arm. "We'll get it." She glares at Gully. "*Won't* we?"

The old man gives a distracted nod as he watches three people turning into wolves before his eyes.

Queen Fiona of Hare

"How will we get past them?" Min asks.

Rain falls steadily on their backs as they lie among rusting pieces of discarded armour and broken weapons on an open hilltop. The dark dawn is cold and threatening. In a broad valley below, Tin's besieging army surrounds the substantial terraced hill of the Hare camp in an unbroken circle of tents, smoking campfires, and corralled horses.

"Getting past the Tin army won't be a problem," Gully says. "It's what Fiona will do when we get in that worries me."

Ouzel flaps his wings to keep his place on Flo's shoulder while she rummages in her pocket. She produces a cube of red ochre, like the one Tara Hand crushed into a paste to colour Flo's skin for her magical rebirthing funeral ceremony. She nudges Gully and shows him. "This is for you."

He looks appalled. "Thank you. That makes me feel so much better about everything."

Flo puts the ochre back where it came from and strokes his face. "You know I love you. I'll look after you. I always have and I always will. Don't be scared now."

Gully closes his eyes and gives a heavy sigh.

"It's time, brother. You've gone far and forgotten much. It's time for you to remember."

"I know." When he opens his eyes, they're brimming with tears. One spills over and rolls down his cheek.

"I'll be here for you. And you never know," Flo smiles, "they might just hand over your staff without any trouble."

"Yes, and pigs might fly."

"I saw a pig fly once."

Gully frowns. "Really?"

Ouzel caws a scornful sound.

"No, you idiot." Flo grins at Gully. Then she gets serious again. "Come on. Let's go and see what's what."

Min gets to her feet and follows them. The wolves move too, and they all walk in a tight little group down the hill towards the Tin army.

"What shall we do when they see us?" Min asks.

"No one will see us," Flo says. "I'm casting a cloak. Stay together and keep quiet. Don't let those wolves go for the dogs on the way in."

They walk straight through the Tin lines without a single human looking their way, although when they pass a corral the horses white-eye them and pull at their tethers. Then they climb the hillside to the Hare camp.

Each fortified terrace is protected by a deep ditch and patrolled by Hare soldiers and their fierce war dogs. They walk past them all silently and as easily as they passed the Tin soldiers.

At every level a new team of dogs starts up a furious racket that confuses and angers their handlers, but Shad and the sisters ignore them and keep close in behind Min.

The camp sits inside a timber stockade on the stepped plateaux that form the pear-shaped top of the hill. Cattle, sheep, pigs, and goats graze in separate compounds on the bigger and slightly lower level, while the people and their poultry live in concentric rings of houses on the higher level.

Driving rain eases to a fine mist that wafts across the hilltop. Min shivers in her soaked clothes. Her hand on Shad's back gives her some security, and she appreciates his comforting shoulder bumps against her side as they walk.

Flo and Gully halt in an open space in the middle of the camp, at one end of a long fire pit filled with embers.

At the far end of the glowing pit, beneath an awning, stands a carved, tall throne of shiny yellow-brown wood. Round houses with pointed thatched roofs over low daub walls surround them.

The atmosphere is tense, but in a focused *getting on with business* way. Small children play quietly beneath wide roof overhangs, out of the drizzling rain. Older children work with adults, weaving, working leather, and preparing food in the doorways of houses.

"I'll do the talking," Gully murmurs. "When Flo lifts the cloak, stay close together and let me deal with whatever happens." He glances at Min over his shoulder. "Can you convey that to the wolves?"

"They understand what you say."

"Okay." He releases a shaky breath and nods to Flo. "Do it."

Nothing changes about the way Min sees the world around them, but Flo's removal of their invisibility is obvious immediately when the nearest Hare people cry out in alarm and three mothers scoop small children to safety inside their houses.

Gully takes a step forward to place himself in front of Flo. He stands straight and proud, fists balled on his hips and his cape of bird feathers rustling in the wind as if it's alive. He juts his chin and glares down his nose at the growling war dogs and warriors who are assembling with a rumble of angry muttering around the edge of the open space.

"Fiona Hare!" His voice is powerful, reminding Min of the way he commanded his troops in Quarter Square the day he stole her song magic. The imposing figure he cuts now is a far cry from the complaining old man she's come to know over the past few days. "Fiona Hare!"

"You still have your balls. I'll say that for you." The queen strides into view between two round houses, flanked by a heavily muscled, nearly naked warrior on one side, and four wizards wearing decorated animal-skin cloaks and helmets on the other.

She's about seventy, Min guesses, with healthily weathered skin and long, iron-grey hair gathered at her nape. The thick torque of twisted gold wire ropes around her neck lends her good posture and a regal bearing, and its flattened terminal rings are decorated with a pattern that matches the hefty gold ring on her right index finger. She heads directly for her throne and sits upon it before aiming a haughty glare at her visitors.

The brawny young champion stands at her side with an expression of calm indifference, while the wizards array themselves behind the throne and glare at Gully. The oldest of them carries a five-foot-long wooden staff covered with intricate carvings and painted symbols.

"You know you're going to die now, don't you?" Fiona's words are spiked with contempt. "This siege we're suffering is your fault, and today you will pay for it. I don't know why you've brought two girls to die with you. Axe wolves I can understand," she surveys the wide circle of frenzied dogs, "although I doubt even they will survive this day. Satisfy my curiosity. Why have you come back?"

"I want my staff."

"This?" Fiona receives the staff from her sneering chief wizard. "Senovara tells me you put everything of yourself into this. He's extracted all your knowledge from it."

The four wizards take up an incomprehensible chorus that they drone together, never taking their eyes from Gully.

Fiona holds the staff horizontally and looks up at her champion, who leans in so she can whisper something in his ear. She turns her attention back to Gully. "This lump of wood is now as redundant as you are. You want it back? You can have it."

The warrior takes the staff from her, weighs it, then draws his arm back and hurls it like a spear along the length of the fire pit.

It strikes Gully in the chest and rips right through him with a sickening, meaty thud, piercing his back until ten blood-dripping inches of it sticks out behind him. He staggers under the impact and falls into Min, who catches him and lowers him to the ground.

Her heart hammers and her own blood sings in her ears as his soaks into her clothing. She is shocked and horrified at the sudden dreadful violence. She feels crushing, suffocating guilt at her part in insisting he must come to this place, to his death. And she is scared.

Gully stares at Flo as the life leaves his eyes.

Instantly, the mood around them changes from barely restrained hostility to open fury. Dogs snarl and leap at them when they're released from their leashes. Men shout. Fiona screams high above the noise, ordering her warriors to kill them, kill them all.

Shad, Tae, and Vua face outwards, placing Min at their centre. They snarl and bunch their muscles, crouching to meet the attack.

Min springs to her feet, panting. Her heart thuds in her chest and throat, and she gapes around wildly as death comes howling for them.

An explosion of pressure in the air brings sudden silence and stillness to the chaos. Everything freezes in mid-movement. Every person and every animal. Min too. She's paralysed. She can see but can't move a muscle. It's as if time has stopped.

Something dark moves in the sky. It rustles like dry leaves in the silence as it passes through Min's peripheral vision above her. Then it comes into sharp focus and lands beside the fire pit.

It's big, huge, like a blackbird the size of a stretch limousine standing up on end. Only it's nothing like a bird. Feathered, beaked, wide-winged, and sharp-clawed, it's all those things but also it has a human shape somewhere within it and a human type of intelligence in its piercing black eyes.

It screeches a sound of rage like nothing Min has ever heard before in all her long life. Then it stalks along beside the fire pit to the paralysed queen.

You are a bad woman! The huge bird blasts the words without uttering a sound. Min hears it in her mind.

Worse than that, you are a fool! The sharp yellow beak juts perilously close to Fiona's frozen face.

You spend all your time and effort fighting the Tin people, when they are the same as you. You spend your people's blood on this stupid war. And for what? For your pride!

The final word is accompanied by another terrible screech, one that rocks the stiffened Fiona hard against the backrest of her throne and echoes in the mist.

My brother told you there are more urgent battles and more important enemies. He counselled you to make peace with Tin and fight those enemies together. What did you do with this advice? You scorned it. You didn't want to hear his wisdom.

Dark clouds gather on the horizon all around and rush in to the hilltop.

And now you have murdered him!

The clouds crash overhead, exploding thunder and lightning into the camp and sending cold rain lashing from all directions in strong, blustering, confused winds.

The blackbird goddess who is Flo and Ouzel together seizes Fiona's champion in one of her terrible claws, lifts him high into the air, and slams him to the earth, and again, and a third time. She throws his broken body aside and does the same to Senovara. Then she seizes the queen and lifts her high.

But she doesn't crush Fiona. She holds her in the air for long moments and watches her getting battered by the storm, then throws her back into the throne.

I won't kill you now. Your people need leadership, and you, foolish woman, are the queen they know. More importantly, Tin knows you. The world is in turmoil, and Hare and Tin have a part to play. Together! I don't care how you do it, but make peace with Tin. Quickly!

You've angered me, Fiona Hare. Don't make the mistake of thinking I will ever forget this day. Don't think I won't come back to destroy you in an instant if you anger me further.

She juts her savage beak into Fiona's face again and glares at her a final time. Then she scoops up Min, Shad, Tae, Vua, and her dead brother's impaled body, and carries them high into the storm.

Lake Sunrise

KENI CROUCHES LOW behind a curtain of willow leaves at the water's edge, watching the mermaid while she watches a boat of midnight-clad soldiers puttering along beside the distant far bank of Lake Erskine.

She is breathtakingly beautiful. The most alluring creature he's ever seen. For now, she remains perfectly still in deep shadow beneath a wooden jetty tucked into a small cove, with only her eyes and the top of her head above the surface. From Keni's vantage point, he can see the swirl of jewelled colours underwater that is her tail keeping her steadily in position while she studies the patrol boat.

That tail is powerful. At dawn, his eyes had widened in amazement at her incredible speed when she swam back to shore from her hunt in the middle of the lake. She was underwater the whole way, but he followed her fast progress by means of the rippling arrow wave she made. And he gasped aloud when she shot from the surface in a glittering stream of water with a big, flapping catfish gripped between her teeth.

It was his first glimpse of her, and he'd been unable to drag his attention away ever since. She'd emerged from the bushes, holding the dead catfish and walking on normal legs like a normal person. Lovely legs, leading up to a beautiful bottom and a strong back, with luxurious black hair dripping rivulets of water down her perfect black skin as she climbed the steps to her cabin.

His chest ached with something like grief until she reappeared, dressed in a flowing white gown that covered most of her body but served only to tantalise him further with its hints of her curves and lines and shadows.

She sat in a deck chair on the jetty and opened a book, which occupied her full attention until soon after the sun passed overhead, when a distant engine noise announced the boat's approach. Then she draped her gown on the chair and slipped back into the water without a sound.

The boat continues its slow, inquisitive journey along the far bank until it passes out of sight. Its engine noise reduces immediately when it goes behind a headland, then fades into the distance.

An upwelling of water from the mermaid's tail fluke suggests she's swimming out to watch the intruders depart.

Keni sits back on his haunches and listens to his thudding pulse. His heart is lost. He wants only to sit here and watch the mermaid for the rest of his life. He won't need food. The hunger that's kept his senses sharp all the way across the wide continent is gone, replaced by a solid lump of excitement in his throat and a thirst for another chance to see her.

He stretches out on his belly to get a drink of water.

A rushing movement below the surface draws his attention, and he's shocked to see the mermaid's face rising straight at him. He slithers back from the edge in a frightened panic as she breaks surface and giggles at him.

The liquid silver tones of her laughter and her wide smile of shining white teeth delight him. His heart thunders. Blood thumps in his temples. His manhood grows and stiffens.

"Hello, golden boy." Her eyes are startling blue, like a flawless summer morning sky.

He falls into them.

She giggles again. "I said, hello."

Her breasts are visible. Beautiful, small breasts with deliciously dark-brown erect nipples.

He gulps. “Hello.”

“You want me to take you to Lake Sunrise.”

“Yes.” What he really wants is to stay with her forever. “How do you know?”

“Young goldens always need me to show you the way.” She extends her long, slender fingers to him. “Come.”

He touches her fingers and in an instant the lake falls upwards to enfold him. The mermaid pulls him down, down, far faster than he can swim. Bubbles stream behind him, his old life streaming away with them. He wants only to be with her forever.

His breath finishes. His lungs are empty. Blood rushes through his veins and his flesh panics, but it’s a remote sensation that has nothing to do with him. All he wants…

She twists them into a sudden stop in the deep water and breathes air into his mouth, forcing him to inhale it and to live, to continue living, to live and go home to Lael.

His beloved’s visual image and her strong presence springs fully formed into his mind, and he returns to his senses.

The mermaid pulls him deeper into the lake, pausing regularly to breathe air into his mouth.

She smiles every time they kiss, and his heart aches for her, but he knows now that she can’t help the effect she’s having on him, and he can’t help being affected the way he is. He also knows who he is again, and why he’s here, and where he’s going, and who is waiting there for him.

Lael.

His muscles jump. They’ve swept through a thin place underwater, and some heartbeats later, everything jumps again when they sweep through another one. Then they’re rushing up through dark water towards the growing and growing and ever-growing pale light above.

They break surface and shoot waist-high into the air, startling two youngsters in a nearby canoe.

"Beryl!" they greet the mermaid then shout her name louder to attract attention and get help for a very weakened Keni.

A golden woman swims out and bears him to shallow water.

He gazes back at Beryl the whole way, and she returns his stare with a sad smile.

When a golden man takes Keni in his arms and lifts him onto dry land, Beryl waves once then dips below the surface and disappears without a ripple. He gives a feeble wave back, then drops his arm heavily and sighs.

The golden lays him on the beach while several others gather around him. He tries to sit up, but his body is too weak and heavy.

"Don't be concerned," the golden woman who fetched him says. "You will recover. What's your name?"

He flops back and looks up at the circle of golden faces with the evening sky above them. "Keni."

"I'm Wan Wah," says the one who lifted him ashore. "Do you have Mountain gold for us?"

"Yes." Care and anxiety lift from Keni's shoulders like birds taking flight. He struggles with the soaking wet waistband fastening but eventually manages to haul off his trousers, untie the knotted pockets, and pull out the nuggets.

He holds the first in an open palm. "I'm taking this one home to Golden Lake." He hands the second to Wan Wah. "This one is for Lake Sunrise."

The goldens smile as one and lay their hands on him, filling him with new strength and reminding him of his last tender moments with Lael and her parents nearly a moon ago.

Wan Wah flies high above the middle of the lake, beating his great golden wings slowly to hold himself in place for some beats before dropping the nugget. It enters the water with a *splunk* and a small splash. He flies back and lands at Keni's side.

"Rest now. You quest is nearly complete. I'll take you home before the full moon rises over your lake tomorrow night."

A golden touches her light fingertips to Keni's eyelids, and he drifts away in peaceful sleep.

A funeral at sea

MIN LEANS INTO the tilt of the deck as *Belle* thunders across racing foam-tipped waves, thanking heaven that she's found her sea legs. Sea stomach, more like. Whatever it is, she's grateful for it, and especially grateful to Lucinda for the tea of secret ingredients that's probably helped more than anything.

The wind blows strong from the west, which is precisely where they want to go in order to round the jagged rocky tip of the Cornish peninsula, so Mister Samson is sailing them in that direction by means of a tight zigzag pattern that leans them first one way then the other at regular intervals.

Astonishingly, she's enjoying the motion.

Lucinda stands beside her while Flo prepares to perform Gully's funeral on the gun deck, out of the cold buffeting wind and flying spray. "You look better."

"I feel it. Thank you for the tea." Min wonders why she didn't offer her secret remedy during those two hellish days in the Irish Sea, from Porthmadog down to Widemouth Bay.

"I was angry with you." Lucinda stares straight ahead. "The first words I heard you speak were untruthful ones about Andrew. I'll never believe he betrayed Joe or any of his friends. But I realise you're as frightened for your man as I am for mine, and when we're frightened our judgement can suffer. Also our tempers."

Flo paints her brother's face, hands, and feet with the red ochre paste. Then she daubs it along the length of his wooden staff. Ouzel perches on her shoulder and watches.

"Mine as well as yours," Lucinda says.

Min nods her acceptance of the sort-of apology. She really hopes the captain is correct. The thought of Andrew deliberately betraying Joe has been tearing a new hole in her already scarred heart.

Flo claps her hands for attention. "I am Flo Crow. Gully Crow is my brother. We have travelled a long way together, and our journey is not yet over."

"How can that young girl be Gully's sister?" Lucinda whispers. "He must have been eighty years old."

"I think you'll understand soon," Min whispers.

Flo squats at Gully's head, puts her fingertips to his temples, and says quietly, "Go with love, my brother." She stares around at the small group of people and wolves who are leaning in unison as the ship turns to a new tack. "This is Gully Crow."

"Why have the wolves stayed...wolves?" Lucinda speaks in a respectful low tone as Flo chants strange words and performs a simple, repetitive dance around Gully's supine body.

"The moon is full, so they have no choice about it for a few nights. They stayed wolf in daylight this morning to help us in the Hare camp, and I don't suppose they had much chance to shift afterwards when Flo flew us back to the ship."

"Ah. That *was* Flo then?"

It must have been a shock for the sailors to have a huge blackbird goddess land on their ship out of the storm clouds and then disappear in an instant, leaving her bedraggled party sprawling like landed fish on the rain-washed deck planks. Especially when one member of that party was a dead man and three of the others were big live wolves. Min's lips twitch at the memory of the faces on those poor sailors. "Yes."

"Thought so." Lucinda purses her lips. "You know, I've the feeling I might be about to lose a valued member of my crew to yours."

Only three people from the *Belle* are attending Gully's funeral. Lucinda is there to pay respect as the ship's captain.

The bosun is waiting to sew Gully's body into a weighted canvas wrap after the ceremony, in preparation for his burial at sea. And there's Red Argument, whose strong presence beside Vua tells his story loud and clear without any need for words.

"How do you feel about that?"

"We'll miss him. A lot. But he's a free man, and I'd say his mind is made up. My concern is, what will happen to him if he leaves with you when we finish our business together?"

Min frowns. "If he'll take the bite, you mean?"

"Yes."

"As you say, he's a free man. No one will do anything against his will, if that's what you're worried about. The Axe are the most honourable people I've ever known. Also, I haven't spoken to Vua about it, but I imagine it's very early days to be thinking of that sort of thing."

The captain sighs. "Okay. I guess that will have to do."

Min finds Lucinda's hand at her side and squeezes it. "If he comes with us, I'll look after him."

"Thank you." She returns the squeeze, then gasps. "Oh!"

Gully's young spirit is rising from his old body, as Flo's did when her old body died in the summer. Her young spirit became the astonishingly powerful force of nature in a child's body that they all know and love today, and Min fully expects Gully's to become something similar. Right now, he's grinning delightedly at Flo, and she's giggling at him while his heavy old staff lifts into the air and burns away to ashes in seconds.

Without warning, Joe fills Min's thoughts. She can almost smell his natural scent and feel his strong arms around her.

Will they ever escape the circle that's bound them for thousands of years? If Joe manages somehow to kill Tyac, what will happen to them? Would Tyac's immortality curse lift from Min with his death? Would her mother's ancient binding enchantment leave Joe then too? Would they enjoy a single mortal life together then pass into peace? Or are they destined to follow the same repeating patterns of death and life forever?

Lucinda is still clutching Min's hand and staring at the boy Gully with her mouth open.

Min chuckles. "Now do you understand the brother-sister thing?"

"I guess so. Who are they?"

"Old gods of western Britain. They've been around forever and they're very powerful. Especially in their pure childlike stage, apparently. Which is a good job, because tonight we're going to need all the help we can get."

"Is it going to be that bad?"

"I think so. I checked online before you lifted anchor. Big professional teams of men have been seen behaving like they're armies about to go into action in three different places in the outside world today. Mount Shasta in California, Lake Erskine in New Jersey, and Looe in Cornwall. That last team are the ones we'll be facing tonight. If we get there in time."

Lucinda gives a definite nod. "We'll get there."

Flying across the ocean

Keni nestles on Wan Wah's broad back between his wings, his arms wrapped loosely around the golden's neck.

Wan Wah holds his passenger's forearms in a mighty grip and flies vertically into the air, high above the land, and within heartbeats high above the ocean, far more powerfully than Keni did at the beginning of his quest.

He feels the true power of a real golden, thrilling at the thought that his quest is nearly complete and soon he will know this power in himself.

For now, his exhaustion is so overwhelming it's all he can do to stay awake. But Wan Wah maintains a firm grip on his arms and Keni doesn't fear anything. He focuses on breathing calmly throughout the flight and uses the slow, regular beat of the golden's wings as a guide.

He remembers the young man he killed, and Jhed killing the young man's father to save him. Again, he regrets throwing the gold nugget so recklessly hard.

"Something is troubling you."

That wakes him up. He didn't know a golden could detect his emotions and talk to him in his mind without uttering words.

"What is making you sad, Keni?"

He tells Wan Wah about his clumsy error and the innocent young man who paid for it with his life. Also about the young man's father.

Then he speaks of Lael's peaceful ways, and how for the first time he thinks he understands her. *"Until my quest started, I always thought being a golden would be about strength and glory. About protecting our people with my might. I used to smile indulgently about Lael's gentle nature and looked forward to the day when I can be a real golden and protect everyone, including her."*

In his mind, he feels Wan Wah smile. *"Many of us feel that way, until we discover what is real."*

"Until we grow up, you mean."

"Don't be harsh with yourself. Life is a series of lessons, to be learned from or not. Becoming a golden is simply another lesson along the way. And there'll be more to learn when you settle into your new way of life. This is normal."

"Still, that young man and his father died because of my mistake."

"You regret it, and you have learned from the experience."

"I look forward to learning peaceful ways to protect our people. I look forward to talking with Lael."

"You love her."

"Yes."

"You are blessed. Few goldens experience the kind of love you and Lael have."

Keni feels her presence so vividly, he opens his eyes to see if she has somehow appeared before him. In not very many heartbeats he will be with her again, where he belongs.

"You and she will grow together in wisdom and protect your people well, I think."

"Are there any real dangers around Lake Sunrise that you have to protect against?"

"Those days are long past, I'm glad to say."

"It's the same on Golden Lake. No threats anymore."

Crescendo

INSTEAD OF LEAVING once he's delivered my breakfast and swapped recorders, Andrew stays with me all day. After listening to yesterday's recording, he pats down his pockets then hands it back to me. "Keep this one safe too, will you?"

I button it into the left chest pocket of my quilted lumberjack shirt. The erased one for today's recording is in the right chest pocket, and I memorise that so I won't mix them up, because today's recording will be the most important of the whole month. Today's event is what this thing is all about, Keni coming home and becoming a golden.

Lunch is another vacuum flask of hot chicken soup for me, and a double pack of chicken sandwiches for us to share. We sit side by side on the log with me wrapped in my blanket, and he encourages me to lean some of my weight against him.

I'll be glad to get some proper strengthening meals inside me when I get back to the outside, although I don't know how the hell I'm going to walk out of the Wild when this is all over. My limbs are still trembling weak. My magical pisky baths take away the pain for an hour every day, but they don't touch the exhaustion.

Will the sickness lift when I leave this place? I hope so, but what if it doesn't? What will I do then? Find out who's put the curse on me and make the bastard remove it, I suppose.

But it'd make more sense to do that before I leave the Wild, wouldn't it?

I stare at Andrew's booted feet planted next to mine and listen to him munching a sandwich. Can he help me? Probably best not to hold my breath. He's as lost and confused as I am.

Who's done this to me?

If Thomas is right about it being someone who doesn't want me to visit the red pyramid again, the strongest candidates have to be the priests. And that young firebrand Noala is my prime suspect.

My head aches just from trying to think in straight lines.

"Quick!" Thomas appears out of thin air and pulls us to our feet. "You too, Doggy!"

He drags us to the northern side of the clearing, where Joan appears from nowhere too and gestures for us to hurry. They're agitated, pressing us to our knees in the undergrowth.

"Doggy!" Thomas is distressed at Ban's haughty refusal to move, or even to look at him.

"Come on, Ban."

He responds to my calm voice, which is a pleasant surprise as he's made a point of ignoring me since we got ill after my jaunt to the temple.

We all huddle together, and I twist to peer at Thomas. "What's going on?"

"Soldiers from the outside." He glares at Andrew. "They followed him into the Wild."

My brain buzzes. "How many?"

"Forty."

Is this more of Merritt's crap? "Shouldn't we hide?"

"We are hidden. Joan and I are cloaking us."

"They can't have followed Andrew in. He's been here with me for hours."

"They waited inside the thin place. Their leader sent two men to track Andrew to this hill, and they've taken turns reporting back to the main group. Our piskies have been watching them all day. The soldiers caught my Uncle Michael this morning.

They killed him and threw him into the bushes like he's a piece of rubbish. They're coming here now."

"Where were you while all this was happening?"

"Joan and I were at a meeting on Dartmoor. Tin and Hare are trying to negotiate a peace and they asked us to be there as neutral observers."

Ban's ears prick towards the clearing entrance. He growls low in his throat.

We all shut up and wait for the soldiers to appear.

*

Belle anchors in Talland Bay as afternoon merges into early evening without any change in the light quality or greyness.

Gully's guided Mister Samson from Land's End up the south coast of Cornwall and into the deep Wild, where Tae's social media observations suggest a mercenary unit is about to attack the people of Golden Lake, and where Joe's recordings indicate he is most likely to be found.

The passage was fast and furious with a strong westerly wind behind them, and the sudden absence of its roar leaves Min's ears numbed when *Belle* turns into the sheltered bay.

Lucinda and Mister Samson waste no time in anchoring, then clearing the spars and decks, and the crew impresses Min with their no-nonsense expertise.

As soon as the ship is secured, everyone arms themselves and readies for battle, except for Mister Samson, his skeleton crew of six sailors, and the old cook. Pistols and cutlasses bristle everywhere. Min even sees four of the old-fashioned sailors carrying modern machine pistols. Goodness knows where they got hold of *them*.

The bosun takes charge of lowering the boats, and the first two gangs of sailors row ashore to set up a beachhead.

*

"No one here," one of the soldiers reports in a confident Texan drawl to the lantern-jawed man in command, who stands with his booted feet planted wide apart and fists on his hips like an invading king in the middle of my clearing, while the others wreck my camp.

"Signs of recent occupation," the soldier continues, "but no indication where they are now."

They all wear the same plain navy-blue combat uniforms and speak with American accents. Do they belong to the same outfit as Keni's *midnight-clad men*? Every one of them is heavily armed and scarily aggressive in that calm, menacing manner always adopted by TV actors playing Special Forces soldiers.

Americans, wearing no identifying insignia, conducting a military operation in the UK. Is this Merritt's doing? Are they his men, or are they operating above and beyond his authority? Are they on an official joint operation of the UK and US governments? And which of these things would be worse?

No contest. A joint US/UK government operation would be the worst.

My guess is that Merritt is just a corrupt public servant on the make, anywhere and anyhow he can grab a piece of the action, and that he's looking to extend his reach into the Wild. The low-rent thugs he employs in his Revenue operation suggest he's more an opportunist thief than a real player with his own mercenary army.

Although, until we blew it up, his forces in Liverpool included a gunboat, so he isn't short of resources.

Whatever he's up to, he's a nasty piece of work who is threatening my parents, and I look forward to taking him down somehow.

But these characters are in a different league.

"Fuck it. We're here for the gold in that lake, not this shit." The commander kicks my upside-down tin bath and raises his voice, drawing everyone's instant attention. "That's our target today, men. To secure the lake. Anything gets in your way, you kill it. Doesn't matter what we find in there or what they throw at us. They're savages. Kill the fuckers. Got it?"

"Sir!" The chorus of growled replies sounds like a single deep snarl.

"Move out."

They form a single file and step down into the stream one at a time. Within minutes, the last man in the line splashes up the hill and out of sight.

Joan stands. "I'll follow them into the deep Wild and lead them a pretty dance in the forest. You warn the goldens."

Thomas's laugh lines are deep creases of concern. "Take care, lover."

"I will. You too." She gives him a quick hug then goes to the stream and disappears.

Thomas sighs from the bottom of his soul.

I'm putting my arm around his shoulders to give him a comforting squeeze, when Andrew squints up and grunts in surprise.

Something dark smashes through the treetops and falls heavily towards us.

Thomas drops to the ground, pulling the tin bath over himself. Ban steps backwards into the undergrowth.

The big, winged creature grabs me around my neck without even landing and flies back up with Andrew and me hanging below it. We crash through the canopy into the darkening sky, veer sharply through a thin place in mid-air, and head straight for the red pyramid.

I can't breathe properly. The creature's grip around my neck allows me only shallow panting breaths, which aren't helped by my terror as the forest flashes by beneath us.

In the bay to our left sits a familiar ship. It looks identical to *Belle*. Why is she here?

We land hard, and I collapse in a bruised heap on the stone platform near the top of the temple, where Thomas and I stood when he took me there by magic. We're on the sacrifice platform.

Andrew struggles to his knees, holding his throat and heaving painful breaths. He stares at the creature and wheezes, "Stone! It's *you*!"

He is powerful and winged like a golden, but not a golden. His skin doesn't glow. He's naked and burned and scarred. He's a man, not a creature. And his name isn't Stone.

It's Mahu.

He swings a heavy punch at Andrew's chin that sends him sprawling across the stone surface. He doesn't bother with me. Why would he? I pose no danger to him. He's made sure of that by cursing me, the bastard.

I lie helpless while he lifts the unconscious Andrew as if he's as light as a child, throws him across one of the altars, and lashes him to it.

He lights a brazier that sends thick, black, oily smoke out to be scattered by the wind, then picks me up and lashes me to the other altar.

The ropes are made of twisted roots. If I had any energy to use my wood magic, I could loosen the bindings. But I have none. No strength. No magic. He's hollowed me out. I'm trapped. At Mahu's mercy. And he doesn't have any mercy. Fear wells up in my chest. Andrew and I are going to die, and I'm helpless to stop it.

Another figure in a dark robe climbs the steps to the platform and throws back his hood just as the brazier catches and flames lick yellow light across his face.

Noala. The tall young priest with branded cheeks. The angry priest who wants rid of goldens.

I knew it.

"Mahu, what are you doing?" He stares at Andrew and me on the altars, then back at the old man. "What are you thinking?"

Mahu is using a fist-sized conical stone to grind herbs or something in the sacrifice dish. "I'm taking back what our weak and foolish ancestors lost."

The young priest's eyes are wide pools of astonishment. "Are you mad?"

I got Noala wrong. Lael is right about him.

But she's got Mahu wrong. The old bastard has fooled everyone.

Noala puts a comforting and persuasive tone into his voice. "We should talk about this. You haven't gone too far. You can come back from this dark place." He reaches behind Mahu's back to touch the wings sprouting from terrible scar tissue.

Mahu spins on the balls of his feet and smashes the pestle rock into the side of Noala's head.

He slumps to the floor without a sound.

Mahu takes a stone knife from the dish and stoops to carve open the young man's chest. Blood spurts over his bare arms, but he pays it no attention. He plunges both hands into the chest cavity, rips out Noala's heart with a horrible wet sound, and raises it to his face as he stands, dripping blood all the way.

He gives me a serene smile before sinking his teeth into it and tearing off a big bite. He chews and swallows, then takes another bite, and another, until he's eaten poor Noala's heart.

Battle in the forest

JOE, WHERE ARE *you? What's happening?"* Lael's anxious voice rings in my mind.

"I'm being held prisoner on the sacrifice platform of the red temple. Mahu is insane. He just murdered Noala and ate his heart."

"No!"

"He's going to sacrifice me and my friend. Help us."

"I'm coming."

"No, wait. There's something else. Soldiers from the loud world are in the deep Wild. They're coming to kill you all and steal the gold from your lake."

"Where are they?"

"Joan the Wad is leading them astray in the forest to give you a chance to organise a defence. Warn everyone."

"Thomas is here telling my parents now. I'll add what you've told me. Then we'll come for you. Hold on, Joe."

*

Keni's homelands spread out below them in the glowing early evening light. Tiny, white-capped waves crash into cliffs, or wash across beaches of pale sand, and glorious trees crowd together in every shade of autumn over hills that roll gently from coast to coast. He's so excited he can hardly breathe.

There's a ship with tall masts anchored in the bay nearest to the beautiful, dark, three-sided shape of Golden Lake.

Wan Wah tips forward and they begin a long, smooth descent, but suddenly the golden's graceful glide is interrupted. *"People are attacking my home."*

Wan Wah's distress makes Keni's heart ache. *"Who?"*

"The same midnight-clad soldiers who were hunting you."

"How did they get through the thin places into Lake Sunrise?" Then his mind's eye sees the same thing Wan Wah is seeing. *"Oh."*

The soldiers aren't in Lake Sunrise yet, but they're trying to get there. They're in Lake Erskine in the loud world, on land in Beryl's cove and in boats out on the lake. Beryl dragged some down to their deaths before others threw pressure bombs into the lake and forced her to swim to safety deep underwater.

Now goldens are bursting from the surface and throwing soldiers into the water.

The soldiers' resistance is diminishing. Some goldens sustain gunshot wounds and are taken back to be cared for in Lake Sunrise, but the midnight-clad attack is failing.

"I think it will be peaceful again soon."

"For the time being," Wan Wah says. *"However, the people who sent those soldiers will send more. Our home isn't safe anymore."*

Golden Lake is close now, but Keni's attention is caught by a pretty light twinkling in the trees immediately below. It reminds him of the warm feeling in his childhood home, before everything became cold and unfriendly. He wants to follow it.

A loud world gun barks somewhere in the forest, and the friendly light winks off. He feels its loss, but only for a heartbeat. Then he can't remember exactly what he saw. He has only a vague memory of something lovely. Something to do with a light.

More loud world guns bark, and Wan Wah shudders horribly. They're falling. Not gliding. Falling. Tumbling uncontrollably to the trees.

"*Keni!*" Lael's fear fills his mind.

Sacrifice

"YOU'RE INSANE." ANDREW is conscious again. At first, he struggled against the ropes holding him down, but now he lies still and stares at Mahu. "Now I see who you are. There's a lifetime of horror showing in your face, but I recognise the youth who shared my fire one night forty years ago."

The hazy full moon rises over distant hills behind Mahu, as he turns from the spectacle he's watching in the forest and smiles lazily at Andrew. His craggy face is smeared with Noala's blood. It looks like dark paint in the firelight.

"You wanted to know about the angels. Well, now you do. They're goldens, not angels. They're mortal, and they have weaknesses like other mortals. They live and they die. Their only advantage is that they can fly. Well, guess what." He spins around and spreads his powerful wings. "I can fly too."

"You're nothing special," Andrew growls. "All these years I've thought of you as my angel, but your envy of the goldens has made you bitter and evil. There are many evil men in the world. They're two a penny. You're nothing special."

"That isn't what you thought when we met in the desert."

"I was only a kid. So were you. I've learned a lot since then."

"Not as much as you think. There are no angels. There's only magic. Our people have always known two sources of magical power, that of the goldens, which is merely borrowed and temporary, and the ritual magic performed and controlled by our priests. But I found a third course. Sylph magic. I've taken it and transformed it."

"You've been sacrificing innocent creatures and eating their hearts to steal their magic. That's how you can fly." I put the picture together as I speak. "And when the Sylph migrated to get away from you, you started hunting and eating piskies. And now you've eaten a human heart too. You're a monster."

Mahu turns back to watch the battle raging below. "All sacrificial hearts add to my power," he says over his shoulder. "This is the old magic of my people. This is *my* magic."

I can't see anything from the altar except the night sky full of racing clouds, Mahu's head and rhythmically flexing wings, and his flaming brazier.

But I hear plenty of gunshots from across a wide area, both single shots and the rapid fire of machine guns, and in my mind's eye I see disjointed flashes of light and movement via Lael's thoughts.

These include the faces of soldiers she and the other goldens are fighting with swords, as well as images of running wolves, pirates engaged in hand-to-hand combat with the attackers, two children slamming soldiers aside with waves of their hands, and, astonishingly, a fleeting glimpse of two women who can only be Min and Lucinda Mercedes.

How did they hook up together? And what the hell are they doing in the middle of a battle between angels and soldiers in the deep Wild?

A burst of clear soprano song rises from the forest, and my heart leaps. No doubt about it. Min's here, and from the sound of it she has her magic back. For the first time since Mahu abducted Andrew and me, I feel hope. More than that, I thrill with love for Min, my Min, who is somewhere nearby.

There's a sob of disappointment in Andrew's voice when he speaks again. "When did it all go bad for you?"

Mahu half turns and opens his mouth to reply, but Andrew talks over him. "Oh, I've heard your legend in Joe's recordings. No need to bore us with that again. What was it all about anyway? Why did you pretend to be Stone, and why insist on me giving you the recordings?"

"I've been broadcasting them every day in your world." Mahu is hugely pleased with himself. "I've learned a lot about various technologies in your world. I knew you as soon as you mentioned your desert experience. I judged you to be a naïve fool, and subsequent events have proved me right. I knew the story of a lake full of gold would attract an army to steal it. And here they are."

He sweeps his arm to encompass everything happening in the forest.

"The goldens are powerful, but well-armed soldiers from your world should be an even match for them. The two forces will wipe each other out. When they're done fighting, I will destroy any survivors on both sides and step into the power vacuum."

"What about your son, you twat?" I know he'll make me pay for this, but I can't resist hurting him if I can. "Your stupid game just cost him his life."

"His stupid idol worship cost him his life. I played no part in that."

"Joe!" The relief in Lael's voice is almost a physical thing. *"Keni's alive. I caught him before he hit the ground and got him into the lake before the moon rose. Not only will he recover, but he brought the sacrifice of his quest home and he's becoming a golden now."*

"That's good news. I'm very happy for you both."

"My father caught Wan Wah in the air, but he was already dead. When this is over, we'll take him home across the ocean to Lake Sunrise."

"I'm sorry."

"Please don't tell Mahu about Keni. Try to keep him occupied for a while longer. Keep him talking, but don't goad him too

much. I'm standing with someone who very much wants you to stay alive."

Her smile shines in her words, and through her eyes I see Min.

Love floods me. Overwhelms me. I've been damping down how much I've missed her during the month of our separation, but now yearning breaks free and fills my existence. *"Tell her I love her and have no intention of dying tonight."*

"She's relieved to hear it. Now we have work to do."

Our connection dissolves.

"What about your friend?" Andrew is back on Mahu's case. "If you won't take responsibility for the death of your boy, how about the one you sacrificed for your own freedom on the Mountain all those years ago?"

This is news to me, so I stay quiet and let Andrew run with it.

"I saw a fast-moving light burning bright from east to west in the desert sky. It went from horizon to horizon in a matter of seconds. Joe's recording of Keni's journey confirmed for me what I saw that night was someone going on a golden quest. For years I believed it was you, because you stumbled into my camp a few nights later, all torn and battered. Those two incidents started me on *my* life's quest, if you like. But I also listened to your story in the recordings, so now I know that your quest started three months earlier. By the time your friend...what was his name?"

"Sona."

"By the time Sona arrived, you'd already betrayed him to the Mountain men, hadn't you? You'd trained for the quest together. You knew he was on his way and when he'd get there. They were expecting him and shot him down easily. The legend you've built is that you took advantage of the confusion and escaped. But the truth is, you bought your freedom with Sona's life. Didn't you?"

Mahu shrugs. He's still watching the battle and obviously doesn't care what Andrew has figured out.

"Sona was your first sacrifice. Then you came home playing the big hero and let Sona's sister nurse you. You married Annam and had a son together. And now you've killed the boy too." Andrew is shouting. "Your whole fucking existence is a lie. You failed to become a golden in your youth, and you've spent the rest of your life hating everyone and plotting your revenge on the world."

"It was never revenge." Mahu growls. "Revenge is a petty human emotion. I lifted myself above such needs and desires. I'm destined to lead my people. Golden magic is a pale imitation of the great power our priests of old built to protect the people. When golden magic failed me, I decided to study the old ways and rebuild that great power in myself."

Andrew sighs heavily. "Golden magic didn't fail you. It was you who failed, you sorry piece of shit."

Mahu moves fast and punches Andrew's face so hard his head bounces off the rock altar. He glares at me as if daring me to say something. When I hold my tongue, he stalks to the front of the platform and stands proud to watch his plan come to fruition.

"These are terrible things we're learning about Mahu tonight."

"I'm sorry, Lael. I know you respected him."

"Truth is truth."

"How's the battle going?"

"On the face of it, badly. But our elders have gathered. They're joining the battle now, and I don't expect anyone will stand against them. We'll come to release you soon."

"What?" Mahu staggers back from the platform edge, his voice cracking with shocked outrage. "What's this?"

Through Lael's eyes I see a host of ghostly golden elders rise from the lake and totally swamp the invading force. All over the forest, skirmishes end cleanly and quickly without a further shot being fired. The awesome presence and power of the elders reduces hardened mercenaries to weeping bundles of shame and regret. Within minutes of Lael making her prediction, it comes true.

"No!" Mahu screams his fury into the night.

Andrew chuckles.

"Don't," I murmur, but my warning is too late.

Mahu whirls on him and rips his shirt open to expose his chest.

Andrew isn't laughing anymore.

Mahu is, though. His laugh is completely unhinged and terrifying. "Don't worry, old man. I have a Plan B. That's what they say in your world, isn't it? Plan B."

Something moves in my peripheral vision. I'm almost too weak to turn my head but manage to lift it slightly and drop it back down, facing the movement.

It's the Green Man. Jack. He's climbed the shadowed side of the pyramid and now makes his way slowly, silently, to my altar.

"As my plan to destroy the goldens and rule my people in this world has been ruined," Mahu tells Andrew, "I will become a god in your world instead."

Jack stands beside my altar and dissolves my twisted rope ties with a single touch.

Mahu is still ranting. "I will gain strength and power in your world by eating as many human hearts as I wish. And I will start by destroying the community I know holds a dear place in *your* heart. Quarter Square, I believe it's called."

Jack holds my gaze and mouths, *"Brother."*

I mouth the same word back and nod my thanks weakly as he turns away.

When Mahu turns to get his knife from the stone dish, he sees Jack shambling back to the dark edge of the platform.

He grabs a burning branch from the brazier and hurls it at Jack, who bursts into flames and falls over the edge out of sight.

No! I squeeze my eyes shut, shaking with grief and anguish. When I reopen them, Mahu is standing beside Andrew's altar, taunting him with the long stone knife.

"Die now, old man. Die knowing that all your friends will follow you into oblivion soon. Know that I will eat their hearts as I am about to eat yours."

I roll off the edge of my altar and grip it to remain vertical. Sylph magic. It's Mahu's strength, and it will also be his weakness. The Sylph can't bear iron. It hurts and weakens them, stops them using their magic. I fish out the two metal recorders from my shirt pockets.

Mahu raises his knife high above Andrew's chest.

I lurch across the platform and drape myself over his back and shoulders, holding him the same way Keni held Wan Wah while they flew, except that I'm using my dead weight to pin Mahu's wings between us and clamping the two metal cases against the bare skin of his chest.

He rages and struggles.

I hold on.

He fights violently at first, so strongly I think I won't be able to hold him. But eventually he starts to weaken. I feel it in his struggles, in his grip on my wrists. Even in his size, although I may be imagining that. He seems to shrink in my desperate embrace. Then he starts keening. He falls heavily to his knees and groans from the bottom of his miserable heart.

I hold on tight with my recorders clamped to his scarred skin.

When he slumps to the stone floor, his wings break off from his shoulder blades, leaving new stumps oozing blood in the old mass of scar tissue.

I check which of my boots has the iron nail in its sole, the right one, and stomp it down on his ribcage to hold him in place until help comes. I grip the altar's edge and hope they won't be long.

They aren't. The first heads appear to above the platform edge are Min's and Lucinda's, followed immediately by four panting wolves, and big Red Argument from *Belle.*

But before they all reach us, Lael's parents fly up from the lake and take Mahu in hand. They wear magnificent swords in scabbards strapped to their backs, but he doesn't put up a fight. He doesn't look like he has one left in him. He can hardly stand unaided.

Lucinda unties Andrew and hauls him off the altar into her arms, while Min hugs me like she'll never let me go.

I don't want her to. I fill my lungs with her lovely scent, my mind with her presence. "I'm never leaving you again. Don't ever try to make me."

"I won't." Her voice is muffled against my chest. "I promise. Never again."

More people appear, climbing the red steps to the sacrifice platform. All the lake people. Hundreds of them crowd up the steps to stand and stare at Mahu.

Among them is the small, quiet figure of Annam. Mahu's wife. Keni's mother. Sona's sister.

Annam crosses the platform and looks down at him. When Myen and Lu haul him upright, he sneers at her. She reaches past him to pick up the long stone knife from the altar and stares into his hate-filled eyes while she thrusts it into his heart.

He dies in silence.

Tyac

GOLDENS FLY US to the lakeside, where I'm elated to see Jack the Green Man sitting in the shallows with Keni and two wounded goldens. The water around them shimmers like flowing liquid gold. Thomas and Joan perch on rocks nearby, talking with child-Flo and a young boy.

"Brother." In any other circumstances, I might have been embarrassed about the squeak in my voice, but I'm too overcome with emotion to care.

"Brother." New green growth all over Jack's body shows the terrible extent of the burns he's suffered, but his beautiful wide grin tells me he's going to be all right.

Child-Flo beams at me. "Good to see you made it okay." She pokes a thumb at the cheerful fair-haired boy beside her who is feeding insects to Ouzel. "I believe you and my brother Gully are already acquainted."

Oh! I look forward to hearing *that* story.

"Get in the water, Joe," Lael says.

Hearing her voice normally instead of in my mind brings me close to tears of relief. The horror is over.

Her eyes fill with tears too. "Mahu's curse is broken with his death. Let the elders heal you."

Jack steadies me when I stumble into the water. I sit, and he puts his brawny arm around my shoulders to pull me close.

Waves of warmth replace the water's natural temperature as golden liquid shapes massage my pain and exhaustion away.

Min sits beside me in the water. We hold hands like teenagers on our first date, smiling with shining eyes.

I'm glad to see Joan is alive and well. "They shot my lamp," she complains.

"I'll make you a new one," Thomas says. "A new lamp is easy." His face crumples. "For a while there, I thought I'd lost you."

"Aw." She hugs him to her bosom and strokes his head while his shoulders shake. "There, there. All over now."

He lifts his head and wipes his eyes dry. "Not really. This place is famous now across the worlds. There'll be more trouble to come."

Because of me.

"No, Joe." Lael heard my thoughts. "Not because of you. Mahu used you and Andrew the same way he's been using all of our people for longer than anyone can remember. You are innocent of any wrongdoing, or poor judgement, or ill intention."

All but one of the goldens has joined us in the lake now, looking truly awesome with those splendid swords strapped on their backs between their wings. They murmur agreement with Lael's words.

"Nevertheless," Lu says, "Thomas is correct. And so was Wan Wah. As he said about the location of Lake Sunrise becoming common knowledge and taking away his people's security, so it is for us here in Golden Lake. Tonight, we defeated the first attempt by outsiders to raid our home, but that won't be the only attempt. Others will come."

Lucinda joins us and catches the tail end of Lu's prediction. "What will you do?"

The goldens exchange measured looks.

"We will consult the people," Myen says. "But I don't think we have any choice other than to move elsewhere and start again."

"There are plenty of other good places still." Thomas has regained his chirpy good humour. "The Sylph are happy in their new home. I can talk to them for you."

The goldens nod to one another.

"Thank you, Thomas," Lu says. "We will consult with our people."

"Where will *you* go?" Lael asks us.

"Somewhere quiet for a while." I squeeze Min's hand. "Do you know about the deal I had to make with Merritt?"

"Yes."

Andrew gives an embarrassed cough. "Something else about that."

Uh-oh. "What?"

"Before I left the house yesterday, one of Merritt's thugs called with another message. Merritt's had your parents flown over from Florida. For their own safety, he says. They're in London."

I should have expected it. Merritt isn't a man who leaves anything to chance, and he won't trust my word unless I have no choice but to keep it. I lift a disapproving eyebrow. "And you didn't tell me this yesterday because...?"

"Because we were going to spend the whole day together and I didn't want you not talking to me again."

Lucinda steers the conversation to safer waters. "Why don't you all come back to *Belle* for a few days? We can catch our breath together, and I'll set you ashore wherever you like."

Andrew's eyes gleam.

I follow Lucinda's glance at a group of four wolves and one big human beneath the tree line farther along the beach. Shad and Ban sit proud, shoulder to shoulder, watching our meeting. Tae watches storm clouds racing across the night sky. Red Argument sits with an arm around Vua's shoulder, and she leans comfortably into his chest. Clearly, there's more than one story for me to hear.

"Hare and Tin want Gully and me up on Dartmoor to help them thrash out a truce," Flo says. "We'd better get there before they mess it up."

Min and I purse our lips at each other and shrug. Why not? "If you could take us up to Plymouth, that would be great," Min says to Lucinda.

She explains to me, "We've got our bikes in *Belle*'s cargo hold, but the insiders have kept all those other bikes the Hare soldiers left in Quarter Square. So you and Shad can choose one each from among them. Also, I want to let Tara know we're okay."

The last golden flies in over the trees and lands on the beach. He addresses the others urgently. "There's a dangerous creature heading this way." He glances at our wolves. "A man-wolf monster in an insane rage."

Adrenaline pumps in my veins, and I meet Shad's serious stare. Will the time be now?

Min jumps to her feet. "It's Tyac. He's hunting Joe, but he'll kill anyone who gets in his way." She takes Myen's hands to get her full attention. "You don't want him here among your people. I've seen him destroy entire communities bigger than this."

Lael stoops to kiss Keni. "Stay here, my love. Let the change continue at its own pace." She stands and faces the other goldens. "We should draw this monster away from the lake."

"Take me," I say. "Let him see you're carrying me, and he'll follow you to the ends of the earth."

"I'm going with you," Min says.

Lucinda calls to her sailors, who are scattered around the lakeside settlement, resting after the battle. "We'll return onboard and get underway," she tells Andrew. "Will you join us?"

He looks at me. "What about Merritt?"

"Go. Take our wolves onboard. We'll draw Tyac away from the lake then come and find you. Merritt can bloody wait."

Everyone is in motion at once. Lael picks me up in her arms as if I'm an infant, and Lu picks Min up the same way.

"You don't want us on your backs?"

"That impedes our wings," Lael says. "Fine for long distances, but not ideal for speed and manoeuvrability."

We take off in a vertical rush that feels like I've left my insides in the lake, but as soon as we clear the trees, we slow down and fly more comfortably, despite the storm of wind and rain that comes howling in from the sea at our backs.

"We want your monster to see us," Lael says in my mind.

"Yes."

The golden who's already seen Tyac leads us, and after a five-minute flight, I see my old enemy tearing across densely packed treetops towards us. Our closing speed takes me by surprise. I think Tyac's strength and agility take Lael by surprise too, because when he leaps high into the air, she doesn't have time to avoid him.

He grabs my dangling left arm.

It's hot agony. His grip is like a steel clamp, his massive weight hanging from my wrist. If not for Lael's tight hold on me, he would have dragged me from her arms.

His roar carries over the storm as he swings his left arm up to try and get hold of me with both hands. He misses the first time, and the second, but sooner or later he'll make it, and I imagine him climbing up my arm to get his teeth around my throat in mid-air.

"My sword."

I crane my neck and squint at Lael through the red mist darkening my vision.

"My sword!"

Its golden handle juts up from behind the near side of her neck. I stretch my free hand up, hoping against hope that Tyac's weight hasn't pulled me too far down for me to reach it.

My fingertips touch the handle, and I stretch farther, farther, farther, while Tyac snarls and growls below me, his swinging weight threatening to snap my arm off at the shoulder.

I grip Lael's sword handle and pull. The sabre leaves its scabbard in a smooth movement that continues as I whip it down in a flashing arc as hard and fast as I can.

The impact is so brutal, for a second I think I've hit my own arm. But I haven't. The razor-sharp heavy blade cuts through Tyac's forearm just above his wrist.

I hold his severed hand as he falls back to the forest and crashes through its canopy, screaming rage all the way.

A promise

THEY LIE IN bed, sharing their thoughts and fears from the month of separation. Min insists he read all her texts. Then she talks him through her long night of healing with Flo and how she's coming to terms with many things.

"I can change." She's melting into his lovely chest and glories in his strong arm around her. "I've already started."

"You're okay, love."

"I haven't been. I really haven't been okay for a very long time. I yearned for you when we were apart. Then I was scared out of my wits whenever we were together. I was so terrified of losing you, I held on too tight and nearly strangled our love. I've done it many times. It's fear that made me so untrusting. I'm still afraid, but I will never again fail to trust you."

He kisses her. "I love you."

"Our love is the centre of my universe. It's what holds everything together." She props herself up on one elbow to let him see the conviction in her eyes. "I know I don't need to hold on so tight. I don't need to hold everything together."

He gazes deep into her eyes. "I love you, Minsilvia of Atlantis. I'll never let myself get frustrated with you again without speaking of it. We'll talk. Always. Whatever the problem is, we'll talk it through. Yes?"

"Yes." Joy fills her heart.

They make sweet love, and then fall asleep in each other's arms.

Sometime in the night, she feels his weight lift from the bed. The moon casts a block of silver light from a tall window across the floorboards to the doorway, where Lael's sabre leans against the wall. It was her parting gift to Joe.

From Min's warm, sleepy place, she watches him walk naked from the bedroom with her phone in hand. She isn't concerned. He'll come back. She smiles and sinks into peaceful sleep.

*

"It's been a few days since my last podcast, and it'll probably seem strange to many listeners for me to finish the story this way, but I only want to say this to one person, and I don't know any other way to do it.

"You know who you are.

"I know you're still out there. You think you're clever, but I know more about your movements than you know about mine.

"I burned your hand to ashes and scattered them in the wind. Think about that, bastard.

"If I have to kill you one chunk at a time, I will.

"I'm hunting you now."

BOOK III
FULL CIRCLE

These people interest me

"WELCOME TO SILCHESTER, the most unaltered Roman city site in Britain." Our tour guide, Sharon, is quick and agile for her age. Sixtyish, I guess, but with a youthful spirit belying the salt-and-pepper in her pixie haircut. She climbs a steep, grassy bank and removes her mask while she waits for us to join her at the top. "This is the amphitheatre, originally constructed of wood around seven hundred AD and then remodelled in stone in the third century."

Min and I are first up behind her, then Shad, Tae, and Vua, with Ban and Red bringing up the rear. We're wearing combat boots and clothes suitable for the late November cold. Each of us carries a well-packed rucksack.

The amphitheatre, enclosed by substantial earthen banks, is a flat sunken circle with a diameter about the length of a basketball court.

"Seating for seven thousand spectators." Sharon's breath clouds when she speaks. "We don't know exactly what entertainments they came to see here, but archaeological evidence from similar sites tells us activities probably included animal baiting, gladiatorial combat, and public executions."

"Animal baiting," Tae repeats.

"Dogs, bulls, and bears." Sharon's cheeks are bright pink. They match her scarf, while her sky-blue cagoule matches her eyes. "Ancient Roman society was brutal compared to ours."

I catch Min's eye. No less brutal nowadays, if you know where to look.

She blinks her understanding.

"The amphitheatre stood outside the town," Sharon says. "Shall we?" She nods to the nearest point, a hundred yards away, of a high stone wall.

"Silchester was settled in the Iron Age," she continues as we approach the ruins. "It was an important centre for the Atrebates tribe. These lumps and bumps are the remains of their defensive earthwork ditches. Pre-Roman coins found here suggest the Iron Age town was built by Commius, a Gallic chief who fought against Julius Caesar in Gaul around fifty BC and later escaped to Britain."

She leads us through a gap in the ancient wall, the remains of an entrance gateway where evidence remains of old door hinges set into the stonework, and up an internal earthen bank to stand upon a twelve-foot-high wall.

"When the Romans settled here, they created the new town of Calleva Attrebatum, which translates as Town in the woods of the Atrebates."

The woods still stand around the ancient place. Their silence calls to me.

"Calleva became a civitas. A regional capital. This wall is one and a half miles long and is one of the best-preserved original Roman town walls in Britain."

The wall does enclose an area of impressive size, bigger than I expected, but there's nothing to see as we walk along the top of it. The ground below is flat and featureless.

According to Min, around two thousand years ago I lived two consecutive lives with these people. Born into the tribe twice, she says, once before the Roman invasion and once again afterwards. I can see her watching to see if the ruins are triggering any memories in me from those lives, but they aren't.

Our guide sweeps her hand across the view in a gesture perhaps grander that the mostly enclosed field of grazing sheep deserves. "Important buildings in the centre of Calleva were always of stone. They included the forum, for religious and political activities and public meetings, and a law court they called the basilica. Buildings farther out from the centre were built of wood originally, until the late third century when the town suffered a bad fire. But they immediately rebuilt the entire town in stone, and it flourished for another three hundred years."

"Until?" I ask.

"Until it was abandoned."

"When the Romans left Britain?"

"No. The Atrebates remained here, and this town thrived as the most important hub in the region. They continued to live as Romans. They even had their own legion to protect their trade routes and borders."

"Until?" I ask again, mildly.

"Until they left."

"Where did they go?" Min asks.

"No one knows."

We don't push anymore. It would be pointless, and unfair. A twenty-first-century tour guide on the outside isn't likely to know anything about historical migrations into the Wild.

Sharon holds Min's gaze, seeming to need someone to catch the magic with her. "It doesn't look much now. All the Roman building stones had already been robbed out by the twelfth century when King Stephen's clerics recorded what they called a small castle in the woods here, which suggests that someone had built a timber fortress or manor house inside the amphitheatre. But beneath the surface are archaeological treasures of knowledge."

Her eyes sparkle. "If you come back in the summer, you'll see the excavations taking place. If you want, I could get you onto a dig for a few days."

Min smiles. "Thank you. We'll consider it."

At the northeast corner of the site, a path leaves the wall and joins the modern main road back west to Silchester Village, a mile away, where we met Sharon this morning after our excellent fried breakfast in a café outside Reading.

"This is where I get off," she says. "Will you walk back with me, or do you want to continue all around the wall?"

"We'll walk the wall," I say, handing over her small fee and doubling it. "Thank you."

"Thank you." She acknowledges the extra cash and leaves us with a wave.

The woods call to me.

"Thin place in there," Shad says as we approach the trees.

I feel it too.

It's on a small wildlife trail, half a mile inside the wood. Not used much but singing its silent thin-place song and twitching my muscles.

We retrieve our weapons from our rucksacks before we step through. I strap Lael's sabre in its scabbard across my back so its handle sticks up over my left shoulder. Our wolves get out the machine pistols they took from dead American soldiers at Golden Lake and check them for safety like they've been handling modern guns all their lives. Min needs only her voice.

The thin place sends a familiar, brief jump through my muscles. The Wild smells even more pure than the already clean air we've been breathing in the outside, although the temperature is noticeably lower. The trees grow a little more densely, perhaps, and are all frosted. Other than that, in the first instance at least, nothing looks or feels any different.

We walk back to where the old, ruined Romano-British town would be in the outside.

I touch trees as we pass, feeling the life of the forest. For it is a forest, thicker and far more extensive than the wood we've left. I feel tree and plant life and wildlife in abundance, and then a single human stepping quietly in our tracks.

"Wow." Min speaks for all of us when we halt at the tree line.

Calleva is big, easily six times the area of the ancient ruin we walked on the outside. Its defensive wall is tall and well-maintained, with vertical archery towers built into it every twenty feet and topped with sloping red tiles. Bigger, red-tiled roofs are visible over the wall, many of them, including that of an imposing wide establishment in the middle.

The town sits in a clear space the size of ten football pitches, beside a straight road that carries the steady traffic of horse-drawn vehicles and foot travellers through the forest.

Armoured and kilted Roman soldiers guard the busily bustling gateway arch that faces us in the town's southern wall, and out beyond the eastern wall is the amphitheatre, into and out of which are marching squads of disciplined soldiers.

It's the place I've been told to expect.

Hairs prickle on the back of my neck. I touch the nearest tree and feel the stealthy presence of people surrounding us. Quietly, I draw my sabre.

The others respond to my action and cock their weapons as we move into a six-pointed-star defence around Min.

The identical sound of cocking weapons issues from the trees all around us as soldiers step into view.

We study each other.

They're all heavily bearded, like Shad and Ban and Red and me, and they wear an assortment of leather or chain-mail armours and helmets, knitted breeches beneath leather-panelled kilts, and heavy-duty leather boots. But despite their lack of a regular uniform, there's no doubting they are Roman soldiers.

Roman soldiers with twenty-first-century machine guns.

A sturdy horse high-steps into view and stops in front of us. Astride it sits an officer, bearded like his men but wearing better quality scaled iron armour over his white tunic and a side-to-side fan of white feathers in the top of his iron helmet.

He glares down at us. "Drop your weapons."

No one moves.

"Drop your weapons," he repeats, anger boosting the practised authority in his voice.

Behind me, Min hums a preparatory undertone.

"We're here to talk with your king," I say.

These aren't weekend hobby soldiers. They look battle hardened and dangerous. I take them seriously. Their expressions and body language say they're taking us seriously too.

I hold eye contact with the officer, whom I assume is a centurion, and wait for his move.

He draws a modern handgun and aims it at my head. "Drop your weapons now or die now."

Everyone tenses, ready to explode into violence.

Min's steady tone grows stronger.

"Hold!" The woman's voice comes from our rear. It doesn't surprise me.

Nor, apparently, does it surprise the centurion. Without lowering his aim or breaking our eye contact, he acknowledges her with respect. "Lady."

Sharon brushes past us and addresses him. "These people interest me. I think the king would like to meet them."

Evidently, her word is sufficient. When weapons have been made safe all around, I slide my sabre into its scabbard. Then the centurion and his foot soldiers escort us across the hard open ground and into the town.

My praetorians too are fearsome

THE IMPOSING ESTABLISHMENT with a high, red-tiled roof turns out to be the town forum. An open square as big as the entirety of Calleva's ancient counterpart on the outside, it's the otherwise ordered settlement's rowdy shopping centre, filled with higgledy-piggledy rows of market stalls, and animals corralled alive in fenced little enclosures or hanging dead from hooks.

Even in the harsh winter cold, hundreds of people are here. The nearest ones pause in their business to watch us being marched to the long three-storey building of pink bricks that forms the forum's rear enclosure.

Our centurion tethers his horse outside the forum. He leads us directly across the middle of the square with his twenty men surrounding us, their confidence suggesting they think any outward show of aggression in the circumstances would be unnecessary, perhaps even demeaning.

"This is the basilica, or civic centre," Sharon says as we enter the long building through an open archway and are turned sharp right along a high-ceilinged corridor, its tessellated mosaic floor ringing beneath the hobnailed boots of our escort. She jerks a thumb back over her shoulder. "Law courts and city administrators' offices that way."

It amuses me that she's still in tour-guide mode. Also, I'm encouraged by the fact that we've been allowed to keep our weapons, which is clearly her influence at work.

She nods at a tall pair of dramatically carved oak doors we march past. "Assembly hall in there." Nodding ahead. "Treasury and assorted shrines along here."

We continue on the corridor.

"And here," she says, when our escort halts us and the centurion raps the handle but of his dagger on another pair of tall carved doors, "is where you will meet Justin, King of the Atrebates."

Two guards open the doors wide enough for us all the enter a spacious waiting room furnished with benches along the walls to left and right, and two more guards stand before a pair of inner doors at the far end of the room. Their uniforms are of better quality than those our escort is sporting and more, well, uniform. One wears what I assume is a badge of rank, a theatrical sideways fan of tall crimson feathers in his polished brass helmet. They all wear calf-length crimson capes. One of them opens an inner door enough to allow our centurion through, carrying his feathered helmet respectfully under one arm, and then closes it behind him.

I take in the garden scenes on wall murals painted around the pleasantly warm room, and the geometric images of its mosaic floor, expecting to sit for a while and thinking the duration of our wait might indicate the king's egotism, or possibly his power-play inclinations. But after only two or three minutes the inner doors open wide, our centurion joins his men and they leave together, and Sharon ushers us into the audience chamber.

It's uncomfortably hot, from an underfloor heating system raging somewhere I expect, and furnished solely with a cushioned couch and chair sitting on a low platform, their crimson fabrics matching the cloaked and helmeted guards who stand around the trompe l'oeil walls, watching us steadily.

Our friends arrange themselves in a loose protective formation around Min and me. We've never planned or even discussed this move. It comes naturally to them.

King Justin reclines upon the couch, wearing a voluminous white toga and propped on one elbow in the classic Roman fashion.

He's about Shad's age, but there's nothing alike about them. While Shad is the strongest, fastest, most powerfully muscled, bravest and fiercest sixty-year-old man I've ever encountered, Justin is running to fat. Where Shad is crowned with a glorious mane of silver hair and beard, Justin's scalp is clipped close in surrender to his baldness on top. In stark contrast with Shad's mahogany tan from his life lived outdoors in all weathers, the scars he carries from a hundred battles, and the recently healed burn marks all over his chest, Justin's skin is pale, unmarked, and soft.

But there's nothing soft about the king's intelligent stare. Also, I see no belligerence there. No defensive aggression. Only calm curiosity.

And then his face fills with delight when Sharon rounds us and skips up his platform steps to embrace him.

It isn't a friend's embrace. Nor is what follows a friend's kiss. Without doubt, Sharon and Justin are lovers.

Pieces fall into place.

She removes her cagoule, scarf, and chunky woollen jumper, laying them across the back of his couch while he shuffles up to make room for her to sit beside him. They hold hands, and then he addresses me.

"I'm told your guard are fearsome when challenged." He gestures at the watching crimson-cloaked men. "My praetorians too are fearsome."

A heavily curtained door opens behind the platform and a man of about my age enters. He's wearing thick outdoors breeches and stout boots, but only a thin shirt with them, which I imagine is an allowance for the room's heat. He gives us a hard stare as he takes the chair beside the king's couch.

"This is my son, Prince Marc," Justin says. "What are your names?"

"I am Joe Walker. This is Min, Shad, Tae, Vua, Ban, and Red."

Justin studies us. "Your names have not come to my ears before."

"Not heard in our land," Marc says. "But as warriors of the Axe tribe, they are known in Tin and Hare country."

"Ah." Justin's steady gaze remains on me. "My son returned recently from the west."

"I was told of a battle at a golden lake," Marc says. His evident physical fitness offers a glimpse of what Justin might have looked like thirty years ago. "In the West Country, you are claimed as triumphant defenders of the Wild in that first battle against an army from the outside."

Regardless of the good things he might have heard about us, his stare is still hard. He wears his suspicion like a helmet visor. "The story tells of men and women who are wolves. Wolves who are men and women."

Justin and Sharon jerk their attention to Marc and then right back to us. The room tingles with tension.

I say nothing.

"I have heard legends of wolf warriors," Justin says. "But before today, I have never met any. Are you here to offer us your service?"

"I'm here to tell you a truth," I say.

"What is this truth?"

"We've been sent to spy on you."

The tension ramps higher.

"I've been sent to infiltrate the Atrebates. Min is my partner in everything. These men and women are indeed wolves of the Axe tribe, and they are our friends. They are here to help us.

We live together. Fight as one. The man who sent me is aware of their existence, but I don't know if he knows they are with me now."

Justin's intelligence burns in his eyes. "Why are you telling me this?"

"I have no loyalty to the man who sent me. His name is Merritt. He holds my mother and father prisoner to ensure my compliance. Until we locate them and secure their rescue, I have to be seen to be obedient."

"So, here you are."

"Here we are."

Sharon's watching and listening intently.

Marc looks ready to jump out of his chair and fight someone.

"What information does Merritt want you to take back to him?" Justin asks.

"His interests are two-pronged. First, and dearest to his heart I expect, is your capability to keep fighting off incursions from outside to steal your lands and resources. Any weaknesses I might detect in your defence structure."

I'm sweating into my winter outdoor clothing and wishing I could remove half of it at least but don't want to interrupt my explanation. "He's a corrupt government official with fingers in many unofficial pies, including his active involvement in invasions of your land by groups that are privately owned, not governmental, but whose operations in the Wild are nonetheless sanctioned and licenced by the outside government. Be warned, he is determined and ruthless."

"I hear your warning. His second interest?"

"Is official. His government masters want to know the truth or otherwise of rumours that you intend to attack London on the outside."

Marc, not as skilled a statesman as his poker-faced father, shoots a glance at him.

Justin maintains his calm study of me. "So, with what intentions do you and your guard come to us?"

"With your permission, we intend to live among you and fight for you. For as long as it takes friends of ours in the outside to find where Merritt is holding my parents."

"How does Merritt expect to receive information from you?"

"Once per month, starting a month from today, someone will arrive on the River Kennet. He and I will exchange information where the river leaves the lake it flows through, four and a half miles north of here."

"One and a half leagues." Sharon converts the distance for Justin.

"I know the place," Justin says. "The Kunnit is our border and main trade route with the Kingdom of West Saxons. The man you will meet is Merritt's trusted agent?"

I rock my hand. "Merritt instructs him, but I doubt he trusts him any more than he trusts me. The man is our friend. He is quietly leading the search for my parents."

Mum and Dad's future safety is in Andrew's hands. I hope he'll come through for us. Min's confident he will. I'm only cautiously hopeful.

Merritt's plan is for me to spend six months with the Atrebates. My plan is to give Andrew three months. If he fails to locate Mum and Dad by the end of February, I'll go back and tear Merritt's corrupt organisation apart to find them.

Min gives me side-eye, alerting me that I'm growling under my breath.

I need to stop doing that.

"You would of course discuss with me exactly what information you intend to send back each time." Justin's statement isn't a suggestion.

"Of course."

"Then I am pleased to accept you and your guard as auxiliaries in my legion for as long as the arrangement is mutually beneficial." He stands, shaking out his toga to cover his bare legs, and extends a hand for us all to kiss the big ruby in his right forefinger ring.

We step forward in turn and kiss it.

His smile looks open and honest. "Welcome."

Everyone goes

A SERVANT TAKES THEM from the basilica across frozen open ground to the amphitheatre and its adjoining garrison town, laid out in an ordered criss-cross street design and nearly as big as Calleva itself, which surprises Min.

Their progress is interrupted briefly by a distressing incident, when a wounded soldier clatters on horseback to the forum entrance and falls into the arms of people who rush to help. He's little more than a boy, barely conscious, and bleeding from what looks like three gunshot wounds in his lightly armoured back. People carry him hurriedly on a makeshift stretcher of cloaks into the forum, while two girls tend to his lathered and exhausted mount.

The servant shakes his head sadly and leads them to the garrison town and the villa they've been allocated there.

Is he a servant or a slave? Min can't tell without asking him, and the circumstances aren't right for that.

Their single-storey square villa is delightful, from its pretty pink bricks beneath a red-tiled roof, green-shuttered windows, and inner walls painted throughout with delicate woodland scenes, to the mosaic floors of its corridors and the pleasant airy rooms leading off them, and especially the gently bubbling fountain and fern-filled urns in its central open courtyard edged by a shaded walkway.

Someone has lit the underfloor heating system furnace in advance of their arrival, and the villa's interior is already warming up.

Many years have passed since Min enjoyed so lovely a home. Many years more since she enjoyed one with Joe.

Six of the rooms contain beds, each big enough to sleep two people in comfort. Min chooses the first one she finds overlooking the courtyard fountain for her and Joe. Vua and Red drop their rucksacks beside the bed in the next room. Tae, Shad, and Ban each claim one of their own.

Min and Joe stand in Shad's bedroom doorway, holding hands and watching him unpack until he notices them there.

"We want you to know our invitation still stands," Joe says. "If you would like to sleep with us, you will be very welcome in our bed."

"Whenever the time feels right," Min adds.

Seeing the badly wounded young man at the forum entrance has reminded them, as if they need a reminder, that the life of a loved one can end in the blink of an eye.

Shad studies a leather strap on his rucksack, stroking it between thumb and fingers, then looks up and smiles. "The time feels right."

Min's heart sings.

Joe gives her fingers a squeeze.

Shad crosses the room to them in three great strides and pulls them into his strong embrace. "Thank you. I love you. We will honour Anya together."

Min hugs him tight. "We will."

Tae calls along the corridor, "Visitors."

Two women in white gowns, one of them also wearing a cloak lined with white fur, wait at the front door with two men in military uniforms. Behind them is an old groom sitting in a single-horse chariot with his sandalled feet dangling from its platform, two more sturdy horses tethered to a post at the roadside. Everyone's breath is clouding.

The cloaked woman invites herself and her retinue in, courteously but with an air of someone accustomed to deciding matters.

She goes directly to the main reception room, where she allows the younger woman to remove her cloak before she sits on the central couch and waits for her audience to assemble.

The young woman folds the fur cloak and lays it over the couch's backrest, then takes a quiet step back out of the attention focus.

Min takes a seat on the couch facing the older woman.

Joe stands beside Min, and the others stand behind them.

The handsomely bearded officers wear brass helmets fitted with fans of fabulous copper-brown feathers, the first front to back and the second side to side. They tuck them beneath their arms and stand smartly against the window wall behind the women.

Their uniforms are similar, clearly of high value and demoting senior rank, and beneath their armour they both wear brown tunics that match their helmet feathers. But there are differences.

The elder, a man of about fifty with the front-to-back helmet feathers, wears gleaming segmented armour that moves with him. The horizontal lines of its highly polished steel exaggerate the width of his shoulders and even suggest a six-pack. Min wonders if it's a dress outfit, more for effect than protection in combat.

The younger, by ten years or so, wears scaled combat armour similar in style and shape to that worn by their escort centurion earlier, but instead of dull iron scales, his are polished bronze.

As she did in the king's audience room, Min looks to see if anything might be triggering memories in Joe. If anything will, it may well be the military uniforms. But it doesn't look like they are. That might be for the best, at least at this early stage in his relationships with people of authority.

She catches herself. No more secrets, she's promised. She must tell him how things once were for them in this part of the country, in a society very like this one, with Roman Britons very like these. When she can, she'll tell him.

"I am Amelia Heaven," the seated woman says. "My husband is Cato Chalice." She gestures with a brief flutter of fingers over her shoulder at the officers.

Min's best guess is that Cato Chalice will be the older of the two. She maintains a politely neutral expression while Amelia continues.

"I have come to see that you are settling in, and to lend you my servant Iovita for the duration of your stay." The same flutter of her fingers with her other hand over her shoulder. She pronounces the young woman's name Y'vita. "She knows where to find everything you might need, and she can prepare food to a satisfactory standard."

Min wonders if Iovita is a servant or a slave.

She stands behind her mistress, hands clasped loosely below her flat belly, calm dark eyes appraising the room's occupants. Her sleeveless gown references Amelia's in the shape and stitching of its neckline, but plain and mid-calf length rather than elegant and to the ankles, it's evidently an inferior version.

Nonetheless, the simple gown is set off to fine effect by her flawless, deep-brown skin with its warm, orange-red undertones, by her well-defined, muscular arms and wide shoulders, and by her cloud of cottony black hair cut straight across above those shoulders like an ancient Egyptian headdress.

In comparison, Amelia's pale skin and her mousy hair, even coiled up as it is in an elaborate arrangement, adds nothing to the visual impact of her fine gown.

Amelia stands. "I trust you will be comfortable here." She casts a vague look around the room while Iovita pins her cloak back on, then turns and pauses for a moment to brush her fingertips down her husband's whiskered cheek before she leaves.

Outside, as the old groom bends his knee with a pained wince for Amelia to step up from it to her chariot platform, the formerly quiet neighbourhood is quickly becoming active and fraught with tension in response to messengers running from villa to villa. The chariot departs at a dignified pace past soldiers, fully armed and dressed for combat, hurrying from their homes, pausing briefly to kiss their wives and children, then leaving in the direction of the amphitheatre.

At the front door of the nearest villa, a mother wraps a colourful plaid blanket around her shoulders and huddles her three small children together under it while they watch their husband and father stride away.

"I am Cato Chalice," the older officer says. "Primus Prime of the Wolf Cohort." He indicates his colleague. "This is Quinctus Luck, Senior Centurion of the First Wolf Century."

"Call me Quin."

Cohort. Primus whatever. The typically pompous Roman military jargon doesn't interest Min. The only word that registers is Wolf.

The officers are studying Shad, Ban, and Red. Quin appears to be weighing them up as fighters, but whether as allies or enemies, Min can't say. He looks like a man of action who will keep his options open until it's time to move, and then do so decisively.

Cato explains. "The legion is mobilising to counter the attack and occupation of our town Anderitum by a force from the outside last night."

"Your entire legion?" Min asks. "It must have been a big attack."

Joe doesn't glance her way, but she feels his interest at her knowledge of the Roman military.

Cato doesn't look at her either. He answers her point but directs his response to the men in the room. "The fort was wiped out and all our iron mines taken. It's essential that we take them back immediately. Two centuries will remain here with the Praetorian Guard to protect Calleva if necessary. Aside from those units, all ten cohorts of the legion are mobilising. You are assigned to the First Wolf Century under Quin's command."

"We're moving now," Quin says. "Can you force march and fight at the end of it?"

"How far?" Joe asks.

"Eight leagues southeast on the Iron Road. An eight-hour march."

Min recalls Sharon converting four and a half miles to one and a half leagues. So eight leagues will be twenty-four miles. In the outside, that distance directly southeast from Reading would take them to the High Weald, where, nearly two thousand years ago, the Romans did indeed mine extensively for iron in the thickly forested region spread across Sussex, Kent, and Surrey, and where she and Joe lived two lives of his.

Two very different lives. The first blissful, the second hellish.

She nips to the bedroom and grabs the body armour vests they took from two dead American soldiers at Golden Lake. The vests didn't protect those men from decapitation by angel sabres, but she likes Joe wearing the bulletproof torso panels. She hands him his, and they buckle them on, then replace their winter coats on top.

Cato frowns.

"Our wolves can easily run eight leagues to a fight," Joe is saying, "but Min and I will do better on horseback."

Quin gives a nod. "Horseback for you two."

Cato squints at him.

Tae, Vua, Shad, Ban, and Red are stripping off their clothes, ready to shift.

"Wait." Cato blinks at all the sudden nakedness. "We don't take women to war. Yours will stay in Calleva with ours."

Joe catches Min's eye, and she flares hers in response. Their recent vow is rock solid. No more separations.

The sisters growl in unison at Cato. They are fearlessly naked, in splendid human form still, but their wolf-like warning is unmistakeable.

Iovita stares at them.

Min touches her hand. "Don't be alarmed. You're safe with us. Make yourself at home here. There's a vacant bedroom you can have. We'll see you when we get back."

"Our women are warriors," Joe says. "They're as good as our men. At least as good. Ten, twenty, probably thirty times better than your best soldiers. Where our men go, our women go. We are one." His voice is steady. Not challenging, but firm. He invites no argument.

Quin lays a hand on Cato's forearm and addresses Tae and Vua as, heedless of the discussion, they crouch to shift. "We have heard of your prowess. I look forward to seeing it for myself. Everyone goes."

Don't expect to arrive unannounced

HORSERIDING IS NEVER fun, but I'd be no use in a battle after a twenty-four-mile speed march through the freezing night, and at least the sturdy animal they've given me is mild mannered.

In fact, when I relax my haunches against the two padded horns on the rear corners of his wooden saddle and grip my inner thighs against the two corresponding horns on its front corners to compensate for the lack of stirrups, it's actually a comfortable ride.

It's taken me only an hour to learn that from watching Quin riding up and down the ranks of marching men and pausing to check on us each time he reaches our position at the back of his century. Then I notice Min's been riding like this all along.

"Thanks."

"What for?"

I chuckle. She genuinely doesn't know. So many things come naturally to her, things I have to learn or relearn from the ground up.

Anyway, regardless of my comfort in the saddle, our journey is only sitting there at a horse's walking speed, while Quin's century ahead of us and the rest of the legion stretching out a long way behind are marching at a demanding boot-stomping pace, and our wolves are trotting along easily down beside us.

It took until late afternoon for the entire legion of four thousand men to prepare their departure, complete with giant crossbows in wooden carts behind the marching ranks and wheeled catapults trundling along heavily behind them.

The intention is to reach Anderitum at midnight, so we set off at four o'clock, which was precisely sunset, although the leaden skies didn't change until the low cloud base got darker while we marched.

Cato rides out alone, ahead of Quin's eighty-strong First Wolf Century, his polished armour glinting heroically in the variable light.

Between his horse and the double-columned ranks, bearing the legion's standard on a pole, marches a tall, powerfully built soldier who wears the skin of a lion. Its head sits proud above his helmet, with its hide draped across his shoulders and back and its tail hanging between his legs.

Might he be a shifter? A *lion* shifter?

No, I think not. The intense interest our wolves have generated in the legion suggest shifting is a novelty to these soldiers. And I can't imagine any shifter in human form wearing the skin of a dead familiar. It would be an insult. Our wolves would certainly never do it.

A symbol of courage for the legion, then, paired with the golden standard of a Latin emblem or whatever it is he's holding high, but not the badge of a lion shifter.

Courage. I don't lack it. Well, to be accurate, while I don't think of myself as courageous, I'm not fearful. What I lack is commitment.

I'm approaching this coming battle with mixed feelings.

On one hand, I have no problem siding with the legion against an invading outside army. My loyalty certainly isn't tested in that respect. But on the other hand, I'm not keen to run into battle again. Ever again. It doesn't excite me. My blood doesn't rush in my veins at the prospect. I'm a different person now to the man who gloried in savagery during the battle for Quarter Square.

Some battles need to be fought. The phrase keeps coming to me, and it's true. The war against end-stage disaster capitalism will never be won if good, caring, compassionate people aren't willing to take up the fight on behalf of our living planet and its billions of vulnerable people and creatures. So yes, some battles do need to be fought. The question I keep asking myself is, what is my role in such battles?

"How's the young soldier who brought news of the attack?" Min asks Quin the next time he rides beside us. "He looked badly wounded."

"He died."

"That's sad."

Quin's expression is grim. "He should have been taken to the garrison hospital. Our surgeons might have saved him, and his news would still have reached the king quickly. But the people in the forum didn't know what to do, so they took him to the basilica and the praetorians let him die."

No love lost there, then.

The road we're riding is dead straight. Its broad surface is of square cobbles that fit together perfectly, and it looks well maintained all along its length. I mention the fact.

"Good roads are essential," Quin says, "for trade throughout the kingdom, for efficient military movements, and this one for iron from the Anderitum mines. Our blacksmiths are the busiest tradesmen in the garrison."

He watches our wolves running comfortably. "They're fine animals."

"They're fine people too," Min says.

He accepts her gentle correction with grace. "I suppose the red one is their leader?"

Because he's the biggest? It's a revealing question.

"Red is a new member of the pack," I say. "Shad is their father."

In the half year since Anya's death, Shad's coat has graduated from its old pattern of light and dark greys to splendid monochrome silver from nose to tail.

Quin regards him. "He's impressive."

"Wait until you see him fight."

Quin's battle grin is fierce.

Sandwiched between him and me, Min gives a small sigh.

We're halfway to our destination when breaks in the clouds allow thin moonlight to illuminate the empty road ahead.

Empty, that is, until four people on horseback come into view, waiting at the side of the road. Cato turns off to join them. At Quin's invitation, Min and I leave the ranks and ride ahead with him to meet the newcomers.

Prince Marc's horse looks splendid in Roman cavalry armour, all polished steel with brass edgings and raised highlights. The man himself is bulked out in full-body panels similar to the vests Min and I are wearing under our winter coats, and he's armed with modern automatic weapons slung about his person.

Beside him, a senior officer sits tall and studies the passing ranks as if they're on parade. His shiny torso armour is segmented like Cato's, and his fan of helmet feathers is a high golden Mohican.

"Who's the peacock?" I ask while we're still out of earshot.

"Joe," Min warns in an undertone.

"Gordian Stern," Quin replies, possibly I think amused by my disrespect, although he doesn't allow it to show. "Praefectus Castrorum."

I squint my lack of understanding.

He explains. "A legion's ten cohorts are each commanded by a Primus Pilus, which is a higher promotion than most centurions will ever achieve. Ours is Cato. The only rank higher than his is the Praefectus Castrorum, a promoted Primus Pilus who is responsible to the king for the training and organisation of the entire legion. Four legions guard our kingdom. Four Praefecti Castrorum. Stern is one of them."

"Right," I say. "Thanks."

On the other two horses are children, bundled up in coats and hats and scarves against the cold. Except of course they aren't children. Min hums a happy tune at the same time as I recognise the old Crow gods of the west.

"You do get yourselves mixed up in some stuff," Flo says, leaning across to kiss Min's cheek.

"You do too," I say when she kisses mine.

She's radiating her own heat. Clever.

Marc observes our friendly greetings. "I see you know each other."

"Fought with each other a few times," Gully says. He winks at me. "Fought *with* each other too."

I catch Min's eye. The loss of our friends in Quarter Square is still raw to us. Gully's an innocent young boy now compared to the angry and betrayed old wizard he was then. I understand he'll never feel the same about our friends as we do, and nowadays he's living some sort of a different life altogether, so I don't even know how much detail he remembers. But regardless of his circumstances, for us the deaths of our friends is no joke.

Flo punches her brother's arm. "Have a thought."

He rubs the impact point. "Sorry," he tells me. And to Min, "Sorry."

Marc has no patience for our small talk. "Flo and Gully have come to help us take back our fort and mines."

Quin and Cato exchange an expressionless look. I wonder if its subject is a pair of children on the battlefield, or a prince and an old general getting in everyone's way.

We all watch our wolves when they trot past, except for Gully, who is staring up into the night sky. "They know you're coming."

"They will expect us to counter quickly," Stern says.

"They're watching you." Gully points up.

In a cloud break, something small and metallic reflects a glint of moonlight. It's moving steadily, independent of the windblown clouds, staying apace with the marching legion.

Of course. Any modern fighting force will be equipped with more than modern weaponry. They'll have drones and who knows what other hi-tech equipment.

Stern produces a small field telescope and focuses it on the flying machine, while Quin draws a modern rifle from its holster behind his saddle.

Flo makes a casual hand gesture, and the drone falls tumbling until it lands with a crunch on frozen ground somewhere in the forest.

The officers stare at her while she repeats the gesture in two different directions, and a second then a third machine reflect flashing moonlight as they plummet.

"Still," she says, "don't expect to arrive unannounced."

"We didn't." Marc heels his horse into motion, then canters forward with Stern and Cato to take position at the head of the legion.

Flo, Gully, Min, and I catch up with our wolves and slot into place among the marching First Wolf Century.

Not your way of war

THOSE DRONES SHOW the sort of thing we'll be up against," I say. "It must have taken some size of army to take out your fort defence and occupy the town and mines in a single night. And they have drones, so I expect they're equipped with more deadly weapons than you've ever fought against."

Quin arches an eyebrow.

"More powerful than the machine pistols your men have lifted from dead soldiers. You can't imagine how much more powerful."

His body language expresses interest, even if he doesn't voice it.

"I'm not in any army, but I've seen the kind of weapons they have." This isn't the time to start explaining that I've seen them in films. "Think of one in the sky that could destroy your town and garrison in seconds with massive missiles."

Now I have his full attention. "You think we will face this kind of weapon tonight?"

"I hope not, but I don't know. All I'm saying is, they wiped out your fort."

He wrinkles his nose in distaste. "Forts are defended by inferior soldiers. Nothing like a legion."

"How many of them were stationed at Anderitum?"

"Five hundred. We are four thousand, and we are Legion One." There's no bombast in his tone, only the certainty of lifelong experience. He clicks his tongue to his horse and rides ahead along his century's line.

I hope his confidence will prove to be well founded, but I have a bad feeling, and it gets worse the closer we get to Anderitum. Eventually I slip off my horse, while Min holds his reins and walks on, so I can leave the road and touch my hands and forehead to a tree.

There's devastation ahead. I can't visualise the destruction, but in their distressed confusion, the trees are telling me it's catastrophic.

I stumble twice on my way to catch up, carrying the forest's pain with me. Getting back into the saddle on the frozen road isn't easy. Back at the garrison, they provided a box for us to stand on, but there's no box now. Trying to jump and swing my leg over the horse's back only adds to my crisis.

A big soldier crouches beside him for me, the body-length shield strapped to his back providing a firm platform for me to boost myself up into the saddle.

Once settled again, I clap his strong shoulder with gratitude and shake my head clear of the forest's confusion.

Quin's here, riding beside Min.

I say nothing. Let him assume I jumped off to answer the call of nature, which of course is true but not the way he thinks. How could I explain what I'm feeling, never mind how I'm feeling it? In any case, whatever's happened, we'll all see it for ourselves soon enough.

Twenty minutes later, we stop upon a raised ridge of ground and a soldier leads our horses away while we stare at the devastation the trees warned me about.

In the twenty-four hours since their attack, the occupying force has cleared a half-mile-diameter circle of churned-up earth around the fort, which now stands alone like a single remaining front tooth in a ruined mouth. The road is sheared off, as if at the edges of two cliffs that have fallen into the sea, one beneath our feet and the other on the far side of the circle where the little mining town stands silent in cold moonlight.

Hundreds of felled mature trees are stacked in great pyramidal piles around the perimeter of the cleared ground, which has been churned up by a fleet of British Army tractors and heavy earth-moving machines that are silent now and all secured together at one outer corner of the fort wall.

I feel again the overwhelmed fear of the forest, but no longer its confusion. As well as the immediate defensive reason for this industrial-grade felling of trees, there will undoubtedly be a commercial purpose following on from it. Under capitalism, a forest has no value unless it's cut down. That fact is at the root of our ecological crisis. And here is the outside spreading its disease into the Wild with massive military force. This is the future the outside government thirsts for.

Cohorts continue to arrive behind us, spreading out to our left and right along the newly made ridge as they hurry to surround the fort. Engineering units are already hard at work, some cutting timber-lined access slopes in the bank for the big catapults and crossbows, others down on the flat constructing wheeled siege towers and stripping felled trees for battering rams.

A series of dull bangs accompanies powerful spotlights above the wall, which come on and light up the deforested area like a football pitch ready for an evening match.

The ridge we're standing on is thirty feet high. A corresponding bank rises steeply to the foot of the fort wall, as if holding a square hub socket for a huge wheel, with one visible access point where a more gradual slope leads up to an arched gateway with its big double gates closed. The cleared area is effectively a five-hundred-metre-wide sunken ring of frosted earth.

"There is our battleground," Quin says. "A legion likes to fight on open ground where possible. Our siege engines will hammer holes in those walls until either they come out or we go in. This is what we train for. The odds are in our favour."

"No." I point at the heavy machine gun placements along the top of the fort wall, each with its silhouetted team of people watching us and waiting. Ten guns cover our face of the wall, with ten more covering each of the other three faces. "They won't engage you hand to hand. Not your way of war. They've made it a killing ground."

We hold eye contact for two clouded breaths.

"Explain," he says.

"Those machine pistols your men love so much? You know what they can do? Think of one of them with a hundred times more firepower. That's those big guns on the wall. Every minute, they'll fire thousands of bullets that'll shred your shields and blow your arms and legs and heads off while you're marching to fight them. Your catapults and crossbows will be in range of them. You'll all be in range. They'll annihilate you before you can strike a blow."

Min moans in distress.

Quin blinks. "You are sure about this?"

"Yes."

He turns and shoulders his way through the massing legionnaires.

I eye the army tractors. They're huge, some of their raised grabber arms and shovels nearly as high as the wall corner they're parked against. Climbing them might be the legion's best way into the fort. Or, if I can get one going, I might be able to smash it through the big double gate. Two ways in will be better than one.

But that's in an ideal world. One where we're not facing those deadly machine guns.

When Quin returns, his expression tells me all I need to know.

"They didn't listen."

"Cato did. He's no fool. We went and told Stern what you said."

"He wouldn't listen."

"No."

"Prince Marc?"

"Cato tried to tell him, but Stern cut him off and ordered us back to our posts."

The legion is going to march to its death. It will be suicide. Quin knows it.

Marc and Stern are off their horses. They slide down the steep bank to the sunken ground below and set off towards the fort. Cato follows them. The standard bearer carries his golden emblem high, right behind Cato. Then Quin scrambles down to lead his First Wolf Century.

Evidently, a legion's commanders lead from the front and on foot. Just as evidently, under those spotlights, Stern and Cato's shiny armour will make a great target for the gunners on the fort wall.

All along the bank, legionnaires slither down its steep face. They form close ranks quickly and efficiently into a great spreading arc of shielded units, like armoured square tortoises behind their respective cohort commanders, and move forward across the broken earth.

We don't follow, Min and me, and our wolves, and Flo and Gully. We bunch together like a rock in the sea of resolute soldiers who part around us before they slide down the bank.

It takes only minutes for armoured tortoises to half fill our quarter of the sunken ring. Then they stop advancing and wait, while others continue to spread around the circle and those still on the ridge with us make corridors for the catapults to be brought up from the rear of the column.

The night is eerily quiet. No human sounds come from the fort or the assembled cohorts. Only the rumbles of ironclad wheels on stone cobbles and the groans and squeaks of heavy timber war machines moving up to our position.

Our wolves twitch their ears and turn urgently before the new noise registers with me, even though I follow their line of sight back along the road. When it comes, the slow *woomph, woomph* sounds are horribly familiar from films I've watched.

Min and I stare at each other, and she mouths the word, "Helicopter."

Two helicopters. They appear suddenly over the trees and fly low above the road to attack the rearmost section of the legion. Their clattering machine guns fill the night with a terrible cacophony as they blast the Roman catapults into deadly splinters then continue along the human column like a pair of giant hover mowers, scything down hundreds of soldiers in seconds.

The formerly ordered cohorts break ranks and run in a panicked mass the only way they can, away from the relentless helicopters, along the road to our ridge, where the press of them pushes waiting soldiers over the edge and down the steep bank.

We struggle to remain on the ridge, our wolves' fierce snarls and snapping teeth persuading people to veer around us.

"They're herding the legion into the moat," Gully shouts. "Between the helicopters and the machine guns on the fort, they'll kill everyone."

Below us, unstoppable pressure from behind is pushing the armoured tortoises forward against their will and the hoarsely shouted commands of their officers.

"That's their plan," Flo shouts. "The forts and mines are bait. They intend to destroy the entire legion."

They exchange a determined nod and fight their way back through the panicked mob, heading for the helicopters, waving aside with magical gestures those soldiers who don't move for them.

The machine guns on the wall open up, and carnage hits the legion's front lines.

Min cries out when in the first barrage old Stern and his lion-helmeted standard bearer blow apart in pieces.

A big soldier beside me groans, at the falling of the standard I guess. He's the one who helped me onto my horse back on the road. We share an *about to die bravely* look.

He thrusts out a hand of comradeship. "Otho."

I grip his muscular forearm as he grips mine. "Joe."

Min gasps, staring at me, and I hear myself growling.

It's the legion's foolish general I'm angry at. I expect the soldiers firing machine guns from the wall and in those deadly helicopters behind us are normal everyday people in the British Army. They're simply following their orders, as are the legionnaires being blown to bits before us. But Quin and Cato warned Stern of this danger. And he ignored them. The blood of thousands like this brave man Otho will be on that stupid, arrogant man's head.

Flo and Gully are up a big tree, standing on sturdy branches either side of its trunk, hers a foot higher than his. They raise their hands to the helicopters and mouth something soundless.

Instantly, the terrible machines whine as if in agony as they lurch up and away from the road.

One crashes into the forest on the far side of the column. It explodes in a ball of fierce red flames and a huge rising cloud of dense black smoke, but Flo maintains her focus on it and quenches the fire quickly.

The other one, Gully's, veers the wrong way. He shouts something to Flo, and she tries to help, but it's too late to prevent the helicopter from crashing at the base of the tree they're standing in. It goes up like a bomb, incinerating their tree and several more around it.

No one can survive such an explosion.

Flo and Gully are gone.

I roar in rage and run down the bank with the wolves. When we hit flat ground, Ban bumps his flank against my hip, and I swing my leg astride him. Min's here, riding Shad and singing for our protection. Otho's here too, bravely riding Red, who looks to be taking his big, unexpected passenger in his stride.

Min's magic works. The carnage continues all around us, but no bullets penetrate her song of deflection. We run like the wind through flying body parts and showers of splattering blood.

When we reach the standard, I grab it and lift it high to rally the legion.

Otho roars an aggressive cheer.

Cato is alive. He's lost an arm and is groaning in extreme pain. Two field surgeons are tending to him with practised urgency.

Marc's here too, sitting on an ice-rimmed fold of earth beside a big wheel rut with his head in his hands and his dented helmet between his boots. It doesn't look like he'll be taking any further part in the battle.

The tractors! I lean towards them, and Ban takes off in that direction with the others right behind us, although the riderless Tae and Vua quickly overtake us all.

A deafening screech sounds, and everything stops.

Ban and I are frozen in mid-stride. My senses still work. My heart thumps like a big bass drum. But I can't move. Can't even muster the strength to try.

Everyone's the same, Min and Shad to our right, Otho and Red to our left, Tae and Vua ahead. Thousands of people seized, freeze-framed, the entire battlefield locked as if in amber.

Two huge birds fly overhead, great black crows the size of estate cars with fan-shaped tails.

Min's told me about Flo's appearance as the Crow god. How she froze everyone in the Hare camp on Dartmoor. It must be her again, this time with Gully too.

One of them flies fast along the top of the walls, sweeping aside machine gun after machine gun and sending them flying out of the fort to crash to the ground far below, smash, smash, smash, smash, together with their crews.

The other one flies straight into the entrance arch and blasts its big heavy timber gates apart like they're balsa wood.

Then a second screech sounds, and our world unfreezes with a jolt.

Ban staggers beneath me, but I hold on as he rights himself and we veer with everyone else to the shattered gateway.

Red races alongside us with Otho still astride him. My new comrade's battle grin is fierce.

I thrust the standard across for him to carry and draw my sabre, flourishing it above my head, still raging, relishing the blood pounding in my veins as we charge into the fort ahead of the legion.

But no one in the occupying army wants to fight us.

We skid to a halt with Quin and his First Wolf Century right behind us.

Hundreds of soldiers in modern uniforms lie face down in the cold dirt, hands clasped behind their heads, cowering under the terrifying glares of two great birds of war stalking among them.

I swing off Ban and stride the compound with my sabre in hand, bellowing rage, still hungry to kill, struggling to swallow my seething frustration at the sudden end of hostility.

No enemy soldiers want to make eye contact with me, any more than they do with our Crow gods or our wolves.

Min touches my arm. "It's over." Her voice is light but powerfully calming.

I take a slow, shuddering breath, and sheath my fury with my sword.

Otho stands with one hand holding the standard high and proud, the other fisted against his armoured chest in a salute to Quin.

Then they both salute our wolves.

And then Otho salutes me. "Lion man."

Born into slavery

IOVITA HAS PREPARED a welcoming home for them in the warm villa. The bedrooms are tidied, rucksacks emptied, and their contents folded up on wall shelves or in chests, and every bed is made up ready. The reception room's chairs and couches are softened by cushions and draped in fabrics. That's where she stands, quietly alert, watching to see if everyone is returning from battle.

Min hugs and thanks her. She senses an initial reserve in the young woman, but it dissolves, and she returns the hug with strength.

Still, though, there's tension in her, clearly counting the wolves, and when they pad into their various bedrooms to shift into their human forms, she watches from the corridor.

When Tae stands naked and tall, rolling her neck and shoulders, flexing her muscles and swinging her limbs vigorously, the tension flows out of Iovita like water from a suddenly unblocked pipe.

She busies herself, preparing a breakfast feast for everyone with Shad and Ban's exuberant assistance, but despite her patience with their messiness and despite her evident ability in the kitchen, she keeps an eye out for Tae.

Min smiles.

"What?" Joe's at the other end of the long timber courtyard table they're carrying indoors to make a dining room of an unused space.

"Nothing." She maintains her innocent expression but twinkles her eyes at him. He'll know soon enough.

He rolls his eyes, and they go back out for the table's matching benches.

Vua and Red wrap up warm and take a walk to explore the garrison. When they return, Vua has exciting news to share. "They have sweat houses!"

Amid enthusiastic cheers, Red looks bemused.

"You'll love it," Vua promises him. To the others, "Communal ones for the ranks and family ones for senior centurions. Fires are burning right now all over the garrison."

"Today we'll sleep," Shad says. "When we wake, we'll find somewhere to sweat."

Everyone cheers again.

Tae catches Iovita's wrists as she passes. "You'll come too."

Efficient and self-contained Iovita looks flustered. Min isn't sure if it's the concept of sweating for pleasure or the invitation itself. Mostly, she thinks, it's who the invitation is coming from.

"Sit." Tae makes room for her on the bench. "Eat with us."

Iovita tries to demure but isn't allowed to.

"Sit," everyone agrees. "Eat."

Shad sleeps in his own bed, which doesn't surprise Min and Joe. They're all exhausted after the battle anyway, and the wolves always use massive amounts of energy in a long shift so need good quality sleep to recover. He's accepted their invitation. He'll come to them when he's ready.

They wake in the late afternoon to find Iovita has prepared a light meal for them and has sought out Quin to discuss their interest in sweat houses. "He uses a communal one with his soldiers. There's a family one behind his villa, but he isn't a family man so never uses it. He's had someone preparing it today while you slept. I'll take you when you're ready."

They're ready. Everyone is already in their rooms, throwing off clothes and shucking naked bodies into winter coats and boots.

Iovita doesn't have a coat. The simple white gown she arrived in is her only garment, and the lightweight open sandals her only footwear.

Tae lends her the parka coat she loves dearly and in its place wears a thigh-length thick woollen jumper. She refuses to hear Iovita's protestations.

The sweat house is far grander that Shad and Anya's, back in the Axe village. Bigger, more substantially built to Roman standards, and furnished pleasantly with curved benches of smooth blonde wood around the fire pit. It even contains a blue-tiled plunge pool, small, but a perfect addition that draws happy *oohs* and *ahhs* from the family.

Quin isn't there. Nor is anyone else. The house is prepared for them and fully at their disposal.

Within seconds, they've all hung their coats on pegs by the door and taken seats on the benches while Shad throws water on the hot rocks and lovely fresh steam billows everywhere.

Iovita's dark brown nipples stand out proudly. Her breasts are small, but her prominent nipples arrest Min's attention. In fact, everyone notices them, especially Tae, although of course no one says anything to embarrass her. In any case, her splendid nipples soften quickly in the intense heat of the room, and she seems unconcerned about their condition whether erect or not.

Hours later, when Min is snuggled up in bed with Joe and Shad, she isn't surprised to hear Tae and Iovita talking quietly in the next bedroom. Talking only for a brief time, though. She imagines that for the rest of the night, their bodies will do most of the communicating.

In the morning, Tae and Iovita, who Tae announces likes to be called Vita, cook another big breakfast for everyone. They wear similar outfits of Tae's dark clothing. Vita is even wearing Tae's second pair of combat boots and has tucked her black fatigue trousers into them.

Fit, strong, agile, and now dressing as the family do, she looks like one of them.

When everyone is eating, Tae has something to say. "Vita is a slave. Amelia Heaven *owns* her."

All around the table, busy knives and forks pause in mid-air.

Min has wondered. She and Vita seem to be the only ones who aren't shocked. Joe in particular is horrified, which is another thing that doesn't surprise her.

Everyone returns to the fry-up, although now the mood is sombre.

"Were you captured, or born into slavery?" Min asks.

Joe lifts his eyebrows at her matter-of-fact tone. It's a conversation she needs to have with him when they're alone.

Vita's reply is equally matter-of-fact. "Born. My parents were too, I expect, although I never knew them. Cato Chalice bought me for Amelia as a wedding present when I was a young girl. They're good owners. Amelia is an aristocrat after all. But I know people whose owners aren't as good, even though the culture of Calleva is generally tolerable for slaves."

She speaks well.

"Did they educate you?" Min asks.

"Yes. I was tutored alongside their daughters. Both have junior centurion husbands now and little children of their own, so there are only us three adults left in the villa, Amelia and Cato and me, together with two girls who clean the house and tend the garden and laundry, as I did when I was their age, and Petie, the groom who lives in the stable."

"What work do you do?" Vua asks.

"I run the household for Amelia."

Breakfast is finished, but no one breaks the thoughtful silence.

Vita makes a move to collect the emptied plates.

Tae stops her with a light hand on her forearm. "You are not a slave here."

Everyone agrees.

Honoured citizens of Calleva

TWO DAYS LATER, my family and I are invited to a promotion ceremony in the king's private audience room. Vita stays home while we walk across to the basilica.

It's more a rectangular hall than a room, furnished with gold-leafed chairs and couches around its walls, although most of the hundred or so elegant people here remain standing. It is, if anything, even hotter than the room where we first met Justin. Foreseeing that, we've worn only lightweight clothing beneath our coats despite the harsh overnight freeze.

There are few people I recognise in the assembly, but I'm glad to see some friendly faces. Quin is here, in his dress uniform with its copper armour scales polished to glowing. Otho, cleaned-up in a new tunic and new boots and a sharp haircut, looks distinctly out of place among the dignitaries and is visibly pleased to see us. Cato sits in a corner, wearing his shiny armour and protecting his amputated shoulder stump from passers-by.

"How are you?" I ask.

"Fine," he says, although his clammy, pale face and awkward posture suggest otherwise. He sits straighter, trying to disguise his wince when he does so, and greets me with a left-handed forearm grip. "Recovering. No infection, that's the main thing."

He watches his wife enjoying a conversation with some other women of rank on the far side of the room. "Amelia's happy."

Because he won't be going into battle again? I recall how she stroked his cheek before we left for Anderitum.

A senior officer I don't know is studying Cato from across the room. Not aggressively, but without trying to hide his scrutiny. He wears an air of effortless authority with his shiny armour, and above his helmet stands a tall Mohican of golden feathers like Stern wore in his.

Is he Stern's successor? Cato's new boss? Unlike Stern, he has the look of a fighting man. A soldier's general.

Another difference is that, unlike Cato, Quin, Otho, and all the other legionnaires we fought alongside at Anderitum, his face is shaved. Unlike Shad, Ban, Red, and me too, for that matter. But *our* beards don't matter because we're not living under legion discipline. At any rate, we don't consider ourselves to be. I suppose a new general might be a clean shave in many respects. Is a culture shift on its way to Legion One?

A praetorian guardsman at the inner doors clears his throat officiously, and the assembled people fall silent before Justin appears.

Amelia hurries to stand beside Cato's chair as I return to my family. When our paths cross, she gives me a look of vague recognition, then lays a light hand on her husband's uninjured shoulder.

Sharon and Marc enter the room with Justin, one each side, she arm in arm with him. They walk at a regal pace, although the king's practiced smile looks to be present in spite of physical pain somewhere, and his son's squint suggests he isn't over his concussion, so I wonder if either of them would want to try a greater speed. Or even, in Justin's case, to walk unaided.

They're wearing immaculate white togas. Justin and Marc also sport a golden laurel leaf crown apiece, but even without one of them, Sharon looks every inch the king's consort. They take their seats on three throne-like chairs set on a low stage, and polite applause ripples around the room until Justin holds up a hand for quiet.

"We are here today to honour some of our finest people. First, Gordian Stern, Praefectus Castrorum, lifelong loyal defender of our kingdom, and my friend for many years."

He pauses for a respectful silence. Then, "We will now appoint Gordian's successor to command Legion One."

Amelia produces a folded handkerchief and dabs her husband's brow.

"I proclaim," Justin continues, "that there is no one better to fill this role than our heroic Primus Pilus of the Wolf Cohort, Cato Chalice."

Cato stands, with discreet assistance from Amelia when he wobbles a bit, and makes his way to the stage while applause swells loud and long and the king stands waiting for him.

A guardsman hands a highly polished brass helmet with a Mohican of golden feathers to Justin, who places it on Cato's head. There are moments of fumbling between the two men and the heavy headgear, but they get there without dropping the thing, and the new Praefectus Castrorum turns to face the cheering people.

Amelia is beaming like a summer sun as he makes his way back to his chair, and her friends are fluttering lacy handkerchiefs at her from across the room. At that level in society, I suppose the promotion is hers as much as his.

Eventually, Justin lifts a hand for quiet. "This leaves us with another high-rank vacancy. Today, I promote to Primus Pilus of the Wolf Cohort, our remarkable Senior Centurion of the First Wolf Century, Quinctus Luck."

On his way to the royal platform, Quin removes his brass helmet with its side-to-side feathers, and a guardsman takes it from him.

Another guardsman hands Justin a new helmet with a copper-brown front-to-back Mohican like Cato's old one, which Quin takes from him and fits firmly himself, earning him a quick grateful smile from the king.

The applause celebrating Quin's promotion is subdued compared to that which greeted Cato.

For one, I think, he hasn't been seriously wounded in a victorious battle only a few days ago. For two, and no doubt more significantly, he isn't married to an aristocrat who swims in the same social pond as these people.

Justin lifts his hand again. "We lost good men at Anderitum. Too many of them. They will be remembered."

A murmur of agreement washes through the room.

"While the legion recovers from our losses, while replacements and promotions are taking place all through the ranks, there is one name from among those ranks that I bring to you today. This man's heroism in Anderitum earned him a field promotion, which I am pleased to honour and validate now. People of Calleva, I bid you recognise Legion One's new standard bearer, Otho Valerius."

People press back to make a path for Otho when he strides forward.

Justin hands him the standard.

When he turns back to the room and holds it high, our family's cheers and whoops more than make up for the aristocratically polite applause the rest of the audience offers. He marches back to stand with us and grins hugely as we clap his back with enthusiastic congratulations.

Justin smiles, as does Sharon, and even Marc eases his frown a bit, all of which I think encourages the audience to go along with it too, even if some of their smiles remain a little frosty.

Justin is ready to continue. "The final honour I wish to bestow today will show my gratitude to a group of people who until only a few days ago were strangers in our kingdom, people who owed us nothing, but who nevertheless fought alongside our legion and showed such bravery as to guarantee our triumph."

Uh-oh. Whatever this is, I wish it wasn't going to happen. My private shame about roaring around the surrendered fort and terrifying those poor cowering soldiers sits rancid in my stomach like dirty oil on ditch water.

"Joe Walker, Min Silver, and Axe warriors, Shad, Vua, Tae, Ban, and Red, I thank you. From today, everyone will recognise you as honoured citizens of Calleva."

The applause is reluctant at first, almost pained, until the royal party stands and raises their hands to clap in our direction, and everyone else in the room follows their example. Except for Cato and Quin and Otho, of course, who are cheering like soldiers do for soldiers, with Otho also thumping the base of his heavy standard pole on the fine mosaic floor to the visible concern of some fine people nearby.

Justin sits and leans back with his eyes closed, evidently in pain. I wonder what his medical condition is. Sharon and Marc sit too. Marc removes his crown, and Sharon removes Justin's, both handing the golden laurel leaves to an attending guard.

It's a signal to the audience, who relax instantly. The volume of speech swells, with delicate trills of female laughter sounding here and there, and the military men remove their helmets. In the next few minutes, a dainty draining of numbers takes place until only twenty of the original toga-clad people remain.

All men, I notice, except for Min, Tae, and Vua standing with us, and Amelia sitting with Cato and Quin, and Sharon sitting with Justin and Marc. Twenty older men with serious expressions.

Movers and shakers? I think so. Everyone finds somewhere to sit. A guard nods for Otho to leave but says nothing to us, so we sit together near the back.

The mood in the hall has changed again. Apart from the praetorian guards around the walls, only our three friends and the stranger are in military uniforms, but despite the predominance of white togas it feels like a war council.

Justin regains his upright posture on his throne. "We welcome Flavius Bronze, Praefectus Castrorum of Legion Two."

The old men around the hall make gruff noises of greeting.

The stranger responds with three smart nods, to his left, and forward, and right, then focuses his attention on Justin. "May I speak?"

Justin gestures with open hands. "You may. I'm keen to hear your thoughts."

Bronze takes a steady breath. "My people complain bitterly about your intention to redeploy Legion Two. Not my soldiers. Discipline holds firm. But a legion isn't only soldiers. Mine have families. Twenty thousand non-military dependents, altogether, many of whom have lived their entire lives in Aquae Sullis."

"Bath," Min murmurs to me.

"Your plan to leave a single cohort manning our fort in the town concerns me on two levels. The upheaval of our people I have mentioned." His brief pursing of lips isn't quite a dismissal of their pain. "More urgently, I question the military wisdom of abandoning all fifteen of our western forts between Aquae Sullis and the south coast. We will be asking too much of the remaining cohort. The wall will be undefended, and the border overrun."

Justin nods his understanding. "The cohort will be tasked to face north, and only north, against any possible incursions from the outside, although at this time we consider even the northern outside threat in that corner of our kingdom to be small."

"The threat from the western Wild isn't small," Bronze insists. He's no whiner, but he isn't scared to argue his point.

"The threat has changed," Justin says. "As your intelligence informed you, and you shared with us, Tin and Hare have negotiated a truce." He gestures at Marc. "Following that development, the prince has negotiated a truce with Tin and Hare. There is no longer any threat to us from the western Wild."

Bronze blinks.

Justin continues. "There is, however, a great threat to our kingdom from the outside. It's concentrated for now in attacks across the northern border into our central and eastern lands.

You'll have heard about the battle Legion One fought four nights ago at Anderitum."

"I have heard. But I'm not sure I'm hearing correctly now. A truce with Tin and Hare? After centuries of constant hostility and many times open war, against each other and always against us, how can we possibly trust that they have changed the historic focus of their hatred?"

Justin looks again at Marc, who copies his father's open-handed gesture. "I am fully satisfied of it."

"Why?"

"Because of the threat from the outside the king has described. It threatens Tin and Hare as much as it threatens us. It threatens all of Britannia in the Wild, but our first and primary concern must be to protect our own kingdom. The ancient West Country gods who cemented Tin and Hare's truce have also cemented ours with them. They trust their gods. At Anderitum the other night we learned that we could trust them too. This is the cement."

Justin takes over. "This time of danger to our kingdom is like nothing seen before. Ever before. We need Legion One and Two to protect our northern border while Legions Three and Four continue to guard our eastern and southern coasts. For now, at least, while we continue to watch for changing threats. We need our iron. We need the permanent presence of Legion Two in Anderitum to rebuild the fort, to repopulate the town, to protect our mines, and with Legion One to strengthen our protection against this grave threat from across our border with London in the outside."

Bronze accepts the inevitable with grace and a brief bow of his head.

"As for your people," Justin says. "I understand their dismay and will do everything I can to make this redeployment a happier event for them. My first act is that each and every one of your legion families, when they arrive in their new home, will receive my personal gift of a household slave. I've allocated four thousand slaves for this purpose. Twelve hundred of them are enemy soldiers captured at Anderitum this week, who I'm sure will be grateful to be employed in such a manner instead of shackled to work in the mines."

Min warned me. She described my former lives with the Atrebates, both times in the outside, several centuries before the tribe migrated to the Wild.

My first life was long and happy, she said, as a woman a hundred years before the Roman invasion. My second, as a man, was short and brutal, a hundred years after the invasion, when the tribe had been thoroughly Romanised and I fought a bruising war against slavery. She stayed at my side, and we attracted a few likeminded people to our rebel band. But we rarely succeeded, except for some isolated actions when we managed to free small numbers of slaves who then escaped into the forest, and I died young in that life.

In battle, I asked, or executed by the Romans?

Murdered by Tyac, she said. Our actions drew his attention.

She warned me how I always respond, whoever I am and wherever in the world, when I encounter slavery. She understands why I'm appalled. It's at my core, and she loves it in me. But she warns that I must take care not to attract Tyac's attention because he knows so well the pattern of my responses.

I'm not convinced by her argument. Not least because if Tyac is as aware of Merritt's activities as we suspect he must be, then he will know exactly where we are right now. And so far, he hasn't turned up in Calleva. He must have his reasons. He might even be lying low to recover from me taking his hand.

That memory still gives me a grim smile, which makes Min anxious every time she sees it.

In any case, we're stronger now, possibly stronger than ever before. Shad and the others know the threat and never let us out of their sight. If Tyac does arrive, I'd back us against him. Some battles must be fought, and if ever there's one I must fight, it's against him.

So, I make no promises about my reactions to slavery in the future, but for Min's sake, right now, I will only observe the despicable practice in Calleva.

When we leave the basilica, it's snowing, heavily enough to settle on market-stall roofs in the forum and the ground in the aisles and gaps between, although people are still getting on with their daily business. Hardy types. I wonder how many of them are free to choose.

Min stands in the doorway, catching soft snowflakes on her tongue, and my heart swells with love. We pull our coats tighter and set off back to the villa.

In the garrison, we bump into Otho on his way to enjoy a sweat with four of his comrades.

"Come with us," he offers.

We're always ready for a good sweat.

"I'm sorry," he tells Min and the sisters. "Not you. It's our century house."

Vua chuckles. "They're frightened of naked women?"

He's embarrassed. So are his comrades.

"Superstition is strong in the legions," Min tells us. Her tone is gentle to Otho. "Vua is teasing you. We understand."

His relief is evident. I like how open and honest he is. Shad, Ban, Red, and I agree to meet him at his century house as soon as we've changed our clothes.

It must be a quiet time of day for a sweat. We're a small group, sitting like old friends on a pair of benches beside one of the partitioned fire pits, splashing water across the searing stones and breathing clouds of steam.

"Are you happy here?" Otho asks.

I gesture around the building with a soundless, *"Duh."*

He mirrors my expression. "Not in here. This is paradise. I mean in Calleva. You're thinking a lot."

Perceptive.

"Is it something I can help you with? Say the word."

I don't know whether to open up to him. Don't know if I should burden him.

He leans back and closes his eyes. "If it's none of my business, I won't pry."

"Slavery."

He opens one eye with a lazy movement and fixes it on me. "What about slavery?"

"I hate it. It makes me feel ill."

He opens the other eye too, to show he's taking my discomfort seriously, and knuckles them free of sweat. "It's how the kingdom is run. Our society has always been this way."

"I know. That doesn't make it easier for me to accept."

"I was born a slave."

Now I pay him my full attention.

"Joining the legion was my way out of it." He nods to the two burly soldiers playing draughts on the bench across the fire pit from us while sweat glistens in their beards and runs freely down their shining bodies. "Same with Brutus and Felix there. The system worked well for us, and for many others. It's how the world goes round."

He waits for me to comment, and when I offer only a small shrug of acceptance, he settles his head back against the bench and lets his eyelids droop. "My life is good," he finishes. "I'm happy."

Many people do like their worlds, I reflect, no matter how dreadful the social engines of those worlds might look to a stranger.

The price is paid in full

DECEMBER IS PRETTILY snow filled, with much of the activity in the garrison town shrinking happily to family time. Min enjoys watching parents and children playing together outside their villas.

It's no surprise when Sharon turns up one day, ostensibly to check on Justin's behalf that they have every comfort they need, although Min thinks she can guess the real reason for her visit.

She invites their guest to sit with her in the cosy candlelit reception room and watch through the window while Joe and the others do their daily workout in the courtyard's cold afternoon gloom.

"They're magnificent," Sharon says.

Min thinks her admiration is honest. They are, after all, genuinely magnificent. She remembers her and Joe's first days with the Axe in their forest village, when they both kept using that word because all their new friends truly did have splendid physiques.

That was only seven months ago. It feels like seven years. Some of Joe's lives are more action packed than others. This one definitely is.

She brings herself back to the present and watches Vita boxing with big Red, dancing around him as the sisters have taught her and jabbing him hard from all directions. Someone judging on size alone might think he could snap her in two. In a wrestling brawl, maybe he could. But out there in the courtyard he's defending himself with real respect for her fast fists.

"Justin used to be like that." Sharon's tone is soft.

Min pictures Marc's strong build, and imagines his father looking the same way in his youth. "What happened?"

"He was badly injured in a chariot race only a year into his kingship, when Marc was a toddler. His wife, Queen Livia, was racing the other chariot in the crash. She died. I don't think Marc remembers his mother at all. Justin's broken bones mended, but his health never recovered."

"Did you know him back then?"

Sharon smiles and indulges Min's curiosity. "I found the Wild when I was a little girl. By the time I discovered Calleva, people here knew I was from the outside, but they accepted me as a harmless kid. So, yes, I knew of Justin since he was a boy prince about the same age as me, but we only met each other properly as adults, three years after his queen died."

She stares into the past, and then blinks herself back to the conversation. "He wanted to know all about the outside. Even had me take him to Reading once. He was hungry to experience a big town for himself, and the plan was to visit London next. But that day in Reading did for him. The busyness of the place made him ill."

"I've known others who've suffered lifelong poor health after an accident," Min says.

"I think he has an autoimmune condition. I researched it online, and the most likely candidate is ME. All his symptoms fit. He's a brave fighter, same as he always was, only now his battles are different. He's survived pneumonia twice. There's no cure, although I'm sure painkillers from the outside would help him manage it more easily. I offered to bring him some to try, but he won't hear of it. His body is weak and horribly painful, but his mind's as sharp as a tack."

"He clearly holds his people's respect."

"Yes, and deservedly so. He's a good king. His father was an okay ruler, but during Justin's reign the kingdom has prospered, and not by accident. I think this will be remembered as a golden age." Her smile fades. "If the Westminster government doesn't ruin it."

Min hears water boiling in the kitchen and goes to make them a pot of tea. She brings two mugs of it back with a plate of Vita's homemade ginger biscuits.

Sharon sips the everyday blend Min's brought in from the outside with a smile of recognition. She dunks a biscuit, a little too thoroughly, but manages to transfer it into her mouth all in one go as it sags.

"I hear one of your wolf women and Amelia's girl are an item." Her tone is light, but they've come to the real reason she's here.

Min keeps her tone similarly light. "Yes."

Sharon cups her mug in both hands and stares into the steaming tea. "I hope she doesn't go running away without an agreement. That sort of thing never ends well."

Min watches Joe doing squats with a heavy rock the size of two footballs clutched to his abdomen, and reflects that Justin's isn't the only sharp mind in the royal partnership.

Next day, she, Tae, and Vua accompany Vita when she goes to see Amelia. The sisters have spent hours braiding Vita's hair in intricate tight patterns, which is something she's never seen before. Judging by people's reactions when they walk through the town, nor has anyone else.

Min loves these reactions because Vita is walking tall and looking like a black goddess. In her combat boots and body-hugging fatigues, the entire confident package is stunning.

Amelia's walled villa is a small palace, one of several occupying Noble Hill, a genteel district on the town's high ground behind the basilica.

The old groom limps out to greet Vita in the entrance courtyard. His painful gait indicates crippling arthritis, and Min recalls Amelia using his bended leg as a step up to her chariot. He places a gnarled hand on Vita's shoulder and looks into her eyes. She gives him a slow nod, as wordless as he, and a gentle expression. He blinks a sad understanding of whatever has passed in their silent communication and returns slowly to his stable.

The villa's interior is decorated and furnished with great style and a conspicuous display of wealth. Old wealth, Min guesses. Flawless white marble features a lot, as carved columns framing painted walls that show undulating countryside scenes, cut into slabs and joined perfectly as floors of the several airy rooms Vita leads them through, and in busts sitting upon plinths everywhere.

The busts have all been sculpted by talented artists. Some are recognisable as characters from classical Roman and Greek mythology. Others bear something of a family resemblance that suggests they are Amelia's ancestors.

In the most lavishly decorated reception room they enter, two girls aged nine or ten run to hug Vita. They are weeping silently. Vita embraces them together, and the threesome stand in tight intensity, until Amelia sweeps in and takes a seat on the room's central couch. Then the young girls leave without a word or a backward glance.

Amelia doesn't welcome her guests or invite them to sit. At first, she says nothing, while she gives Vita a slow look up and down, and then does the same to Tae, Vua, and Min.

They simply look back. No one is daunted. Of course they aren't. After a minute's silence, Min detects a crack in the woman's self-confident shell of lifelong privilege.

She focuses her attention on Vita. "What do you want?"

Vita's voice is calm but strong. "I've come to take my freedom."

Amelia blinks in pretend astonishment. "You're asking...?"

"I'm not asking. I'm taking it."

Her former owner's blinking increases to rapid for several seconds as her focus darts back and forth between Vita and her companions, whose impassive stares remain steady.

She thinks Vita has taken the bite, Min realises. She's scared.

Amelia tries to restore her confident tone. "The price—"

"Is paid. I have paid you with thirty years of enslavement. The price is paid in full. I'm here only to do you the courtesy of informing you."

Amelia's swallow is a gulp.

Min keeps her expression blank. *She's thinking a slave would never talk like this or even think this way if she hasn't taken the bite.*

Amelia's attention flickers to each of the four women once more, and then suddenly she stands. "Very well. Goodbye." She sweeps from the room faster than she came in.

The deed is done.

Vita says her sad farewells to the sobbing young girls and in the courtyard to the old groom, and then she walks free.

That night, in their bed, Min listens with Joe and Shad when in the next room Vita takes the bite from Tae.

We've made some good friends

AT THE END of our first month in Calleva, the day before Andrew's scheduled arrival on the River Kennet to exchange information, a messenger comes to the villa with a courteous summons for me from the king.

We meet in yet another overheated private room, this one smaller and more intimate than any others I've seen in the basilica. Despite its fine furniture of carved bone structures cushioned with crimson velvet and the rich earthy reds of its walls, it's clearly Justin and Sharon's living room. If I'd needed any proof of this, a small wooden bookcase is crammed full of paperbacks from the outside, and a small circular table bears a chessboard of ebony and ivory with a game paused in mid-play.

When a praetorian guardsman lets me in, Justin is alone, sitting in one of the chess table's cushioned chairs. I don't take its partner, supposing it to be Sharon's. Instead, when he gestures me to sit, I choose a similar chair opposite him.

"We must discuss what intelligence you will pass to Merritt. I trust you not to betray my people intentionally, but I'm taking a risk."

"In your place, I would feel exactly the same way."

"Good. Obviously, you will confirm the enemy's failure to occupy Anderitum. You should provide all the details of the battle. Including, I think, your own involvement. That will satisfy Merritt of your honesty to him, and it will let the Westminster government know we are more able and willing to defend our kingdom than they thought."

"I won't mention Flo and Gully." I've barely talked with Gully since we met in Wallasey, but as an old wizard, he was keen to avoid appearing on Merritt's radar, and I expect this will still be so. "Their existence, never mind their involvement in the battle. No enemy soldiers escaped? Your people are sure of that?"

"They're sure."

"Then no details will have got back to Westminster. In the radio silence since the battle, they'll assume their incursion failed but will have to assume your legion was fully able to defeat their force. We should confirm that. No need to mention old Crow gods of the west."

"I agree. We'll let them think we crushed their invasion with no requirement of assistance. Also, don't mention my redeployment of Legion Two. Not a word of that. Or of Legions Three and Four. Nothing whatsoever about our troop movements. Let the total defeat of the invasion speak for itself."

"Understood."

"With your military intelligence seemingly limited to specifics of the single battle in which you were involved, might they want to know about anything else?"

"I won't know until I see Andrew tomorrow. I expect he'll bring me questions from Merritt." I wrinkle my nose. "Knowing Merritt, he'll want particulars of your trade. What, who with, and how? That sort of thing. He's a state-licensed pirate really."

"What details of our trade have you learned?"

"Not much. Obviously, I know about your iron supply from Anderitum. And I remember you saying the River Kennet is your main trade route with the Saxon kingdom to the north."

"Ah, yes. Don't mention any of that. Our trade with the West Saxons, or the river barge route. Leave them out of it."

Interesting. Justin would make a superb poker player. His expression reveals nothing. But I have to wonder if, after Anderitum, he's now talking with the West Saxons as well as with Tin and Hare about a joint defence against outside armies. Or even a joint attack.

"I told you when we first arrived that Merritt's government masters want confirmation or otherwise of rumours about you planning an attack on London in the outside."

"You've heard nothing about that."

"Merritt will expect me to have tried."

"Nevertheless, you have discovered nothing. You wonder if that means there is nothing to discover."

"Understood." Only too well. I need to find my parents and get them out of London, now more urgently than ever.

"I'll send an escort with you tomorrow. To ensure your safety."

"Thank you."

We don't need an escort, of course, and when I tell the others later, they're amused at the notion. We enjoy a long afternoon in Quin's sweat house, followed by a leisurely meal and an early night.

Before dawn next day, we're joined by twenty legionnaires from the First Wolf Century, who, along with their grizzled centurion, watch with pride and admiration when our wolves pad from the villa. Six now, including Vita. She's fast and strong, and her sleek coat is darker even than the sisters. As our escort marches beside the centurion and Min and me on our sturdy horses, the legionnaires keep looking out for fleeting glimpses of the wolves running through the trees.

The road we ride for three hours is nothing like the Iron Road. The difference is like ancient Roman versions of a motorway and a B road. But it's well maintained and as straight as an arrow through the forest to the river.

"How ya doin'?" Andrew sits waiting for us on a fallen tree trunk near the riverbank, wrapped up as if he's on an arctic expedition, his breath clouding in the still air.

Beyond him, anchored at the far side of the lake, is the welcome sight of *Belle,* her crew watching our meeting from the upper deck and on its raised stern section the familiar figures of her captain and first mate studying us through telescopes. They're all dressed for arctic weather too. Lucinda returns my wave.

I hadn't expected to see *Belle,* but my reaction is nothing compared to that of our escort. They're astonished at her size, and vocally so.

There are ice-coated barges moored in the lake and some of them are big, but none with anything like the height and graceful curves of *Belle*'s hull. None with three tall masts carrying great rolls of furled canvas, and a cat's cradle of rigging, and a row of cannon muzzles pointing across the lake.

Certainly, there are none like the big inflatable boat with a snub, upturned, black nose and a substantial engine housing behind its central steering wheel, which has clearly been Andrew's transport from the ship and is now tied to the riverbank near his fallen tree.

The man sitting at its wheel has handsome Asian features. He wears high-leg combat boots, a black beanie hat, and panelled body armour like ours. The machine pistol slung around his neck sits comfortably against his chest. His posture is relaxed, but I don't buy it. He looks like a very capable military man of the twenty-first century outside.

Andrew introduces him. "This is Chun-Kit Tam."

"Call me CK."

"Merritt sent him to be my driver and guard." Andrew counts our wolves as they emerge from the forest and notes without comment our new midnight-black one. "Keep me out of trouble and report back on what I get up to. We were supposed to come all the way in his boat. What Merritt doesn't know is, CK has joined Lucinda's crew with me. His boat is now *Belle*'s boat. The crew call her *Bertha.* She's gutsy. Towed *Belle* all the way upriver from the Thames to here without breaking a sweat."

CK sends me a casual salute. He's more interested at first in our Roman escort, and then much more interested in our wolves, especially when Red and Andrew embrace like old friends with a big history. The sight of a huge red wolf greeting the American with such enthusiasm may well lift Andrew in his estimation.

Our wolves and legionnaires surround us in an outward-facing wide semicircle, while CK covers the opposite riverbank with his machine pistol, and we get down to business.

"So, you've deserted Merritt."

"Yeah. Only been hanging on until I located your ma and pa. We know where they are now, so it's time to get you out of here and them out of there."

"Where?"

"London. An insider in the Red Rose haven found them living in a big old house in Rotherhithe with direct access to the Thames. CK and I went and checked. They're there."

He gives me his phone, which shows a photograph of my parents standing together at the low-walled bottom of a garden lawn at sunset, staring out across the broad river. They look okay.

"When did you take this?"

"Day before yesterday."

I frown. Mum and Dad have on thin woollen jumpers, hers blue and his green, like the V-necked lambswool ones they'd usually wear for an autumn walk. "What's the weather like there?"

"Mildest winter I've ever known in Britain." He gives a dramatic shiver inside his big duffel coat and heavy cable-knit roll-neck jumper. "The house is right near a thin place on the river. And Merritt's security people there are complacent. Getting your folks out will be a piece of piss."

He shoots a glance at CK, who returns an expressionless nod. Whether at Andrew's assessment of the situation or his usage of the military-sounding slang, I don't know. Maybe both.

"So." Andrew stands up and gestures at *Belle*. "Let's go."

"Not so fast." I hand him his phone. "We need to say our goodbyes first."

Andrew squints. "Yeah? This bunch got your loyalty, have they?"

"We've made some good friends." Also, which I choose not to say in the centurion's hearing, I don't know how Justin would react if we simply got on *Belle* and left without a word. His kingdom is on a war footing. If he decides we're betraying him, we might find ourselves attacked all along the river. "We can be there and back in seven hours, by sunset. Or tomorrow morning if that will suit Lucinda better."

"Make it today, eh?" Andrew is intense suddenly. "You don't know what's been happening while you've been here. Big shit going down, and fast. There's a migration from the Wild, thousands of people and even some creatures arriving in London and all across the English Midlands. I don't know what's going on where they come from, or what they think they're going to find on the outside, but they keep coming. North London's a powder keg. Riots every night. Curfew. They're policing Tottenham like it's Gaza."

"You mean with police snipers?"

"Yeah."

"That's war on civilians."

"Undeclared, but yeah. Birmingham's in full lockdown, claiming in the media that it's the coronavirus fifth wave, but through the havens we're hearing rumours of concentration camps and martial law executions there."

"Fuck."

"Shit's going down in other countries too. The US is on fire. No official news coming out of there, but I'm guessing civil war, with the Wild folks caught in the middle of it."

He squeezes his eyes shut and rubs away tears of distress or anger with two swipes of a knuckle. "We need to spring your folks tomorrow and get the hell out. That's why Lucinda brought me here for you, so we can do your extraction and their escape all in one move."

I nod to the centurion, who is hearing everything. "Let's go."

We make fast time back to Calleva and straight to the villa, where our wolves shift to human form while the centurion goes to report Andrew's news to his command, then we pack our gear and eat everything available in the kitchen. When we arrive at the amphitheatre, the legion is getting busy, and four praetorians are waiting there to escort me to Justin.

"I've heard," he says without preamble.

My winter outdoor clothes are instantly uncomfortable in his hot living room.

Sharon is sitting beside the bookcase with her nose in a novel, but I doubt she's reading it.

"What are your intentions?" Justin wants to know.

"We're going to rescue my parents and escape with them into the Wild."

"Back here? Sharon is going to stay with me now. You too, and your family, will always be welcome in Calleva."

Sharon lifts her head and gives me a quick smile.

"Thank you," I say. "I don't know. There's a lot about this we can't plan. We'll have to take things as they come."

I'm not being completely honest. My instinct, like Andrew's I guess, is to take our people somewhere safe and peaceful in the deep Wild. I've come to think of Justin's kingdom and the lands of Tin and Hare as the shallow Wild. It's a war-torn region near to the outside, not unlike much of the outside, in fact, and getting worse now so many people are armed with automatic weapons taken from dead outsiders.

News of serious civil disorder in London might be precisely the catalyst needed to start a coordinated attack on the city. And anyone who thinks an attack like that won't bring revenge attacks back into the Wild on an enormous scale is only fooling themself.

The danger of an all-out war is very real.

On the ride back from the river I settled my thoughts. My loyalty is to my loved ones and our true friends. That does include the ones we've made in Legion One, but their loyalty to their homeland makes them complicated.

None of which I can share with Justin.

"Take care," he says.

"We will."

"My legion will protect your ship for as long as you are on the river in my kingdom. I wish you could stay and tell me of the great ship. Its description has captured my interest. But you must go now, so go in safety. I'll welcome the day when we meet again."

Sharon hugs me, and then I hurry back across hard frozen ground to the amphitheatre.

They've ramped up the noise and movement in the military camp. Its command building is a hive of busyness and the parade ground a mass of ordered activity.

Quin is outside the building, talking with my family. He hauls me into a bear hug and holds me for a good long while. "Stay safe," he growls in my ear. "You and yours mean a lot to me and mine. Do what you have to do, but come back to us in one piece."

Someone calls to him from inside the command building, their tone respectful but urgent.

His *me and mine* means the legion. It's his family.

"You too," I say while we hold each other's shoulders with fierce grips and share an intense stare. "There's war coming. You know, don't you? You come out the other side of it in one piece too."

He nods, brushes my whiskered cheek with his, and disappears back inside.

Otho takes his place. He crushes my ribs in a hug, urges, "Come back to us, Lion Man," and brushes a tear from his cheek as he strides away.

Min tries to hide her unhappiness when he calls me that.

Cato's there, watching us all but particularly Vita while he waits to say goodbye.

I grip his left forearm with my left hand, feeling more strength in his return grip than last time when his wound was only days old.

"Your woman influenced my wife to free her slave," he says quietly. There's no rancour in his tone, but it isn't exactly warm.

"No, she didn't. Vita and Amelia conducted their negotiation without interference."

"Amelia was scared. She knows nothing of magic or violence."

"There was no magic and not even a hint of violence. But whatever Amelia's reason, she did the right thing. Slavery is disgusting."

He blinks. "Our economy runs on slavery. Always has. It works. And our slaves are treated well."

"Just because you've always done something doesn't mean you always have to do it. Slavery is an unnatural state of affairs. Any system that denies human beings their freedom is wrong."

He shakes his head. "I don't know what you mean by unnatural. What could be more natural? There will always be people at the top of a system and others at the bottom."

Min's gesturing behind Cato's back for me to get a move on. A new centurion has turned up with fresh horses for us to ride and twenty more legionnaires to escort us back to *Belle*.

"It isn't natural," I say. "Slavery is a fiction written by men and lived in by other men. You should free your old groom."

"Petie? He's been in Amelia's family since she was a girl. He taught her to ride. Why would we want to get rid of him?"

"He's old and crippled with arthritis. His pain is terrible. He sleeps in your unheated stable. Amelia uses one of his horribly painful knees as a step to climb into her chariot. You might not agree with me about slavery in principle, but how long will you keep that sick old man living in such terrible conditions? Until someone goes to look for him one morning and finds him dead in the hay? You should free him today and pay him a good pension to reward his years of forced service."

He blinks again.

Petie is only one slave and Cato only one owner. It's as much as I can do.

Concentration camps in Birmingham. Civil war in America. Slavery in Justin's kingdom. Frankly, I'm ready to let the outside and the shallow Wild go to hell together.

Cato and I are still gripping each other's forearms. I give his a squeeze. "Stay safe."

"Stay safe," he replies and returns my squeeze.

The centurion rolls his eyes at Min.

"Joe," she says.

"I'm coming."

Parallel obsessions

THE THIN PLACE is a hundred metres downriver from the target." CK is standing at an easel that displays his simple diagram of the house and its surrounds while the family, the landing party as he calls them, sits cross-legged around him on the lamplit gun deck.

Two of *Belle*'s sailors are crewing *Bertha,* towing the big ship at a steady speed along the river. There's no wind so the going is as smooth as silk, which makes Min happy. Joe hadn't known she suffers from seasickness. She can get so bad she's useless, she'd explained, and she hates being useless nearly as much as she hates being seasick. But thankfully, Lucinda has some magic medicine tea for if the sea gets rough after the rescue. Or even before then, if the Thames is lumpy when they reach it.

"*Belle* will stay this side of the thin place," CK says, "and we'll take *Bertha* through. From the house we'll look like river police."

He studies the party, one by one, pausing at Shad and Ban. "You two will need to tie your hair back like the women and tuck it up into your hats or something."

"We have hats like yours," Ban says. He and CK hold each other's steady gaze for a moment.

Min noticed them doing that earlier, on the upper deck before it got dark, when CK was instructing them in small arms firing into the West Saxon riverbank.

"When we go through the thin place it'll make you sort of jump. Both directions, in and out, like a muscle jump all over.

It only lasts a second and won't do you any harm. Don't let it affect your concentration."

No one embarrasses CK. He isn't to know that what's a new sensation for him is already an everyday part of his audience's lives. He's preparing them the way he knows how to, equipping them with every bit of information they might need on the operation, and doing it well.

After the briefing, Lucinda and her cabin steward Wendy arrive on the gun deck with supper for the landing party. Joe moans with pleasure when he smells Jamaican coffee, which apparently is heavenly. It's the property of someone called Johnson, who Min learns was Wendy's predecessor, Lucinda's beloved old retainer, killed by Merritt's thugs.

She lets the conversation flow around her and sees Ban and KC catch another glance then look away quickly. They're cute. If they manage to get past the action-man reserve they both wear so naturally, she won't be surprised to see KC join the family.

"You were in the army?" she asks him.

"Twenty-two years a Royal Marine." He smells and sips his coffee with evident appreciation. "Retired last summer."

There's a slight musical accent in his well-spoken, educated English. It's attractive, but she can't place it. "Where are you from?"

"I was born in Hong Kong." His smile is pleasant, his dark eyes shining in the lamplight with liquid warmth. "Came here when I was a boy with my mum and dad. They're both gone now. Mum a few years ago and Dad in the coronavirus first wave."

"I'm sorry. Any family over there?"

"Some, but we lost touch after Mum died. I wouldn't know how to find them now. With the Hong Kong revolution still going and China kicking shit out of the place, I don't expect I ever will."

Another one all alone. Yes, maybe her family will become his too.

"Don't lose hope for your homeland. People have come together and changed whole countries in the past. Even China. Just like in Hong Kong, the Chinese Revolution of 1911 started with a student-led uprising. Brave kids, back from studying abroad, seeing their country with fresh eyes, determined to change things and prepared to sacrifice even their own lives to achieve their vision of something better."

He studies her. "You sound like you were there in 1911." He looks almost embarrassed at voicing what he clearly thinks is a daft notion.

She watches Joe getting to his feet and smiles too. "I used to know someone who was."

"Early start in the morning," Joe announces. "Get some sleep and we'll meet back here at six."

Min is grateful to Mister Samson, who again has vacated his cabin for her, and this time for Joe too. Its single bunk is wide enough for them to spoon snugly.

She's drifting off to sleep, lullabied by Andrew's sad flute from Lucinda's cabin next door, when Joe says something quietly in her ear.

"Sorry, what?"

"What happened in our past that upsets you when people call me Lion Man?"

She thinks for a minute, staring into the cabin's darkness and deciding what to say. She's promised always to be truthful, and this is one of those times when she must put her controlling instinct firmly aside. "Twice, in ancient Egypt three thousand years ago, in two consecutive lives, you became a lion."

He says nothing, but his instant tensing speaks loud and clear.

"We were in service to the pharaoh Ramesses the Second, you a soldier prince and me a royal witch, and naturally, we were lovers. He was a powerful pharaoh who honoured you in your first of those lives as one of his most fearless warriors and highly favoured among his many sons. Then, without me knowing until it had happened, you sought out a desert lion called Maahes and took the bite from him. Maahes was what the ancient Egyptians called their lion god of war. I don't know if the one you found was the god or just named after him. I don't know. Never met him. Only knew him through what you told me."

She holds herself together, nearly crumpling but determined to tell the story he wants so badly to hear.

"After the bite, you became more of everything that Ramesses gloried about you. Bigger, stronger, faster, famously majestic in battle. Everything. And your successes added to his glory. So, when you became obsessed with hunting down a monster that was killing hundreds of people along the Nile, a monster you and I knew was Tyac, then Ramesses became equally obsessed with the quest. I wanted us to run away, but you were fired up like I'd never seen you before, and your father the pharaoh kept throwing fuel on your flames."

She feels the tremor in her voice and pauses for a minute.

He doesn't hurry her. Just holds her gently and waits.

"You found Tyac. He let you, I think, and when you did, he destroyed you. After your death, Ramesses honoured you as the lion god of war, Maahes. He built lion statues with your face."

The memory stabs like a knife in her aching heart.

"And then, within a year, when you were born to his youngest royal wife, I knew the moment I looked into your eyes that you were you again. And you knew it too, immediately, from birth, the only time that's ever happened. It was like you were born to complete a task, and I was terrified from the moment go."

"I was a prince."

"You were. Twice. A splendid boy who that second time grew into an even more splendid young man. You were godlike.

They worshipped you. Your painted likeness was everywhere. And we were lovers again. I would have done anything, *anything*, to attract you off the road of your obsession. Being your older lover was no hardship. But it didn't work. You sought out Maahes again, and he gave you the bite again, and Ramesses gloried in you again as the living embodiment of the lion god of war."

She can almost hear him trying to remember. The darkness feels electric.

"I hated Maahes. If I could have found him, I would have killed him. But I couldn't. And our parallel obsessions tore us apart. I tried to deflect you with my magic, but you rejected me, despite knowing who we were, and I lost my mind. It wasn't the first time, or the last, but it was the longest. While I was gone, you went hunting Tyac in the Nile marshes, and he let you find him again, and he destroyed you again."

The pillow is sodden with her silent tears.

Joe says nothing. On a different night, his regular breathing might persuade her that he's asleep, but he isn't. He's processing what she's told him.

Heaven alone knows what road he'll take now.

We didn't want to believe it was true

I RECOGNISE THE OLD riverside house from Andrew's photograph as soon as CK drives *Bertha* through the thin place at Rotherhithe.

The change from the Wild to the outside is the starkest one I've experienced, in its temperature rise more than the visual difference between uninhabited meadowland for miles on both sides of the river and its instant transformation into twenty-first-century London. The relative warmth of a mild winter day is welcome, although, as always, the outside's air quality is noticeably poorer. And now it contains a strong taste of burning that must be coming from the black cloud over the north of the city.

CK sees me looking. "Tottenham."

Pen and Poke live there, somewhere under that cloud. Knowing them, they'll be out on the streets every night in this unrest. Bill lives in Wimbledon, and I guess she'll be staying safe at home. I hope they're all okay. Wish I could check, but contacting them would be dangerous, even more for them than for me, probably, so I don't even flirt with the idea. If Tyac identified them as my friends, he'd tear them to pieces. Regrettably, I have to hope they're okay in this turmoil and leave them in my past.

CK maintains a steady course and speed in the middle of the broad river, we his passengers sitting still and looking out for a police or military presence on the river or its banks. We see none. When we get opposite the house, he turns and drives us directly at the slender mud beach.

Everything goes according to plan. Shad and Ban are first into the water, then Vua and Red. They splash through knee-deep shallows and drag *Bertha* up onto the wet mud. CK kills her engine as Tae and Vita and I run over her nose and sprint to reach the low wall and cover the others while they run up the beach. In less than a minute, Min and CK are out of the boat too. All nine of us roll over the wall together and fan out across the garden lawn as we jog watchfully up to the house.

Its windows reflect the bland morning light. No security personnel are visible anywhere. Steps lead to a tatty old wooden deck and a newer patio door, which Shad slides open to exclamations of surprise from inside as our landing party piles in.

I step into the room, my sabre in hand. A single security man is pinned against its far inner wall by Ban and CK. His coffee cup has spilled across the dining table, and he hasn't had time to draw his handgun, which Vita plucks from his shoulder holster. The room's other occupants are my parents, sitting at breakfast, their faces frozen in alarm.

"Mum," I say. "Dad."

"Joe!" they chorus.

"You need to come with us," I say. "Quickly. Don't worry about collecting your things. We can replace everything. Just come now."

"We certainly will not." Dad's alarm is replaced by anger.

"How many security people in this house right now?" CK asks the man against the wall.

When he presses his lips firmly together, CK twists his hand into a painful shape and applies pressure for a few seconds until he blurts, "Two."

"You and one other?" CK wants it confirmed before he releases the pressure.

"Yes."

On cue, the second security man opens the internal door and enters without realising what he's walking into until it's too late when Vua and Tae slam him against the wall and relieve him of his handgun. His expression is only a little more shocked than Mum and Dad's.

"Oh, Joe." Mum sounds incredibly sad. "We didn't want to believe it was true."

"What was?"

"That you're a terrorist," Dad says in disgust.

I chuckle without mirth. "Let me guess. Merritt told you that."

"Evidently, he wasn't lying," Dad says.

"Mister Merritt has been good to us," Mum says. "All this time while you've been missing, his people have looked after us and he's been kind whenever he visits."

"Where is he now?"

Mum and Dad compress their lips just like the security man did.

CK twists his prisoner's hand. "Where's Merritt?"

"Birmingham," the man squeaks.

"Tie them up," I say.

Red and Vua cuff one of the men in a dining chair with a cable tie behind his back, while Tae and Vita do the other. Then they strap them to the dining chairs with masking tape.

Mum and Dad still haven't moved. Mum stares at my sabre.

I sheathe it. "We need to go now."

Dad's resolute. "No."

Mum's still staring at my sword's handle sticking up above my shoulder.

Min has remained at the open glass door. So far, she's taken no part in the action of conversation. Now she sings.

It's as beautiful and heart lifting as ever. I imagine it has the same effect on everyone in the room. Certainly, Mum's and Dad's expressions soften. They stand and accompany us without another word, Min walking beside them singing softly.

"Wow," CK breathes.

She stops singing when we're all in *Bertha* and back on the river. Mum and Dad sit quietly behind the powerful engine, resigned to the inevitable, although Mum stares around my fearsome family and Dad glares at me, until we go through the thin place and they both jump hard.

"Is this the Wild?" Mum stares at the empty countryside, sounding more curious than scared.

I'm surprised she's heard of it. "Yes."

She picks up on my tone. "It's on the news every night. I don't know where you've been these past months. But the world has changed a lot." She catches Dad's eye and holds his gaze. "I don't know if we'll ever be able to go back to Florida."

He shakes his head sadly. "Things sound bad there. I don't know what would have happened if DCI Dawson hadn't brought us home when he did."

"Is he still working for Merritt?" I ask.

Dad looks across the water, pointedly away from me.

"As far as I know," Mum says. "We haven't seen him since we arrived in England. They must be very busy with all the riots and..." her voice drops, "...terrorism, and everything."

The sudden drop in temperature had probably been their biggest shock after CK powered us through the thin place. Then they see beautiful *Belle* under full sail on the otherwise empty river and their mouths open soundlessly.

Our transfer to the big ship goes as smoothly as everything else has. Before Mum and Dad know it, they're sitting in a circle with all of us in the enclosed gun deck, on chairs supplied by the friendly crew, drinking mugs of steaming hot tea and bundled up as we all are now in heavyweight woollen clothing topped with duffel coats and sea boots.

Min sees me looking at her mug of Lucinda's medicine tea. "Mister Samson is expecting what he calls stiff weather and lumpy seas when we leave the Thames. Atlantic winds in our face all the way to Cornwall. Ugh."

"Are you extras?" Mum asks no one in particular.

I don't know what she means. Film extras? Is she confused, like I was the first time I stumbled into Quarter Square?

Dad's watching the gun deck crew bolting cannon ports shut with practised efficiency as *Belle* increases speed and leans over into her course downriver. "Is this a pirate ship?" he asks Min when she sits beside him.

She wrinkles her nose and rocks her hand. "Depends who you ask. For many years, *Belle* was a lawful trading ship importing cotton, tobacco, and rum from the Caribbean to Britain, until Merritt made her illegal because the captain wouldn't give him a cut. Rather than surrender to his corruption, she became a smuggler."

Mum leans forward and listens with interest past Dad. He looks like he's being too polite to scorn the nice young woman to her face.

"Here she is now," Min says. She introduces Lucinda and Andrew to Mum, who is visibly impressed with the stylishly dressed captain, and Dad, who looks like he thinks he's woken up in a pantomime.

"So you *are* all extras," Mum says.

"Give me an hour with them," Min tells me. "I'll take them somewhere quiet and sing them our history."

She leads them away across the gently tilting deck, even Dad once she starts singing, despite his initial reluctance to go anywhere with anyone.

"What are extras?" I ask Andrew.

"It's what the media is calling folks from the Wild. Short for extraordinary, although no one says that anymore. The phraseology's moving as fast as events. On the street, people call them trubs. Short for trouble." His eyes search my face. "What was it like?"

"Easy. We were in and out like that." I snap my fingers. "I'm surprised Merritt's people weren't more prepared."

"Good. I'm glad. I reckon you and your parents are one of Merritt's unofficial projects, so he can't call in a heavy military presence. But I meant, what's the city like?"

I think about my answer. "The river was quiet for a midweek morning. Felt more like an old-fashioned Sunday. Big black cloud over Tottenham. We didn't see any violence or evidence there has been any where we were."

"It's focused," he says. "For now. Feels like the police and military are working together to a plan."

"Whose plan?" Does he mean a coup? "Theirs or the government's?"

"The government's. The all singing and dancing Government of the United States and England."

"*What?*"

"Happened last week. Emergency ballot in Westminster with only a handful of no votes. The Scottish MPs all went back home that same night, and the English dissenters walked too. It's a done deal. England is now the fifty-first state, although English politicians are claiming it's a partnership between two equal countries. Of course they are."

I'm staring. "What about Scotland, Wales, and Northern Ireland?"

"That happened just as fast. Ireland is re-unified. Scotland and Wales separated from England that same night and have applied to join the EU as independent countries."

I close my mouth with a pop. "Why?'

"Westminster? All bought and paid for."

"I mean what's the official reason?"

"They say the two countries are facing the same problems. By which they mean immigration from the Wild. And while there are obviously security and housing and tax and whatever angles they like to keep talking about, I'm not convinced it isn't all a smokescreen. In fact, it wouldn't surprise me if the entire wave of refugees thing was dreamed up in Washington and Westminster anyway."

"So is it Wild people rioting in London?"

"Nah. It's Londoners, nudged along by brutal policing. All the pieces are moving into place for a police state, fast, over here same as in the States." He stares sadly at the deck between his boots.

Lucinda takes his arm and snuggles in to comfort him.

I go up to get some fresh air before we hit rough seas, and to think about the shocking news. CK is leaning against a rail, staring out across the river and empty marshlands.

"Andrew's told me what's happened," I say. "England joining America. Is that why you left Merritt's department?"

"Merritt's a twat. Didn't take me long to see that, so I've been on the lookout for something better while the whole world's been turning to shit these past months. Andrew's a good bloke. A bit weird but okay. Lucinda Mercedes is a good captain with a good crew." He pats the timber rail. "And *Belle* is a good ship. Job done."

Mum and Dad come looking for me. Dad stands back and watches while Mum hugs me hard. "You should have told us about the monster," she whispers fiercely.

"I'm sorry," Dad says when Mum finally loosens her hug. "I should have believed you."

Mum lets go so he and I can hug. It's been a long time. My eyes are brimming.

"I'm sorry," he says again, his words muffled into my duffel coat.

"It's okay. We're together now. We'll be okay."

He leans back and searches my eyes. His are brimming too. "How can we be? How can anything ever be okay again?"

Honestly, I don't know. But Mum and Dad need some assurance.

"We'll never give up. There are more of us than the hundred you've seen here on *Belle*. Many good people. Nothing is over yet."

Nothing is permanent anymore

IT'S A HUGE relief to reach Cornwall.

For Min, obviously. She didn't once complain about the rough seas, but despite Lucinda's medicine tea, she's quite green around the gills, as my Dad puts it, by the time we thunder past the little river mouth at Looe and turn into Talland Bay. So I'm relieved for her.

But I'm much more overwhelmingly relieved that *Belle* has made it safely to the end of our westward passage. Of our tacking back and forth with only slender shapes of canvas on the yards, slamming and surfing and slamming again without relent, three-day passage into cold ocean winds and through several deep Wilds, where the weather differs sometimes in details but it's still January everywhere. And for that entire exhausting time, I've been imagining that Merritt would send helicopters or jet fighters or even submarines through thin places to find us and sink us.

He didn't. Maybe he tried and failed. Maybe his people didn't know where we'd gone and the heavy weather shielded *Belle* from detection. Maybe he's had his hands full with more urgent events on the outside. Maybe Andrew's right that we're an unofficial private project so he can't access big military resources to throw at us.

Whatever it is, my relief drains me of energy, and I lie on our bunk for an hour thinking of absolutely nothing while routine shipboard noises put me at ease, until Mister Samson's voice calls from the upper deck where he's setting anchor watches, and Min comes to say CK is readying *Bertha* to take us ashore.

Golden Lake is nothing like the peaceful place I remember. I stop on the hillside, the others bumping to a halt in single file on the wildlife trail behind me, and take in the change. The lake's shoreline is filled all around with hundreds of canvas tents and makeshift little wooden shacks. It looks like a refugee camp.

I lead our landing party to the open grassy ridge from where during my first days in the grove I used to watch the community below, and we study the busy scene.

A small, ordered camp of tents next to the village is home to a band of Iron Age warriors who sit beside their campfires, cooking, eating, sharpening swords and daggers, cleaning machine guns.

I have no desire to go among them.

"Tin and Hare soldiers are one army now." Lael lands on the ridge and hugs me tight. "It's good to see you."

She turns to the others and greets everyone she knows, in turn, by name, while Mum, Dad, Vita, and CK stare open-mouthed at the sight of a magnificently winged, gloriously naked, splendidly beautiful golden angel hugging everyone and crying golden tears of joy. I make the introductions, and she hugs the newcomers too, leaving them speechless and nearly tearful themselves.

"Tin and Hare live here at the lake now?" Min asks.

"The tribes are living together in Tin's cliff fort on Rame Head," Lael says. "Temporarily, I imagine. Nothing is permanent anymore. They send war bands in rotation to help protect our lake from further attacks. So far, none have been attempted here, although we hear many have occurred elsewhere. Perhaps the presence of these warriors is sufficient. For now, at least."

Min looks as enthusiastic about the soldiers as I feel. Her experiences with the Hare tribe were even worse than mine. Although I suppose that, as I do, she accepts the need for them at the lake. "Are Flo and Gully here?" she asks.

"They come and go. I believe they're in great demand these days, in many places."

"Queen Fiona of Hare?" Min glances sideways at our Axe family. "King Owen of Tin?"

"No, we don't see them at all."

Good. The last thing we need is Shad having to defend his decision to betray Owen before the battle for Quarter Square.

"What do Tin and Hare ask of you in return for their protection here?" Min asks.

She and Lael seem to share a quiet moment.

"We help their wounded warriors to heal in the lake."

Min blinks her understanding. It feels like they've just conducted a conversation filled with wisdom and knowledge that their few spoken words only hint at.

"Come," Lael says. "We'll find you a place to stay."

I touch her arm, thrilling at a sudden electric-tingle-like echo of the connection we shared during my weeks in the grove. "Thank you, but for now we're living on *Belle*."

"Come to the lake anyway." She appraises each of us in turn. "Some of you are carrying hidden wounds. Come sit with your feet in the water and let us help you to heal them."

It's a welcome offer.

Villagers greet us with friendly calls and waves, as do the other goldens, including Lael's parents Myen and Lu, and Keni, who now stands as stunningly powerful a warrior angel as they.

The elder goldens swirl like brilliant rainbows twining below the surface.

Lael lands in waist-deep water and encourages us to put our bared feet into the steaming lake.

We sit on flat edging rocks below the village. The water is pleasantly warm. Within a minute or two, Mum starts crying quietly. Dad does too, and Min and all the others.

Me too. I don't try to hide my tears. Certainly, I don't want to stop them. They're part of a gentle cleansing, a healing process. It feels like a warm glow that starts in my feet and grows up through me.

Some hidden wounds hurt more than others, judging by the groans and cries from my family and friends. New wounds and old, I guess.

Before long, Ban is sobbing his heart out. CK takes him in his arms and rocks him. Shad too. Min hugs him and sings softly into the crook of his neck through her own tears. Tae and Vua break down in each other's arms, with Red and Vita each stroking their partner's back. I feel a strong awareness of Anya, the warm memory of her, here with us now at the lakeside.

When a wail comes, I lean forward to see Lucinda comforting Andrew. And then, on my other side, Mum and Dad both sobbing and reaching for me to embrace them together.

Deep healing.

Later, villagers prepare a communal meal and share it with us on cushions and blankets spread across their flat area above the lake. They want to thank us for our part in saving them from the outside attack when we were last here.

Thomas Appleleaf and Joan the Wad arrive when we're about to eat. I don't know if they're invited, but the villagers are happy to see them and make room. The pisky king and queen greet us with delight.

The goldens don't eat, but they participate in the reunion from the water, until, after everyone has eaten, they turn as one to stare into an unoccupied glade along the bank.

Two sylphs appear there with a dazzling white light that fills the space then dims to reveal them in all their finery.

Tall and slender, dressed in rich, dark velvet, their shoulder-length hair perfect and their skin glowing like polished marble with its own inner light, they look exactly like the pair who visited Thomas and me in my grove. Although I can't say for sure that they *are* the same ones, because they're like a mirror image of each other, for a start, so I don't know if all sylphs are handsomely, androgynously identical.

Why am I gibbering? I shake my head to clear it of awe.

The goldens greet the sylphs and beckon us to join the meeting. I don't know if they mean all of us, but no one objects when we all go, Thomas and Joan too.

Soldiers in the Tin and Hare camp are watching, too far away to hear whatever conversation we're about to have, but clearly curious about the theatrical visitors and our meeting with them.

"Have you told them of our plan?" one of the sylphs asks Lu.

"No. We wanted to let the villagers thank them first."

The sylphs show haughty disapproval. "There is no time to waste. Tell them now."

Lu responds with dignity to the arrogant command. "The community of Sylph is relocating to a new home in a Wild," he tells us. "It's so deep they believe no one has ever been there before. They invited us to live there with them."

No one else replies, so I ask the question. "They invited who, exactly?"

"First," one of the sylphs says with an elegant bow to Thomas and Joan, "our cousins the piskies."

Thomas clarifies the agreement in a firm tone. "All of our people, not only piskies but also our friends who share the forest with us. Jack-in-the-Green and his family, and everyone else who wants to come."

The sylphs concur with synchronised nods.

"Our entire Golden Lake community is going," Lu says. "Including our elders, and as many as want to from among all these other people who have come to us seeking safety. Also, the people, goldens, and elders of Lake Sunrise."

"My friend Jhed and his clan," Keni adds. "And Beryl, the mermaid of Lake Erskine. The goldens of Lake Sunrise have agreed to bring them all over the ocean with their own community before we depart."

Lael addresses us. "You are all invited, along with everyone from your communities who wants to come."

Shad and Ban give me the nod.

So does Min. "Quarter Square," she says.

I speak to the sylphs. "There's a community called Quarter Square. Do you know it?"

"We know of it."

"If we come, we will want to invite them too."

They accept, with imperious nods. "*If* you come." One repeats my words. "Would it help you to see our new home before you decide?"

"Yes."

"You too, Captain Mercedes?"

Lucinda purses her lips. "I'll see the place before I put your invitation to my crew."

"Very well," the sylph says. "Here it is."

I don't know how many thin places we flash through in a single second, how deep is the Wild we find ourselves in, or how the sylphs transport us all so effortlessly. But here we are, standing on a grassy hill, surveying the prettiest island I've ever seen.

It's big, beautiful, and tropically warm, sitting like a great jewel in an otherwise empty emerald sea. My impression is of a country-sized landmass. Wales-sized? It's a cliché, but yes, probably. Behind us, reaching high for clear blue skies a few miles inland from the gentle curve of foothills upon which we've arrived, stands a range of prettily snow-capped mountains. Before us are ancient forests, green plains, sparkling rivers, and slender white beaches.

"The island is bountiful," one of the sylphs says. With a look to Lucinda, he continues, "As is the sea. Together, they will support everyone we have discussed today, and more, although we reserve the right to decide exactly who is invited."

Shad eyes him. "So you'll be in charge?"

He returns the look with calm composure. "Not, I think, in the way you mean. Our queen has no interest in governing this land. Only in continuing to reign among the Sylph, as is our nature. We are choosing carefully when inviting communities here, so we do not anticipate anyone trying to claim a rule over anyone else. We expect that relationships between our various communities will grow organically over time, and we trust that it will happen peacefully.

Min gives me a mischievous nudge. "Will you cope without coffee?"

"I'll have to." But I pout at the thought.

One of the sylphs heard us. "We like coffee. We are growing it here on the island."

Paradise!

Lael points to a big lake reflecting sunshine. "A new Golden Lake." Then to a second one, the other way along the curve of foothills. "And a new Lake Sunrise."

"Will you still send questors to the Mountain?" Andrew asks her.

"No. We think our elders living in these lakes will be sufficient to introduce and maintain healing properties in their waters. The Sylph believe so too. We shall see."

At my side, Mum is moaning with delight and hugging Dad's arm, while he gives me a happy nod over her head.

At my other side, Min is singing softly. Her vision fills me with joy. I see again in my mind's eye the beautiful island country of ancient Atlantis, and before me now the similarities she's undoubtedly seeing too.

"New Atlantis," she murmurs.

"That is a good name for this land," one of the sylphs remarks. "Let us return now to Golden Lake."

In a flash, literally with a flash of light of course because these are sylphs, we're back at the lakeside.

Soldiers in the camp are all staring now.

"Are the Tin and Hare tribes coming too?" Min asks.

The sylphs and goldens exchange looks.

"We don't know," Lu says. "We're waiting to hear back from Queen Fiona and King Owen before we extend a formal invitation to them. There will be negotiations about their behaviour and future intentions."

"Don't bother," Flo says, appearing with Gully in the treeline as if they've walked here through the woods. "They're not interested."

I thought we might get some hugs, but they're standing back, looking emotionally distant. Disappointed. Irritated, even.

No one wants to annoy the old Crow gods. The sylphs greet them with a synchronised graceful bow, which Flo and Gully barely deign to acknowledge.

"Frankly," Flo says, "we're pissed off that you're all running away. Abandoning our Wild. Surrendering to the outside even when there's open war broken out all across the Midlands. Tin and Hare will stay with us and fight. As will many others."

Gully's intense glare suggests he's growing back rapidly into his full terrifying power. "If you're going, go. We won't hinder you, but don't expect our blessing."

With a final look of contempt that takes in all of us, they turn and walk back into the forest.

I'm shaking. As, no doubt, are the others. No one says anything until all sight and sound of the angry gods has gone.

Personally, I've reached my Rubicon, and it's time to cross it. No more war for me. No more running into battle like some berserker. There are people who need to fight, have to fight, like we had to that night in Quarter Square. I support them in their struggles against evil. But I've learned that the thick of battle isn't my place.

I remember Pen and Poke telling me about hopepunk. How it involves cooperation, gentleness, kindness, and self-awareness. Bravery and strength, yes, but while caring for others. Softness. Comfort. Hygge. And empathy. Always empathy. "It's anti-cynicism," Pen said.

As a comparison, that cold day when we were chained to a bridge in London, she described for me the classic hero's journey in literature. "A chosen one, a noble warrior hero battling evil and leading his people to victory. Aragorn in Lord of the Rings."

Then, "Hopepunk doesn't have a chosen one. They're more likely to be a facilitator. Someone who inspires, encourages, supports, or enables people to work together and keep fighting the evil. Samwise Gamgee."

I've never been a chosen one. Certainly no noble hero. I'm a Sam Gamgee.

"The act of choosing hope and cooperation over despair distinguishes the hopepunk movement," Poke said. "It's how we'll win this war without innocent people getting hurt."

I feel like ever since my conversation with those peaceful people, I've been moving towards that state of being. I'm far from perfect. Some days, I'm nothing like the gentle revolutionary I want to be. Many days. But being aware of my imperfection while trying to move in the direction of hope feels like the route I should be walking.

Flo and Gully say there's a war being fought right now. People will be getting hurt. Innocent people as well as warriors. Quite possibly some of the warriors I've come to know and care for. I wish they weren't, but at the same time I know it isn't my job to fight for any of the violent nations in this war.

For the innocents, yes. I want to fight for them. But not with a sword in my hand. How can perpetuating violence ever bring real peace?

Hopepunk feels right for me. New Atlantis feels like the right place for me, certainly now and quite possibly forever, with these people I love.

"I'll consult my crew and let you know what we decide," Lucinda says. She and Andrew leave.

CK looks torn, wanting to go with his captain and also to stay with Ban.

"Go," Ban says. "Your place is with *Belle*'s crew. We'll be together soon in..." he glances at Min, "...New Atlantis, but right now we have separate responsibilities."

CK blinks his agreement. They touch hands, and then he jogs after Lucinda and Andrew.

"Let us discuss this with your friends in Quarter Square," one of the sylphs says, and in an instant, with the customary flash of light, we're here.

I *have* to learn how they do that, but for now there are important conversations to have.

Leaving forever

IT'S A SAD event for everyone. Most of the insiders have chosen to make New Atlantis their home, and to do it immediately, on the same day they've come to their collective decision. But even those who've chosen not to come with us are moving on to other havens. By the end of today, Quarter Square will be empty.

I find Andrew and Fliss sitting in the garden, on a log by the cold ashes of last night's fire, watching the surrounding houses they and their friends have spent years maintaining with their sketching and threading magic. Already, the fabric of structures is visibly fraying at the edges all around. The rate of change looks faster than I've seen before, almost as if the place knows its abandonment is a done deal and the enchantment is surrendering to the inevitable.

"How long will it take to disappear altogether?"

Andrew doesn't respond to my question, but Fliss does. "It's happening right now. I think if we came back tomorrow, we'd find most of it gone."

A single tear rolls down Andrew's cheek, and she hugs him.

There's an email I want to send. I borrow Andrew's throwaway phone, leave through the theatre door, and walk down towards the harbour until I find a wi-fi signal.

> *Hi Bill*
>
> *I'm emigrating to somewhere nice and warm. Thought you and the kids might like to come with me. It's a safe place with good people.*
>
> *Simba*

It's been eight months since I last emailed Karen. Feels more like years. A lifetime.

Plymouth's Barbican is unnaturally quiet. The insiders say the outside war hasn't reached this far down the West Country, at least not yet, but the police have got heavy-handed, and the army are around too. People are frightened, they say. I can feel it.

The phone dings with Karen's reply.

> *Hi Simba*
>
> *We've already emigrated, in the opposite direction from you by the sound of it. My sister urged me to come home, and the kids came with me.*
>
> *Love to you. Be safe.*
>
> *Bill*

So that's that. Karen, Pen, and Poke are safe in Scotland. I wish them well.

Back in the square, the final three families are all packed up and ready to move. I walk with them into the Wild, where my friendly sylph waits on the other side of our nearest thin place to take them home.

Arryn is a young one. Every bit as haughty in appearance as his peers, when we got talking about the practicalities of transporting groups of people through very long jumps, he showed that you can't read a sylph's personality by their face any more, generally speaking, than you can with other people. That insight will be useful when I'm dealing with sylphs in future.

"Are you ready?" he asks.

I am, with his watchful support of course. We've decided my six guided jumps are enough training for me to take this last one from start to finish.

I get the families to shuffle up close together in the thin place clearing, ensuring all the children are within their parental perimeter. One little one is crying. Her mum picks her up and murmurs comforting words.

Arryn gives me the nod, and I take them through.

The flash is part of the process. It doesn't even embarrass me anymore, although once we've got all the insiders to their new home I intend to figure out if I can do away with it.

Appreciative *oohs* and *ahhs* come from my passengers. We've arrived safely. Min and Cindy take charge of them, and I return to receive Arryn's courteous congratulations.

On the path back through the trees, I meet Andrew and Fliss.

"That's it," Andrew says. "Everyone's gone. Only Jimmy left back there."

"He wants to say bye to the theatre with you," Fliss says.

I understand.

They go on to the thin place, and I walk back through the deserted square to my theatre.

Jimmy's sitting on the edge of the empty stage with his head in his hands. When I arrive, he wipes tears away. "I've turned the water and electric off."

I don't make a performance of it. I simply sit with my arm around his shoulders and stare out into the shadowy auditorium.

This is where it all started, that night I spent trying to sleep on the stage floor. Lonely, scared, with absolutely no idea about the fabulous people I was going to meet and the amazing direction my life was going to take.

"It's a sad day," Jimmy says. "Everything. Leaving the haven, like, but there's always another haven, and at least most of us are going to New Atlantis together. But this place." His sigh is heavy. "I was so proud of what we did with it. Really thought we'd finish the job and get paying punters in. I really did."

"We'll build a new theatre in our new home," I say.

"Promise?"

"You and me and all the others, anyone who wants to be involved, we'll build one. I know just the place for it, along the beach from where we'll be living, on a raised headland looking out over the ocean. Maybe we'll have open-air performances as well as in-house."

His cheery smile is back. "Sounds good."

"It will be." I jump down from the stage. "Come on. Let's go."

In the foyer, we snap our fingers in unison to open the magic door, and let it swing closed again behind us. His shoulders droop again at the sight and silence of the empty square, so I nudge his arm and we don't look back as we set off with a positive stride across the garden.

The dart hits my neck like a hammer blow. I'm falling before I know it.

Jimmy shouts in alarm and plucks out the dart. He tries to drag me to my feet, but that's not happening.

On another day, I might be wearing my body-armour vest with its high stiff collar, but I'm stupid. Stupid. I do have my sabre strapped to my back with its handle poking up from behind my shoulder, and on a luckier day the dart might have struck that instead of my neck, but it didn't. Bad luck. Good marksmanship.

My head's on the ground and I'm seeing everything sideways, including four twenty-first-century soldiers sprinting from the house next to the theatre. Big Luke's house. I see him being fantastic in the battle to save our home, standing head and shoulders taller than everyone else and leading the charge against Hare warriors who are jumping down from his roof. I see him carrying old Flo to her funeral, carrying her as gently as he would a baby. I hear violins playing a fast jig and see everyone dancing and drinking and singing and laughing. Will's here.

I can't hold any one image for longer than a few seconds. My mind's like liquid, like oil, like oil in water.

Jimmy's still trying to drag me into the trees, but the soldiers are already halfway across the garden, and we're not going to make it before they reach us.

"Go!" I tell him. "Run! Tell Min..."

Who got him?

"MIN!"

She hears Jimmy scream her name before the flash fades. Fliss is already with her and the wolves on the hillside, and they run to where he's kneeling with his palms on the ground, spitting bile, while Joe's new sylph friend Arryn stands by looking worried sick.

"They got Joe," Jimmy wails. "Darted him. I couldn't carry him."

Her heart pounds like a drum of doom. "Who got him?"

He takes a shuddering breath.

"Jimmy! Who got him?"

"Soldiers. They ambushed us. Shot a dart in Joe's neck. He fell, and I couldn't get him up."

Karn and Keira lead the Axe pack at the run across the hilltop to where people are gathering around Jimmy.

"You left him?" Andrew is there.

"He told me to," Jimmy sobs. "I couldn't lift him. I tried but I couldn't, and they were coming fast. He told me to go, to tell Min."

Joe's parents stare at her in horror. She doesn't know what to say to them.

Wolves are stripping off all around, and not only Min and Joe's family, including Red and Vita as naturally as if they've been with them all their lives. The entire Axe pack is shifting and waiting for sylphs to jump them all to Quarter Square.

"Those soldiers will be working for Merritt," Andrew says.

Or for Tyac, Min fears. Merritt would be her preferred option. "We ready?"

Everyone's ready.

Arryn jumps them through.

The darkest of dark niches

I'm in a cave. Naked, cold, bound at my wrists with my arms stretched out horizontally, brutally, standing upright against a rock wall.

When I move my head, something jabs into my cheek. A firm plastic tube, connected to a plastic bag of clear liquid suspended over my shoulder. Drinking water, I hope, because my thirst is raging and my head's splitting. I suck. It's cold water with an on-demand valve.

While unconscious, I've vomited down my front. I dribble and then spit water at it for a minute in an unsuccessful attempt to rinse it off, but then decide I'd better save the water for drinking because I don't know how long it'll have to last.

The room-sized cave is silent and unlit. Pale daylight reaches some planes of its natural walls, from how far away I can't guess, but even in the few minutes since I awoke it's already dimmed steadily.

Thinking is difficult, but I need to push through the woolly-headedness and get my brain working. Those soldiers shot me with a tranquiliser dart at about four o'clock. The fading light suggests that sunset is now easing into twilight. If the cave's somewhere near Quarter Square, or maybe in a similar time zone of a Wild somewhere, it will mean I've been out for between thirty minutes and an hour.

My family will be looking for me now. Tracking me.

The darkest of dark niches in the cave draws my attention. It's straight opposite me. I can't see into it, can't make out any shape or form within it, but once I've seen it, I can't look away.

I know who's in that deep darkness. I listen for his breathing and eventually hear it, slow and controlled.

Then he opens his terrifying red eyes and glares hatred at me.

A new spoor

MIN RUNS WITH the wolves along a wildlife trail. Joe's captors must have left a strong spoor, because after the wolves cleared Quarter Square in a matter of minutes, they massed in the garden then plunged into the woods.

Shad bumped into her hip before they left the square with an invitation to ride him, but for now she can match the pack's steady pace and she wants to run.

A thin place makes her jump. She hasn't encountered this one before and doesn't know exactly where they were, or where they are now, but the wolves don't hesitate to go through, so she goes too.

On the other side they're all running to and fro, back and forth, on and off the trail, sniffing the earth intently until Tae and Vua alert the pack to something they've found at a fork in the trail.

Vua shifts and calls to Min without even taking the time to stretch out her cracking joints. "A new spoor. The four who carried Joe here went off that way and left him with the new spoor. It's Tyac."

Min's stomach lurches. "You're sure?"

The pack waits, some sniffing the ground and trees, others sniffing the air, jostling one another in a state of high alert and readiness.

"Tae and I tracked him before, remember? Outside our old village when you first came to us. We found two related spoors back then, one weak and one strong but definitely the same creature. It was Tyac the man with a thin scent of the monster, and Tyac the monster with a thinner scent of the man. This is Tyac the man."

Ban howls from up ahead.

"Tyac's shifted," Vua says. "It's the monster carrying Joe now."

She crouches to shift back, then the pack sets off hard with her and Tae in the lead and Min riding Shad.

You have a choice

"I WANT TO DIE."

The disembodied voice is familiar, but I can't quite put a person to it. Not quite. It speaks calmly, without emotion. Not deadpan. Not depressed, and certainly not dramatic. Just stating a fact.

"I've tried to kill myself hundreds of times in many different ways, but that bitch's curse won't allow it."

Who *is* that? I can so nearly link a face to the voice.

No light reaches into the cave now. Tyac's bloodshot eyes glare at me from the blackness without changing in mood or moving in place.

I didn't know he could talk like a human in his monster form. Then the penny drops in my fogged brain. He isn't talking. He's playing me a recorded message.

"For thousands of years, I've been desperate for this hell to end, and I have long been convinced that you are the only person who will be able to kill me."

Give me a chance and I will, you bastard.

"I've been trying to get you to end my torment all through this eternity. To terminate the abomination you see before you."

Tyac stands and steps out of the blackness of that niche into the lesser gloom of the cave. The murderous hatred in his eyes doesn't match the matter-of-fact tone of his recorded voice. Of course it doesn't. The voice is a man, murderous but reasonable, to a degree anyway. The monster is a monster.

"I've destroyed you time and time again, so many times, and not only because I hate you. I killed you because you were a weakling. Every one of those lives was a wasted opportunity, so I cut them short."

The monster growls, low and long.

I say nothing and keep my face straight. Try to keep any possible expression from my eyes. I don't want to anger him worse than he already is while I'm tied up and probably still drugged, about as defenceless and vulnerable as I can possibly be.

"In only two of your lives did you get even close to being my equal, three thousand years ago, as a lion in ancient Egypt. You must become a lion again in this life. It's my only chance of finding peace. Finally. It's therefore your only chance to survive. Become a lion and fight me. Live or die."

My heart is hammering.

"The lion pride you need is in this Wild. Not far from this lair, which is why we're here. You have a choice. If you refuse to become a lion, I will end this life and we'll move on to your next one. Sooner or later, you'll do it. You have to. You know you do."

The monster walks towards me, swaying with a rolling gait as he approaches and rocking his huge head from side to side but never dropping his glare. His right forearm ends at the healed stump where I cut his hand off. He stops with his face mere inches from mine and thrusts the stump up between us.

I go cross-eyed from trying to focus on it, and also trying to breathe without inhaling the stench of raw meat and blood from his maw.

His growl is so menacing I have to clench hard and long to not lose control of my bowels.

"When this recording ends, the monster will probably let you live. I make no promises, because when I'm a beast I don't always follow the same logic paths as when I'm a man. But this is big. So, I think I will probably retain the knowledge that this time you need to live through the night."

That growl again.

"Don't antagonise me."

He draws back his unmaimed arm and smashes his huge, clawed paw across my face.

We'll find him

THEY'VE SEARCHED ALL night. In the deepest cold before dawn, they huddle together and warm her with their bodies while she sobs silently.

She's in a poor state. Her instinct is to push on, of course, but it's essential that she be strong enough to sing her magic when they find Joe and Tyac, so she doesn't fight the pack's decision to warm her up and rest her for an hour.

Meanwhile, some pairs of wolves go off to extend the search.

Tyac climbed a tree. They lost his trail hours ago. The wolves couldn't follow him up the tree. Min could, but once up there, she couldn't follow his scent.

For all she knows, by now he might have taken Joe through several Wilds. They could be anywhere.

Shad shifts and holds her close in the middle of the pack. "We'll find him. If Tyac was going to just kill him, he would have just killed him. There's something else happening with that bastard. I don't know what, but whatever it is, it gives us time. It gives Joe time. We'll keep looking. We'll find him."

She wishes she had his confidence.

Ready to talk now?

I'M BEATEN NEARLY to death. Feels like it anyway. Although the monster's attacks through the night, looking back on them when the first faint light of dawn starts to play tricks with my vision and he finally leaves me alone, seemed calculated to inflict only severe pain on me, not death. I believe he derived savage enjoyment from it, exacting revenge for thirteen thousand years of torment, for which he blames me.

Which isn't to minimise the effects of his violence. My face is pulped, my eyes swollen to slits, and my limbs beaten nearly useless. Worse, his hundreds of hammer blows to my ribcage makes breathing agony and have wrenched my shoulders so that now the tiniest movement of them sends searing pain right through me.

My sabre stands in its scabbard, leaning against the cave wall. For what it's worth. Even if I wasn't tied with strong ropes to iron rings set into the rock, I'm too badly beaten to hold the thing, never mind wield it in action. I'm just glad he didn't use it on me.

A new sound penetrates the silence and makes my ears twitch. Sharp cracks, accompanied by muted grunts. It reminds me unmistakably of the noises our family's bodies make when they shift from wolf to human. It's distant, possibly, or maybe closer than it seems but distorted by angles and dull echoes from the rock walls inside the cave system. That's where I think it's coming from, somewhere deeper underground.

Where Tyac is shifting.

Will he leave me all day and return after dark to continue my torture? My water bag's been empty for most of the night. I'm very thirsty and will be in trouble by nightfall. Not that such a thing will worry him, the bastard.

Silence. I hang my head. He must have left me.

I release my bladder for maybe the last time from the water I drank before I sucked the bag dry. The warmth of urine splashes lasts only a second before the cold intensifies on my wet feet. I'm going to freeze.

Then comes another new sound, of someone walking on the rock floor of the cave system. Someone wearing shoes. Quiet steps, but not stealthy. Confident. Coming closer.

I don't see where he comes from, but he appears before me.

Detective Chief Inspector Ian Dawson. The man who interviewed me cleverly yet courteously after Carole and Tony were murdered, who later mourned the same mutilating murder of his colleague Detective Sergeant Jennifer Smith, and who later again went to Florida on Merritt's instructions and brought my parents home to force me into compliance. Mum's favourite polite policeman.

He's dressed the same way he was back in that interview room, in a nondescript dark suit with an open-necked white shirt and black leather shoes. An everyday outfit for an everyday detective, except that with the suit jacket carried over one shoulder, his rolled-up shirtsleeves reveal that his right forearm ends in a healed stump.

His smile is grim. He's enjoying watching me realise who he is. Who he always was.

He folds his jacket over a protruding lump of rock and performs a spinning jump to kick me unbelievably hard in my agonised ribs.

I cry out. I tried so hard to make as little noise as possible all through the long night's beating, but now it escapes me.

"In case you thought the pain was over," he says.

I pant, trying to bring it under control.

That's why I couldn't place his voice on the recording. The Scottish accent is gone.

He sneers at me. "Ready to talk now?"

"If you stop kicking me long enough to let me breathe."

He spins and hammers another kick into me. I don't know how long it takes me to not black out, but when I can see straight again, he's standing there watching me. This time, he lets me recover until I can talk.

"Why don't you just give me my sword and say here, kill me?"

"That would constitute suicide. I told you, the curse won't let me do it. Keep up." He feints another kick and sneers when I flinch. "Are you going to become a lion?"

"There's a problem."

"What?"

"Min. She's totally opposed to it."

His scream of rage is barely human, and he lays into me for I don't know how long. I'm not sure I stay conscious for all of it. When it's over, when I can focus, he's sitting cross-legged in the same niche where he sat as the monster last night.

"Min's totally opposed to it." He mimics the whine in my voice. "Ask yourself why that is. Why she likes the status quo." He waits for me to ask myself. When I don't respond, he carries on. "It's all right for her, isn't it? She doesn't have to live in torment like me, and she doesn't have to keep dying like you."

It's true, but not the whole truth. Only his twist on it. His understandable twist, because he's insane.

"You want to be a lion, don't you? It's time for you to decide if you're going to do it in this life or not."

I do want to be a lion. I need lion strength to beat him, to kill him, to finally destroy him once and for all. My wood magic is gentle and passive. It's useful and powerful in its own way, but it will only ever help me to evade him. And I'm totally over running away from him. Some battles need to be fought. This is mine. If anything is ever going to give me the edge over him, at least to meet him on equal terms, I'm convinced it will be a combination of my wood magic and lion power.

He stands and studies me. "Well?"

It's either say yes or die right now. At the very least, saying yes should give me some breathing space from him. Some healing time. Planning time. Just time.

He slides my sabre from its scabbard and gives the air a few experimental slashes. "Last chance. Yes or no?"

"Yes."

It's the first time I've seen a gleam of life in his eyes. He pokes the sabre into my stomach, pokes it and keeps poking, until suddenly a new agony pierces me. And he keeps pushing, concentrating on what he's doing as my blade enters deep into my abdomen.

I scream.

"Shut up."

I'm panting in fear and hideous pain.

"None of your vital organs are damaged, but when I withdraw it, you're going to start bleeding. Inside more than out. You're strong and fit, notwithstanding your condition after last night, but everyone's different when it comes to blood loss so there's no knowing how long before you'll die."

He slaps my face to make me focus, and points along a narrow dark corridor in the cave system. "That's your way out. You'll find the pride in the forest out there. Or they'll find you. Whatever, that's where they are, and you need them. You need to take the bite before you die. Got it?"

"Yes."

He pulls the long blade from my stomach. As slowly as he pushed it in. It's hot agony. Then he slashes my ropes in two fast swipes.

My legs give way. I fall to my hands and knees and stare at the ground below me, my little world swimming alarmingly, dangerously.

One of his feet lifts from the ground beside my head and there's the unmistakable sound of my sabre snapping across his knee. It lands on the ground in two pieces.

He kicks me hard in my side and laughs when I collapse.

I'm barely aware of him leaving.

It doesn't matter

THE SEARCH HAS failed. The wolves gather, their movements and demeanours subdued. The trail went cold hours ago. No one has any fresh ideas. There's nothing more to try. Hope is gone.

Shad gives a long mournful howl, which the entire pack takes up.

Min collapses and curls up in a ball, her agony a continuous keening note that nothing can get past.

She's aware of a sylph presence, of being transported with the wolves, of them shifting on the hillside. They're back in New Atlantis.

It doesn't matter where they are. It doesn't matter where she is. Because Joe isn't.

Maahas

THE NARROW PASSAGE goes through a thin place underground. Only the shivers across my tortured flesh keep me focused long enough to stay upright and get to it, and once I'm through the thin place only the growing promise of daylight ahead keeps me staggering along the passage, keeps me getting back to my feet when I fall, even though it gets slower and closer to impossible every time.

My torn shoulders keep screaming at me to stop bouncing off the rock walls, although I half think this specific pain, as awful as it is, helps me maintain my determination to get out of the cave and find the pride. It's also a different and entirely more manageable pain than the terrifying one radiating from deep in my belly.

I pinch my stab wound closed. Don't know how much it will help. There's not a lot of blood escaping anyway, but Tyac said the bleeding will be inside, and I have no reason to disbelieve him. He certainly knew what he was doing when he stabbed me. For all I know, somewhere along the line he might have trained as a surgeon. Anyway, keeping pressure on my belly feels the right thing to do.

The air I'm breathing isn't the clean, fresh deliciousness that normally welcomes me into the Wild. It's more like Tottenham's fire cloud was in the outside. Where is this cave system? I step cautiously into the light.

The passage opens under a stand of tall beech trees on high ground. Not very high. A small hill, overlooking a plain of devastation that makes what the British Army did at Anderitum look compassionate by comparison.

It's like a diagram of early Victorian industrialisation in an old history book. Working coal mine towers and factories occupy the scarred land for as far as I can see. Modern machinery, but evidently free of modern environmental laws and requirements. There's no vegetation. No trees. No greenery. All is mud and darkness on the ground, and in the air only a pale yellowish glow hinting of sunlight through thick, black smoke from hundreds of industrial chimneys and heavy diesel lorries. Pollution coats my tongue and throat with a bitter tang. It's disaster capitalism in the raw. The noise is a constant collective growl from everywhere.

I touch one of the beech trunks. The world is holding its breath. There's no wildlife in the region, big or small. No birds. Only insects, and they're mostly burrowed. The tree trunk is slick with grime.

"You're on Barr Beacon in the Black Country."

I jerk around and cry out when the sudden movement does something bad to my insides.

My lion is here, with his pride standing behind him. They're all staring over the destruction spread out before us. Only he is looking at me.

"We've seen this before, you and I, although not together until today. The Black Country in the outside was a scar man inflicted upon nature once before. Now here is he, doing it again in the Wild."

He's talking in my mind, the same as Lael used to.

"You're badly hurt. Shall we go somewhere more peaceful so I can look at your wound?"

"Yes."

We're there. Here. Somewhere. I don't know. My strength deserts me, and without knowing I was falling I'm looking up at the clean sky through a canopy of ancient trees.

My lion sits tall and proud at my side, waiting for me to focus. Then, *"My name is Maahas. The last time you and I communed, you knew me as Maahes, which is what your people of that time called me."*

"In Egypt."

"Yes, although thousands of years earlier, in our first home of Atlantis, you knew me by my real name. I am Maahas, father god of forest folk, of your family, Cayal."

"In this life, my name is Joe."

"Joe." He regards my wound. *"What are we going to do about this?"*

"You know Tyac?"

"I do."

"He stabbed me. Says I'll bleed out quickly unless I take the bite from you."

"He wants you to take the bite?"

"Yes."

"Interesting. More to the point, do you want to take it?"

"Yes."

"You know it will be painful?"

"I didn't."

"Not the bite itself. The process of transformation afterwards. I will stay with you. Are you ready?"

I take a steadying breath. *"Yes."*

*

I'm walking to school, past quiet houses I've known all my life. I'm a boy. I'm also a man, dreaming of my boy-self dreaming about walking to school. My lion sits where he always sits, watching me. This time, I turn to see him. Big, sleek, fabulously muscular, with his majestic dark mane ruffling in a breeze, he is Maahas.

"You've changed."

It's a struggle to open my eyes. The pain isn't anything like as bad as I expected, but the exhaustion is overwhelming. *"Hm?"*

"You are much changed since Egypt."

"How so?"

"Then, you were youthful. Prone to anger, to violence. Excited about everything. About life, and death, and especially about your power through taking the bite. Now, you are quieter in mind and spirit."

Hopepunk.

"What's that?"

I explain.

"Yes, this is what I sense in you. It gives me hope. Perhaps this time will be your time. Perhaps it will be mine too."

"How so?"

"After Tyac the priest murdered you in Atlantis, your mother asked me to protect you in your future lives. I was always fond of your people, of your family. Your mother was a particular favourite of mine. I was pleased to grant her request. It's been a long life for me, Joe. I'm tired. I would like to rest, but I made my promise to your mother in good faith, and I will keep it. When your cycles are complete, mine will be too."

"You'll die."

"I will rest."

*

The pain is big. The pride watches me change. Maahas stays with me, powerful as ever, faithful as ever, supporting me and protecting me in my time of great vulnerability.

When, for the first time, my pain ends, although it's hardly an end because more than anything ever this is a new start, my senses are big.

The world is mine for the taking.

Or not. That's a temptation, a pridefulness I gloried in once before, twice before, which on both of those occasions proved to be my downfall. Mine and that of those who loved me and depended upon me.

The world isn't mine for the taking. My physical power is big, but to make the fullest use of it, for the greatest benefit of all concerned, I must temper it with wisdom and compassion.

*

The pain of transformation is over. The joy is here. The joy of running, running wild and strong and free, with Maahas at my side and the pride running with us.

None of them are like me. I'm the only one. They watch my change with keen interest, accepting me for who and what I am, but we all know I will never be one of them.

Maahas is magnificent, a king of beasts and so much more. While the pride teaches me by example how to live as a lion, he teaches me through his awesome presence to grow and become everything I can be.

One evening, when the pride rises to hunt, he doesn't.

"My time is now."

"You're dying?"

"I'm resting. It's good."

I sit beside him, paying respect, already grieving before he leaves.

"Do not. My time is here, and it makes me glad. Your time is here too. Your time to do that which you have set out to do. Go well, Joe. Young Cayal the woodsman, son of my favourite forest folk daughter. Be great. Be humble. Be powerful. Be compassionate. Be wise."

He closes his eyes and slips peacefully into his rest.

That's why you're a lion now

MIN SITS ON her hill of fine white sand above New Quarter Square's crescent beach, gazing out across the ocean as the morning sun warms her face. This is pretty much where she lives now. Some nights she lies here and stares up at the stars until dawn. Rousing herself is becoming more difficult by the day, so her loved ones are making sure she's fed and hydrated and keeping clean with a daily swim.

They're worried about her. Many New Atlanteans are. They understand her pain, of course they do, but some want to try and help her heal somehow. That this grief won't heal in time, in any time, that she has never once healed in all her many periods of grief, they don't understand.

Some things in life can't be fixed, only carried.

Thirteen thousand years she's been living with this condition, in this condition, and for more than half of them, she's lived without him. She can't not live on. It's her curse.

Her lifelong experience is that she will rouse, eventually, probably, because those times when she doesn't are always the worst. So she will. Eventually. Probably. But not yet. It isn't quite three months since he was taken. In three years, she might start dragging herself out of this black hole. But not three months. Three months is a single hour in the dark, lonely night of eternity.

Jimmy comes to sit with her. He isn't one of those who feels the need to talk. Along with her wolf family, he knows that words won't help. Neither her nor him. He's living with his guilt. No matter how his loved ones tell him it wasn't his fault, he was there when Joe was taken. He sits in his own silent pain and stares out to sea.

Two silhouetted figures walk on the raised headland at the end of the beach, along to the clifftop where Joe intended to build a new theatre. It's his parents, hand in hand, facing into the sea breeze that's often stronger up there, his mother's shawl flapping like a bird's wing until she clutches it closer around her. They, too, are carrying their grief in their own way.

"How will you find him in his next life?" his father asked after the first month had passed. Ever the practical one, he'd accepted the likelihood of Joe's death before his wife did. Ever the kind husband, he said it out of her hearing.

Min doesn't know, exactly, because she doesn't know where he died. It's one of those worst-case scenarios, but she didn't have the heart to tell his father that he might live some lives alone.

One thing is sure. When he's born again, he won't know to look for her in New Atlantis, so she can't stay here.

Shad says the Axe think he was taken to the West Midlands in the Wild of England. It's a big slash of a region, devastated and depopulated by invasive industry from the outside. The wolves are still searching there, faithfully, if rather forlornly. It's where she'll go when the time comes to start looking for him in his next life.

When will that be? She doesn't know. The paradise of New Atlantis has no hold on her now, but neither does anywhere else. Her friends and loved ones are here, so for now it will do.

Jimmy tenses. He looks past her, along the beach.

A male lion is walking towards them as the longest last touches of waves reach up the white sands to caress his paws. He's huge. His coat is golden in the strong sunlight, and his breeze-blown mane dark brown. His gaze is fixed on Min.

Her heart is in her mouth.

Is this Maahas, the Atlantean god who gave Joe the bite twice in ancient Egypt, come with news about him? Or can it be…?

Can it?

She sits as still as stone, waiting to learn, scared to even think what she is desperately hoping for.

The great beast climbs the dry sandhill and stops before her. He sits tall and proud, his big, intelligent, amber eyes looking steadily into hers.

Her heart is pounding fit to burst.

"Lion man?" Jimmy breathes.

The lion butts Jimmy gently on his cheekbone, then returns his full attention to Min.

"Joe?" She whispers it, scared to say his name aloud in case she shatters the spell of her suddenly burning hope.

He nuzzles his snout into her neck. His breath is sweet.

She throws her arms around his powerful neck, sobbing, and hugs him tight. "Joe!"

Shad, Vua, and Tae are here, running to greet him. He stands, butts his snout into them, and pants gruff chuckle noises, clearly happy to see his family.

His parents are here too. His father stands back warily, but his mother strokes his head and murmurs soothing noises and says, "You have to fight the monster, don't you?"

Min jerks her head up. What? This, already?

Joe's mother is talking quietly. "You have to do this. I understand. You can't let the terror destroy any more lives. You have to release yourself and Min from it. Release all of us from it. That's why you're a lion now."

Min's swallow is a dry gulp.

His mother embraces him. "Come back to us, Joe. Go fight your fight, and then come back here to live with us in peace. We love you."

Barr Beacon

JUMPING THE SYLPH way gives me a big advantage, I think. Especially now that I've perfected my method of going from inside one tree to inside another. I can cover great distances this way, or small ones, without revealing my presence. I can jump from place to place inside one Wild, or between different Wilds. Can even change direction in mid-jump. It's all about visualisation and intention. I don't need physical thin places.

I did wonder if I'd need to shift to human form to blend into a tree. But no. Lion form is fine. The fact is, it isn't like I used to see it, with my normal body squeezed inside a trunk. When I'm inside a tree, I truly become part of it. When I jump, I'm part of the next one.

The beech stand above Tyac's lair is my ideal cover. I don't know the extent of the cave system, or all its entrances and exits, and I really don't know if this is where I'll find him, but it's the right place to start looking. I relax inside my tree as pre-dawn light pales the polluted sky, and wait.

The pride wanted to come with me, but I have no intention of letting Tyac kill any more innocent creatures, so I persuaded them to remain in the deep Wild, and we said our goodbyes with fondness and respect.

My wolf family weren't as easy to persuade. Shad, Vua, and Tae were determined to fight at my side in this final battle. They kept reminding me that the day after Tyac killed Anya, we vowed to hunt him down and kill him together, for her. My decision to remain a lion throughout the exchange frustrated Shad enormously, but I had my reasons. Their vocal wall hit my wordless wall, and we stayed locked there, until Min stepped in and backed me up, despite our vow that we will never again be separated. She was prepared to put the vow on hold, this one last time, in the desperate hope that it really will be the last time we'll need to be apart. In the desperate hope that I'll come back alive.

Her fear was evident. As was her bravery. In the end, it was her vulnerability, I think, that persuaded our family to stay with her.

For which I'm glad because I didn't want to disappear the Sylph way without their knowledge. I wanted our parting to be filled with love and hope, and it was.

Finally, and surprisingly for a moment, although I shouldn't have been surprised, Lael and Keni wanted to accompany me. Lael and I communicated with our minds, the only clear speech conversation I had in New Atlantis because I'd decided in advance that I would remain in lion form there to help Min accept my imminent departure to confront Tyac.

As with the others, I was determined not to put Lael and Keni in danger. In their case, it was the golden elders who influenced their acceptance of my decision to face Tyac alone. And I was enormously grateful to the elders for feeding me with love and strength when I bathed in New Golden Lake before I left.

It's May now. The beech trees are filled with the vigour of new life, of growth and strength, while at the same time they're watching surrounding events with dread. I suspect it's only Tyac's unseen but undoubtedly felt presence that's saved this hilltop from the destruction the great Midlands forest of the Wild has suffered. Destruction that's still happening, far worse than when I was in this spot a month ago. There's smoke, fire, and fumes belching constantly from chimneys everywhere. It's hell on Earth. And still spreading. There's a ten-mile-wide managed fire burning fiercely on the eastern horizon.

May. It's exactly a year since I first stumbled into Quarter Square. Since I first met Min in this lifetime. Since I found my new family. An anniversary. A birthday.

Not a day to celebrate, although I'm content in my beech tree. Content but alert. If Tyac appears in human form, I'll have him.

He doesn't appear. By mid-morning, I'm ready to explore his caves. If he's sleeping in there, I'll have him.

I leave the tree as a lion, which is how I intend to remain until this is over, one way or the other, and pad into the narrow passageway through which I exited after he tortured me. The ropes are still here, tied to iron rings set into the rock wall. The broken halves of my sabre are still here too, where he dropped them after he stabbed me. Dark smears on the rock wall below the rings are probably my blood.

I explore the entire system and locate three more entrances. His freshest scent overlays mine, so he's been here since I left. As recently as last night, I think. I spray urine everywhere, then return to my beech tree and wait.

The first signs of non-human life moving in the devastated land stirs my recognition. I know these creatures. It's a patrol of nine Axe wolves, working their way cautiously past pit towers and foundries and factories and growling truck routes in their approach to Barr Beacon.

They're sad. Not listless, searching diligently, but with none of the exuberance I know and love in our wolves. This patrol can't have heard yet that I turned up in New Atlantis. They're still looking for me.

They fan out and climb the gentle incline, sniffing and snuffling with intense new vigour and alertness when they detect Tyac's scent everywhere.

One of them pauses at my tree, investigates it thoroughly, and then sits and stares at it. She knows, I think, that I've been here. Does my lion scent carry tones of my human scent? I don't know, but from the intensity in her stare I think it must.

I'm tempted to ease myself from the beech and reassure her, reassure the others who join her briefly in studying my tree, but then someone finds the narrow passageway and they all pile into the cave system.

Their search is silent at first, but it's evident that they've cleared the entire system for signs of danger when they start giving yips and yaps of excitement. There's no doubt that they know they've found one of Tyac's lairs. No doubt that they've also detected fresh signs of me in there.

When they tumble out, they all mark the entrance and all around with their urine. Several of them join my discoverer with a final long look at my beech, then they trot away with purpose. A good way off, I feel them go through a thin place.

Well, so much for secrecy. Very soon, everyone back in New Atlantis is going to know exactly where I've been recently.

Will they honour my determination to fight Tyac alone? I don't know. The Axe are stubborn buggers. I'll have to take it as it comes. At the very least, though, this will give Min a location to start looking for me in my next life, if this one ends tonight.

I look out at the polluted hell from the top of the tree. What kind of life would that be? Heaven only knows.

Thin places will do us

THE PACK HAVE found one of Tyac's lairs. Joe's been there." Min's heart lurches as Shad's words rouse her from meditation. "Where?"

"As they suspected, in the West Midlands of England. It's a cave system. They believe Joe is watching one of its entrances from inside a tree."

"We're going," Tae says. She and Vua stand at Shad's side, all three haloed by the setting sun.

"You promised him you wouldn't." She won't argue the point strenuously. She'd rather they were there to help him. But she feels obliged to mention it.

Shad shrugs. "Not really. We accepted his position reluctantly. He did, after all, vow with us a year ago that we would kill Tyac together. Then yesterday, he used emotional blackmail on us about our first priority being to protect you. But now the entire pack is here to protect you, even if you were in any danger. Us three going to help Joe won't reduce your protection."

She agrees.

"Do you know how he jumps so far and fast?" Vua asks.

"No. He learned it from the Sylph."

Shad looks along the beach, to the forest where the Sylph have made their new home.

"We shouldn't waste time," Tae tells her father. "You know how sylphs like to negotiate and bargain everything. The pack told us exactly where he is and how they got back from there. Thin places will do us."

Shad nods his decision. "Let's go."

Forever only has an hour left to live

TYAC'S DISTORTED ROARS of rage inform me. He must be rampaging through his cave system smelling the Axe scents everywhere, and beneath them my scent everywhere. His lair must feel invaded and spoiled. I don't expect he ever needs a safe place, but if I'm wrong, if he does, then this one will no longer qualify.

Increasing clarity and volume in his fury announces his imminent appearance in the passageway opening. He tears out of there and spins, searching the beech stand for me, for any intruders, hungry to kill, frustrated that no living creatures await him in the still evening air.

He drops to the ground, and his search becomes intense. Every intruder scent is noted, investigated, inhaled with urgent snuffling noises, and tasted with his tongue. Eventually, inevitably, the search leads him to my tree.

As my Axe friends did, he squats and studies it, but not for as long or anything like as patiently as they. He springs up and climbs to the top of it, as high as the slender uppermost boughs will take his weight, then returns to the ground and studies its trunk intently.

His bloodshot eyes are only inches away. I absorb the smell and taste of his breath, feel the rough rasp of his tongue when he licks the bark precisely in front of where my face would be, if I had a face right now.

It's exactly the same situation we were in a year ago, when I grew Min and me into an oak for the first time and he examined that tree. Then, I was terrified. Now, I'm calm. He can't get me when I'm part of a tree. Of any tree. I suppose he could destroy the tree. I hope he won't, but he could. He still can't get me, though, because I would simply jump to another one.

He's impotent in this regard. That's what informed me when he raged in his cave, and it's what helps me stay calm now. The advantage is mine.

An experiment. I jump to my tree's nearest sibling. The transfer is a mere three feet, but I'll be surprised if any physical evidence shows of it. Tyac doesn't flinch. His attention remains on the first tree. I jump back across the stand to a tree on the other side of my original one. Again, Tyac doesn't react. Good. Advantage: me.

His stomach rumbles. If I had human or leonine ears inside the tree, their muscles would twitch at the sound. He doesn't respond to his hunger for a while, but he'll have to do so eventually. He'll need to feed, quite urgently, I expect, to maintain maximum strength for the night ahead. Sure enough, after a few minutes more, he abandons his futile inspection of my first tree trunk and lopes away through the small stand of trees.

Following him without detection across the denuded landscape isn't going to be as easy as if he were moving through a living forest. There are broken bits of destroyed trees strewn around everywhere, but none of them are as big as the living trunks I'm accustomed to inhabiting. This will be a new challenge.

I make my first jump into open ground, to a torn tree stump beside a muddy riverlike road carved by the big heavy vehicles that keep growling past at short intervals.

Tyac proceeds at his normal jogging pace, outside the flaring glare of truck headlights, straight past the stump, evidently unaware of my proximity.

That's good, but far better is my discovery of the surviving root network. Millions of trees and shrubs have been destroyed above ground, but they live on below the surface, and they're all comfortably inviting for me. Furthermore, their communication is intact. Even beneath the raging fire that's destroying great swathes of forest away to the east, life remains in the soil, and communication continues from the roots and fibrous networks of those poor burned trees.

That's where I want Tyac. My instinct is to guide him to those flames. Unsure why right now, but it feels right. I think that's how I'll maintain my advantage.

He's hunting a human. His raised alertness communicates itself to me disgustingly well, and I feel all the life signs of his target before I see the man.

It's a truck driver, taking a break in his cab, eating his supper and listening to music on headphones. He's pulled his vehicle off the main mud-river thoroughfare and killed his engine, while heavy traffic continues to rumble past only a hundred feet away. He has no warning of the horror that's coming for him.

I jump ahead into a splintered old forklift pallet half buried in the mud near the truck and watch Tyac approaching. There's no sense of gathering my strength, no bunching of my muscles, because inside the timber my muscles don't exist, but when Tyac jogs past my position I burst from the pallet in lion form and take him down.

His surprise doesn't reduce his violent response. I'm prepared for it. Dragging him to the ground, with my front legs pinning his arms to his torso and all my weight bearing him down, I grip the back of his neck in my jaws, biting hard, twisting hard. If he were human, his neck would snap like a dry twig. But he isn't human. He's a monster. He wriggles furiously to meet my teeth around his throat with his around mine, his first attempt thwarted by my thick mane.

I jerk my head back and swipe a great clout of one clawed front paw across his face, then again with the other, satisfied that the two rapid blows make his eyes cross for a heartbeat, and by the time he recovers from them, I've freed myself from his clutch and grown instantly back into the pallet.

He's raging. Roaring. The truck's engine snarls into life and the big vehicle rumbles away in a hurry. But Tyac wants me, not some human. He casts around, spittle flying from his maw, eyes burning insane red in the polluted night.

I jump from the pallet to a broken tree some way away and emerge from it, standing proud until he sees me and comes at a run. He's fast. I know he is, but even prepared as I am, I have no time to waste growing back into the timber before he reaches my new position and searches around furiously.

I continue this pattern, attacking him from out of nowhere and disappearing back into nowhere, inflicting more injuries on him than he inflicts on me, infuriating him, drawing him always to the east, ever closer to the burning forest.

My plan is to move across the wide face of the fire until we reach its end, then to take him beyond it, behind it. Maybe even into the path of the flames, although I'm not sure about that yet, but if I can keep him sufficiently angry, keep him reacting with rage, not logic, I definitely want to lead him into living forest. I relish the prospect of attacking him from every angle when he won't know where I'm coming from next. That's when I'll stop angering him and start killing him.

A quarter mile past the northern edge of the fire, the ancient forest is still physically unharmed, for now, although its trees are traumatised by the pain and destruction they've witnessed in their siblings and know is coming to them. I emerge from a tree and lead Tyac into the green.

He senses my end now, I feel. He thinks I'm trapped in here. Little does he understand.

It's time to turn defence into attack. He doesn't know where to look next, can only twist to meet my repeated fast assaults with fury and vicious teeth and his clawed front paw, which although single is still dangerous. He tries to surprise me by springing up trees and down again, and his enraged roars grow notes of increasing insanity, especially when I bite and tear his remaining hand to bloody shreds.

We're in the fire's path now. I still don't know exactly what I'm going to do. One thing's for sure: he doesn't care about the flames. He wants only me. His wily cleverness as a man seems to have deserted him for pure strength and speed and fury as a beast.

I'm not foolish. All my power and strength as a lion make me only his equal. Possibly his equal. Definitely not his superior in killing. My intelligence and awareness give me an advantage, but they don't overrule his millennia of experience in dealing death, or his terrible brutal recklessness. I'm cautious. Only one of us will leave this burning forest today. I don't want it to be him.

The wind has picked up from the west. Cinders in the air. The fire is coming faster.

If I can't beat him in equal combat, and I probably can't, perhaps I can destroy him through sacrifice.

Maybe I can keep him here and die with him.

I watch him from a tree and consider this option. Am I prepared to die to wash the world clean of him?

Yes. Yes, I am.

Decision made, how to trap him here is easy. The next time he stalks past my tree, I reach out and drag him into it with me.

He's terrified.

I feel it, can't help knowing his fear, for he is as much a part of this tree as I am. We're in here together, joined as never before. While I understand our situation, he knows only breathless claustrophobia and fear, and it doesn't go away. He can't calm himself. Can't think it through. He's already dangerously insane, although functionally so. I think if I were to leave him in here, he would lose his mind forever.

Except that at the current speed of the forest fire's approach, forever only has an hour left to live.

I can't leave him in terror. No matter what he's done to me, time after terrifying time, I can't do that to him. It isn't who I am. I move him inside the tree to free his face from the living wood so that he can at least feel the air. Then I step from the tree altogether and sit before him.

We can't talk. But once his fear subsides a little, once his futile struggles cease, I see him reach a degree of understanding. He regards the distant fire. Then he watches me with all the hatred of his entire being.

A long howl comes from the west. Shad. Through the trees, I see and hear and feel him, Tae, and Vua standing below the beeches on Barr Beacon.

I roar back. They turn to face my greeting, then come at a fast run.

I sit and watch Tyac while we wait.

It appears he is picking up at least some of the tree senses too, for he looks to the west with the bloodshot insanity in his eyes having reduced quite noticeably.

The fire is half an hour away when my family arrive. They survey the situation in seconds before greeting me with nuzzles and rubs of their necks and shoulders against mine. Then they sit with me to study Tyac.

He studies us back.

I don't think his being encased in the tree will allow him to growl and snap, even if he wants to. I don't know. His demeanour is calmer than I've ever seen in him before. But again, I don't know. I'm not about to be fooled into putting aside his thirteen thousand years of murderous hatred because he's been forced into quiet immobility and has seemed calm about it for the past few minutes.

I walk around the back of the tree and shove him a little more out of it.

He takes great, shuddering breaths, then roars, snapping his jaws and struggling violently to release himself all the way, but I was careful, so only his head and upper torso are free of the tree. As long as we stay out of range of his snapping teeth, we'll be safe.

I can't kill him. Not because I'm weak or scared. I can't kill him because of who I am. Of whom I have become. He's a trapped creature. A monster, yes, and not one I'm prepared to set free to continue his reign of terror, but still a trapped, temporarily helpless, living creature. I don't kill such beings. It isn't who I am. His terrible treatment of me hasn't turned me into anything like a version of him.

Nor can I leave him to burn alive when the fire gets here. That isn't who I am either.

I meet Shad's stare. It's flinty hard. His message is clear. I give a nod of understanding and consent, and step back to allow him the space he wants.

Tyac regards him too. He knows what's coming. I'm sure of it. Does he remember that night a year ago when he killed half of the Axe pack while they protected Min and me? I suspect he does. His full attention now is on the big wolf bunching his muscles and launching himself.

Shad rips open Tyac's throat. It's over in seconds. The monster's head hangs lifeless from the tree trunk.

I shift. I want to see this with my human eyes. I want to remember it always with my human senses.

He's dead. It's over.

Shad, Vua, and Tae shift too. We stand looking at Tyac's sad remains hanging from the bark and dripping blood like some hideous sort of woodland decoration.

The fire is nearly here.

I gather my family and prepare them for a long jump. "Let's go home."

Full Circle

MIN AND I sit on her favourite sandhill, watching the silver moon sail across our velvet sky. My arm rests around her shoulders, and her head rests against my chest. I kiss the top of it, inhaling her exquisite citrussy scent, and she murmurs a small noise of complete happiness.

New Quarter Square sits comfortably at the edge of the forest behind us. It's late into the night, but some lights still burn there, and noises of safe domestic life reach us from inside the houses.

At the end of the pale crescent beach, up on the cliff, our new theatre stands clean and quiet, partly built, but fully what Jimmy and I have been dreaming of. A couple stroll hand in hand along the headland to the theatre. Mum and Dad. These days, they're the happiest I've ever seen them.

Belle sits at anchor in the bay. She looks magical in the moonlight. Andrew's flute carries sweetly across the water from an open window in Lucinda's gently lit cabin.

We've talked our way around and around the future, Min and I, and always come back to where we started. Will Tyac's immortality curse on Min have died with him? If so, will her years from the time of his death end in her own a natural death one day? Will I continue being reincarnated? We don't know. We can't ever know, until we find out in real time. It's pointless talking it over and over, so we reached a wordless agreement to leave it alone now. One day, it will become clear. Until then, we'll live in love and peace, enjoying each other to the full.

We're like everyone else in that regard. We're normal people now, and speaking for myself, I'm very content with that. I believe Min is too.

We watch the moon sailing across the endlessly deep, endlessly starry, velvet night sky, and enjoy true peace and safety for the first time in thirteen thousand years.

About the Author

David Bridger settled in England's West Country after twenty years of ocean-based mischief, during which he worked as a lifeguard, a sailor, an intelligence gatherer and an investigator.

Then he got hurt, came home a bit physically broken, and for good measure caught a severe Myalgic Encephalomyelitis (ME) virus in a military hospital.

Now he writes science fiction and fantasy novels. Sometimes they're informed by his experiences out on the crinkly blue.

He writes what he loves for readers who love what he writes.

He is a Quakerish ecosocialist, a spoonie, an adopter of donkeys, a lifelong Liverpool FC supporter, a lover of blues and jazz, a browncoat, and a Whovian of the 9 and 10 era (starting with Rose and ending with Donna).

Social Media

Twitter: http://twitter.com/DavidBridger

Instagram: http://instagram.com/davidbridger1

Facebook: https://www.facebook.com/DavidBridgerAuthor/ and https://www.facebook.com/groups/478381059398631

Publisher: https://www.beatentrackpublishing.com/DavidBridger

By The Author

The Honesty of Tigers

Damage Control

Quiet Resistance

Storywalker

Gifted

A Flight of Thieves

Space Train

David Bridger's Science Fiction & Fantasy Collection

Wild Times

Beaten Track Publishing

For more titles from Beaten Track Publishing,
please visit our website:

https://www.beatentrackpublishing.com

Thanks for reading!

Lightning Source UK Ltd.
Milton Keynes UK
UKHW040634101221
395407UK00001B/150

9 781786 454881